SEVEN SISTERS

Berkley Prime Crime Books by Earlene Fowler

FOOL'S PUZZLE
IRISH CHAIN
KANSAS TROUBLES
GOOSE IN THE POND
DOVE IN THE WINDOW
MARINER'S COMPASS
SEVEN SISTERS

For Martha —

SEVEN SISTERS

Trails!

EARLENE FOWLER

BERKLEY PRIME CRIME, NEW YORK

SEVEN SISTERS

A Berkley Prime Crime Book
Published by the Berkley Publishing Group
a division of Penguin Putnam Inc.,
375 Hudson Street, New York, New York 10014

The Penguin Putnam Inc. World Wide Web site address is
http://www.penguinputnam.com

Book design by Carrie Leder.

First Edition: April 2000

Library of Congress Cataloging-in-Publication Data

Fowler, Earlene.
Seven sisters / by Earlene Fowler.
p. cm.
ISBN 0-425-17296-1
I. Title.
PS3558.0828S4 2000
813'.54—dc21 99-33283
CIP

Printed in the United States of America

10 9 8 7 6 5 4 3 2 1

For

Debra Jackson, my wonderful baby sister
and the real quilter in the family

and

Helen May,
dear friend and one of the most
courageous women I know

ACKNOWLEDGMENTS

I never forget that books and lives are not written completely alone. Some of the people below have helped me with gifts of information and technical advice, some with personal support and friendship, many with touches of both. To each of them I extend my gratitude and also confess that any mistakes in the manuscript are mine alone:

O, Lord, our Lord, how majestic is your name in all the earth!

Clare Bazley—for your precious friendship, insightful comments and for the great information on quarter horses, and

Tom Bazley—for giving me one of the best lines in this book.

Tina Davis—for your special friendship and cheerful, giving spirit.

Karen Gray, deputy district attorney, San Luis Obispo—for sound legal advice, and research help above and beyond the call of duty (with an extra thanks for being such a tremendous friend).

Jo Ellen Heil—for your Spirit-filled friendship, your graceful suppport, and your prayers, I truly give thanks.

Christine "Nini" Hill, the Queen of everything—for a friendship that defies description: No one makes me laugh like you do.

Steve Himmelrich, detective, San Luis Obispo Sheriff's department.

Robert A. Jakucs, retired LAPD detective, Pacific Division.

Lynda Kay, M.D.—for expert medical advice.

Dean James and Donna Houston Murray—much treasured writing buddies.

Jo-Ann Mapson—beloved friend, writer, and shopping partner.

Mike and Magaline Messina and Lisa Marrone, fire captain, Department of Forestry—for showing me the Carrizo Plains.

Pam Munns, officer, California Highway Patrol, and Janice Mangan, officer, San Luis Obispo Police Department—for generously sharing your life and experiences.

Judith Palais, my ever remarkable editor, and Deborah Schneider, my wonderful agent.

My husband, Allen—who proves to me every day that love isn't only someplace that you fall, but something that you do.

SEVEN SISTERS

The Seven Sisters quilt pattern, like many others, was most likely designed from an observation of nature. The Seven Sisters, or Pleiades, is a fairly loose grouping of stars in the constellation Taurus. Although seven stars can be seen with the naked eye, binoculars or telescopes reveal it actually consists of several hundred more. The quilt pattern itself, a single six-pointed star surrounded by six identical stars, has been seen as early as 1845. It became popular again during the Depression era, when hand-piecing difficult and challenging patterns was popular. It is also known as Seven Stars, Evening Star, and Seven Stars in a Cluster. An interesting phenomenon of the Seven Sisters star cluster is though they appear to be close together, they are, in fact, quite far apart.

THE BROWN FAMILY

First generation:

JOHN MADISON BROWN—judge, father, and husband (deceased)

ROSE JEWEL BROWN—96 years old—wife of John Madison Brown, mother of seven daughters

Second generation:

CAPITOLA "CAPPY" JEWEL BROWN MATTHEWS—75 years old—oldest Brown sister (took back her maiden name when she divorced her husband)

WILLOW JEWEL BROWN D'AMBROSIO—74 years old—second Brown sister

ETTA JEWEL BROWN—73 years old—third Brown sister

DAISY JEWEL AND DAHLIA JEWEL BROWN (first set of twins—deceased)

BEULAH JEWEL AND BETHANY JEWEL BROWN (second set of twins—deceased)

Third generation:

SUSANNA "SUSA" JEWEL MATTHEWS GIRARD—47 years old—Cappy's daughter

CHASE MADISON BROWN—48 years old—Cappy's son

PHOEBE JEWEL BROWN D'AMBROSIO—Willow's daughter (deceased)

Fourth generation:

BLISS JEWEL GIRARD—22 years old—Susa's daughter

JOY JEWEL GIRARD—22 years old—Susa's daughter

ARCADIA JEWEL D'AMBROSIO NORTON—29 years old—Phoebe's daughter and Willow's granddaughter

GILES NORTON—35 years old—Arcadia's husband

"BUT WE'RE IN love," my stepson said, his dark chocolate eyes burning bright with the passionate angst of a nineteen-year-old male in full-blown heat.

"Oh, Sam," I said, trying to choose my words carefully. "You're still so young." I reached down and scratched behind my dog's soft brown ears. Scout was a part Labrador, part German shepherd mix with a suspected itinerant coyote grandparent. He gazed up at me with adoring ocher eyes.

"You were nineteen when you married Jack," Sam replied.

There was no way I could argue that point with any sort of genuine conviction. I had indeed married my first husband when we were barely nineteen, and it had been a warm, loving relationship working together on our ranch for fifteen years until he was killed in an auto accident two and a half years ago. Since then, I'd moved to town, married Sam's father, Gabriel Ortiz, San Celina's police chief, and acquired a new life. A life that included being, or attempting to be, a proper police chief's wife, curator of San

Celina's folk art museum, still occasionally wrangling cattle on my family's ranch, and often acting as the buffer between my volcanic husband and his equally explosive son.

Now it appeared love was in the air. Or a reasonable facsimile. And it wasn't even spring. Like the haunches of old mountain lions, the hills around San Celina were spotted with early September golds and tans, adhering to the old Central California Coast joke that this region possessed only two actual seasons, green and brown. Downtown streets were equally covered with new Cal Poly University students flush with excitement, hope, and abundant checking accounts. It was a natural fact that the hills would retain their dusty colors a good deal longer than the students did either their excitement or their bank balances.

"So who is this mystery woman?" I asked, leaning back against the sofa in the Spanish-style bungalow Gabe and I had called home for the year and a half we'd been married. We'd recently begun the frustrating task of house hunting because though this house was fine for one five-foot-one-inch widow lady with minimal luggage, it was spatially challenged for the burgeoning possessions of a married couple. Unfortunately we'd discovered in the twenty houses we'd viewed so far that our individual opinions as to the perfect house were as different as his silver-streaked black hair was to my strawberry blond. Yet another mid-life relationship challenge.

"She's so great," Sam said, flopping down on the sofa next to me. "You'll love her. Actually you two have met." The wide, gorgeous grin on his gingersnap-colored face made me instantly suspicious.

"We have?" I racked my brain trying to remember who I knew around his age who might be in the running. The redheaded girl with the pierced eyebrow who worked weekends at Blind Harry's Bookstore where Sam also worked?

The cute waitress with the wide blue eyes at Liddie's Cafe? The vegetarian girl in hemp clothing at Kinko's I'd seen him flirting with when I'd picked up orders for the museum? Sam, like his father, was a very attractive man, so the possibilities were endless.

"Yep."

I frowned slightly at him, gripping to my chest a suede pillow decorated with a bucking bronco. "I hate guessing games. Just tell me."

He ran his long fingers against the hair on Scout's neck, making it stand up. Scout's tail thumped agreeably on the tan carpet. "It's kind of complicated."

Apprehension rippled down my spine. "How complicated?"

"She's kind of pregnant."

I groaned loudly and threw the pillow at him. "Sam, how could you?"

He dodged it and went back to playing with Scout's hair, refusing to meet my eyes. "Dad's gonna kill me."

I didn't dispute his statement because I couldn't guarantee his dad's reaction. If not death, then tar and feathering was a distinct possibility. My place in this scenario, as it had been before, was to see if I could convince these two stubborn, emotional men to sit down and discuss the problem rationally. A headache, the first of many I was certain, started tapping on my skull's inner walls. I touched my temples with my fingertips and started rubbing small circles.

"Well," I finally said. "What are your plans?" Since he had just started his sophomore year at Cal Poly, worked part-time at my best friend Elvia's bookstore, and lived in the bunkhouse at my family's ranch, his ability to care for a wife and child was, to say the least, skimpy.

"Guess I'll just take each day as it comes."

Resisting the urge to strangle his tanned, muscular neck, I said, "Sam, you're pretty much past taking each day as it comes. You have a child on the way who will need bottles and diapers and health care and a car seat and . . ."

"Geeze, Benni, I know all that. I was hoping for a little more support from you. Lectures I can get from my dad."

And you will, I promised silently. "This girl you're in love with, how does she feel about being pregnant? Has she told her parents yet?"

"She told her mom. Her mom's kind of a hippie-type and thinks it's totally cool. Her dad's living up north in a commune or something. He's a carpenter and grows stuff in his garden to sell on the side."

I didn't dare ask what kind of stuff. What kind of family was he marrying into? "Her mom lives here in San Celina?"

"Yeah, on a ranch over in Amelia Valley. It's a winery, too."

Amelia Valley was south of San Celina about fifteen miles, on the eastern side of Interstate 101 across from Eola and Pismo beaches and Port San Patricio. Famous for its temperate climate and excellent soil, it was some of the most beautiful and valuable land in San Celina County.

If they were ranchers, then they were possibly people I knew, if only casually. Our county's ranch community was a tight, small group. "So, who is her family? Who is she?"

He stopped playing with Scout's hair and looked directly into my eyes. "Promise you won't get weird or anything."

"Sam, I'm not getting weird, I'm getting annoyed. Just tell me."

He dropped his head and mumbled a name.

I ducked my head lower to hear him. "What did you say?"

"Bliss Girard."

"What! Please tell me you're pulling my leg." If I had

another pillow within reach, I would have held it down over his face.

The absolute fear in his eyes was real. As well it should be. “I’m sorry,” he whispered. “But we love each other. Really, we do. We want to get married.”

“Sam, how in the world am I going to tell your father that you got one of his best rookie cops pregnant? You want to answer me that?”

“Not really,” he said.

SAM LEFT, WITH the promise that he'd be back about five p.m., so we could share the joyful task of telling his father that he was going to be a grandfather. I hoped Gabe would be in a congenial mood since this was the first time in weeks he'd managed to steal a day to work on his master's thesis in philosophy. Sam was smart about one thing—Sunday was definitely the best day to drop this bomb on his father. Hopefully some of the sermon Gabe and I heard at church this morning on forgiveness and tolerance was still resonating in his brain. But just to be safe, I started baking M & M cookies. Gabe adored M & M cookies, and I figured after his favorite dinner of chiles rellenos and smoky pinto beans topped off by a beloved dessert, he'd be in a mellow, cholesterol- and sugar-sated stupor before we broke Sam's news. As I mixed the stiff cookie dough, I thought about Bliss Girard and her family.

Though they were an important presence in San Celina's agricultural society, I didn't know them well since they had never been cattle ranchers. Their combination quarter horse breeding ranch and winery was called Seven Sisters because, I assumed, of its location. From their magnificent Julia Morgan–designed house, which I'd visited once years ago during a holiday homes tour, there was a breathtaking view of the ancient Seven Sisters volcanic peaks that stretched down to Morro Bay, the last peak being Morro Rock.

It was only recently that I'd connected Gabe's youngest and newest officer with the Seven Sisters clan. At a departmental picnic last June she and I had a short conversation about the best way to treat shin splints in horses. She had overheard me talking to Gabe's assistant, Maggie, who owned a cattle ranch with her sister in North County, and offered an opinion about the overuse of anti-inflammatory drugs without regard to the serious consequences down the road. That worked into an interesting conversation about the burgeoning popularity and controversy of a more holistic approach to horse and cattle health. It was during our conversation she revealed her relation to the Seven Sisters dynasty, as it was known in San Celina County. In fact, her maternal grandmother was the renowned Capitola "Cappy" Brown, former rodeo star and respected quarter horse breeder.

"You didn't grow up around here, did you?" I'd asked. She was much younger than me, twenty-two to my thirty-six, but the agricultural community in San Celina isn't that big, and I was sure I'd have heard her name or seen her somewhere through 4-H, the Cattlewomen's Association, at a Farm Bureau function, or in connection with one of my gramma Dove's eclectic groups of which Cappy Brown or one of her two sisters were often members.

Bliss shook her head no. She was a small, muscular woman with thick blond hair pulled back in a neat French braid. Delicate features and large gray eyes gave her a fragile, sheltered look, and I wondered if that was a difficult persona for her to overcome as a cop. "I grew up on a commune outside of Garberville. That's north of San Francisco." Looking at the ground, she relayed the information with a wry, slightly embarrassed tone, her pale skin flushing pink to the edge of her downy hairline.

"I heard it's real pretty up around there," Maggie said.

"It is. My dad still lives there," Bliss continued, "but my mother moved back to Seven Sisters when Grandma Cappy fell off a horse and broke her arm six months ago. Mom's a nurse-midwife. I left the commune when I turned eighteen and worked as a groom for my grandma while I went to Alan Hancock College in Santa Maria. I've wanted to be a cop ever since I can remember. One time when I was eight I was out with my dad, and he was pulled over and busted for possessing some marijuana. I was really scared, but this old cop, he was really nice to me. He told me that they wouldn't hurt my dad and waited with me until my mom came to pick me up. He didn't look at me as if I were a piece of trash, and, well, I decided I wanted to be just like him. His name was Lyle, that's all I remember." Then, as if realizing she'd revealed too much personal history to her boss's wife, she tightened her lips. Her face remained rosy-colored, and a forced scowl only made her look more vulnerable.

I kept my face serious, hoping to reassure her that her revelations wouldn't affect my respect for her. "We all have people in our lives who we can say influenced us. Actually, your grandmother was a real inspiration to me as a girl."

"Why's that?" Maggie asked.

"Cappy Brown was a trick rider in the rodeo during the forties and fifties, and for a while taught a barrel-racing school out at her ranch. That's how I really came to know her. She used to take her students around the state to compete in amateur rodeos. The best show I ever saw was one she put on for four of us girls in an empty arena one morning in Bishop. She did things on her horse I'd never try, and she was in her fifties. She used to tell us that anything we wanted to do was possible, that there were no 'boy' jobs or 'girl' jobs, only jobs."

Maggie's head nodded in approval. "Sounds like my kind of woman."

Talking about her grandmother softened Bliss's expression. "She'd tell us grandkids to always ride tall in the saddle. I bet I've heard that a million times."

"And, girl, you've sure as shootin' had to heed that piece of advice a few times at work," Maggie said.

The frown reappeared on Bliss's face. "They've learned not to mess with me."

"They?" I inquired.

Maggie chuckled. "This poor little child has been hit on more times than those old mission bells. You can't blame those besotted fools at the station. Just look at her."

Bliss's frown deepened. "All I want is to be a good cop. I don't have time for a boyfriend."

Well, I thought, as I mixed the M & M's into the cookie dough, *apparently she found a little time.*

Gabe, bless his experienced little cop's heart, was immediately suspicious when he sat down for dinner at our pine kitchen table.

"So, what's up?" he asked, digging into the steaming chiles rellenos. "Did you find a house you know I'll hate?"

"Nope."

"Seriously, you're buttering me up. Why?"

I wouldn't tell him, changing the subject every time he brought the conversation back around to it. When he was almost through eating, when I was in the middle of describing the latest house the realtor had shown me, Sam knocked on the front screen door.

"In the kitchen," I called out, smiling widely at my husband.

Gabe's wary, blue-gray eyes traveled from my face to his son's, then back to mine. A small groan rumbled in his chest. "I should have known. Just what are you two plotting?"

"I'm starved," Sam said, opening the cupboard and taking out a blue-and-white stoneware plate.

"Let's finish eating," I said, patting the top of Gabe's hand.

Gabe shook his head and took another bite, his expression stern. "You'd better not be quitting school again or tell me you're on drugs or in trouble with the law."

"It's not any of those things," Sam said quickly, taking a seat across from Gabe. "I swear."

Gabe's face relaxed as he pushed aside his empty plate. "Then anything else is a piece of cake."

I unwrapped the foil-covered plate and held it out to him. "Have a cookie."

His eyes lit up at the sight of his favorite dessert.

"Better make it two," Sam encouraged.

"I'M WHAT?" GABE bellowed.

Sam yelled back, the timbre of his voice an eerie, younger version of his father's. "I said you're going to be a grandfather. Get over it."

I pushed my way between the two glowering Ortiz men, resting my hands firmly on Gabe's chest. "Gabe, we can work this out. It's a little inconvenient maybe, but . . ."

"I should have expected as much from you," Gabe said over my head. "And just who is this girl you got in trouble?"

"She's not *in trouble*," Sam snapped. "She's pregnant, and we're going to get married. No big deal."

"Married! And what do you plan to do then? Where are you going to live? What are you going to eat? How are you going to support this girl and her baby?"

"Dad," Sam said, his voice lower. "I love her, and it's my baby, too."

I moved from between them and watched as the realization of what Sam said hit Gabe. His Adam's apple moved once in a convulsive swallow. He cleared his throat and asked in a less harsh voice, "Who is she?"

Sam looked at me in desperation. I nodded in encouragement but kept a hand on Gabe's forearm.

Sam straightened his spine and said in a composed voice, "Bliss Girard."

Gabe's left eye gave a single twitch, then not a muscle moved on his face. I knew he was shocked, but I also knew he was drawing on every ounce of his cop's experience not to react.

Sam shifted from one sandaled foot to the other, his face flushed under his deep surfer tan. "I'm not going to ask you for money. Bliss and I will work this out."

Gabe gazed back at his son for a long minute, then turned and walked out of the room.

Sam wiped a bead of sweat from his upper lip, his brow wrinkled in confusion. "I thought he'd go ballistic when he found out who she was."

I shrugged one shoulder, unable to explain his father. "He's tired, Sam. Things have been busy at the station these last few weeks with school just starting and that homicide over near the train station. He's under a lot of pressure."

"He's really mad, isn't he?" Sam's face became sad. Then, as rapidly as a summer rainstorm, it turned angry. "I don't care if he is. It's not his life. Bliss works for him, but he doesn't own her."

I gave his waist a quick hug. "The worst is over, stepson. It'll take some time, but Gabe will get used to it. Then mark my words, he'll be the most doting grandpa you've ever seen."

"Thanks, *madrastra,*" he said, using the affectionate Spanish term for stepmother. He ran his fingers through his black, cropped hair. "One parent down, one to go."

"You haven't told your mother yet?"

Gabe's ex-wife, Lydia, was a prominent defense attorney who, after a recent divorce, had moved from Newport Beach and taken a position at a Santa Barbara law firm specifically to be closer to Sam. Because of her busy schedule, we still hadn't met. Sam went down to Santa Barbara to visit her a couple of times a month. The only picture I'd ever seen of her was one of Sam and her when he graduated high school two years ago. If I'd been given twenty-five words or less to describe her I would have said: black hair, black eyes, thin, tall, gorgeous, and Saks-Fifth-Ave–classy. It was easy to see how her and Gabe's combined genetics produced a parade-stopper like Sam.

"How do you think she'll react?" I asked.

"She'll be irritated, but not as much as Dad. She was always more into damage control than Dad. Prevention is more his thing."

I raised my eyebrows, but didn't reply. Prevention, in this case, would certainly have been the more prudent action, but I wasn't about to get into a discussion about birth control or abstinence with my nineteen-year-old stepson. That was definitely in the realm of biological parental privilege. "When are you going to tell her?"

"Tomorrow. Me and Bliss are having lunch with her in Santa Barbara. Then I guess Dad and her will have a powwow."

The first of many, no doubt. My stomach churned slightly at the thought. "Well, good luck. And, Sam . . ."

He sighed extravagantly, resigned to hearing one more piece of advice.

"Everything will work out. You and Bliss will make great parents. That's gonna be one lucky baby."

A slow smile spread across his face. "Thanks, Benni. I really needed to hear that."

In the bedroom, Gabe was sitting on our bed staring at

the floor. I sat down next to him and rubbed small circles on his solid back. "Friday, it's a baby. It's not the end of the world."

"He's so young and irresponsible. And one of my own officers! It's just too much of a coincidence. What was he thinking? What was she thinking? What . . ."

I laughed out loud, grabbed the back of his neck, and squeezed it. "Thinking? Friday, they weren't *thinking*, anymore than we were when we were so *in lust* a year and a half ago. Remember how many people whispered about us when we got married so quickly? Did we care? Not one bit because all we could see was each other. We were in blind love, just like Sam and Bliss. It's just a fluke that she works for you. I haven't heard how they met, but I'm guessing the first time was last year when he and I tried to stop those jerks from wrecking your dad's truck. I also bet they've really worried about how to tell you about their relationship. I've talked to Bliss a few times, and she doesn't strike me as being a frivolous woman."

"She isn't," Gabe said, his face thoughtful. "I imagine this has been difficult for her. She must care a great deal for Sam to risk it."

"Not hard to do. You Ortiz men do tend to be irresistible."

He turned and pushed me down on the bed, covering me with his heavy, warm body. "By the way, what do you mean *were* in lust? What's with the past tense?" He bent down and kissed me deeply, his tongue hard and sweet and tantalizing.

"Okay, okay, *are* in lust," I murmured, as his lips moved down my throat, setting a line of electric sparks on my skin.

"And don't you forget it," he said, unbuttoning my shirt.

"Hmm, this will be something new. I've never made love with a grandfather before."

He undid the last button and pulled my shirt back, his blue eyes bright against his mahogany skin. "That, *niña*," he said, "is something you won't be able to say an hour from now."

AT THE MUSEUM the next morning, before tackling my accumulating paperwork, I called the ranch.

"Did Sam finally tell you?" I asked Dove. I'd called her last night and after swearing her to secrecy, told her about the baby.

"Yes, he told me and your daddy at breakfast," she said. "I pretended to be surprised, but I suspected something was going on. He'd been off his feed for about a week. When he turned down a second helping of my banana-cinnamon rolls morning last, I knew something fishy was up. I'm already looking through my patterns for a crib quilt. What do you think of Tumbling Blocks?"

"Can't think of a more appropriate pattern, but maybe you should think about a marriage quilt first." I doodled interlocking circles on the scratch pad in front of me. "Maybe the Wedding Ring pattern."

"That's too predictable. The Broken Dishes pattern is nice, and I could make one a lot quicker."

I laughed and started coloring in one of the circles. "Not

to mention it could be a prediction of what's in their future. Are you coming into town today? Want to have lunch?"

"Wish I could, honeybun, but I'm brainstorming down at the senior citizen center all day trying to figure out a way we can earn the seven thousand dollars we need to replace our kitchen."

"Didn't the insurance company cover the fire?" One of the members (a *man*, Dove and the ladies immediately pointed out to anyone who asked) had attempted to fry some tacos and started a grease fire that gutted the kitchen.

"They covered it, but they're wanting to do it the cheapest way possible. We need the money to upgrade and enlarge our capacity."

"So, any great money-making ideas yet?"

"This is the most pathetic, unimaginative group of busybodies I've ever laid eyes on. Can't think beyond bake sales and quilt raffles. We need big money fast. Like I said, we're brainstorming today. I told them that this dang committee has six hundred years of experience between them. Land's sake, we should be able to come up with something more clever than selling cupcakes."

"Well, good luck."

"Luck is for the birds. We need cold, hard cash."

"Put me down for twenty bucks."

"Huh, big spender," she said, hanging up on my laughter.

Next I called Elvia at the bookstore and told her about Sam and Bliss.

"Did you take Gabe's gun away before telling him?" she asked, not entirely kidding.

"Tell him what?" I heard my cousin Emory's voice in the background.

"What's that low-life journalist doing there so early in the morning?" I asked. She'd been dating my cousin,

Emory, a writer for the *San Celina Telegram-Tribune*, for almost a year now. He'd moved to California last year from Sugartree, Arkansas, to wine and dine her, and apparently that's all that has taken place. We'd certainly been counting on attending a wedding soon, but we'd hoped it would be Emory and Elvia's. Emory was crazy in love with my best friend, and I was pretty sure she loved him, too. It was getting her to admit it that was the horsefly in the liniment.

"He's trying to tempt me with almond scones," she said.

"Is it working?" I asked hopefully.

"We'll see. So, how about lunch?"

"Noon at Liddie's. Bring the journalist if you want."

"So he can pay?" Elvia asked, laughing.

"Of course, what else is he good for?"

Emory's voice came on the line. "What's going on, ladies? My ears are positively flaming."

"You fill him in, Elvia," I said. "I'll see you both at noon."

I'd finally settled down to my paperwork and was composing yet another grant request when JJ Brown, one of the newest additions to our artists' co-op, knocked on my door frame.

"Got a minute, Benni?"

I glanced up from my new laptop computer, grateful for the interruption. "Sure," I said, gesturing to the black vinyl and metal visitor's chair across from my desk. "I've been fiddling with the line spacing on this blasted thing for fifteen minutes and am about ready to toss it in the trash and sharpen a pencil. Any interesting diversion is definitely appreciated."

She grimaced at the gray plastic machine on my desk. "I am the original technophobe. I'm determined to be the only person in my age group who never learns to use a computer."

"Right now I know how you feel. So, what can I do for you?"

She settled back in the chair and gazed at me thoughtfully. JJ was a welcome, though sometimes controversial addition to the group of forty or so rotating artists who belonged to the co-op sponsored by the folk art museum. In the three months she'd belonged to the co-op, her hair color had changed no less than four times. She was fond of East Indian–style skirts, sixties' bell-bottoms, and belted, rayon dresses that I vaguely remember my elementary schoolteachers wearing. Of course, on JJ they looked decidedly funkier when you added her spiky, fluctuating hair, her blue, green, or black nail polish, and the fake rhinestone beauty marks she placed in surprising spots on her body. Some of the more conservative co-op members found her off-putting at first, but her gentle sense of humor, her generosity and willingness to work, not to mention the beautiful and exacting details of her hand-sewn storytelling crazy quilts quickly changed people's minds. Her true gratitude for being included as a co-op member touched me and immediately made me like her.

"Can I close the door?" she asked.

I nodded and settled back in my chair. This sounded serious. I hoped that someone hadn't really hurt her feelings and she was going to leave the co-op. We needed our younger artists to keep the co-op from becoming too set in its ways. Her unusual crazy quilts had caused quite a controversy in craft circles. Rejecting the traditional silks and velveteens of most crazy quilts, she used a combination of vintage and modern fabrics, conversation prints, leather, bones, and antique buttons to create a modern crazy quilt that defied even the controversial pattern itself. Each of her creations carried a theme celebrating life's most important moments—birth, first day of school, marriage, divorce, death—and were starting to get noticed by certain parts of professional craft circles. All it took for an artist was to be "discovered" by a respected, well-connected folk art collector, and her career was on its way. I hoped that happened for her not only because she deserved it but, selfishly, so our folk art museum would benefit from the publicity, making it slightly easier to obtain those ever-elusive grant funds.

She sat down and twisted her legs together under her thin, flowing skirt. "Guess I'll just spit it out. I wasn't exactly truthful to you on my co-op application."

"Oh?" I said, sitting forward and lacing my fingers together.

She looked down at her hands, her face tinted rose. Her stiff, olive green, spiky hair reminded me that I'd promised Gabe I'd make asparagus this week for dinner. "I'm so embarrassed," she said.

"What did you lie about?" I prompted, feeling slightly alarmed.

"Nothing about my art," she said quickly, looking up at me with clear pewter eyes.

"So, what was it, your age? Are you really sixty-five?" I laughed, trying to set her and myself at ease. She couldn't be more than twenty-two or twenty-three. Whatever she lied about couldn't possibly be that serious.

She laughed with me. "No, I really am twenty-two. I . . . It's that . . . Actually, the person I put as my next of kin, my dad up north . . . He is, well, sort of . . . but not the nearest next of kin . . ." Finally she blurted out, "Bliss Girard is my twin sister."

"Oh." I sat back in my chair. Not a serious lie, but definitely a surprising one. Her twin? I'd never have guessed it. They couldn't look more different. "So, I assume you've heard the news."

She straightened her spine. "Bliss and Sam came by last night. They said they told you and his father yesterday, so I figured I'd better come clean."

"Why the big secret? You're not ashamed of your family, are you? Cappy's a great lady."

She nodded vigorously. "Don't get me wrong, I love my family and I'm very proud of them. That's why I use Brown as my professional name. They're just so overwhelming at times. I think that's why my mom took off with my dad when she was seventeen and lived up north while me and Bliss were growing up. She'd always felt overpowered by Grandma Cappy and her two sisters and especially Great-Grandma Rose."

I nodded in understanding. Rose Jewel Brown was more than just the matriarch of one of our county's richest and most influential families, she was practically an icon. Without her years and years of hosting charity events, General Hospital's children's wing would have never been built or sustained. Even now, the Harvest Ball she started back in the forties was still one of the premier charity events in San Celina County. I'd only attended it once, last year, since before that not only were the society people who supported it out of my social league, the ticket price, two hundred and fifty dollars per person, was way beyond my financial range.

"How is your great-grandma?" I asked.

"She just moved to a retirement home outside San Celina. You know, the one on the way to Morro Bay."

I nodded. I'd taught quilting classes at Oak Terrace Retirement Home over two years ago. Or at least I threaded needles for the already talented quilters. Before I married Gabe, I'd also stumbled across a homicide among the residents, an incident the ladies in my quilting circle there still loved to discuss.

"Why did she leave the ranch?" I asked. The Browns were extremely wealthy people who could afford to hire full-time home care for Rose Jewel.

JJ shrugged. "It's what Great-Grandma Rose wanted. Says she doesn't want to die at the ranch. She didn't even want to visit anymore. All the sisters, Grandma Cappy, Great-Aunt Etta and Great-Aunt Willow weren't thrilled, but Great-Grandma Rose always gets her way."

"That's odd. Most people *want* to die in their own homes. How old is she now?"

"Ninety-six." JJ's dainty young face looked amazed at anyone being that old. "Anyway, between the perfect Rose Jewel, Cappy and her horses, Willow and her politics, and Etta and her winery, I think my mother just wanted to escape to someplace where she could breathe. Not to mention the ever-present Silent Sisters, as Bliss and I used to call them."

"The Silent Sisters?"

"The sisters who died. Two sets of twins. Add them up and you get the seven sisters the ranch was named for."

"I thought it was named for the volcanic peaks."

"Well, I'm sure that had something to do with the name, too. When my great-grandfather came here from Virginia right after WWI, he just called it the Brown Ranch. The two sets of twins died after they moved here. Cappy was about eight at the time, my great-aunts a few years younger. Great-Grandpa Brown changed the name to honor them. They died really young—right after they were born. No one had twins in the family again until Bliss and I were born."

"That's right," I said, an old memory coming back to me—when I first met Bliss I asked her about her name. "Bliss said she had a twin sister named Joy."

JJ grinned. "That's me. My full name is Joy Jewel. She's Bliss Jewel. All of the Brown women have the middle name

Jewel in honor of Great-Grandmother. I like JJ better. It's what my dad calls me."

"So that's where Seven Bars Jewel came from," I said. The stallion they had standing stud was well known and in demand because of his ability to produce not only winning racehorses, but also superior cutting horses. Daddy had considered breeding his quarter horse mare, Reba, to Seven B, as they called him, but the five-thousand-dollar stud fee the stallion commanded was definitely more than we could afford. "He's a beauty."

"Yeah, he's the cornerstone of Grandma Cappy's breeding operation. He has direct lineage to Three Bars."

Though I didn't know much about quarter horse breeding, even I'd heard of Three Bars, one of the most famous quarter horses that ever lived. He'd produced extraordinary offspring in racing, halter, and cutting events.

I searched her dainty features for a resemblance to Bliss. "Are you fraternal twins?"

She laughed and untwisted her legs, relaxing again. "Actually, we're identical, but we've done everything to avoid looking alike. Our parents always encouraged our individuality."

I peered closer at her face, decorated with bold, bright makeup and was surprised to see that underneath she and Bliss did indeed have the same bone structure, eye color, the same arch of eyebrow.

"I fit right in with our parents' hippie lifestyle," JJ continued, "but Bliss has rebelled since she was a kid. She would alphabetize our canned goods and use her birthday money from Cappy to buy file folders to organize her school papers. She drove Susa and Moonie insane trying to turn the commune into her version of *The Brady Bunch*."

"Susa and Moonie?"

JJ colored slightly again. "My mom and dad. Their conventional names are Susanna and Brad. Anyway, Bliss moved in with Cappy the minute she turned eighteen. Frankly, I think they should have let her live with Grandma earlier. She probably would have been a lot happier, but my parents believed in keeping the family together. It's not what people think. We didn't grow up without morals. My mom took us to the evening folk mass every week at a little Mexican church near the commune, and she and my dad really loved each other. Even their split-up wasn't vindictive. I had a wonderful, if slightly irregular, childhood." The last sentence was said with a hint of defiance. She'd obviously been forced to defend her parents' lifestyle before.

"Are you and Bliss close?" I asked, curious. There were no two identical twins who could look and act more different, so I couldn't imagine how they'd relate.

"We've always gotten along great. What annoys her to no end in our parents doesn't seem to bother her with me. We've seen each other once a week since I moved back down here when Susa did. Bliss and Susa live out at the ranch, but that's just a little too much family for me, so I rent a house downtown. Sometimes Bliss stays with me if she has to work a double shift and is too tired to drive home."

"How's your family taking the news about the baby?"

"Susa's excited, of course. She's been looking for something to focus on since she left Moonie. Cappy's in the middle of racing season and is always training some horse or another, so she's distracted. She just said she trusts that Bliss will do the right thing and handle it fine. She and Bliss are just alike. I can imagine Grandma Cappy having a baby in the morning and breaking a green filly that afternoon without batting an eyelash. Great-Aunt Willow and her granddaughter, my cousin Arcadia, are scandalized, being the conservative society branch of the family, and Great-Aunt Etta's too busy with grape harvest and the crush to pay attention to anything unless it has to do with wine."

"How's that working out, having both a winery and a horse-breeding operation?" The struggle between cattle ranchers and wineries for available land was a hot topic these days in San Celina County.

"It's been nine years now, and Seven Sisters Winery is rapidly taking over the family, which is causing a lot of problems between my grandma and her sisters." She shifted in her chair, scratching around a red, paste-on jewel on her neck. "The ranch is run by a trust left by my great-grandfather, and there never was a source of conflict until Great-Aunt Etta started the winery. My mom's brother, my uncle Chase, is involved with the winery, too, and has voted at times against Grandma Cappy. They begrudge her every penny she spends on the horses."

Chase Brown, Cappy's son, was a local lawyer, former city council member, and a regular at the political shindigs I was often forced to attend these days with Gabe. He was in his late forties, never married, and handsome in that alcohol-flushed, decadent, aging-movie-star sort of way that appeals to some women.

"Didn't your great-grandfather intend it to be only a horse-breeding farm?"

"Yes, but even though Cappy's got a great reputation, I guess quarterhorse racing took a big plunge in the early eighties, and that hurt her as a breeder. She's slowly built the business back up, but it's never been the same. The winery has its ups and downs, too, apparently. Both need a lot of money to operate, but it seems like the winery is slowly becoming the family's main business."

"Wine is certainly taking over the county, that's for sure," I said. It was a sore spot among ranchers, and I heard about it constantly from Daddy, more so, it seemed, in the last year or so. Daddy and his friends called the wine people "those grape assholes" whenever Dove wasn't around to reprimand them.

She stood up and smoothed down her thin skirt. "Well, times change. We can either float with the current or drown as Great-Aunt Willow loves to say. I don't necessarily like it, but she's got a point."

I shrugged, not willing to delve any further into something I felt so conflicted about. I'd had enough changes in the last two years to last me a lifetime. Things staying status quo for a few months looked pretty appealing.

"So," she said. "What I actually came in to do besides confess was invite you and Gabe to dinner at the ranch tonight. Grandma Cappy thought it wise that we all get together and meet each other since we'll be related soon. I know it's short notice, but she figured we'd better start making plans."

"Have Bliss and Sam set a date? He didn't say anything to us."

"I think that's what's on the agenda tonight. Will you come? Oh, and ask Dove and your father, too."

"We wouldn't miss it for the world. I'll call Dove right now."

I caught Dove just as she was leaving and told her quickly about the invitation. "Are you and Daddy busy?"

"We'll be there with bells on. I haven't seen Cappy in a month of Sundays. Now we're going to be kin. That just tickles me."

"It'll be interesting, that's for sure," I replied.

I finished up the grant application and watered my scraggly fern before going out to the central co-op room. The co-op studios, once the Sinclair hacienda's stables, were separated into small storage and workrooms that accommodated the woodworkers, painters, potters, and other folk artisans. The main studio was usually filled with quilters, since it was the only room big enough to hold our two quilt frames, which could extend from crib to king-size with the adjustments of a few screws. We'd taken to renting out the room and quilt frames for a small hourly fee to various quilting groups. It was one of the small ways the museum could supplement our always fluctuating sources of revenue. I loved it when the local quilt groups rented time, because they always showed up with some wonderful snacks—quilters are often award-winning cooks. Sure enough, the room had filled with quilters since I entered my tiny back office three hours earlier, but I resisted the lemon bars on the counter, telling myself that lunch was just minutes away. Maybe there would be some left for my three o'clock sugar fix.

The San Celina Cotton Patch Quilters were working on a huge quilt in the dominant colors of purple, burgundy, white, gold, and green. Each square was an appliquéd scene of vines, grapes, and leaves representing a different variety of grape grown in San Celina County. The exotic, romantic-sounding names of the grapes were embroidered at the bottom of each square—zinfandel, cabernet sauvignon, chardonnay, pinot noir, grenache, viognier, merlot, syrah.

"It's beautiful," I said. "Who's it for?"

"It's a raffle quilt," a silver-haired woman in a Hopi storyteller quilt vest said, looking up from her work. "The Harvest Wine Festival in Mission Plaza is this weekend, and the money goes toward the free clinics in Paso Robles and San Celina. The winner will be announced on Saturday at the Zin and Zydeco event."

"Gabe and I have tickets," I said. "He loves zydeco music. Not to mention wine."

"You'd better buy some raffle tickets, then," the woman

said. "A dollar a piece or five for five dollars."

"Gee, what a deal," I said, pulling a five out of my faded Wranglers.

She took my money and handed me five numbered tickets. "We thought about making it five for six dollars to see if anyone fell for it, but Edna there is making us toe the line. Still thinks she's a guard at the county jail."

Edna, a titian-haired lady in her late sixties, raised matching red eyebrows. "You gotta watch these ladies. They'll do anything to get good health care for needy kids."

"What a lawless bunch," I said, laughing.

At Liddie's Cafe downtown I wiggled through a group of tourists perusing the specials written on the blackboard in the cramped 1950s' lobby. Liddie's "25-Hour" Cafe had been the locals' favorite eating place since before my family even came to San Celina in the early sixties. Fancy restaurants and trendy cafes have come and gone, and still Liddie's survived. With its taped red vinyl booths, Formica tables, faded pictures of 4-H lambs on the wall, and country classics on the jukebox, it was more than a tradition; it was almost a shrine to the way things were. Buck, the eighty-year-old owner, didn't believe anyone worthwhile recorded songs after Tammy Wynette and George Jones in their prime, though he consented, when a few of us younger regulars complained, to allow Dwight Yoakam, Emmylou Harris, and Dale Watson a place on the roll.

And then there was Nadine.

Standing behind the counter, she eyed me over her pointy pink eyeglasses. Her matching pink uniform was crisp and clean and had one of those handkerchief name tags that no one ever sees waitresses wear anymore except on television. Or at Liddie's.

"They're in your usual booth," she said, nodding toward the back. "You ask Emory how long he's gonna put up with that girl a-teasin' him, like a kitten with a broken-legged grasshopper."

"No, thanks," I said cheerfully. "I'll leave that fine and nosy question to you." Everyone, especially Nadine, was dying to find out when Emory and Elvia would tie the knot. Little did she know that another wedding was on the horizon before theirs. I relished having information before her.

"I'll fine and nosy you," she called after me. "What will you be wanting today, Miss Priss? They've already ordered."

"The chili any good today?"

"It won't give you ptomaine poisoning, if that's what you're asking."

"Extra cheese and onions, Miss Nadine. I surely thank you." I turned and blew her a kiss.

She grumbled under her breath, then snapped at the tourists. "For cryin' out loud, people, you've got two choices—take it or leave it." Then she yelled my order to the cook.

In the booth, Emory and Elvia were sitting side by side, not speaking.

"Everything okay?" I asked, sliding across from them. Nadine had already brought my water and large Coke. I sipped at my water and looked from Emory's face to Elvia's—her face was neutral, his troubled.

"Fine," Elvia said, but the tone of her voice told me otherwise. Her full red mouth turned downward.

Emory's green eyes were miserable and a little resigned. I wondered just how long my blond, urbane, Arkansas Razorback–obsessed, and very rich cousin would continue to pursue my beautiful but reluctant friend. It had been eleven months of one step forward, five steps back, and though he was a patient and optimistic man, his fuel gauge seemed to be moving precariously close to empty. I knew the reason she was so wary of men, a devastating relationship with a sabbatical replacement professor when she was twenty-three—one who'd told her he was single, but she later found out was married with five kids and no intentions of leaving his family. There'd been a couple of relationships since then, but none that had any power over her emotions. Until Emory. He was different, she knew it, and that scared her to death. There were so many things I could explain to him about her, but didn't. Her history . . . and her feelings for him were something she had to tell him.

Oh well, the road to love was a bumpy one—I certainly knew that. Thank goodness things had smoothed out for me and Gabe in the last few months. Maybe some gossip would take their minds off their personal problems. "You'll never guess what I found out only minutes ago about Bliss."

Elvia put a phony, interested expression on her face and straightened the collar of her forest green wool suit. "Tell us."

Emory sipped his black coffee and remained silent.

"She's an identical twin. Her sister is a member of our co-op, and I never knew they were related."

"If she's an identical twin . . ." Emory started.

I held up my hand. "I'm telling you, Emory, they're like a German shepherd and a poodle. I noticed the resemblance after JJ told me, but honestly, it was a surprise to me. JJ's a quilt artist. You might have seen some of her work around town. She makes very untraditional crazy quilts that kind of tell stories."

"You mean JJ Brown?" Elvia said. "I bought one of her quilts to hang in the children's department at the store. It portrayed some of the original Grimms' and Hans Christian Andersen fairy tales. I liked it because she stayed true to the stories—they weren't all Disneyed up. Cinderella's stepsisters go blind in the end."

"Never heard of her," Emory said. "What does she think of Sam's dilemma?"

Before I could answer, our food arrived. Elvia had a salad and vegetable soup, Emory, his favorite Western omelette with a side of avocado. Nadine beamed at Emory. "Anything else, sweetie?" she asked him.

"No, ma'am," he said, giving her his best Karo syrup smile. "It all looks so delicious I swear I don't know where to begin."

"Saved that avocado for you 'cause it was the best of the bunch."

"My dear Nadine, you are a queen among women, and I gratefully offer you my heart."

I snorted at his words.

Nadine whacked me in the shoulder with the back of her hand. "Missy, you could take a lesson in manners from your cousin here. And it wouldn't hurt you to remember that *tipping* is not a country in China." With that, she turned and marched away, her thick-soled shoes squeaking across the old linoleum floor.

Elvia laughed out loud, causing Emory to beam. The tension between them eased a bit.

"So, find out anything else?" Emory asked, digging into his omelette.

"Not much. I'll probably find out more tonight, though, since Gabe, Dove, Daddy, and I are invited to the Seven Sisters ranch for a get-acquainted dinner."

"Don't you know the family already?" Elvia asked.

"Dove and Cappy—that's Bliss and JJ's grandma—belong to some of the same clubs. I've seen Bliss's uncle around, but he's in his late forties, so we never ran in the same crowd. Bliss, JJ, and their cousin, Arcadia, are in their twenties, so they're quite a bit younger than me. Except for

Dove and Cappy, our families have never had any reason to connect."

"Until now," Emory said.

"Until now," I agreed.

"That name Arcadia sounds familiar," Elvia said.

"She and her new husband, Giles Norton, are frequently pictured in the *Tribune*'s society section," Emory supplied. "Cappy's younger sister, Willow, had a daughter named Phoebe who died in a plane accident with her husband about twenty years ago. They had one child, a daughter named Arcadia, who was nine at the time. She went to live with her grandmother Willow. A few years back, Arcadia married Giles Norton of the ultra-snobby Napa Valley Nortons. Demands to be called a 'vintner' rather than winemaker, which is the more favored term among wine people in this easygoing little county. His father is William Giles Norton of Napa Valley fame. The family has owned wineries in Napa Valley for a hundred years. Giles is currently running the Norton Winery over the grade in Paso Robles. The winery's not very old, but everything in it is the best. Word on the grapevine, so to speak, is that he's itching to become a large presence down here in San Celina County, and he doesn't care how he does it."

I looked at my cousin, amazed. He'd only been living here eleven months and he already knew more about most of the inhabitants than I did. "Well, I'll be meeting the whole clan tonight. I'll give you both the full report tomorrow."

Elvia left first since she had a sales rep due at the store. Emory and I stayed longer, sharing a cherry cobbler à la mode.

"So, what's going on with you two?" I asked.

He shrugged his shoulders under his tailored Hugo Boss sports jacket. "We're at an impasse. I want more commitment. She's happy with things the way they are."

I didn't answer because I didn't know what to say. I loved both of these people so much, and though a part of me was thrilled they were together, I also knew it could spell disaster. Already things had become a little awkward between me and Elvia since we couldn't dissect this relationship-in-progress like we had with other men she'd dated. I didn't want her hurt, but I also didn't want my cousin, who was more like a brother to me, to be hurt either. I sighed and patted his hand.

"Enough about me," he said, setting his spoon down. "How's this unexpected pregnancy affecting you and the chief?"

It was my turn to shrug. "He's upset, of course. Thinks they're too young and too irresponsible. He'll cool down. They both have very concerned families, so I'm guessing too much help will be more their problem than not enough."

He looked at me steadily. "No, I mean how is this affecting you and Gabe personally?"

I knew what he was talking about and wanted to ignore it. But Emory, who'd been my bosom buddy since our preteen summer together at the ranch the year his mom died, knew better than anyone the mixed feelings I had every time someone I knew became pregnant.

"More to the point, are you okay?" he asked.

Another sigh escaped my chest. "Emory, you know how it is. We had the tests, and they say there's nothing wrong with either of us. Obviously it isn't him. He has a son. The next step is all that fertility stuff, and I'm not sure I want to do any of that."

"Why?"

I carefully folded and unfolded my paper napkin, not looking at him. "All that poking and prodding. The drugs. You know how I hate going to doctors. Maybe I don't want it bad enough to go through all that. If it happens, then great, but if it doesn't . . ." I ran my hand over the napkin, smoothing it. "Maybe that's just how things are supposed to be."

"You'd make a great mom."

I continued to play with my napkin, reluctant to confess, even to this man who had been my closest confidante since childhood, the sadness inside of me at the thought of having a child. How my mother's death so early in my life left me terrified about repeating that with my own child, how a part of me was secretly glad the decision had been taken out of my hands.

"Do you and Gabe ever talk about it?"

"Some. He's mostly concerned that I'm happy, and right now I am happier than I've ever been, so I'm just going to deal with what's on my plate right this moment and leave the rest to God."

"Wish I could be that wise," he said, crumpling his own napkin and tossing it in our empty dessert bowl. "I just want to grab Elvia by the hair and haul her down to the justice of the peace."

The image made me laugh out loud. "You'd better hope these tables aren't bugged, 'cause if my feminist friend ever heard you say that, you'd be seeing her taillights fifty miles down the highway before you could blink those gorgeous green Southern eyes of yours."

THAT EVENING I performed a scenario familiar to every woman on earth—standing in front of the closet an hour before the big event, moaning I had nothing to wear.

"You should go shopping more," Gabe said practically, tying a patterned silk tie in front of our long mirror. He always had the appropriate clothes for everything. Tonight it was gray wool slacks, a blue-gray tweedy jacket, and a dark gray shirt.

"I hate to shop," I said, but knowing he was right.

With Elvia's voice in my head giving me directions, I finally decided on a pair of black wool Anne Klein pants she'd made me buy, a lapis-colored silk shirt, my good Lucchese boots, and a pair of silver, turquoise, and lapis earrings by Ray Tracey, a Navajo jeweller from New Mexico whose clean lines and unusual combinations of stones appealed to me. They were a gift from Emory, who'd once interviewed the artist for an article he did for *Southwest Indian Arts and Crafts* magazine.

On the drive to Amelia Valley, Gabe casually mentioned that he had talked to Lydia earlier that afternoon.

"Oh?" I murmured.

"She's upset about Sam, of course, but I calmed her down. She doesn't know Bliss, thought she was some young girl trying to trap him. I set her straight." He glanced over at me.

"Oh," I repeated noncommittally. There was no way I was being pulled into commenting on anything to do with his ex-wife.

"She's coming up this weekend. She's staying at the San Celina Inn."

"An article in the *Tribune* said they've just redecorated. I'm sure she'll like it."

He gave a low laugh and said, "If she doesn't, they'll hear about it."

At least I had a few more days before I met this assertive and gorgeous woman. I'm not a particularly jealous person, but I had to admit it would have made me a lot happier if she didn't look quite so much like a *Vogue* model or wasn't so incredibly successful, not to mention having a child in common with my husband. I picked at a piece of white lint on my knee. In some ways I envied Sam and Bliss. It was so much easier when you're young and have minimal history to cloud a relationship.

"So," I said, changing the subject, "tell me everything you know about wine so I don't appear unsophisticated around these people." I had a problem. Not only did I not particularly like wine, I didn't like grapes—grape anything—the fruit itself, grape juice, grape jelly, not even that horrible grape soda pop Gabe and Sam loved so much. "There's red and white, that much I know. Now, quick, tell me the rest so I can fake it."

Gabe laughed and maneuvered his sky blue '68 Corvette down the interstate off ramp and headed down a long, twisting country highway. "That's one of the things I love about you, *querida*. Your complete confidence in your ability to pull one over on people even though your confidence is significantly greater than your ability."

I whacked his biceps with the back of my hand. "Do what the lady says or you'll be sleeping in the doghouse with Scout."

"He sleeps in the kitchen," Gabe said amicably. "At least I won't have far to go to the coffeepot in the morning."

"Wine, Friday. Tell me about wine. I don't want to insult Sam's in-laws-to-be. Tell me what I should do."

"Be yourself, sweetheart, with a few alterations. Drink what they put in front of you and say it's marvelous. Smile a lot. Try not to make your cauliflower face when you drink it."

My cauliflower face was what he called my expression when I taste something I can't stand. Faking it has never been one of my strong points.

"I can do that," I said.

The sky had faded to a lavender dusk when we came to Seven Sisters Road. Two-hundred-year-old oaks, leafy ash, and a few scattered maple trees canopied the narrow, twisting road and formed long, jagged evening shadows. Though it was still only the latter part of September, there had been a slight frost a week ago, and some of the maples had turned reddish-yellow, adding an unexpected color to the dusty green of the oaks. After five miles of winding road, we came to the entrance of the ranch. A white wrought-iron arch was topped by the Seven Sisters brand—two back-to-back interlocked S's. Underneath the arch, swinging from two chains, was a simple wooden sign: SEVEN SISTERS RANCH—EST. 1922. Underneath that sign dangled a slightly larger one carved with the outline of seven peaks: SEVEN SISTERS WINERY—EST. 1985. We drove through the open gates, passing still-green pastures with a few horses contentedly browsing the ground. Farther down the road, the pastures turned into rows of grapevines. Set among the rows were two gray-and-white farmhouses with window boxes filled with bright red flowers, too far away for me to name. One of the houses had tiny, blinking white Christmas lights scattered throughout the small bushes in front of the wraparound porch and a Volkswagen van painted with a colorful mural parked in front.

"California fireflies," I said, pointing at the lights.

We went by a row of stables and then drove up a slight incline, passing the tasting room—once the original landowner's residence. Its whitewashed adobe walls and red tile roof were a twin to the folk art museum. We turned a corner where the "new" ranch house perched on top of a hill overlooking the valley. The Craftsman-style house was painted shades of tan and brown, blending in with the oaks and pines growing tall and lush around it. A sprawling three stories, and lit up bright as a ballpark, it looked large enough to house three or four families. In the circular driveway were parked a half dozen cars, including one of

Daddy's blue Ramsey Ranch trucks. We pulled in behind a gleaming maroon Jaguar.

Gabe eyed the Jag and whistled under his breath. "The gang really *is* all here."

"What do you mean?" I asked.

"That's Lydia's car. She said she wouldn't be able to reschedule the trial she was working on, but apparently she did."

I looked through the windshield at the sleek, expensive car, my heart sinking, my armpits growing damp, thankful that it was almost dark so Gabe couldn't see what was, no doubt, the cauliflower look on my face.

THE DEEP-SET front porch was comfortably crowded with some bent willow tables and chairs, a long porch swing, and three Adirondack benches. All were covered with identical green plaid cushions. A large, triangular dinner bell, the kind Dove used to call Daddy and the hands in from the barn, hung next to the porch steps.

"This is some place," Gabe said in a low voice.

"Eighteen thousand square feet," I said, for some reason remembering that fact from the long-ago home tour. "Designed by Julia Morgan herself. She and the judge were personal friends, I heard."

"Who's Julia Morgan?"

"You've never heard of Julia Morgan?"

His face was blank.

"She only designed the Hearst Castle, a ton of YWCAs, some big conference center up in Pacific Grove that's supposed to be the biggest arts and crafts–style complex in the country, and a good deal of the houses in Berkeley. Never got the credit she deserved, probably because she was a woman."

He groaned under his breath. "Don't tell that to Lydia, or we'll be hearing a lecture half the night on how men keep women down."

"Which might do you some good, *el patrón,*" I said, my voice slightly mocking as I knocked on the carved front door. *Maybe I'd like this Lydia after all.*

Cappy herself answered. She was dressed in neat black Wranglers, a black cowboy shirt with yellow roses embroidered on the yoke, and shiny black round-toed riding boots. Except for the occasional newspaper photo, I hadn't seen her for probably ten years, but she hadn't changed much with her cropped, iron gray hair, wide, strong jaw, and tanned skin, whose real beauty was found in the deep lines radiating from her clear, gray eyes and faintly overbitten smile.

"Benni Louise Harper, I swear you don't look a day over eighteen," she said, putting a wiry arm around my shoulders, giving me a hearty squeeze. "You still riding every day? Still practicing your rope tricks?" She looked up at Gabe. "You would be surprised what this one can do with ropes."

Gabe grinned at me and winked. "Is that right? We'll have to talk about that."

Cappy held out a short-nailed, age-spotted hand. "Cappy Brown here. You must be her police chief."

"That would be me," he said, taking her hand. "Gabe Ortiz."

"Pleased to make your acquaintance, Gabe. I've heard through the grapevine you're doing a bang-up job policing San Celina. Come on back to the big room and we'll get you a glass of wine." She nodded over at me. "Let me tell you, Chief, you're darn lucky to have corralled this one. She comes from good stock."

Gabe laughed and took my hand. "My grandfather was the best horse trader east of Dodge City, Kansas. He taught me if they had strong legs and good teeth, you can't go wrong."

"Sounds like a man I'd be proud to trade with. Come along now."

"Good teeth?" I said under my breath, elbowing him in the side. "You're going to pay for that remark, Friday."

We followed her down a long hall past a dark wooden staircase toward some open double doors.

The room was large and airy with an open-beam ceiling, reminding me of the sitting room of an expensive Montana hunting lodge. The sounds of people laughing and the tinkle of glassware washed over us the minute we stepped over the threshold. The deep brown leather sofas and wingback chairs were well used and comfortable-looking with bright, geometric Pendleton pillows tucked in the corners. Old, probably priceless, Navajo rugs were tossed casually over the backs of straight-back mission oak chairs. An antler chandelier, the lightbulbs cleverly hidden among the horns, lit the room with a warm glow. Behind a dark oak bar, a picture window stretched from one end of the room to the other, framing a breathtaking view of the Amelia Valley, its orderly seams of grape rows, and the Seven Sisters volcanic peaks, shadowed blue and gray in the waning evening light.

"Wine at the bar, and appetizers are over on the sideboard," Cappy said, pointing to the south side of the room where a small group of people gathered. "Help yourself. It's some of our 1988 vintage. A good year for the pinot noir, Etta tells me, though I've always preferred the '91 estate chardonnay. We're barbecuing a top block of beef and chicken and, for those with more exotic tastes, some wild boar my son, Chase, and our ranch manager, Jose, shot a few days ago. We have wines to match anything you care to eat, of course." She glanced at an antique grandfather clock next to us. Tiny carved racehorses, necks stretched for the finish line, ran around the clock face. "We'll probably be eating in another half hour or so. Chase will pour you whatever you want." She gestured to the man behind the bar.

Chase was dressed casually in an expensive sports jacket and white golf shirt. His blotchy face and loud laugh made me guess he'd been sampling the wine long before the first guest arrived. He stood in front of seven or eight wine bottles, each bearing a version of the silver-and-white Seven Sisters label—the seven volcanic hills with three horses connected tail to nose, running in front. "If you're not a wine drinker," she continued, "we have a full liquor cabinet, and Chase once worked as a bartender on a cruise ship. So if you drink it, he should be able to make it." She rolled her eyes. "One of his many unsuccessful forays into the world of real work. The rest of the time he practices law. I keep telling him if he practices enough, he might get halfway decent at it. My two sisters are late, as usual, but they'll eventually slither in." She looked up at Gabe, her mouth twisting into a sly, scheming grin. "You and my baby sister have tangled, I'll venture to guess."

"Who's your sister?" Gabe asked.

"Willow Brown D'Ambrosio. She was one of the city council members who voted against the budget initiative that would provide the city with more money for additional police. I can give you the license plate of her Lexus if you like. She's always parking in handicapped spots using our mother's sign even when Mother's not with her."

"Well, as to the voting, it's a free country," Gabe murmured, letting his voice drift off, not addressing the illegal use of the handicapped placard.

She winked at me and gave a deep belly laugh. "He's being a politician now, isn't he? I bet he wants to string her up by her diamond-studded ears. Probably would do her good. Shoot, she might even enjoy it."

I laughed at the somewhat shocked look on his face. I'd known there was no love lost between the sisters, since I could remember Cappy talking this way when I was a teenager. Old age and maturity obviously hadn't softened their attitudes toward one another.

"I think I'll go see how Jose's coming with the meat. Let me know if you two need anything and don't let Giles, Willow's no good grandson-in-law, talk you into buying stock in the company. No matter what he says, we're not selling out to his daddy's corporation."

"She's certainly something," Gabe said, watching Cappy stride across the room.

"That's mellow for Cappy," I said. "You ought to see her when she's really aggravated." I stared after her curiously. "Wonder what that remark about selling out was about."

Gabe shrugged. "Family squabbles. What would you like to drink?"

"Anything. I just need something to hold." I never could eat or drink comfortably at parties where I didn't know the people, especially when gorgeous ex-wives lurked in the bushes.

I spotted Dove and Daddy over by the natural stone fireplace gazing up at an original William Matthews watercolor of cowboys herding cattle through a pebble-strewn creek. Daddy held a glass of wine, gesturing up at the painting, nodding his head at something Dove said. I quickly scanned the rest of the room, looking for other people I knew and, if truth be told, for Lydia. I wanted to catch a glimpse of her before she saw me. There didn't seem to be anyone resembling the woman in Sam's picture, but I did see Sam and Bliss over by the picture window. He looked unusually subdued and even surprised me with his appearance. I don't know who helped him pick out the clothes—Gabe certainly hadn't—but he wore dressy dark slacks, a slate blue linen shirt, and black leather loafers. It was hard to believe this handsome, neat young man was the kid whose normal attire was either baggy surf shorts or faded Wranglers. Bliss wore dark green tailored pants and a thin, off-white shirt, her pale hair hanging loose and wavy around her shoulders. Sam dipped his dark head a moment, listening to something she said, his eyes drinking her in. They were a physically striking couple, no doubt about it—not just because of their youth, but also because of the stark difference in their coloring. I studied them a moment, contemplating what their child might look like.

Behind me Gabe said, "You look wonderful, as always." His voice was low and pleasant, his practiced public voice. Through the thin silk of my shirt, I felt his large hand on my elbow. "Benni, I want you to meet Lydia."

I turned and faced her, licking my suddenly dry lips. She was even more striking in person than in Sam's photo, though, I was happy to see, not as beautiful. Taller than my five feet two by about five inches, her black hair was cut in a straight, shoulder-sweeping style, making the most of its glossy ebony shine. Perfect makeup softened her sharp features, her face dominated by the deep brown luminous eyes she'd passed on to her son. Her red designer suit—Armani, Anne Klein, Chanel, Elvia would know—fit her frame without a bulge. Though she was eight years older than me with skin that, I gleefully noted, showed it, I still felt like a mixed breed ranch horse standing next to a champion Kentucky Thoroughbred.

She held out a French-manicured hand. "I'm happy to finally meet you," she said. Her handshake was firm, dry, and assured, befitting a successful professional woman. "I've heard so many wonderful things about you."

I paused for a moment. "Me, too," I finally said, thinking, *Oh, very clever reply.* That should send her running to the hills in intellectual terror and intimidation.

Gabe said, "I'm on the way to the bar to get Benni a drink. Would you like something?"

"That would be wonderful. Just bring me my usual."

"Chardonnay is apparently one of Seven Sisters' specialties," he said.

Her deep-throated laugh caused a glimmer of recollection on his face, obviously bringing back an intimate memory. That and the fact that he actually remembered what she liked to drink intensified my feelings of not exactly jealousy . . . More like anxiety.

She laughed again, teasing him with the memory. His nervous returning laugh tempted me to smack him.

Oh, geeze, forget anxiety. Jealousy is exactly what it was.

After he left, attempting to be mature, I said, "Cappy says their '91 estate chardonnay is very good."

Her lips curved in a half smile. "Are you a wine aficionado?"

Don't even try to compete in that arena, a small voice inside me warned. "No," I said, for once heeding the sensible voice. "Cappy just told us that. Actually, I know next to nothing about wine. Don't even like it. Don't even like grape juice."

She laughed again, heartier this time, a there's-no-male-to-impress female laugh. "You're honest, I'll give you that.

If you want to know the truth, Benni Harper, if I wasn't a more secure person, I'd hate you. Not only did you manage to snag Mr. Evade-All-Emotional-Entanglements over there"—she nodded at Gabe's broad back—"but my son practically worships you. I do appreciate you taking care of my two men so well."

Her two men? I cleared my throat, stuck for a comeback. Gabe hadn't been *her man* for almost nine years now. Before I could think of a retort, Gabe returned with a glass of wheat-colored wine for Lydia and a club soda for me.

"The appetizers are really something," he said. "You ladies should check them out."

"Thank you," Lydia said, taking the glass from Gabe, her hand lightly brushing his. "I think I will after I reconnect with my son and future daughter-in-law." She sipped the wine. "Umm, this *is* very good. Ms. Brown certainly does know how to make wine." She looked up at Gabe, her expression serious and worried. "We need to talk about Sam."

"Call me at work tomorrow. We'll compare schedules and get together."

"I'll do that." She turned back to me. "It was so nice finally meeting you, Benni. We'll see each other again soon, I'm sure."

"I'm sure we will." I took a huge gulp of my club soda, annoyed at myself for acting like a tongue-tied junior high school girl.

"She's very worried about Sam and Bliss," Gabe said, watching her walk toward their son. "I think she's going to try to talk them out of getting married."

"And what do you think?" I asked, trying to be calm and mature about everything, attempting to ignore the explicit and very appealing mental picture of her falling off

San Patricio pier and being eaten by a passing great white shark.

"She should be worried. They are young and naive. Then again, I'm proud he wants to take responsibility for this baby. Makes me think that we did some things right as parents."

I tucked my arm through his. "You did a lot right in raising him. Sam's a wonderful person, and so is Bliss. Everything's going to work out just fine."

"Your optimism is appreciated, though not necessarily shared. I spent too many years in a patrol car going to family disputes caused, in part, by the stress of immature children trying raise their own children. Not to mention that he's marrying into a family that appears to already have its share of animosity."

"Oh, go chow down on the appetizers, you cynical old cop. And drink some sweet wine while you're there to brighten your outlook."

He kissed the top of my head and headed back toward the oak bar. I walked over to Dove and Daddy, who were now comfortably situated on a long leather sofa next to an open window.

"Hey, honeybun! I swear, isn't this place just like out of a magazine?" Dove said, patting the sofa next to her.

"Hey back." I gave each a quick hug and sat next to her. Daddy stood next to the window, eating some barbecued Portuguese sausage. "I think it was in a decorating magazine once on California ranch estates. Maybe it was *Country Living* or *Sunset*."

"I think it was *Sunset,*" Dove said. "I remember Willow a-braggin' about it at some historical meeting. She used to attend real regular, but I hear she spends most of her time either doing city council stuff or taking care of her mama. I guess Rose Jewel is a real handful over at Oak Terrace."

"Really, why?"

"Apparently nothing is ever right to suit her. Willow's over there almost every day. Would've been a lot easier if they'd just kept her here."

"She didn't want that," I said, tucking my arm through hers. "JJ, Bliss's sister, told me that she didn't want to die on the ranch. She won't even visit anymore. I guess that's why she's not here tonight."

"Well, that's odd," Dove said.

"I know."

"How do you know Bliss's sister?" Dove asked.

"I thought I told you. She's one of the artists in the co-op. I just found out today that she and Bliss are twins, though you'd never guess it by looking at them."

Another couple had arrived, so I said, "Okay, tell me who everyone is." Dove's memory for faces and names, even of people she'd only met once or twice, was phenomenal.

"I'll start with the two who just walked in," she said in a low voice. "Now pay attention, 'cause I'm not going to repeat myself."

Daddy let out a chuckle, the whole situation amusing him to no end. The one thing you had to say about my father was society or money didn't impress him in the least. If you took care of your family, weren't cruel to animals or children or people weaker than you, worshiped God, worked hard, respected the land and paid your bills on time, you were okay by his book no matter how much money or status you had. If you didn't, you were plain white trash, no matter what color your skin happened to be.

"The woman in that flowy pink dress is Willow's granddaughter, Arcadia Norton. Handsome fella with her is her husband, Giles Norton."

"Snooty old Napa Valley wine family, I heard," I commented. Arcadia had an all-American, shampoo-model prettiness with long, light brown hair and ivory skin. Giles was dressed in a pair of pressed khaki pants, a starched button-down shirt, and suede tassel loafers. Very Ivy League–looking. Thanks to Emory, I knew Arcadia was twenty-nine. Giles looked to be in his late thirties.

"Rumor has it among the grape assholes . . ." Daddy started.

Dove shot him a severe look. He grinned and gave me a broad wink. "Word among the grape *growers* is that he's trying to merge Seven Sisters with Norton Wine Group. Wants to go national within two years and international within five and that Willow is for it and Cappy is fighting tooth and nail against it. Don't know where Etta stands. They've got some real fine pasture land up in the foothills they're clearing to plant more grapes. Gonna take down about two hundred oak trees I heard, though the greenie-beans are fighting it with some of their fancy lawyers." Greenie-beans is what Daddy calls the most rabid environmentalists. He shook his head, amazed at the whole thing. "We ranchers are lookin' pretty good to the greenie-beans these days. At least they can't accuse us of killing oaks."

"That explains a comment Cappy made to me and Gabe about Giles," I said. "Which one is Etta?" She was the third and youngest sister, the unmarried one. The one who had taught home economics for years at Amelia Valley High School until she retired back in the early eighties and started making wine as a hobby, learning as she went along from articles and mail-order wine books. I remembered seeing bottles of her homemade wine at the MidState Fair back when I was a 4-H kid showing my lambs and calves. Her wine always won blue ribbons.

Dove pointed across the room. "Etta's over there, talking

to Sam and Bliss and that pretty Spanish lady."

I grabbed her finger and pushed it down. "Very funny, Dove."

"Did you meet her?" Dove asked.

"Yes, and she's very nice."

"You best watch her. I don't cotton to how she's a-lookin' at your husband."

"I told you, she's very nice. We had a nice talk."

"Heed my words, honeybun. She looks like one who could surely nice you to death."

"Enough about her," I said, trying not to let my irritation show. "Etta's the one in the black velvet blouse and skirt, I'm assuming." Her outfit was plain except for her fist-sized Navajo squash blossom necklace.

"That's her," Daddy said. "They say she's a genius with wine, that the winery would be nothing without her. Drives the other wine fellas crazy, Bob down at the Farm Supply says. A lot of them old boys have fancy degrees in some kind of wine culture or something, and she runs circles around them. Wins all the big awards. And to add flies to the manure, she's a woman."

Dove and I glared at him simultaneously.

He held up his hands in apology. "I was just reporting what the boys at the Farm Supply say."

"Viticulture," I said, remembering the chapter I'd read on it years ago when I was taking classes for my minor in agriculture. "The study of cultivating and growing grapes is called viticulture."

"Whatever," Daddy said, eating his last sausage, then using the toothpick on his teeth. "Whatever that degree is, she ain't got it, and they do, and she still makes better wine than any of 'em. Apparently that woman can make wine out of raisins. I say more power to her."

"Here, here," Dove agreed.

Etta looked like a protégé of Georgia O'Keeffe. I guessed that Bliss, with her pioneer spirit, was probably Cappy's favorite and that maybe JJ, being an artist, might be her great-aunt Etta's favorite relative, especially since Etta had never married and had any children or grandchildren of her own.

My assumption proved correct when JJ came in from the back patio and Etta rushed across the spacious room and took JJ's face in her large hands. Following JJ was an earthy, fortyish woman with lush graying blond hair flowing down her back. She watched Etta's enthusiastic greeting with an uneasy expression. The earthy woman looked enough like Bliss and JJ that she had to be their mother, Susa—the ex-hippie nurse-midwife. Tonight she looked like any slightly artsy, upper-middle-class San Celina matron with a preference for autumn-toned gauzy dresses and handmade bead jewelry. She stood quietly watching her daughter chatter with her aunt, as much a part of the exchange as if she'd been a stranger at a bus stop.

Behind us, Cappy started tapping the side of her wineglass with a silver knife, continuing until the noisy voices quieted down. Dove and I stood up and faced her.

"Everyone's here but Willow, and she said she'd be here as soon as the city council meeting is over, so I think we'd best get on with the toast and go eat that delicious barbecue Jose has been slaving over. As the oldest member of the Brown family here, I welcome you all to Seven Sisters Ranch. We are—"

"And winery," Giles broke in, causing a few titters in the group.

Cappy stared at him a long, uncomfortable moment, her eyes boring holes in his forehead. Then she smiled. "Of course, Giles. Seven Sisters Ranch and Winery." She said the last word slowly, deliberately. "We are here to celebrate the engagement of our own sweet Bliss to a fine young man, Sam Ortiz." She held up her glass, and we all followed suit. "Long life, easy trails, and much happiness. Now, let's eat."

I searched the crowd, looking for Gabe, wanting to catch his eye. He was standing next to Lydia, Etta, and JJ. I watched as he clinked glasses with Etta and JJ, then turned and did the same with Lydia. She smiled at him, and he smiled back. Then they walked over to their son, whose face was flushed with excitement and embarrassment. Gabe hugged Bliss, and Lydia hugged Sam. Then Sam and Gabe hugged. At that moment, Giles passed next to Bliss and whispered something in her ear. Her face flushed pink and she gave him a look that, had she been wearing her gun, might have proven dangerous. Then Sam turned back to her, and in an instant her smile returned. Giles moved over to the bar and poured a glass of wine, then leaned against the bar watching Bliss and Sam with narrowed eyes.

"Why don't you go over and stand with your husband?" Dove whispered in my ear.

"He's busy right now," I said, determined not to appear the paranoid second wife.

"And going to get a might busier if'n you don't get over there and guard the rooster roost."

"I trust him," I said firmly. "This situation is something he and Lydia have to work out. Sam is their son."

Dove made a disbelieving sound deep in her throat. "All I have to say is you'd better keep your eyes open on this one."

"Nothing to watch, Dove. They just want to work out what's best for Sam."

"Let's eat," Dove said. "I do believe you're getting lightheaded."

"Daddy!" I turned to him, exasperated. "Would you please talk to your mother?"

"Don't look at me, pumpkin," he said, setting his empty plate and glass down on the arts and crafts–style coffee table. "Your gramma gets something in her craw, may as well try to wrestle a bobcat as change her mind."

"Just be nice to her," I grumbled in Dove's ear as I took her arm and we walked out to the patio.

"Me?" Dove feigned shock and hurt. "Honeybun, I'm always nice to everyone."

I scanned the sky.

"What are you looking for?" Dove asked.

"The cloud holding the lightning bolt that God will strike you dead with for lying."

She smacked my hand. "You are more stubborn than a roomful of Baptists. And that's all you know. If God wanted to strike me dead, He wouldn't need a cloud."

Laughing, we walked out to a brick patio overlooking the neat vineyards with the Santa Lucia mountains in the distance. It was almost dark, but the patio, thick with clay pots filled with flowers and ferns, was cleverly lit by recessed lighting and electric lamps made from old mining lanterns. Part of the patio was glassed in, facing west with a clear view of the Seven Sisters peaks. The rest of the patio was tiered with steps leading down to deep second and third levels, plush with emerald grass. The second level had long tables covered with white tablecloths and set with china plates, silverware, and linen napkins embroidered with the Seven Sisters brand and huge bowls of green salad, coleslaw, wild rice salad, San Celina sourdough bread, spicy pink pinquito beans, sliced avocados, tomatoes, and ripe strawberries the size of small apples. In the middle of it was a cake inscribed with Bliss's and Sam's names and a detailed picture of two horses nuzzling—one a deep, dark brown, the other a palomino. At the bottom level, with only a white rail fence separating the grass from the grapevines, a traditional Santa Maria–style cast-iron barbecue was being manned by a thin Latino man in his sixties and a younger man who looked like his son. We helped ourselves to the food and made our way back up to the top level where round tables were set up.

"I'll go eat with my husband if it will make you happy," I told Dove.

"Doesn't make no nevermind to me. It's your life," she said, shrugging.

I found Gabe at a table inside the glassed-in porch where he was sitting with Bliss and Sam. We were joined shortly by Lydia, Cappy, and Willow, the third sister, who'd left the city council meeting early. She was dressed elegantly in a navy tailored pantsuit with a maroon blouse. An antique watch hung from a thin gold chain around her neck. Her hair was the same iron gray as Cappy's but cut in a soft wavy halo around her head.

"I'm going to sit right here next to the chief," she said, smiling mischievously. "See if I can convince him to loan me some of his officers for a charity fashion show the Monday Club is putting on."

Gabe smiled his politician smile, but I knew he'd rant about her nerve to me later on that night.

The conversation wasn't as awkward as I feared it might be. Lydia was subdued and pleasant and didn't hog the conversation or make any more veiled references to her former relationship with Gabe. Sam clearly loved his mother and was excited to have both his parents in the same place, even under the strained circumstances.

After we'd eaten once and people were milling around contemplating seconds, I excused myself to find a bathroom. I found a guest bathroom right off the front hall and was coming out when I heard an argument on the porch. The front door was partially open so only a screen door separated me and the people arguing. Nosiness getting the better of me, I paused to listen.

"Don't think I won't," a man's voice said, low and mean.

An older female voice answered in a tone so low I couldn't make out the words. I edged a little closer, telling myself it wasn't being rude, that I was looking out for my stepson and that any conflict in this family would eventually concern him.

". . . not by you," the man answered, his voice louder. It was then I recognized it was Giles's voice. "I'll do it tonight if I have to."

"You won't," the female voice answered. Cappy's? Etta's? Their voices sounded enough alike I couldn't tell. Then there was silence.

I ducked back into the bathroom, afraid they would come through the partially open door and find me behaving so tacky. I combed my hair and inspected my makeup for a good five minutes before emerging. I glanced out to the porch. It was empty except for a fat calico cat licking one paw. One thing for sure, I didn't envy Sam's entry into this turbulent family.

When I got back, Chase offered to open the tasting room for a private tasting and Dove, Daddy, Gabe, Lydia, Susa, and Sam accepted. Willow, Arcadia, and Etta went upstairs, and I decided to take Cappy up on her offer to show me the horses. With Bliss riding in the backseat, Cappy drove down to the stables in her faded blue Jeep Wagoneer.

"I've had this baby since 1972, and she's never broke down on me once," Cappy bragged, dodging a pothole in the dirt road leading to the stables. She gave a cheerful honk to the group walking down the long driveway toward the winery and tasting room.

"Sam's mother is quite a looker," she said, glancing over at me, a mischievous glint in her eyes. "No doubt Sam got the best of both parents. I can see why my granddaughter would fall back on her heels for him. Just like you did for his father."

"Grandma!" Bliss said in an aggrieved voice.

I stuck my tongue out at Cappy. Bliss gave an uncharacteristic giggle.

"Benni Harper, you haven't changed a bit since you were sixteen," Cappy said good-naturedly.

"That's not true," I said, turning to grin at Bliss. "I know way more cuss words now."

She and Bliss laughed, and for the first time this evening, it seemed as if Bliss relaxed a little. About a half mile from the house, we reached the stables. Cappy had built a beautiful setup—a row of freshly painted double stalls, enough for forty horses, two hot walkers, an outside wash rack, three corrals, a separate tack room, a graded half-mile training track, and plenty of shade trees.

"Are you full up?" I asked as we walked through the first stall row. A black-and-white long-haired barn cat followed us, darting between our legs, mewing loudly.

"Almost," she said. "We've got six free stalls, but they'll be filled soon." She bent down and picked up the complaining cat. "Figaro, you're almost as big a nag as Giles. You don't need one more saucer of cream." The cat purred as she stroked his black head.

I reached over and scratched under his chin. "He looks like he's wearing a hood."

"He's a criminal, all right," Cappy said. "Stole our hearts a long time ago." The cat purred a reply.

"Grandma's been taking in boarders this year," Bliss explained, stopping to fondle the nose of a strawberry roan filly with a pencil-thin blaze. She put her face close to the filly's and blew softly in the horse's nostrils.

"Quarter horse breeding isn't what it was," Cappy said. "Not since the early eighties when they took away the tax benefits for racehorse owners."

"JJ mentioned that this morning. How would that affect you?" I asked.

Bliss jumped in with the answer. "It affects everyone involved with racing or breeding. If rich people can't use racehorses as tax write-offs for their other businesses, then they don't buy them anymore, and people lose jobs all the way down the line—trainers, grooms, pony girls, breeders, feed brokers, people who work at the racetrack, farriers and tack suppliers. I could go on and on. A lot of people are involved with the business of horse racing and breeding who don't work directly with it and usually they don't have the education or means to find jobs anywhere else so they end up on welfare or robbing liquor stores." She smiled. "Which, of course, gives *me* job security. One thing about being a cop, there's always bad guys."

Cappy smiled and passed me a handful of carrots. "Got her trained pretty good, don't I?"

"You sure do." I took the carrots, breaking them in half as I followed her down the center aisle of the stalls. "I understand what she's saying. It's like when beef consumption goes down. It affects more than just the ranchers who raise cattle. And most of the jobs involving cattle are the same as with your industry, people who can't get jobs in other industries. Not everyone can be a computer programmer."

"Exactly," Cappy said. "I wish a few politicians understood that."

We walked from stall to stall, feeding carrots to the

horses as she relayed their histories, showing me the ones she had high hopes for and the ones she intended to run in claiming races.

"Claiming races?" I said. I'd been to a few horse races in my life, but didn't know much about the intricacies or terminology of the industry.

"That's when the horse is basically up for sale in a race," she explained. "People can make a bid for the horse by filing a claiming form and leaving a certified check on deposit before post time. The purse"—she paused and looked at me—". . . that's the money awarded to the winners of the race, goes to the owner who entered the horse, but the horse will legally belong to the successful claimant so even if the horse gets injured during the race, it's the responsibility of the new owner. It's a gamble, though. But if you know your stuff and have a good working crystal ball, you can pick up some great deals in claiming races. We've bought two claimers that went on to become stakes horses and bred them into our line."

"What's a stakes horse?" This was a whole new world to me. Good ranch horses only needed three qualities—excellent health, no fear of cattle, and a willingness to learn. Some of our best ranch horses were uglier than a bucket of mud, but they had a magic sense when it came to working cattle.

"In simple terms, a stakes horse is one that, after it's shown exceptional talent by winning races and clocking some fast times, can run at the big money. Stakes horses are the best of the best." Cappy stroked the nose of a muscular bay with friendly "people" eyes.

"This business sounds about as predictable and profitable as cattle ranching," I said, stroking the neck of a young mahogany-colored horse who had finished his carrot and was tossing his head for more. "Young man, that's all you get tonight." I held out my empty hand. "See, all gone."

"That's Churn Dash, a two-year-old we're planning on running in a few races this year. He foaled out late so we've waited on entering him. His mama was Seven Sisters Dash. She wasn't a great runner herself, but she sure can produce them."

"He's beautiful," I said, rubbing my fingers along the star and stripe on his face. "What a great name. Did you know it's a quilt pattern?"

"Actually, I did," Cappy said. "In my office I have a quilt made by Mother in that pattern. We named him in honor of her."

"I never got to know Great-Grandma Rose that well," Bliss said, coming over and running her hand down Churn Dash's neck, scratching his withers. "I wish Susa hadn't moved us away when we were so little." Her tone was slightly bitter.

"Your mother always was one who had trouble taking the bit," Cappy said. "Guess she wanted her own life."

"Your great-grandma is certainly a famous person in this county," I said to Bliss. "They practically have a shrine to her down in General Hospital's children's wing."

"She raised most of the money that built that wing," Cappy said. "And she started both the candy striper volunteer group and the home nurse program. Health care in this county, especially for children, owes a lot to Mother."

We went into the tack room and working office, and I couldn't help but admire the rich assortment of shiny, well-cared-for tack. As Cappy listened to her answering machine messages, I walked past the long row of photos of winning horses on the panelled wall. In the center was a large, expensively framed photograph of Seven B winning a race by a length. A photo underneath showed a younger Cappy and a bunch of other people posing in the winner's circle with the horse and his trainer, a strong-looking blond man with a thick, reddish mustache. Everyone wore wide smiles.

"That was taken fifteen years ago," Bliss said. "When Seven B won the All-American Futurity. That's the biggest quarter horse competition in the world. It's a million-dollar purse."

"How exciting that must have been," I commented.

Cappy came and stood next to us. "Yes, but like anything else this competitive, you're only as good as your last win. Seven B hasn't even produced a stakes winner in a few years. We're hoping that will change soon. Believe me, when you aren't winning at the track, only the feed man knows your name." She checked her watch. "We'd better get back and see to our guests. They're probably ready for dessert about now." At the Jeep Bliss hung back.

"I think I'll walk," she said. "I need the exercise."

Cappy, her face aggravated, started to say something, but I broke in.

"Want some company? I could use a walk, too, after that fabulous spread."

Bliss shrugged. "I don't mind."

"Okay," Cappy said. "I'll see you two in a few minutes." She reached into the glove compartment of the Jeep and took out a small flashlight. "Take this. There's lots of holes in the road."

"Oh, Grandma . . ." Bliss started.

"Don't you, 'Oh, Grandma' me," Cappy countered. "I'm only—"

"Thanks," I said, breaking into her sentence and taking the flashlight. "We'll be careful."

"She's already driving me nuts," Bliss complained as we watched her grandmother drive up the road, a small cloud of dust trailing after her. "She's the last person I expected to be treating me like I was a piece of expensive crystal."

"She's just concerned," I said, falling in with her irritated strides.

"She was breaking green horses when she was pregnant with my mom. Great-Aunt Willow said they considered locking her in her room the last three months."

"Maybe that's why she's so concerned about you. 'Do as I say and not as I do. If your friends wanted to jump off a cliff, would you? Don't make that face, young lady, or someday it will freeze that way.' All the things mothers and grandmothers say to us to try and keep us from being hurt. What they're actually saying is—'I'm afraid the world will hurt you the way it did me and I don't want that to happen.' Of course, they can't stop it and they know it, so they tell us dumb things and for the moment they're saying it, they feel better."

She was silent, and I thought I'd gone too far in my mini-lecture. "Then again," I added, bumping her shoulder with mine, "they could be just trying to keep us from having any fun at all."

She laughed and bumped me back. "I think that's it."

We continued walking up the gravel road toward the house. The flashlight illuminated the path as we looked up to the September sky, wild with stars, trying to remember constellations we'd learned in science class.

"Too many years ago for me," I said, after only being able to find the Big and Little Dippers and Orion and the planet Venus. Bliss picked out Aries the Ram and Aquarius the Waterbearer.

"Did you know that there is a cluster of stars called the Seven Sisters?" she asked.

"No, I didn't."

"My dad showed them to me." She pointed up to a spot in the sky where a faint grouping of stars was visible. "It's in the Taurus constellation. It's also known as Pleiades.

Seven stars can be seen with the naked eye, but with a telescope or really good binoculars you can see that there's actually a couple of hundred. Look, they appear to be close together, but actually they're really far apart." She gave me a slight smile. "As my dad says, just like Cappy and her sisters."

"Seems like the name of your ranch has all sorts of hidden meanings."

"No kidding," she said.

The hint of sharpness in her voice caused me to glance at her in surprise, but she kept walking and didn't elaborate.

Sam, I thought, *what have you gotten yourself into?*

"Let's stop here for a moment," she said when we reached a weathered wooden bench in front of a large metal building. A small security light bathed the area in a stark white glow. "I'm feeling a little sick."

I sat down next to her. "Want me to go get the Jeep?"

"No, it's not that much farther. It's just that I seem to be getting my morning sickness at night. Lucky for me, I'm on day shift for the next three months."

We sat silently for a moment, uncomfortable with the mention of her pregnancy. The fact that I was married not only to her future father-in-law, but also her boss caused an awkwardness between us that was hard to breach.

"So, what building is this?" I asked, turning to look.

"It's part of the winery. We store barrels of fermenting wine here. My uncle Chase has his office here." She put a fist up to her mouth, her face grayish-green in the harsh light.

"Should I go get Sam?"

She swallowed hard, and her coloring came back. "No, it's just a spell. Really, I don't do this very often. I've found a good doctor, and he says I shouldn't have any problems, that this feeling sick is perfectly normal and should pass in another month. I'm going to be able to work until the baby's born." She turned pink, which looked a whole lot better than green. "I'll tell the chief that myself. I'm not trying to, like, pull strings or anything. I've made an appointment with him next week to talk about my schedule."

I touched her hand. "Bliss, you don't have to explain anything to me. What happens between you and Gabe on a professional level is not my business. Gabe is adamant about keeping his personal and work life separate."

"I guess Sam and I have screwed that up, haven't we?"

I gave her an encouraging smile. "I doubt it's the first time this has happened in a family and I also doubt it'll be the last."

Not answering, she looked over at the dark vineyards. In the cool darkness, we watched a partial moon rise over the vineyards, the Santa Lucia mountains craggy and black behind them. The heavy scent of ripe grapes sugared the air, giving it a flavor you could almost taste. In the distance, a horse whinnied, the sound causing a nervous echo from another horse, then another and another. Like cattle, horses were such group animals. When one of them was afraid or agitated, it passed through the herd like fire in parched rye grass.

"The hills remind me of a quilt pattern called Moon Over Mountain," I said, just to break the uneasy silence. "It's a simple one, with clean lines and not a lot of pieces. But it doesn't really capture the beauty of mountains. Mountains have such wonderful three-dimensional peaks and valleys that are impossible to capture in a flat pattern. Like the difference between a cartoon character and a real person. We get the bare essence, but nothing else."

"I'm scared, Benni," she whispered so softly I wasn't sure I heard her right. She didn't look over at me, but continued to stare at the dark hills.

I reached over and took her hand, squeezing it gently. "I know." What else could I say to her at this moment? Take heart? Things will work out? You're stronger than you realize? *I know.* The only thing we can truly tell another person who is afraid or in pain. I know the unknown is terrifying. I know what fear is. I know what pain feels like. *I know.*

What I didn't realize until much later was she wasn't talking about Sam or the baby.

6

WE WERE STILL sitting on the bench when the urgent clanging of the dinner bell reverberated through the valley. I didn't think anything about it, assuming Cappy was calling everyone back up to the house for dessert, until Bliss jumped up, her face twisted with panic.

"What's wrong?" I asked.

Without answering, she took off running up the gravel road toward the house.

I caught up with her, my heart pounding, and asked again, "Bliss, what's going on?"

"She only rings the bell in an emergency. I know a shortcut through the fields." She took off running through the rows of grapes. I followed her, keeping my eyes on her blonde hair bobbing through the lush green vines. Prickly branches caught at my silk blouse, snagging it in places that would irritate me later, but at that moment my only mission was to keep up with Bliss.

My side felt splintered when we reached the front porch. Bliss dashed in ahead of me, calling out for Cappy. Her grandmother appeared, followed by Etta and Willow from behind the closed doors of the living room we'd occupied a few hours before. She closed the doors behind her and said calmly to me, "You'd better find your husband."

Her serious tone caused Bliss and me to glance at each other in apprehension.

"Why?" I asked.

"There's been an accident."

"Who?" Bliss asked.

Her grandmother's face was sober. "It's Giles. He's dead."

Before she could elaborate, we heard a mixture of voices out on the porch—Gabe, Dove, Lydia, Sam, Daddy. They were laughing at something, obviously unaware of the dinner bell's ominous purpose. They entered the hallway, and Gabe's smiling face turned instantly serious when he saw us.

"What's wrong?" he asked. Sam went over to Bliss, who was standing motionless as a trapped fawn, her hand grasping her side as if searching for the weapon that wasn't there.

"It's my grandson-in-law, Giles," Willow said. "We need to find my granddaughter, Arcadia, and—"

"She was down at the tasting room with us," Dove said. "Until about a half hour ago. She said she was coming back up to the house."

Cappy's face looked troubled. "Gabe, you'd better handle this." She opened the door, and Gabe entered the room. We all pushed forward, stopping only when Gabe commanded us to stay where we were.

Lying on the floor in front of the fireplace was Giles in a rapidly spreading pool of blood. A .38 revolver lay a small distance from his body. He lay on his back, the gun above his outstretched hand, as if he were reaching for it. The entry point of the bullet could barely be seen, but I knew the force of a .38 bullet. If we turned him over, half his back would be splayed open, his insides a tangled mess. Gabe bent down and pressed his fingers to Giles's neck. I watched my husband's face, trying to gauge by his reaction whether Giles was actually dead. Behind us we heard Susa's soft exclamation.

"Let me by," she said. "He might be alive." She pushed past us and ran over to Giles. She kneeled down next to him, her eyes rapidly surveying his chest wound.

"He's dead," Gabe said quietly, pulling his hand back and standing up.

She ignored his words and gently pressed her fingers in the same spot Gabe had. Moments later, she said in a choked voice, "Oh, no."

Gabe looked over at Cappy. "Where's the nearest phone besides this one?" He nodded at the phone on a side table.

"My study," she said, pointing down the hall. "Last door on your right."

He looked over at the rest of us, which now included Chase, Jose, and Jose's son, who seemed to have appeared from nowhere. "I need all of you to go out on the front porch and stay there." He walked over to me and said in a low voice, "Benni, I left my cell phone in the car. Go into Cappy's study and call nine-one-one. I don't want to leave the scene."

Arcadia picked that moment to walk up to the crowd. Her soprano voice rang out. "I was upstairs powdering my nose when I thought I heard the dinner bell. What's going on?" When she moved around the crowd and saw Giles lying on the blood-soaked carpet, a strangled cry came from her throat. We all stared at her, morbidly compelled to watch her reaction. She started toward Giles's body, but Gabe gently blocked her way. "I'm sorry, but you'll have to stay back." He nodded over at Willow, who took his cue and rushed over to her granddaughter.

"Grandmother?" Arcadia said, her voice strangled. "What happened? Who did this?" Willow put her arm around Arcadia's shoulders and murmured softly in her ear. Arcadia started sobbing, her slight body convulsing.

"Benni, nine-one-one," Gabe reminded me. He turned and looked at everyone and said firmly, "Everyone out on the porch, now. And no talking, please."

As everyone started slowly moving toward the porch, I went to the study and made the phone call. The dispatcher replied that sheriff's deputies would be there in a few minutes, that an officer was only a few miles away. When I came back into the hallway, the hallway was empty, and Gabe had closed the living room's double doors.

Gabe walked over to me. "What's the deputies' ETA?"

"The dispatcher said a few minutes. I told them you were here."

He nodded his approval.

"So, what do you think?" I asked in a low voice.

The skin around his prominent cheekbones tightened. "I think my son has picked one heck of a family to marry into." He put his hand on my shoulder and massaged it gently, more, it seemed, to comfort himself than me. "Why don't you join them outside? I'll be out after I talk to the sheriff's deputy."

Out on the porch, I went over to Dove, who was sitting at the far end in one of the Adirondack chairs. Daddy stood next to her, his face subdued, holding his white dress Stetson in his hands. "Are you all right?" I asked.

"Just fine, honeybun. What's Gabe got to say about this?"

"All he said was he wasn't thrilled about Sam marrying into this clan."

On the other end of the porch, on a padded bench, Willow sat next to her granddaughter, Arcadia, who was quietly sobbing into a small lacy handkerchief. She rubbed Arcadia's back, whispering into her ear. Bliss stood next to Arcadia, her face ashen. Sam, his face fighting panic, bent down, murmured something in Bliss's ear, then lay his hand tentatively on her back. Her face relaxed slightly, and a small shudder ran through her. Lydia stood on the top porch step, her expression uncertain.

"Bliss, honey," her mother said. "Why don't you sit down?"

"I'm just fine," Bliss replied, her face going stiff again.

The sharpness in her tone surprised me, but Susa's genial expression didn't change. She just patted her daughter's arm and went over to where her mother, Cappy, sat on the other side of Arcadia.

A few seconds later two sheriff's patrol cars pulled up behind Gabe's Corvette. A uniformed officer stepped out of each and, after a brief talk, strode up to the porch, heading toward Lydia, who would be the first one they'd encounter. I moved around her and met them, informing them I made the 911 call and that Chief Ortiz of the San Celina Police Department was inside.

We silently watched them enter the house. A few minutes later Gabe came out and said, "The detectives and the investigative team are on their way. They'll need a statement from everyone. Please refrain from talking to each other until they've had a chance to question you." He went back inside the house.

In about fifteen minutes, another vehicle arrived. A truck, actually. A big red Dodge. The man who stepped out appeared to be in his late thirties and wore a tan cowboy hat, sharp-pressed Wranglers, a Western-style sports jacket, and golden brown ostrich cowboy boots. When he came up the porch steps, he nodded at us genially, then walked into the house without a word. About a minute later, one of the uniformed deputies came back outside, probably assigned to keep an eye on us and discourage talking. I leaned my head against a wooden post and sighed, knowing we were in for a long night.

Ignoring the deputy's presence, Lydia walked over to me and asked in a low voice, "You seem to understand my son. Should I go over to him?"

I stared at her, surprised. Asking my advice about her son was the last thing I expected. *Oh, geeze, don't turn out to be nice*, I thought.

"He'd probably deny it with all his Latin machismo," I whispered back, "but I'd say having his mom stand next to him right now would definitely make him feel better."

The sheriff's deputy frowned at me and Lydia, shaking his head. I felt like a school kid caught passing a note.

"Thanks," she murmured. Pointedly ignoring the deputy in a way I couldn't help admiring, she walked across the porch, said something in Sam's ear, then lay her hand on his shoulder. Sam's tense face eased at her touch.

By the time Gabe and the cowboy detective came back out on the porch, more cars had arrived, and soon the yard and house were full of crime scene personnel. Gabe came over and stood next to me while the detective cleared his throat to get our attention.

"Excuse me, folks." His voice had a soft Texas twang, like an electric guitar slightly out of tune—not enough to be unpleasant, but enough to notice. "I'm Detective Hudson. I know this has been a hard night on all y'all, but please bear with us a little longer. Since we don't really know what happened yet, we're going to have to question each of you on an individual basis. Just some standard questions so we can try and figure out what happened.

There's three of us, so it shouldn't take too much of your time."

His voice was so friendly and easygoing it was almost easy to forget that this wasn't an accident, but was most likely homicide, and there was a good chance that someone standing on this porch had committed the crime.

After a quick consultation with Gabe, the two other detectives asked Dove and Daddy to step into the house. The rest of us waited, a deputy still watching us. About a half hour later, Dove and Daddy were given permission to leave, and they came over to me to say a quick good-bye.

"Call me tomorrow first thing," Dove said, hugging me hard.

"I will."

"See you soon, pipsqueak," Daddy said, kissing my cheek.

Probably because they knew I was with Gabe, I was one of the last to be questioned. My interview, almost three hours later, took place in Cappy's office off the front hallway. The Texas detective had placed two deep-green leather visitor chairs side by side in front of Cappy's large oak executive desk, slightly turned toward each other in a non-intimidating way, as if he and the witness were just having a pleasant chat.

"I'm Detective Hudson, Mrs. Ortiz," he said, reaching out to shake my hand. His palm was smooth, warm, and a little damp. "I'm sorry this has taken so long."

"It's okay. You can call me Benni," I said, not wanting to go into the fact that although I was officially married, I wasn't officially an Ortiz.

"Great, Benni, then. Please have a seat." He gestured to one of the green chairs. After sitting down, I tried to get my bearings, by glancing around Cappy's office. It was a mixture of funky cowgirl kitsch, Native American elegance, and colorful Mexican folk art, organized in a way that looked straight out of a magazine spread. A brown-toned framed poster of a Pendleton cowgirl riding a bucking bronco shared wall space with a bright acrylic painting of an Indian warrior and a folk art cross painted with happy scenes from a Mexican wedding. A loveseat upholstered in a tan, brown, deep green, and red Pendleton blanket fabric sat between floor-to-ceiling oak bookcases. In a corner, a burnished mahogany-colored tooled sidesaddle rested on a fancy oak saddle rack. Above it was a gallery of framed win pictures, Cappy smiling proudly in each one, and an oil painting of Seven Bars Jewel. Behind the desk hung the Churn Dash quilt—made of brown and gold calicos and pale muslin—that Rose Jewel Brown had created and was the inspiration for the name of the two-year-old colt I'd seen earlier.

The detective cleared his throat to get my attention. "Excuse me, ma'am. Can we get started now?"

I jumped slightly, felt myself flush. "Oh, I'm sorry. The room distracted me."

He nodded and glanced around the office. "It is somethin' else. My mama would love it. She's an interior decorator in Dallas." He looked down at the palm-sized wire-ring notebook in his hand. The front was decorated with the characters from *Beauty and the Beast*. When he looked back up, he caught me staring at it and smiling.

He turned it over and scrutinized the cover, laughing himself. "It was all I could find," he said, sitting back in his chair and crossing his legs, ankle to knee. His golden brown ostrich boots had deep brown shafts. "I think it was left over from my daughter's last visit. I reckon I should have just torn the cover off, but as my dear old daddy would say, if a man can't act like a girl sometimes, then he ain't a real man."

I thought about his comment for a moment, trying to decide if it was insulting to women.

He grinned at me, an amused twinkle in his dark brown eyes. "Now, why don't you tell me everything you saw and heard and what you were doing, say, the half hour before y'all heard the dinner bell callin' you to the house."

While I talked, he made notes in his cartoon notebook, his smooth-shaved, country-boy face screwed up in a concentrated frown. He reminded me of the type of boy in school the teacher always picked for Tom Sawyer's part in the class play. The kind who would pull your braids, then look so cute and wide-eyed innocent when accused that the teacher glanced back at *you* with suspicion.

"Then we ran through the wine fields because Bliss knew a shortcut and we found Cappy, Willow, and Etta standing in front of the double doors," I finished.

Nodding, he made a few more notes, then looked up at me, his boyish face thoughtful. "Now, if you don't mind, I'd like to pick your brain for a moment. Off the record."

I became instantly wary. He apparently forgot I was married to a cop. There was no such thing as "off the record." Especially in a homicide investigation. I waited for his question, nervously jiggling my foot.

"You're pretty connected in the agriculture community here in San Celina County, right?"

"I guess. I've lived here most of my life, and my gramma and daddy have owned a ranch here since the early sixties."

He grinned again. "That Dove, she's a real kick in the pants. You know, she got me to commit to a donation for their senior citizen center's new kitchen before I even asked two questions. That's the first time anyone has finagled a charity donation out of me during a homicide investigation. I was tempted to swear her in as an honorary deputy and set her to questioning folks. We'd have this wrapped up in time for biscuits and gravy."

"She's one of a kind," I agreed, laughing. "How much did she shake you down for?"

"A hundred bucks!" He shook his head. "My own dear grandma Hudson, the Lord rest her soul, would have loved her."

I smiled, then involuntarily yawned. "Sorry, it's been a long night. Are you through?"

"One last question. Take some time thinking about it and answer it now if you want or call me at the office." He pulled a business card out of the inside of his jacket and handed it to me. "I just want your input on what is going on in this family."

I thought for a moment, torn between the loyalty I felt toward Cappy because of our past association, not to mention the general loyalty among the agricultural community who'd, with good reason, often viewed government officials with more than a little suspicion.

"Well," I said, "there was probably some friction between Giles and Cappy, because the two things they do are so different, and there might be some disagreement as to how to utilize the resources on their land."

"Such as?"

"Whether pasture land should be used to raise horses or be covered with wine grapes."

"Can't a big place like this do both? Ms. Brown said . . ." He flipped back through some pages in his notebook. "This property is about eleven hundred acres. Isn't that enough for everybody? Forgive my agricultural ignorance, but I'm a Houston city boy. My father was an accountant. The only agriculture I'm familiar with was my mama's prize-winning roses."

"A good part of their land is probably not productive,"

I said. "And often the best pasture and feed-growing land is also the best land to grow grapes. Not to mention the problems with the property being reassessed once they grow grapes on it, which puts it in a higher tax bracket. Keeping Seven Sisters a horse-breeding ranch would definitely keep the property taxes down. That's about all I know about it. Doesn't seem like much of a motive for murder. They seem to be working it out okay, from what I've heard." There was that little jibe that Giles made during Cappy's toast, but that didn't seem important enough to mention. And there was the comment JJ had made in my office about the winery causing a problem among the sisters, but no doubt he'd found that out when he questioned JJ.

"What about Etta and Giles? How did they get along?"

"I have no idea, Detective. I don't really know the family well. I mean, our families have known each other for years, but we're not intimate friends. We don't run in the same social circle, if you know what I mean."

He nodded. "I understand this Giles Norton comes from a pretty famous wine family up in Napa Valley."

"I heard the same thing," I said, leaving it at that.

He gazed over my shoulder to the saddle behind me, staring at it until I thought he would bore a hole in the thick leather. "Something's not right with this whole scenario."

"Oh?"

He turned his attention back from the saddle to me. "Don't you find it all just a little too . . . neat and organized?"

I sat back in my chair, a bit confused. "Organized? I don't know what you mean."

He gave his head a small shake, reminding me of Cappy's horses. "Never mind, just some ramblings of a suspicious old Texan. Anything else significant you think I should know?"

I hesitated, then said, "I did overhear an argument, but I'm sure it's nothing."

He nodded at me to continue, and I told him what I'd heard outside the bathroom.

He asked, "You're sure you couldn't recognize the female voice?"

"I told you, it could have been Cappy or either of her sisters. Have you heard their voices? They all sound alike. Besides, I was just passing by and only caught a bit of their conversation. I didn't actually stop and . . ." I paused, realizing I'd just begun a lie.

He grinned, as if he could see the moral struggle inside my head. "So maybe you had to tie your shoe or something," he said, looking down at my pull-on boots. "Happens to me all the time. Then you just happened to overhear a little more . . ."

"That's all I heard," I snapped, embarrassed.

He uncrossed his legs, his face suddenly serious. "I'll be in touch if I need to ask you anything else."

"One more thing," he said when I reached the office door.

I turned around, waiting.

"If you hear anything or someone inadvertently drops a remark about this situation . . . or you remember something else about that *accidently* overheard conversation, you will give me a call."

His face was open and friendly, but his voice had taken on a definite authoritarian tone I recognized. Cops. When they're sworn in I think they're given a transfusion of dictators' blood.

"I always cooperate with the authorities," I answered.

I waited for Gabe on the porch with Lydia and Sam,

who'd already been questioned. While we were waiting, a man with a leather medical bag arrived. The family doctor had come to see Arcadia, who was understandably in bad shape. I guess when you were high up enough on society's ladder, doctors still made house calls.

"Why don't you call in sick tomorrow?" Gabe said to Bliss as we walked down the gravel driveway to our cars.

She stood a little straighter. "I'm fine, sir. I'll be at work as usual."

"Maybe it would be better . . ." Gabe started.

"He's right," Sam said. "You should stay home and rest."

"I said I'm fine." Her voice had an edge to it.

"Bliss," Gabe said, his voice taking on his no compromising *el patrón* tone. "I really think . . ."

"Hey, guys," I said, interrupting. "She knows how she feels."

Gabe and Sam shot me an almost identical frown.

"Benni's right," Lydia said. "And so is Bliss. Let her decide if she feels well enough to work."

They turned and frowned at Lydia, whose black eyes remained unmoved by their irritation. "Boys, how many times do I have to remind you that most women do have the mental capabilities to make quite complex decisions? Especially when it concerns their own bodies."

To my consternation, I was beginning to warm up to Lydia.

She turned and held out a hand to me. "Not quite the best circumstances to meet, Benni, but I'm glad we did. We should have a nice long lunch and get to know each other better."

"Certainly," I said, taking her hand and thinking, *I'm not that warm yet, sweetheart*. I turned back to Gabe. "Let's go home. I'm tired."

On the drive back home, he was silent, and I knew he was worrying about Giles's murder, Sam and Bliss, and how it would affect their lives. He was already in the process of moving her in his emotions from being an employee to being his daughter-in-law, the mother of his future grandchild, part of *la familia*. I sighed, worrying about Bliss, too, wondering how she would manage juggling the two. I wanted to bring up the question of whether she should even be working for the San Celina Police Department if her father-in-law was chief, but figured this wasn't the time to ask. To take my mind off our escalating domestic issues, I turned it to something even more disturbing—Giles's murder. I had a feeling Detective Hudson didn't understand how little the Brown family and mine saw each other socially. Being a city boy, he obviously didn't know that within the ag community there was just as much social hierarchy and class distinction as anywhere. And the Brown family was way above my family socially, even if we did occasionally cross paths during common charity and agricultural events. Then again, now that Bliss and Sam were going to be married and with Gabe's political status as a police chief, the Ramseys were moving on up the social scale. I rested my chin in my hand and stared out at the dark hills slipping by. As much as I liked Cappy and Bliss, the thought of my family being connected with the Browns, even in the most peripheral way, troubled me. Detective Hudson was on the right track. Something in that family wasn't right, and whatever it was, it was bad enough for someone to commit murder. And I didn't want any part of it.

At home, after taking Scout out for a quick walk and giving him a dog biscuit to make up for his lonely evening, Gabe and I settled into our own bed.

"What's going to happen next?" I asked, turning on my side to face him, too agitated to sleep.

"The detectives will go over the statements to see if anything doesn't match up. Most likely that's what they're doing right now." He settled deeper into his pillow. "It'll be a real pain-in-the-ass investigation, what with the prestige of the people involved. Glad it's the sheriff's baby, not mine. And I'm especially glad I don't work a homicide detective's hours anymore."

"Who do you think killed Giles? Except for us, there was no one but family members there. Most homicides are committed by family members; I've heard you say that. Who would you put your money on?"

"I'd put my money on it's not our problem."

"It *is* our problem in a way. Sam's marrying into this family. We need to find out which one of them is a murderer before he does." Gabe's breath, slowing down as his body neared sleep, smelled like spearmint.

"So, what did Detective Hudson ask you?" I prodded.

"The normal questions."

"Like what?"

"He probably asked me the same things he did you."

"Detective Hudson seemed to think I had some sort of insider view of the ag community and of this family."

"What did you tell him?"

"That the Browns ran in a different social circle. That I didn't really know them that well. Well, I know Cappy pretty good. And JJ somewhat. But what I know about the rest of the family is just stuff I've read in the papers. He asked me to let him know if I hear anything."

Gabe's head shifted on the pillow. I could feel his intense blue gaze in the dark. "And you said?"

I laughed softly in the darkness. "That I *always* completely cooperate with law enforcement whenever it's requested."

His hand reached over and tickled my side. "Sure you do. Just like the first time we met."

"I do," I protested, wiggling away from his hand. "I cooperate with you at least three times a week."

"Benni, you know it's extremely important for you to tell Detective Hudson everything you know."

"I *did*."

"And whatever you find out."

I was silent.

"Benni." All his don't-interfere, this-is-none-of-your-business, leave-it-to-the-professionals, you're-going-to-really-get-hurt-someday lectures were summed up in that one word. Marriage shorthand. You gotta love it.

"Benni," he repeated.

"All right, all right," I promised, laughing.

He grabbed my waist, pulling me toward him. "Ms. Harper, what am I going to do with you?"

"I seem to remember you asking that very same thing the first time I was called into your office."

"So I'll do now what I was thinking about then."

Some time later I said in a groggy voice, "That, Chief Oritz, was highly unprofessional of you. It might even be against the law."

"So report me to Internal Affairs."

7

THE NEXT DAY at the folk art museum, before I'd even taken off my Levi's jacket, the phone started ringing. Though the murder happened too late to make the *Tribune*, it had been carried on the local morning news. Naturally my first phone call was from Emory.

"I'm goin' to take your name out of my will," he said, his Arkansas drawl thicker than normal this morning, probably because he hadn't had his requisite three cups of espresso. "Why didn't you call me when all this was happening last night? I could have come down and gotten a scoop."

"For one thing, Gabe would have killed me. He loves you to pieces, Emory, but he hates your career choice. Two, you aren't even the paper's crime reporter, so what do you care? Three, you wouldn't have gotten your lazy butt out of bed to do it anyway, so why are you bellyaching?" I chewed on the tip of my pen, unperturbed by the dramatic noises sputtering through the receiver.

"Since when has what the chief thinks about your escapades ever stopped you? I may not be the crime reporter, but I could have clued her in and garnered a favor of the gargantuan variety, and for your information, I wasn't in bed, but you are right, I was doing my best to get there."

"So how did your date with Elvia go?"

"We went to the melodrama down in Oceano. Dastardly deeds and damsels in distress. Reminded me of a day in the life of Benni Harper."

"Very funny. Actually, last night did remind me of a crazy melodrama. People all over the ranch when the shooting took place, a rich, crazy family, and a detective straight out of central casting. A Texan, no less, wearing honey-colored ostrich cowboy boots and writing in a *Beauty and the Beast* notebook. I tell you, Emory, it felt like a TV episode penned by a sleep-deprived, schizophrenic script writer."

"Now I'm even more perturbed. I would have surely enjoyed the spectacle. Why wasn't I invited? I'm family."

"Don't blame me. I didn't make up the guest list. Though we recognize the fact that your father and my grandfather were first cousins by marriage and that your father also married my mother's first cousin qualifies you as immediate family, I'm not sure they would. Believe me, you'll be meeting the Brown dynasty at some point in the future since our families are now loosely, soon to be tightly, connected. I'm not sure how Giles's death is going to affect the marriage plans of Sam and Bliss. It's no surprise that no one got around to talking dates or anything."

"What a nasty little bed of cottonmouths your stepson has stumbled into. So, who do you think did it?"

"Is that my cousin asking or a reporter?"

"Depends on the answer. Seriously, one of our reporters got a weird call about the Brown family shindig yesterday evening. Seems something was going down at the Brown estate that night, and this person wanted a reporter to be there to record it."

"Something going down? That sounds like bad movie dialogue. Who called?"

"That famous fella Anonymous. Anyway, the reporter who took the call brushed it off as a prank, then could have kicked himself when he heard what happened."

"Do you think Giles's murder was planned? No, that couldn't be it. Who would plan a murder, then call the press to come cover it?"

"Good question. Let me know if you find out the answer."

"Seven Sisters is scheduled for a full slate of wine activities starting this weekend. I wonder how Giles's death will affect that."

"It'll triple the amount of people who go," Emory said. "I have only my column to write, which I was thinking might have something to do with the inconsideration of family members who have inside tracks to breaking stories that could help the careers of their loved ones—"

"I have no inside track," I interrupted. "You're as bad as that detective. Believe me, no one knows less about this situation than me, and I plan on keeping it that way. I have enough on my plate with Sam and Gabe circling each other like deranged coyotes, not to mention Mama Coyote herself slinking about."

"Was she there? I thought you said she wasn't coming up until next weekend."

"Apparently she pulled some strings and got her pending cases continued so she could check on her son. For that I have a begrudging respect for her. At least she's putting her son before her job."

"Tell me," Emory said, his voice settling into that intimate, confidential tone that said he was ready to hear some dirt. "What is the dragon lady like? Did you spill a drink on her Armani suit? Grind your boot heel on her Ferragamo pumps? Tell me everything."

"There's nothing to tell, you old gossip. She's a very nice woman. We had a nice talk. She was very supportive of her son. She's very—"

"Yeah, yeah, nice. Don't forget who you're talking to, sweetcakes. I know the Southern definition for nice. Any Southern lady worth her crystal egg plate would rather eat dark meat chicken salad made with storebought mayonnaise than be called *nice*. Were her insults very clever?"

"Not so very," I said, allowing him that much. "A couple of gibes reminding me of her connection to, as she put it, her 'two men.' "

"You'd better watch out, my gullible little pullet. If she's just coming off a divorce, she might be feeling unsettled enough to want to renew old ties with something familiar, namely your handsome Latino husband."

"Give me a break. They were divorced over nine years ago. Gabe said they wanted completely different things in life. She hated what he did for a living."

"Which was?"

"He was working undercover narcotics then. She wanted someone more conventional, someone who wore a suit and went to work every day like a normal person. She liked parties and social stuff. She didn't want to be married to someone who stumbled in at all hours all stressed out because of some drug bust, smelling like a sewer. She wanted someone—"

"Someone who is, say, the highly respected and socially prominent chief of police of a pleasant little town like San Celina?"

I froze, silent for a moment, his words articulating thoughts I'd been denying. "Okay, you're right, he's probably more now like the man she wanted then, but anything between them was over long before Gabe and I started our relationship. Don't do this to me, Emory. I don't need it right now. Things are finally running smooth between me and Gabe."

Emory sighed over the phone. "Sweetcakes, I'm not trying to cause problems between you and the chief. I just don't want anyone to rustle your husband when you're not paying attention."

"He's not a prize bull, Emory. No one can steal him from me. He's with me because he wants to be." I said the words with conviction. I didn't fool my cousin one second.

"Better buy yourself some new lingerie," he advised. "And start cooking his favorite meals more often."

I growled at him over the phone. "You are such a man!"

"Yes, I am," he said calmly. "And if you're smart, you'll listen to me."

"I'm hanging up now."

"Benni—"

"I repeat, I'm—"

"Lunch?"

"Only if you promise this subject is closed."

He was silent a moment.

"I mean it, Emory."

"Okay, okay, closed for the day. But not forever. How about Thai on the Run?"

"You know I hate Thai food. McClintock's."

"You and your hamburgers. Noon."

"And it's your treat since you're being such a jerk."

"Since when do you ever pay for a meal when we dine together?"

After almost three hours of diligent paper-pushing and phone work trying to get our next exhibit arranged, I wandered into the main room of the co-op studios to watch the finishing touches being put on the wine quilt that would be auctioned off at the Zin and Zydeco gathering Saturday night. I half expected to see JJ today, but certainly understood why she probably wouldn't come in. The co-op group was a pleasant one, but they loved gossip, and I was sure she didn't want to face the curious looks and questions.

After a quick foray through the museum, which was showing a display of original wine label art created for Central Coast wineries, I went out the heavy Spanish front doors and headed across the parking lot to Gabe's old 1950 Chevy truck parked under a graffiti-scarred oak that was probably older than the hacienda. I was unlocking the front door when a red Dodge Ram 1500 V8 Magnum truck pulled into the lot. Since I knew the vehicles of just about everyone who volunteered at the museum or belonged to the co-op, and Tuesday morning was rarely a time for casual visitors, I watched it curiously as it pulled next to my truck. There was something that was vaguely familiar about it, but the windows were tinted, so I couldn't see who was driving until the door opened and a foot wearing a forest green lizard skin cowboy boot appeared. Detective Hudson's brown head and the rest of him followed seconds afterward.

"Hey, glad I caught you," he said, smiling widely. He wore a pale green tailored Arrow shirt and another neatly pressed pair of Wranglers.

I walked around and met him at the tailgate of my truck. "What's up?"

"Just wanted to update you. They're sending the recovered bullet and the gun down to the crime lab right now. Well, actually I'm taking them there myself."

I waited for a moment, not sure why he was telling me this.

"Bein' used to a big city, it seems weird not having a

crime lab right close. I have to go to some town down south . . . Golatta, I think it's called. And I have to wait for it since the Browns are such famous and respected people in this town. I'm pretty sure there's more to this than anyone realizes, but the sheriff wants it cleared up ASAP. And, he said, he'd prefer the killer not be a family member. I'm guessin' they're a big financial supporter of his, and he doesn't want the till dried up. What do you think?"

"The town's name is Goleta," I said, not answering his question. "It's a little north of Santa Barbara."

"Santa Barbara. Isn't that where that singer Michael Jackson has that weird ranch of his? With carnival rides and circus animals?"

"I don't imagine the city fathers would prefer that to be *the* thing they are internationally known for, but, yes, his estate is in the general area. Actually it's closer to Santa Ynez." I glanced at my watch. I had exactly fifteen minutes to get to McClintock's. "Was there something specific you needed to ask me, Detective Hudson?"

"You want to tell me about this argument you heard between Mr. Norton and that woman again?"

"I told you everything I heard last night."

He looked at the ground, gave a good ole boy kick at the dirt, then looked back up and grinned at me. "Please, bear with me, ma'am, but I'd just like to hear it one more time. For my own clarification."

"Okay," I said with an exaggerated sigh, thinking how much alike cops are. It was the same thing Gabe would have done. "But there's nothing different today than what I told you last night."

He nodded as I talked, watching my body language in that way I'd grown used to since being married to a cop. He took out his *Beauty and the Beast* notebook, flipped through the pages, and wrote something down.

"Is that it?" I asked, jiggling my keys with impatience.

"For the time bein'. Just one more thing. Since you're kind of on the fringe of this family and I'm takin' it you'll be seein' more of them, I was wondering if you'd just kind of keep your ears open and let me know if you hear anything that doesn't sit right with you. You know what I mean." His friendly brown eyes smiled at me.

"You're asking me to snoop around my stepson's future in-laws." This guy was starting to get on my nerves.

"Well . . ." He gave an apologetic but hopeful look. "You do it so well."

I glared at him, completely annoyed now. "What?"

His country-gravy grin spread across his face again. "Your reputation precedes you. I've only been with the department about five months, but I wasn't here but a few weeks when I heard the stories about you."

I felt my face grow warm. "First piece of advice about San Celina: Don't believe everything you hear."

"Now I do apologize from the bottom of my heart. I never meant it as anything but a compliment. Why, I admire the tenacity and vivacity with which you solved your many homicide cases here in San Celina. You're a legend, you know."

I narrowed my eyes at him. "The molasses is running a bit thick here, Detective Hudson."

"Since we're working together on this case, please call me Hud."

I raised my eyebrows and scratched my neck. "Hud?"

"Yes, ma'am. Like the movie."

"What movie?"

"What movie? How can you say that? *The* movie. One of the greatest movies ever filmed. *Hud.* With Paul Newman. It's a *Western*, for cryin' out loud. I can't believe you never heard of it."

"I thought Hud had something to do with low-cost housing." I really had seen the movie. It was just fun teasing him. Besides, I hated that movie. It was depressing. Paul Newman plays a bad guy who is never brought to justice.

He gave me a disparaging look.

"Hud's a dumb nickname. What's your real name? And for the record, I never agreed to snoop for you."

"My first name's Ford. But I've always been called Hud."

"Ford? Like the car?"

He nodded.

"Ford Hudson? Were your mom and dad nuts?"

"Now, that is something we could discuss at length sometime over a big ole cup of strong coffee. My mama is the finest lady to walk the Texas earth. My old man was unique, no doubt about that. And, yeah, they were both a tad nuts. It could have been worse. If I'd've been a girl, they were going to name me Cadillac."

I grimaced. "Cadillac Hudson?"

"Yeah, good thing the little guy sperm won the race, huh?" He faked a sympathetic expression. "And I understand about the snooping. Chief Ortiz would most likely take away your allowance if he found out."

I frowned at him. "Gabe and I don't have that kind of relationship."

"So, you don't do whatever he says?"

"Of course not!"

"So, if you hear anything, you'll call me?"

I wanted to strangle him. He'd managed to maneuver it so if I didn't, it looked like I was under Gabe's thumb. "I told you, I *always* cooperate with law enforcement. Why are you singling me out, Detective Hudson?"

"Hud. Like the movie."

"Detective."

"Well, me bein' new here on the Central Coast and to the sheriff's department and this bein' my first homicide case, I figured I'd need someone in the know. You seemed like a friendly, intelligent face." The expression on his face was so open and earnest I couldn't help but relent a little. Men who were secure enough to admit they needed help held a certain type of power over women. Then again, the guy was a player, no doubt about it, and his aren't-I-cute Tom Sawyer act probably fooled a lot of people . . . likely most of them women.

"No one would ever believe it if I told them you asked me to help you. Not to mention my husband would have your head."

"You're right on both counts, which is why I'll deny to my dyin' day this conversation ever took place."

"Let me get this straight. You're asking me to help you on this case by snooping around, which, if my husband found out, would give him the conniption fit of the century, and never get any credit for it if anything comes of it because you'll deny you ever asked me to help you."

He nodded. "That's about it in a nutshell."

"You want to tell me why you think I'd even consider it?"

He thought for a moment. "Personal satisfaction for a job well done?"

"I don't think so."

"Justice for a man killed in his prime?"

I just raised my eyebrows and didn't answer.

"How about I'm guessin' you won't be able to help yourself, and you're gonna get involved anyway, no matter what your hubby thinks?"

"Thanks, anyway, Hud-like-the-movie, but my detecting days are over."

"Yes, ma'am." His voice was so smug and disbelieving I wanted to smack him.

"I mean it."

"In that case," he said complacently, "do you know of a good place to eat lunch and kill some time in Goleta?"

"YOU'RE LATE," EMORY complained. "I ordered for you already."

"I was detained by the authorities," I said and told him the whole story. By the time I finished, my hamburger and fries and his turkey sandwich had arrived.

"Hud?" Emory said. "You mean, like the Paul Newman movie?"

"Believe me, he's no Paul Newman. And there was a book first. It's ten times better than the movie. *Horseman, Pass By*. Larry McMurtry wrote it."

"You don't say?"

I rolled my eyes. "If you want to marry Elvia, you'd better bone up on your literature, my friend. Cliffs Notes don't count. Apparently, this cop's given name is Ford Hudson."

"Oh, lordy, and I thought being named after a school and a woman's nail care product was bad."

"I can think of worse nicknames for a Texan."

"Like what?"

"Bubba, for one. Joe Bob. Tex."

"You've got a point." He reached over and snatched one of my steak fries. "Are you going to tell Gabe that this sheriff's detective, this Hud"—he shook his head and laughed again—"is putting you on his payroll?"

"I never agreed to anything and since I don't plan on *doing* anything, I don't think it even warrants repeating to Gabe. Especially when he has so much to worry about with Sam and Bliss."

Emory chewed thoughtfully. "Whatever you say."

"Let's forget about this problem that isn't really ours and concentrate on the ones that are. Has Dove approached you about any money-making ideas for the senior citizen center?"

"She was askin' about a walkathon, but I told her that the paper's already sponsored three this year, and though a new stove, refrigerator, and Martha Stewart wallpaper might be important to them, it would have a hard time competing with muscular dystrophy, diabetes, and breast cancer. She made me ask anyway, and our editor-in-chief nixed it."

"I told her I'd try to come up with an idea. The problem is there are so many fundraisers that it's hard to think of one that hasn't been done. Are you going to the Harvest Wine Festival this weekend?"

He pushed his lunch plate aside. "Yep, I've got a full week with the crush activities starting Friday. Seems like every winery in San Celina County has something going on, and my esteemed editor-in-chief wants as many of them covered as possible for a special insert. I'm suspecting the powers that be in the local government are pressuring him to play up the wine aspect of our fair county to better compete with big brother Napa up north."

"That's all we need, something to bring even more tourists into the county," I grumbled.

He patted my hand. "The times they are a-changin', sweetcakes. Cows are out, grapes are in."

"I know, but I don't have to pretend to be happy about it."

We were on our way out when we ran into Bliss and Miguel, one of Elvia's younger brothers and a four-year veteran of the San Celina PD. They were waiting at McClintock's long wooden bar under the TAKE OUT sign. Seeing him in his dark blue uniform carrying a loaded gun and steel handcuffs never failed to amaze me since the memory of cuddling him in my thirteen-year-old lap and singing him to sleep when he was three was still so strong in my mind.

"Hey, Miguel, Bliss," I said. "Who's protecting the streets of San Celina while you two are goofing off?"

"How's it going?" Miguel said, pulling out his wallet when the waitress walked up with two brown paper sacks. Bliss handed him a ten-dollar bill. She nodded at me without saying a word.

"Okay, I guess." I turned to Bliss. "How are you?"

"Just fine," she said, her voice tight. "Have you seen JJ today?"

I shook my head no.

"We had breakfast this morning in town, and she said she was going into the museum to talk to you. Something about giving you tickets to a reception she's going to."

"Oh, yeah, the barrel tasting and artist's reception at the San Patricio Resort in Eola Beach. She was supposed to get me a couple of tickets."

"I'm covering that for the paper," Emory said. "Sunday afternoon, right? Seven Sisters and a bunch of other wineries are hosting a tasting from some vintages that will come out in a couple of years and showing some of the label art being produced by local artists."

"JJ's designing some new labels for the syrah and pinot noir vintages," Bliss said. "One's named after Churn Dash. She's been watching me train him for months, taking pictures and making sketches."

"Who's Churn Dash?" Miguel said, counting out her change.

"A two-year-old quarter horse they'll be running at the track soon," I said. "He's a real beauty."

"I'm working him every evening and the weekends," Bliss said. She lifted her chin slightly and looked into my eyes, as if to say, "we've got nothing to hide." "Whenever you're free, come on out and watch."

I smiled at her. "I'd love to. Is it all right to bring my dog with me?"

"As long as he doesn't go crazy around horses."

"No problem, he's extremely well trained. I'll surprise you one day and take you up on it."

"Ready to split?" Miguel said.

She nodded, taking her paper sack from him. "See you at the ranch," she said to me.

"Count on it," I said.

Outside, Emory clapped me lightly on the back. "Very good, Detective Harper. Now you have free access. Hud will be right proud."

"I'm not going out there to snoop," I said, pulling on my leather barn jacket. "I'm just trying to establish a relationship with the girl who's marrying my stepson. That's all. And the horses do interest me."

"Take a notebook," Emory advised. "Believe me, at our age relying on our memory is death." He laughed. "Whoops, bad choice of words."

"Oh, go find a grocery store opening to cover," I said.

"Now, now, as dear Aunt Garnet would say, let's not let the nasty bird land in our apple tree. Where are you headed?"

"I'm dropping by the Historical Museum to pick up some research one of the ladies there has done for me on early California Chinese folk art and Hmong quilting. We're thinking about having an Asian exhibit next spring."

He kissed me on the cheek. "Be careful in your investigating, sweetcakes."

"I'm *not* doing any investigating," I called after him. His laughter was drowned out by two Ford Ranger pickups dragging down Lopez.

In front of the old brick Carnegie Library building, which Dove and her historical society friends had managed last spring by somewhat radical means to lease from the city for the next twenty years, I ran into JJ coming down the stone steps.

"Benni! What a lucky break for me. Now I don't have to go out to the museum. I have your tickets right here." She opened her small crocheted purse.

"Thanks," I said, taking the tickets. "It's Sunday, right?"

She touched her hair, the green slightly less bright today. "I'm so nervous about it. I'm showing my designs for the new labels and I'm always apprehensive about people's reactions. This is the first time Aunt Etta's let me design the labels, so I want to do a good job. I'm going to actually be working on one there—a watercolor of Churn Dash running, with Great-Grandma's quilt in the background."

"I'm sure they'll be great. How are things at home?" JJ was much easier to ask than Bliss, and for a split second I couldn't help but wish it was JJ Sam was in love with, not Bliss. On the surface, it seemed as if they would be better matched. Then again, I knew better than anyone else that love never paid attention to who matched and who didn't.

"Everyone's in a tizzy, of course. That weird detective left a message for me on my answering machine. Said he wants to talk to me again. Is that normal? I told him everything I knew the night it happened." She rubbed her lips together, slightly smearing her burgundy lipstick.

I stuck my hand deep into the pockets of my coat. "It's not just you. He dropped by the museum this morning to talk to me, too. I couldn't tell him anything else either. I think he's just fishing."

"Giles's family is having a fit about it, as you can imagine. His father is a very powerful man. He flew down in a private jet as soon as he was told. I wasn't at the ranch when he arrived, but I called Jose, and he said there was quite a shouting match between him and Cappy. He claimed we were harboring a murderer."

She was understandably upset by the accusation, obviously not wanting to face the fact that he was probably right. I couldn't help asking, "Who do you think might have wanted Giles dead?"

JJ's face twisted in thought. "I have no idea. He was a jerk, but exactly the type of guy I'd expect Arcadia to marry. Bliss would probably know more than me. She's lived here since she was eighteen. I've only been here a few months."

"I just saw her and Miguel at McClintock's buying lunch. We didn't talk about Giles, but then, Miguel was there and so was my cousin Emory. Emory writes for the newspaper, so that would tend to keep her from saying anything."

"I'm worried about her."

"We all are, but she'll be okay. Pregnancy isn't a disease. She and Sam will work things out."

She reached up and fiddled with the four silver dangly earrings trailing down her left ear. "It's not just the baby.

She's been upset about something else, and she won't tell me what. That's not like her. She usually tells me everything."

"Have you asked her about it?"

Her dark lips turned up in a wry smile. "Get Miss Closed-Mouth Cop to talk when she doesn't want to? I figured it had something to do with work. I knew about her and Sam, so it wasn't that. And she told me when she first suspected she was pregnant, even before she told Sam. Like I said, we usually tell each other everything."

I gave a deep, dramatic sigh. "If it has to do with her work, welcome to the wonderful world of law enforcement relatives. We should start a group. Cop-Anon."

She giggled. "I forgot, you know all about that."

"Trying to get them to talk to you when they don't want to is, as my gramma Dove would say, like trying to milk a two-thousand-pound bull. Ain't possible. Also, don't forget, she's got Sam now, so that might be where some of her confidences are going."

"He's her first boyfriend, you know. I always knew when she fell it would be hard."

"If it makes you feel any better, even though he's young, he's a really decent human being. And I'm not just saying that 'cause he's my stepson and I happen to be crazy in love with his dad."

She touched my forearm lightly. "I know, Benni. It just seems like so much has changed so fast."

"I hate to break the news to you, but as you get older, it only gets worse."

She shook her head, her earrings making a soft, tinkling sound. "What a depressing thought."

• • • •

I WALKED THE three blocks to the Historical Museum where I interrupted a meeting of the San Celina Senior Citizen Kitchen-Raising Committee, the honorable Dove Ramsey presiding.

"Sit down, honeybun," she said, pointing her gavel at an empty chair in front. "We're almost done."

After an excruciating half hour of listening to the seven people on the committee carp and pick at each other's suggestions, Dove brought the gavel down with an angry slam. "People, the bottom line is we need twenty thousand, we've got three, and the insurance will pay ten. We need seven thousand dollars and we need it fast."

"What's the hurry?" I asked.

"The kitchen has to be rebuilt soon," Sissy Brownmiller said. "There's lots of seniors who depend on the hot meal they get there. It's sometimes their only good meal of the day. It's already been shut down a month. We've borrowed the kitchen at First Baptist, but they're getting kinda restless about us going back to our own place."

"I'm telling you," Dove said, "we need something that no one's ever done here before. I'm sick of bake sales and quilt raffles. We need something that'll stand out. Something people really want. Something they're willing to shell out lots of their hard-earned money for."

"Like what?" Sissy countered. "Bake sales and quilt raffles are all we know how to do."

Dove smacked the gavel down again. "Ten-minute break! Get something to eat and drink, and we'll study on this some more."

At the dessert table, filled with apple turnovers, oatmeal cookies, cream puffs, and Sissy's blue-ribbon–winning black walnut–chocolate chip coffee cake, I grabbed a cream puff, a slice of coffee cake, and a cup of Folger's coffee. Though this group was high class in their home-baked goodies, they'd never bought into the baby boomers' addiction to gourmet coffee. Theirs was hot, black, and strong. I put an extra dollop of milk in it to cut the stoutness.

Dove pulled me aside. "Have you heard how things are doing at Seven Sisters?"

"I just talked to JJ. She's pretty agitated, with good reason. She doesn't want to admit it, but everyone knows the killer had to be someone in the family. I don't think she's ready to face that yet."

"It's hard thinking one of your kinfolk would have that kind of meanness in them, but it wouldn't be the first time. That little Texas boy working on the case is a sharp one. I fathom he'll ferret out the bad apple in the bunch right quick. His mama raised a good boy. He donated a hundred dollars to our new kitchen."

"With a little arm twisting from you, I heard."

She opened her eyes wide in mock innocence. "Why, honeybun, a person can't make another person do something they don't want to do. It was purely voluntary."

"Right, kind of like the military draft. Anyway, if you'll tell me where the information Mrs. Shandon left for me is, I'm outta here."

"There's an envelope with your name on it near the cash register."

"Thanks."

By Friday, Giles's murder had been relegated to second-page news since there was nothing new to report. It was still on people's minds and lips, though, according to Elvia. Her mystery reading group at the bookstore had spent more time talking about San Celina's real-life mystery than their fictional English one. Gabe and I didn't even discuss it since his department wasn't handling it. We did, however, talk at length about Sam and Bliss, their impending marriage and parenthood.

"At least she'll be covered by insurance," Gabe said. "Lydia and I are relieved about that." We'd sat down for a rare breakfast together. Usually he jogged with Scout and ate before I got out of bed since I rarely had to be at the folk art museum before nine o'clock, but the telephone had jarred me awake at six-thirty this morning while he was still out jogging. My grouchy hello had been answered by Lydia's sensuous contralto voice.

"Benni? Did I wake you up?"

"Uh, no, I was . . . just . . . taking a sip of coffee." I sat up in bed and ran a hand through my tangled curls, smoothing them down, as if she could see their wildness. "Gabe's not here."

Her laughter grated in my ear. "Out jogging for five miles before his two cups of coffee, bagel with grape jelly, glass of juice, and a quick glance at the front page and sports section."

It irritated me slightly that she knew his morning routine that well. "I guess some things never change."

"Actually, the jogging is new in the last few years, but everything else is the same. If nothing else, our Gabe is predictable in his unpredictable way."

Our Gabe. Yikes. Someone lock the knife drawer. "Want me to have him call you?" I said as sweetly as I could manage without any caffeine in my system. "It's Lydia, right?"

"Right. Lydia Ortiz. Tell him I'll be at home for the next hour, then at the office. He has both numbers."

"Ortiz?" I said without thinking. "I thought you got remarried."

The sexy laugh again. "His surname was Dembrowski.

I figured Ortiz suited me better. Besides, it's been my professional name since I was twenty-two. Gabe and I parted on amicable terms. I don't have any animosity about his name."

"Oh," I said, the irony not lost on me. My husband's ex-wife had his last name, not her second husband's, and I, his current wife, still had the name of my late husband. "I'll tell him you called."

"Thanks, Benni. I'll let you get back to sleep now. Sorry to wake you. Good-bye."

"You didn't wake . . ." But she'd hung up before I could finish my protest.

Gabe found me fifteen minutes later, standing in the kitchen wearing one of his old blue LAPD T-shirts and watching coffee drip into the pot.

He came over, lifted my hair, and nuzzled the back of my neck. "No woman has ever looked better in my T-shirts than you." His warm tongue licked a cool, wet circle on my neck.

I turned and snapped, "And just how many women have you seen in your T-shirts?"

He jerked back, surprise widening his eyes. "Whoa, let's start over. You are the most beautiful woman I've ever seen not"—he held up his hands—"that I *ever* look at other women to compare, because I don't, but *if* I did, you would be the most beautiful, I'm absolutely sure."

Glaring at him, I poured a cup of coffee. His dark face was glossy with sweat, his damp cotton shorts clinging in a way that was not unattractive. The sincerity in his blue-gray eyes was real, and his white, slightly crooked smile seduced me, as it first had in Liddie's parking lot that cold November night a few years ago. I held out the mug of coffee to him. "You're lucky I'm in love with you, Friday."

He took the coffee, then kissed me on the cheek. "PMS,

sweetheart?" he whispered. "Shall I fetch the Godiva chocolate?"

"Oh, man, you're asking for it now," I said, swatting at his stomach. "Bad cop, no doughnut."

He laughed, and Scout, who had been watching our exchange with his one German shepherd ear straight up in worry, barked. I took a dog biscuit out of the jar on the counter and tossed it to him. "Good Scout. I wasn't talking to you. You are the one male in this house who knows how to keep his mouth shut."

"And why are we so cranky this morning?"

"We are *not cranky.* Do you want some toast?"

"No, I'll have a bagel." He opened the refrigerator door. "Are we out of grape jelly?"

I growled inwardly, then said in an even voice, "By the way, Lydia called while you were jogging. She said she'd like you to call her back. She'll be at home for the next hour, then at the office." I poured myself some coffee and pushed my way around him to get the milk, taking it over to the kitchen table.

"So that's what's wrong," he said, his voice amused. He faced me, the jelly jar in his hand, his expression searching. "Was she rude to you?"

I sat down, propping my elbows on the table. The wooden chair was cold against my bare thighs. "No, Gabe, she was perfectly gracious. I just need a cup of coffee. Call her."

When he came back from calling her, he sat down at the table across from me. I was well into my second cup of coffee and feeling a bit more genial toward the world, even one that held perfect first wives. "So, what did she want?" I asked.

"She's coming back up here to spend the weekend. Says she wants to get to know Bliss better, that last weekend was not a good way to start an in-law relationship. She wants us all to go to dinner tonight."

"I agree that it was a rough start to a relationship. Do you think Sam and Bliss will go?"

"I called Sam already, and he's not working at the bookstore. I know it's Bliss's day off. He says he's sure she'll want to come. Lydia'll be staying at the San Celina Inn, so we're just going to eat there."

"Their pot roast is great. It's usually crowded on a Friday night though. You might want to make reservations."

"So, are you free?"

"Me?"

He nodded. "Lydia specifically told me to tell you that you were included."

"How thoughtful of her," I said, thinking, *Bland face, Benni, bland face*. "But this doesn't really have anything to do with me, so I'll pass."

"What do you mean it doesn't have anything to do with you? You're my wife. You're Sam's stepmother. Of course it has to do with you." A tinge of irritation crept into his voice.

I went over and pushed my way onto his lap. "Let me attempt to be a mature human being about this. You go to dinner with your son and his fiancée and your gorgeous ex-wife and let me just trust you, okay? I'll grab a sandwich and harass Elvia at the bookstore if she's not on a date with Emory."

He buried his face in my neck. "I'd rather have you come with us, but it's up to you. Lydia may be gorgeous, but don't forget she dumped me a long time ago."

I laid my cheek on his damp, black hair, my heart troubled, thinking, *that's my problem, Friday. I'd feel a heap better if* you'd *dumped her*.

• • • •

LATER AT THE museum, in the early afternoon when I'd finally caught up on all my paperwork, I decided to take Bliss up on her offer to watch her work the horses. Since I knew it was her day off, I called the ranch, hoping she was there.

"Come on down," she said. "You're welcome anytime. I'll be exercising Churn Dash in about an hour," she said. "We'll be down at the training track."

I went by the house, picked up Scout, and arrived at Seven Sisters stables a little before two-thirty. Scout, his nose quivering with new, tantalizing smells, reluctantly obeyed my command to heel as we walked behind the stables and down the short path to the training track. Bliss was jogging Churn Dash around the freshly graded black dirt. I waved to her, and when she waved back, he took the opportunity to crow-hop and dance around, generally behaving squirrelly. She scolded him verbally and gently brought him back under control with firm, experienced hands.

I climbed up on the metal rail and watched her start around the track at a lope. With the cool, early-afternoon ocean breeze sweeping over me, I felt myself relax and really enjoy the pure, incredible beauty of a young horse's muscles at work. He fought her, aching to break into a run. You could see the pleasure in his neck and ears as she rode him around the half-mile track. I knew enough about horses to see this one had something special—that unpredictable, unknowable thing you couldn't breed into an animal, the thing that made them go the extra mile, make the extra effort, the thing that made you suspect they'd keep going until they collapsed. That thing some people called heart.

After two times around the track she walked him for a while, cooling him down. Then she rode him over to my perch on the railing. She pulled off her jockey helmet and shook out her blond hair.

"Glad you could make it," she said, reaching down and patting his neck. "What do you think?"

"He's something special, no doubt about it."

She nodded, her hair blowing wild around her head. "We sure think so. Like Grandma Cappy said, we haven't had a stakes horse in a few years. We're hoping Dash will change that."

She climbed down and led him toward the gate, which I'd already opened. I followed her to the tie stall where she untacked him and slipped on a baby blue halter. She stopped briefly, touching her hand to her stomach, her face tightening for a moment.

I hesitated before saying, "Are you okay?"

"Fine," she said. "Just a little sick spell."

Knowing it was none of my business, I didn't say anything about the safety of riding a racehorse so early in her pregnancy, but I couldn't help wondering if it was a wise choice.

"Can I clean him up?" I asked, thinking she could at least rest while I did that. "I kinda miss doing that on a regular basis now that I'm a city girl."

Her eyes were disbelieving, but she said, "Sure, if you want."

We led Dash over to the wash racks, and she leaned up against an oak tree as I hosed him off.

"Why aren't you coming to dinner tonight?" she asked, scratching behind Scout's ears.

I ran the slow-flowing water over Churn Dash's brown back. "I thought it might be easier for you to get to know Lydia without me there."

She wrinkled her nose as if she smelled something bad. "Designer suits and those perfect nails. And she's a defense lawyer. I can't believe she and the chief produced Sam. Frankly, she scares me spitless."

I laughed in recognition and camaraderie. "I know the feeling. I still feel that way about Gabe's mother. But we get along okay. Of course, there are two thousand miles between us."

"I'd feel a lot better if you were going."

"Sorry, but I have a dinner date with Scout tonight."

"I'm jealous."

She watched me silently for a moment, then said, "Can I ask you something? Just between us?"

Thinking it was another mother-in-law question, I said, "Sure."

"What do you think is more important, your family or your job?"

I answered without hesitation, "Why, your family, of course." Then I instantly regretted my quick response. "Unless . . ." I started, thinking *Unless your job is to uphold the law.* She looked like she might dissolve into tears at any moment. There was no doubt she knew or suspected something about Giles's murder, and it was clearly upsetting her.

"Unless what?"

I turned off the hose and reached for the scraper hanging on one of the metal posts. "Bliss, I'm not sure I'm the person you should be asking about this. Maybe you should talk to Gabe."

"No! No way!"

Her emotional response surprised me. "Bliss, I know it's your family, but if you know something about Giles's murder . . ."

"Forget it," she said, pushing herself away from the tree trunk. "It's not your problem. Put Dash on the hot walker when you're finished cleaning him up and let Luis know.

I have to go take a shower and get ready for tonight. Thanks for your help." Her tone was clipped and businesslike, but her expression belied her voice. Her gray eyes were full of fear.

"No problem." I turned back to Dash, trying to hold back my anger and embarrassment, and started scraping water off his back and flanks. I was irritated at her giving me just enough information to get me involved and curious, but not enough to do anything about. When I was through, I led the horse over to the hot walker, clipped his halter to it, and turned it on. Luis was in the second barn shoveling clean shavings into a stall. After informing him of Dash's whereabouts, I whistled for Scout and headed for my truck.

Glancing in my rearview mirror at the house on the hill, I had to agree with Gabe. Sam had picked himself one heck of a family to marry into. There were times I really liked Bliss and times I felt like smacking her upside the head. I smiled to myself. In general, I tended to feel that way about most cops, including my own husband.

After dropping by the museum to pick up my laptop computer with the vague thought of working tonight, I took Scout home and fed him. After puttering around the house for a few hours, trying not to worry about what Bliss had told me, I finally decided to walk the five long blocks downtown, grab that sandwich, then visit Elvia at the bookstore. Scout gave me a baleful look when I hooked the leash to his leather collar.

"Sorry, Scooby-doo," I said, giving him a quick belly rub, which made him happy. "But this town has leash laws, and we're a law enforcement family. We have to set a good example."

At six o'clock, downtown was busy with tourists just arriving for the wine activity weekend, Cal Poly students already hitting the bars, and families out for a stroll and an ice-cream cone. The city had declared the crush an official city celebration with flags hung from the wrought-iron lampposts depicting grape clusters and wineglasses. Even Blind Harry's had gotten into the spirit with their display window filled with wine books, crystal and pewter wineglasses, decanters, antique wine bags, and carafes, and huge piles of artificial grapes.

The San Celina Inn, a restored old hotel with a mission-style theme and one of the most popular restaurants in the county, was a little over a mile north, up near the train station, so I walked with Scout down Lopez with no fear of running into Gabe and his ex-wife. I was proud of the mature way I was handling her presence in our life. I bought a roast beef and Swiss cheese sandwich, planning to take it to one of the many benches lining San Celina Creek, which meandered through the center of town, past the mission, and eventually ending at the ocean. Luckily I was across the street when I spotted them at Geppetto's, a new Italian restaurant next to the ice-cream parlor. Gabe, Lydia, Sam, and Bliss were sitting next to the window, laughing at something Sam was describing with exaggerated hand gestures. I froze, staring at them, people weaving their way around me. They looked so . . . right. Unaware of the tight grip I had on Scout's leash, his low whine brought me back to reality.

"Oh, I'm sorry, boy," I said, loosening my hold. I stooped down and rubbed behind his floppy Labrador ear in apology. He licked my hand in forgiveness. "Let's go before they see us."

I ducked into Gum Alley, a local artistic landmark created and maintained by generations of gum-chewing college kids, to Blind Harry's back door and punched in the security code. Leaving Scout in the stockroom on a rug that Elvia had provided especially for his visits, I walked through the children's department to the wooden stairway leading down to the basement coffeehouse. All the way downstairs, while waiting for my coffee order, and winding my way through the Friday night crowd to a table in the back corner, I talked to myself about the picture I'd just seen—there was nothing to worry about, Gabe loved me, I *was* invited and chose not to go, and, yes, they looked great together, but looks weren't everything, were they? Okay, so they had history, too, but that was a long time ago. A long, long time ago. Okay, they had a son together. One child. *One*. He was grown now. And *he* liked me, too. I was so involved in my silent pep talk between bites of my sandwich I didn't notice anyone around me until a chair next to me scraped across the wooden floor. I glanced up into Detective Hudson's smiling face.

"Is this chair taken?" he asked, sitting down before I could answer. In the background, the folk singer started crooning "Blue Moon." Detective Hudson cocked his head and listened for a moment. "My mother's favorite song. She's a music teacher in Abilene."

"I thought you said she was an interior decorator in Dallas."

He rubbed his chin and grinned. "You've got a good memory. Where's your husband?"

My jaw tightened, and I looked away, pretending interest in the folk singer's performance. "Out to dinner with his son."

"And his ex-wife?" he inquired, his voice softly mocking.

I turned and stared at him, unblinking. "Are you following me?"

He shifted in the tall wooden library chair. "You're right, it's none of my business. Just hate seein' such a pretty woman look so sad."

"Would you cut the bull and tell me what you want?"

"Just wanted to know if you'd heard anything new on our case."

" 'Our' case? I told you, I'm not involved." I picked up my sandwich and took a small bite.

He unzipped his black leather jacket, leaned back in his chair, and crossed his legs. Tonight he was wearing bright red bullhide boots. Black shafts stitched with rainbow-colored swirls peeked out from under his Wranglers. No Arrow shirt, only a pure white T-shirt.

"Those are the ugliest boots I've ever seen," I said. "They look like something a pimp would wear."

He grinned at me. "Thank you." Then he leaned forward, placing both boots flat on the floor. The folk singer finished her song and started another, an Emmylou Harris song, "Even Cowgirls Get the Blues."

"You went out to Seven Sisters ranch today."

"You *are* following me!"

"Did you find out anything?"

"I wasn't trying to find out anything."

"Sure."

"Detective Hudson, listen up, because I don't plan on repeating myself. I am not going to snoop for you. Not now, not ever. Got it?"

His face turned serious, and I caught a glimpse of an intensity that startled me. "Benni, I have something important to share with you and I'm telling you because your husband probably already knows or will shortly, and you need to know it, too, whether he thinks so or not. We aren't dealing with a heat-of-the-moment homicide like it first appeared."

"We aren't?" I said, before realizing he'd won and pulled me into thinking of this as something we were doing together.

"I suspected as much Tuesday when I was taking the gun and bullet down to the lab in Goleta."

"Why?"

He said slowly, "The bullet didn't match the gun. The gun found at the scene was a .38 revolver. The bullet came from a 9mm semi-automatic pistol. They cause similar wounds, which is why no one questioned it at first. I'm kind of a gun nut so I knew when the bullet was recovered that it was a FMJ pistol bullet and not a lead round nose or partially jacketed revolver bullet."

"What?"

"A full metal jacket. Also, we didn't find a casing at the crime scene, so they must have taken it with them. Add that together with the switching of the guns and you have a premeditated murder, darlin'. Unless you or one of your family members had a grudge against Mr. Norton, it appears one of *his* family members most definitely had this planned all neat and pretty or was a pretty quick thinker." He couldn't resist adding, "Just like I told you that night."

"But it doesn't make sense," I said. "Why would someone take that chance when all of us are there? They could have killed him when he was out in the fields or in his office alone or any number of better times than when a party is going on. I think you're stretching the facts to fit your theory."

His face stayed genial. "You don't want to face the fact that someone in one of your most prominent families, a family your stepson is marrying into, is nothing but a cold-blooded killer."

I stood up. "I think this conversation is over."

He caught me again upstairs in the art section where I was glancing through a new book on Outsider artists from the South.

"Anything worth reading?" he commented from behind me.

I didn't turn around. "Don't you think you'd be serving our county better harassing someone who had some genuine involvement in this case?"

"Just one more thing before I take your subtle hint and leave. Aren't you wondering even just a little who called the paper *hours* before Mr. Norton was shot to say that there was something going down at Seven Sisters?"

I didn't answer and in a few minutes I could tell he was gone. I took the Outsider artist book to the front counter where Elvia stood leafing through a book catalog.

"Put this on my account," I told the clerk working the cash register.

"What's up with the rhinestone cowboy?" Elvia asked. "You two were really going at it over there."

"Let's go outside," I said.

We sat on the bench in front of her store, and I told her what he said and how I didn't want to get pulled into this whole mess.

"Looks like you already are, *amiga*. And what else is wrong?"

"What do you mean?"

Her look could have withered a hundred-year-old rosebush. "This is your *hermana*, you dope. I've known you since second grade. I know when things aren't right with you."

I described the happy little scene in the Italian restaurant.

She clucked under her breath, causing me to laugh because she sounded so much like her mother, though I wasn't stupid enough to say that out loud.

"She wants him back," she said.

"Dove thinks so, too."

"Listen to your grandmama, then."

"And do what?"

"Don't let her have him."

"Are you, of all people, telling me to fight for my man? Elvia, that's the most unliberated thing I've ever heard you say. I'm going to report you to the feminist police. They'll revoke your NOW card."

She laughed, poking me with one of her red nails. "Benni Harper, feminist or not, if and when I ever decide a man is *mine*, you can bet *mucho dinero* that I'll never let any other woman have him until *I'm* through with him. If you need it, I have a great book on poisons at the store."

"Maybe I'd better warn Emory."

Her smile turned into a tiny frown. "He's not even close to being important enough for me to poison, so don't worry about it."

We made plans to have lunch at her mother's next week, then I went back inside and reclaimed Scout from his bed in the storeroom. The walk home went quicker than usual since my mind was reluctantly worrying over the case. Who had called the paper hours before the murder, claiming something was going to happen at the Brown estate that night? Did someone know Giles was in danger? Why not warn him directly, then? Had the killer called? No, it didn't make sense that anyone planning to kill Giles would want a newspaper reporter there. Unless there was some other announcement that was going to take place. Certainly it wasn't Sam and Bliss's engagement that would bring a reporter out to Seven Sisters. Maybe the announcement that the company was going to merge with Norton Winery? As earth-shattering to the Brown family as that might be, to the rest of the world it was merely another family business being eaten up by a corporation. In this case, a corporation owned by one of their in-laws. That information might make the financial page, but it certainly didn't warrant a reporter being sent out after regular business hours. Then there was that conversation I had overheard—"I'll do it tonight if I have to," Giles had said. Do what?

I was settled into bed reading my new book when Gabe came in at a little before eleven o'clock.

"How was dinner?" I asked, watching him pull off his leather jacket.

"It went really well. I'm feeling a little better about things, though Sam still doesn't have a clue as to how difficult his life is going to be."

"Neither did we at that age."

He smiled. "No, I suppose not."

After he was in bed, he asked, "What did you do this evening? I missed you, by the way." He nuzzled my neck.

"Walked downtown with Scout. Went to the bookstore and listened to some music. That folk singer I like who sounds like Emmylou plays on Fridays, and I need to tell you about . . ." He kissed me long and deep, cutting off my words before I could tell him about talking to Detective Hudson. That was my excuse anyway.

As we made love, though I fought it, my mind flitted over images of him and Lydia, how beautiful they looked together, how they had made love just as we were doing now.

"*Querida,*" he whispered, his shadowed eyes watching my face as his wide, calloused hands cupped my waist. I wondered what he had called Lydia in bed.

Looking down into the strong, familiar planes of his face, an image of Jack came to me, the only other man I'd made love with. Our fifteen years together went so fast. I barely remembered what his lips felt like on my skin.

Gabe closed his eyes, and I wondered if he was thinking of Lydia, of the other women he'd been with, of me. Life with this man was so much more complex than I'd ever imagined it could be, not just because of the complicated adult life he brought with him, but also because of our very different histories.

Then I gave myself over to him, something I never found hard to do with this frustrating, often unfathomable man who made me feel safer than anyone ever had, and for that moment, lost to the hands and lips that had come to know my body so intimately, I told myself the lie all lovers tell themselves, that I was special, that no one had ever made him feel the way I did and no one ever would.

"I'M GOING TO the office to catch up on some paperwork," Gabe said at breakfast the next morning. "What time is that wine thing? What's it called?"

"Zin and Zydeco. It starts at six-thirty. I'll give you your ticket now, and we can meet there." I slid the white ticket across the table. "I'll save a dance for you."

He put it in his wallet, took one last swallow of coffee, and kissed me on the lips. "No way."

"For your next birthday, I'm buying you dancing lessons," I said.

"Oh, by the way, I ran into Detective Hudson last night. He told me something interesting."

"What?"

I told him what the detective had found out about the bullets. Gabe's face sobered as he slipped on his jacket. "That's not good."

"So I assumed."

He looked at me intently. "Why did he tell you this information? Were you questioning him about his case?"

"No, he offered the information without me putting bamboo shoots under his nails."

Gabe didn't look convinced. "Please stay out of this."

"I am!" *Tell him about Detective Hudson*, a little voice inside me encouraged. But the expression on his face told me that it was doubtful he'd believe me. Not with my past record. "I swear I'm avoiding this like poison ivy."

Still looking skeptical, he left for work.

Frustrated, I picked up his breakfast plate, throwing a bagel piece to Scout, then stacking the dishes in the dishwasher. That was enough chores for me today. I hadn't been out to the ranch for a couple of weeks so I pulled on jeans and a pink cotton tank top, since the news said it would be in the upper eighties, and called for Scout.

We dropped by the folk art museum first to check on things. Saturday was usually a big day for both tourists and the artists. Many of our co-op artists worked full-time at other jobs during the week and tried to catch up on their inventory over the weekend. True to form, the gravel parking lot was almost full, and I was forced to park in a space near the empty back field. Out front, D-Daddy, my loyal and very inexpensive assistant, was hosing out two oak half barrels once used to age wine, preparing them for plants. He was a seventy-five-year-old Cajun man who'd spent forty years captaining a fishing boat off the coast of Louisiana and was the most dependable assistant I'd ever hired. His daughter, Evangeline, was a member of our co-op.

"I been thinkin' maybe some nice red geraniums," he said, turning one barrel over to drain. "Maybe some impatiens. What do you say, boss lady?" He gifted me with one of his dazzling smiles. With a thick head of white hair he babied with every sort of potion you could imagine, a lean, fit body from years of hauling up fishnets, and the stamina to dance all night, he was, according to Dove, quite in demand down at the Senior Citizen Friday Night Dance Socials.

"Whatever you want, D-Daddy. I know who the *real* boss is around here."

"The real boss is the boss who bosses the boss."

"Ha, he doesn't boss me. Only thinks he does."

"I was talking about Dove," he said with a cackle.

"Okay, you got me there. Are you going to the Zin and Zydeco event at the mission?"

"Wouldn't miss it, *chèr*. Save me a dance."

"You can have 'em all, D-Daddy. *El patrón*'s got two left feet."

Inside, all three pottery wheels were churning away with clay artists waiting, a tan snowstorm of wood dust thickened the air in the woodworking room, and two quilts were set up in the large room, a double and a queen size. The double was a log cabin made with retro western prints from the thirties—little buckaroos lassoing cattle that reminded me of the pajamas I wore as a girl. The queen was another wine quilt—this one was an appliquéd silk and taffeta Dresden plate pattern featuring the signatures of local winemakers. In the middle of each Dresden plate a cluster of grapes was embroidered. The colors were vibrant reds, greens, yellows, blues and burgundies, salmons and pinks. With a black background, the effect had the stark simplicity of an Amish quilt combined with the richness of a Victorian crazy quilt. I stood over the quilt admiring it, looking for names I recognized. I spotted Etta Brown's neat, small signature in one circle. Two circles away, next to his father's was Giles's bold scrawl.

"Quite a tragedy out at Seven Sisters," a quilter wearing trifocal glasses commented. "Heard you were there." The women surrounding the quilt all looked at me expectantly.

"It is a tragedy," I agreed, then turned and walked down

the hall to my office, closing the door behind me. I sat down in my chair, resting my chin in my palm, wondering what was going to happen in the Brown family when one of them was charged with murder.

Though I hated admitting it, it appeared that Detective Hudson was right. One of the Brown family had probably killed Giles. And if that was true, there would be repercussions that would follow Sam and Bliss their whole lives. What a way to start a marriage . . . or a family.

A rap on my door interrupted my philosophical thoughts.

"Benni?" JJ's voice called from the other side.

I jumped up and opened the door. "Come on in."

She closed the door behind her and shoved an envelope at me. "Read this." Her voice was high and agitated.

I opened the crumpled envelope and took out a sheet of thick ivory stationery with the Seven Sisters logo printed on top. It read:

I'll use it if I have to. Tell Cappy.

"It's Giles's handwriting," she said. "There's more."

I looked back inside the envelope and pulled out a sheet of cheap white typing paper. It was a crude crayon gravestone rubbing showing a single lily of the valley.

"Where did you get these?" I asked.

She ducked her head. Her hair lay flat and soft today, a deep red/brown merlot color. Without her spikes, she appeared younger, more vulnerable. Her kohl-lined gray eyes glowed with fear. "It was in Bliss's suitcase. I admit I was snooping, and she'll never forgive me if she finds out, but she's been so upset, and I've been worried sick. She won't talk to me, and so I went to Sam, and he says he feels like she's holding something back from him, too. I have to put it back before she gets off duty at three, but I had to show it to somebody. I'm so afraid this somehow will make the police think Cappy had a reason to kill Giles."

I studied the note, then the gravestone rubbing. "Do you have any idea of the significance of these flowers?," I asked.

"No," she said, rubbing her eyes, smearing her makeup.

This would not look good for Cappy if the sheriff's detectives saw it. Bliss's question about the importance of job versus family made sense now. "Did you show it to Sam?"

She shook her head no.

"Good, don't. He doesn't need to be pulled deeper into this." I chewed on my bottom lip. To be honest, I wish she hadn't shown it to me.

Tears welled up in her pale eyes. "Oh, Benni, I'm so sorry to drag you into this. It puts you in an awkward position, but I didn't know where else to turn. I thought about going to my mom, but she and Cappy have such a prickly relationship that I don't know what this would set off. I swear, everyone in my family hates each other." She put her face in her hands and started crying softly. I led her to a chair and sat down next to her, rubbing her back like you would comfort a small child.

"It's okay," I lied. "We'll figure something out."

I went over to my desk and ran both sheets through my fax machine, making myself passable copies, then handed the originals back to her. I stuck my copies in the pocket of my jeans. "But, JJ, the reality is that someone did kill Giles, and sooner or later the sheriff's department will figure out who."

She raised her tear-stained face and looked at me with such trust that I felt like crying myself. "What should we do?"

I sat back down beside her. "Let's take it one step at a time. It appears from Giles's note that he knew something about your grandmother that he thought he could use to blackmail her. We need to find out what that is."

She settled back in the office chair, folding her hands in her lap like a child trying to behave. "I know a few things, Benni, but Susa and Moonie left Seven Sisters before Bliss and I were even a year old. We came back for occasional visits, maybe three in my whole childhood, so there's a lot that's happened in the family that Bliss and I don't know about."

"Tell me what you do know."

"Great-Aunt Cappy and Great-Aunt Etta have been fighting over the trust fund since Etta started the winery. Cappy didn't mind it when Etta's wine was a hobby. She even seemed proud of Etta's blue ribbons, but when Etta started wanting money for the winery and it came at the cost of Cappy's horses, there were fireworks."

"When did Giles come into the picture?"

"Arcadia met Giles at some wine dinner up in Napa Valley. It was apparently love at first sight for my cousin, and they got married three months later at a huge affair at his father's estate. About a year or so later I started hearing through Susa's conversations with Cappy that Giles was making noise about merging the wineries."

"How did Etta feel about that?"

"I think she was all right with it. All Etta wants is to be left alone to make her wine. It's more than a job for her. It's like a calling or something. She's obsessed with making the perfect bottle of wine."

"Sort of like producing a champion race horse," I commented, thinking how much alike the two sisters were. "So where does your great-aunt Willow fit into this?"

"Ever since Arcadia's parents died when she was nine, Great-Aunt Willow has tried to compensate by treating Arcadia like a little princess. Whatever Arcadia wants is whatever Willow wants, providing it doesn't hurt her image in San Celina society."

"So Arcadia marrying into a Napa Valley wine dynasty was definitely something that made Willow happy. That might eliminate her as a suspect. Killing Giles would be like killing the proverbial goose with the golden egg. Besides, I honestly can't imagine Willow shooting someone."

"That's how much you *don't* know about the Brown women," JJ said grimly. "All of them were taught to use guns early in their lives by my great-grandfather. That's one of the reasons my mother moved away so young, I think. She's always hated guns and anything to do with hunting. Willow and Etta are just as capable of shooting someone as Cappy, believe me."

I looked at her in surprise, struck dumb for a moment. Then I asked, "What about Chase? Did he and Giles get along?"

"They liked to drink together. And they were hunting buddies. I never saw them argue, if that's what you're asking."

"How did Chase feel about this merger with Giles's family's winery?"

"I think that Uncle Chase would be fine as long as no one cut off his allowance." She said the words without rancor or bitterness, just stating a fact. Then she thought for a moment. "Cappy was counting on him to vote her way at the next family meeting. From what Susa said, the executor of the trust fund said that someone was going to have to start cutting back, that the trust can't afford to support two unprofitable businesses."

"So the winery isn't doing well either?"

"It's up and down, I guess. They had a bad year a couple of years ago, lost sixty percent of their grapes to an early frost. It's a business that's always on the edge."

"Like horsebreeding and racing."

She nodded, her hands still grasped tightly in her lap. Her skin was pale under its bright makeup. A sheen of tears brightened her eyes.

I thought for a moment. "Okay, what about Arcadia? How were things between her and Giles?"

"They had their fights from what Bliss told me. He wasn't exactly faithful."

"Anyone in particular?"

"From what I hear, he wasn't particular. Bliss once said that he and Chase hunted more than just wild boar together, but she never went into detail. The only thing I ever heard about was she caught him a few months back with one of the tasting room girls. Grandma Cappy and my aunts put a stop to that, though I heard they didn't fire the girl. That surprised me, actually. I guess Giles had more power in the family than I realized 'cause Arcadia is Willow's little darling. Bliss said Cappy wouldn't let them fire her. I have no idea what *that* was about."

"So, Arcadia certainly had a motive and as much opportunity as anyone at the party. Can she shoot? Do you think she'd have the nerve to do it?"

"I have no idea. It seems like I remember Susa saying Arcadia's father fit into the Brown family perfectly, that he was a gun nut like everyone else in the family. But she was nine when he died, so I don't know if he ever taught her to shoot."

"Just out of curiosity, what's the story on the men in this family?"

She held out a hand and started counting them off on her blue tipped fingernails. "My dad's up north. Cappy's husband, Stephen . . ."

"You mean your grandfather."

"Right. I never met him, so he's only a name to me.

Anyway, he ran off to Taos in the late fifties to be a painter. My mom was just a little girl. He died in the sixties, I think. Aunt Willow's husband . . ."

"Arcadia's grandfather."

"Right. He was a rodeo rider. The story is he was gored to death by a bull in Reno, but the truth is he was shot by a jealous husband in Barstow."

"Prim and proper Willow Brown was married to a rodeo rider?" I couldn't help laughing at that incongruous picture.

JJ joined my laughter. "I guess we all have our weak moments, and he was Great-Aunt Willow's. Cappy apparently teased her unmercifully about it until Willow flew to Taos and seduced my grandfather and made sure Cappy heard all the details. There's a family rumor that there's a nude painting of Willow painted by my grandfather somewhere, but I've never seen it."

"So there's no love lost between Cappy and Willow."

"Not much, though they mostly stay out of each other's lives. Aunt Etta is the peacemaker, but Giles moving in on her territory caused some friction between her and Willow at times. He must have been really obnoxious about the merger, because Etta's not someone who gets mad easily. But nothing's ever meant as much to her as the winery."

I looked into her eyes. "How much of this did you tell the sheriff's detectives?"

She gazed squarely back at me, unflinching. "Why, none of it. It's personal. I couldn't tell family problems to one of those detectives. Cappy and the rest would kill me." She swallowed hard, her face blanching when she realized the double entendre in her words.

I was beginning to see just how difficult investigating a crime within a family could be. As Detective Hudson suspected, there was much more to this situation than met the eye, and this family was expert at covering up and making things look good on the surface.

"You realize I have to tell Gabe what you told me, and he'll probably tell Detective Hudson. I can't hide anything from my husband."

She scrubbed at her eyes, causing her mascara to smear. "I wouldn't expect you to. I just feel better that someone knows. But can you at least not tell them where you heard it? I don't think I could face talking to that detective about all this stuff."

I contemplated her for a moment, wanting to reach over and stroke her nervous hands quiet. "I'll do my best. That's all I can promise."

She nodded and stood up to leave. "Thanks."

On the drive out to the ranch, I tried to sort out all the information she'd given me. I'd heard the saying that the rich were different, and there was no doubt that the Seven Sisters clan had their problems involving money, but I also knew that families had squabbled and killed over two hundred dollars just as much as twenty million. The amount of money didn't seem to matter; the power struggle was the same, and that was formed when the family members were children, scripts written and parts assigned often before people were even born.

At the ranch it appeared that Dove was entertaining. A half dozen cars were parked in the circle driveway behind Dove's new little red Ford Ranger pickup with a vanity license plate: DOVESTRK. The house was empty, but her red-and-white country kitchen showed evidence that supported my theory with the long breakfast counter covered with plastic-wrapped sandwich platters, casseroles, pies, and cakes. After picking through them and nabbing a miniature pecan pie, I went through the back screen door and across the yard to the barn. Crackly music poured out of the open double doors. Inside I found Dove sitting on a kitchen stool shouting through one of my old San Celina High Stallions cheerleading megaphones.

"Step, step, pause, step . . . Emmett, it's step, step, not step, shuffle! Lift up those feet, old man! You're supposed to be a teenage gang member! Dang it, Melva, how many times do I have to tell you? You're a Jet, not a Shark. Get over to your own side."

"What's going on?" I asked, coming up behind her.

She turned and frowned at me, her pale peach face disgusted. "Land's sakes, I swear I'm going to sell myself on the street corner. I'd make more money than we'll bring in trying to put on a play."

"First, I think Mac might disapprove just a little of the president of the Women's Missionary Union hawking her wares down on Lopez Street, good intentions and Mary Magdalene notwithstanding, and second, what possessed you to put on a play, and am I guessing right that it's *West Side Story*?"

"Ten-minute break, kids. Don't go too far—we've got hours of rehearsing still to go," she yelled through the megaphone. Emmett Penshaw, apparently the head Shark, made a disparaging gesture with his liver-spotted hand and mumbled something to the snowy-haired Jet next to him.

"I saw that, Emmett," she called through the megaphone. "Give me ten push-ups."

He ignored her and shuffled out of the barn toward the house.

Trying not to laugh since I didn't want her irritation turned on me, I asked calmly, "*West Side Story*, Dove? Are you sure this is the easiest way to make money?"

"No," she said, setting down the red-and-black megaphone painted with my high school mascot—a fire-breathing stallion. "But I've about come to the end of my tether, honeybun. Everyone's counting on me to think of something, but whenever I do, they fight me the whole way. All these people want to do is eat coffee cake and complain about their bunions. We have to make some money fast or we'll just have to settle for what the insurance company will pay us, and end up having to turn folks away who need a hot meal. I need to light a fire under their sorry old butts."

I put my arm around her shoulders and hugged her. "Dove, you know I'll do anything to help, and so will my friends. Maybe having some younger people involved will help your friends get more excited about it."

Her mouth turned up slowly into a big, crafty smile. "Out of the mouths of babes. Honeybun, you have just given me an answer to my prayer. I asked the good Lord for a sign, and your suggestion is it."

"What?"

"I wasn't sure if it was okay with God, but I've got the green light now. Mac told me he thought it was all right, but now, after what you just said, I know it is."

"What are you talking about?"

Her smile grew wider. "You'll find out soon enough." She leaned over and kissed my cheek. "Thanks."

I followed her back to the house where her friends were indeed already halfway through the refreshments and comparing knee and hip surgeries. I was pleased that I'd helped her, though I had no idea how. After eating a tuna sandwich and a brownie, I went out to the porch and called for Scout. He came bounding down the driveway where he'd gone to mark some of the towering oak trees. Lydia's shiny Jaguar slowly followed him. I stood on the front porch and watched Gabe step out of the driver's side and Lydia climb out of the passenger's side.

"Hi," Gabe said, coming up the porch and kissing me

on the cheek. "Lydia came by the office and wanted to know how to get out to the ranch, and I thought it would be just as easy for me to drive out here with her."

She smiled at me. "I wanted to see where my son's been living so happily for the last year." She wore plum-colored slacks, matching linen top, and black, thin-strap sandals. Her hair was pulled back with large Hopi silver barrettes.

I smiled back, determined to stamp down the jealous feelings of seeing them together *again* with positive thoughts and the assertion that she had always been a part of Gabe's and Sam's lives and always would be. I'd better get used to it. It would have helped, though, if my husband hadn't looked quite so happy.

"I can't guarantee the cleanliness of the bunkhouse," I said. "Dove stays on them, but between him and the other hands, it can get pretty grungy."

She laughed, touching her smooth throat with her hand. A large diamond dinner ring flashed in the sunlight. "Benni, you don't have to tell *me* that. I lived with his grime for eighteen years."

That made me feel really stupid. Of course she knew what it was like to have a boy around. Better than me. The obvious fact that she was a mother and I wasn't reared its head again.

"I have to get back to the museum," I said to Gabe. "Do you need a ride back?"

"No, I'll drive back with Lydia so she doesn't get lost. You go on to work."

I tried to quell the slow boil inside me. "Guess I'll see you this evening at the wine thing."

"Wine thing?" Lydia asked.

Gabe turned to her, his face animated. "It's one of the harvest events. Zin and Zydeco. You might still be able to get a ticket. What do you think, Benni?"

"I have no idea. I suppose you can try."

"Don't worry," he said to Lydia. "I am not without influence in this town. I'll get you in."

"Wonderful," she said, beaming at him.

Oh, yes, wonderful, I thought.

"I am not without influence in this town. I'll get you in," I mocked Gabe to Scout while driving back to town. "What a pompous thing to say." I growled and made a face at my dog. Scout whined and loyally licked my hand. I ruffled his head and blew him a noisy kiss. "You're the guy for me, Scout. Always and forever."

I drove past the museum, not feeling like facing either paperwork or the million and one questions and requests that always dogged me at work. Before I realized it, I found myself turning off on the road that led to the Seven Sisters ranch.

You're not snooping, I told myself. *You're just going out to visit Bliss, see the horses, maybe tour the wine-tasting room that you missed the night of the engagement party.*

It was almost three o'clock when I stopped at the stables where things were pretty quiet. A Mexican groom was preparing to wrap the legs of a bay mare with a swollen fetlock. Figaro, the masked barn cat, greeted me by weaving around my legs. I bent down and stroked the long black stripe on his back.

"*Donde* Señorita Bliss?" I asked the groom.

He shrugged his answer—I don't know.

"Señora Cappy?"

He jerked a thumb up the road. "*En la casa grande*."

In the big house. "*Graçias*."

I wandered around, petting the horses, then decided to walk the quarter mile to the wine-tasting room and the rose garden, which was quite famous among San Celina's flower set. It was a warm, pleasant afternoon, the temperature hovering around eighty. Walking through the garden might give me the time and solitude I needed to think about what I should do with this new information I'd acquired. The one person I was definitely going to avoid was Detective Hudson, who seemed to have an uncanny ability to sense when I was holding something back. I'd give this information to Gabe and let him talk to the sheriff's detective.

It was a smart move leaving my car at the stable, because the parking lot was completely full and the winetasting bar as crowded as an airport at Christmas. Tourists were well into their wine weekend on this Saturday afternoon. There were two dark red limousines from Will's Winetasting Tours parked in front of the rugged adobe tasting room. Chase, Etta, and two female employees were all pouring wine and chatting with customers. It appeared Emory was right. The murder had only caused business to pick up. Either that or a lot of these obviously out-of-town customers hadn't heard about it yet. I left Scout comfortably situated under the shade of an ash tree with the command to stay and stepped inside the cool, spicy-scented tasting room.

Though the outside was adobe, the gift shop and winetasting room duplicated the Montana lodge theme of the big house. The gift items ran the gamut of pewter wine corks shaped like horse heads to glassware etched with the Seven Sisters logo to local salsas and hand-tinted postcards of the magnificent Brown house and rose gardens. I picked up a brochure that explained the history of the adobe structure and the rose gardens.

The long dark oak tasting bar with a brass foot rail and brown-and-white cowhide barstools must have set the family trust back a pretty penny. Hanging behind the bar, an original Donna Howell-Sickles watercolor of three cowgirls with strong thighs and sky-sized grins also told me no expense had been spared. A built-in fireplace was at one end with a dozen or so padded mission-style chairs surrounding it. Over the carved mantel was a professional portrait of the entire Brown family. I weaved my way through the chattering wine tasters and stared up at the photograph. Everyone's smile was flawless and I couldn't help but wonder how many shots it took the photographer to achieve this polished picture. I stepped closer. The smiles were perfect, but there wasn't a genuine bit of emotion in one of them.

I stared a little longer at Giles's face. What had he done that caused one of these people to murder him? Was it blackmail like his letter implied, or something else? Maybe Arcadia, as dramatic as her reaction had been that night, had, in reality, become fed up with his philandering. The switching of the guns did sound planned, as Detective Hudson said, but it could just as well have been a quick recovery by her grandmother and great-aunts who by no means lacked the nerve to pull it off.

I made a note to call my friend Amanda Landry, who was also the volunteer attorney for the folk art museum, to see if I could finagle her into loaning me her investigator, Leilani, for a day to see what kind of history she could find on Giles Norton, his family, and his extracurricular activities.

"Can I help you with something, Benni?"

The man's voice startled me, and I turned, laughing nervously, to face Chase Brown. His face was already flushed with the explosive red color of a habitual drinker. Like his picture in the portrait above us, his lips smiled, but his eyes remained blank. He held a glass of dark red wine. "Are you here for a tasting?"

I shook my head no. "I came to watch Bliss work with

the horses, but she's not here, or at least the groom doesn't know where she is. I was going to go on up to the house, but I decided to walk over and see the wine-tasting room and garden since I missed it the other night . . ." I paused, suddenly aware that a small group of people were inching closer, listening to us.

"Why don't we go outside?" he said in a low voice, taking my elbow. I tried pulling away politely, having always hated that controlling gesture, especially in men I didn't know well. He let go when we got outside. "People are bottom feeders," he said, taking a big gulp from the wineglass.

"I guess it's been hard on everyone," I said.

"You said it," he said, gesturing toward the tasting room with the wineglass. A bit splashed out, staining his hand. He impatiently wiped it on his dark slacks. "Giles was basically a pain in the ass when he was alive, and he's proving to be even more so now that he's dead."

I didn't answer, hoping he'd continue. It was a well-known fact that Chase was half drunk most of the time, and there was no better place to get information than a partially drunk, irritated person.

"Don't get me wrong," he said, looking down at me out of red-veined eyes. "We had us some good times, me and Giles. The guy could shoot, no doubt about it. And hold his whiskey. He could hold his friggin' whiskey."

I nodded, as if agreeing that it was indeed a legacy to be proud of, the ability of one's liver not to completely collapse while drowning in alcohol.

"But he was pushy," Chase said, "and didn't know when to take no for an answer. The man hated the word no."

"I heard he wanted to take the winery international," I said, trying to make it sound like casual chitchat.

"You heard right. Would've been a real coup for Seven

Sisters. Lots more money. Lots more prestige. I could see the advantages better than some people."

"So," I said, hesitating only for a moment before barging in with my question, knowing this might be the only time I'd ever get a chance to ask. "You were going to vote in favor of the merger?"

He drank from his glass again, emptying it. "Where are my manners? Did you want any wine?"

"Not this early for me, thanks."

He laughed and twirled the stem of the glass in his thick fingers. "There's no cocktail hour for wine, honey. Why, there are places in Europe where people drink it for breakfast."

"Well, I've never claimed to be a sophisticate. About the merger . . ."

"It pissed off the Amazon queen, no doubt about it. But the last few days he had her almost convinced to vote for the merger. Willow and Etta, too. Don't know how he got the queen to even think about changing her mind, but he did."

"The Amazon queen?"

"My dear mother, Capitola, herself. That's what we call her. Not to her face, of course. The queen and her consorts. Giles and I did have our laughs. He was the only man who'd come into this family in a long time who wasn't ball-stripped and beat into compliance by the women in this spider's web. Caused him a good deal of grief, and if I had some wine, I'd toast him." He held up his empty glass.

Before I could answer, a twentyish woman in tight red Wranglers and a silky print blouse walked up to us. "Chase, someone wants a taste of the '92 Merlot, and you said no one's supposed to pour that but you."

"Be right in, honey," he said. "Me and Ms. Harper here are having a little talk. Give us some privacy."

She glanced at me, her pretty, freckled face frowning slightly before turning around and going back into the tasting room. Her irritated walk spoke volumes about their relationship.

I raised my eyebrows in a silent, inquiring gesture.

He twirled the glass by its stem and tried to look chagrined. "She's kinda possessive. Which is ironic considering how free she is with her favors."

I wasn't about to touch that remark. "Who is she?" I asked.

"Just one of the tasting room girls. Giles brought her on. When he was through with her, she and I dated a few times, had a few laughs, a roll or two in the hay—literally." He gave a cynical laugh. "She thinks that constitutes some kind of relationship. But she's a good worker and usually a pretty fun gal. Sure you don't want any wine?"

"No, thanks." I held up the brochure in my hand. "I think I'm going to take a stroll through the rose garden, then go look for Bliss again."

"No problem. You come by any time." He gave me a wet, lopsided smile and moved his face within inches of mine. His breath was sour and stale-smelling. "My casa is always your casa."

I took a step backwards, inhaling a shallow breath. "Uh, thanks."

As I watched him walk back up the steps into the tasting room, I added his information to what JJ had told me. I had been surprised to hear that Cappy interceded for the tasting room girl when she was caught with Giles. Usually it's the weaker person in a relationship, invariably the woman, who ends up losing a job or reputation whenever there's an illicit affair. But I knew Cappy was a fair woman and the least pretentious of the sisters. Maybe she was truly trying to be egalitarian about the situation—assigning blame to both sides where it should be.

Then again, I thought, following a group of khaki-clad wine tasters toward the rose garden, maybe Giles had had something really big on her . . . or the family, giving him the kind of power that would keep his ex-lover employed even under his spoiled wife's aristocratic nose. Did Arcadia perhaps have some knowledge about what Giles had on the family? Why else would she put up with one of her husband's lovers working so closely with him in the winery?

It took me about an hour to see the entire garden, which, according to the shiny brochure, contained ten acres of every type of rose imaginable. Many bushes were in full bloom because of the late summer weather. The sheer number of them was breathtaking. Reading the names of the roses—Apothecary's Rose, Yankee Doodle, Bride's Dream, Secret, Golden Wings, Don Juan, Magic Carrousel—reminded me of the names conceived for wines and quilts. In the center of the garden was a great old queenly rosebush thick with large, heady-smelling blooms—white with red tips. Surrounding it were seven slightly smaller bushes in shades of pink, yellow, and red-orange. The way the flowers were planted almost duplicated the actual Seven Sisters quilt pattern that I'd looked up this morning in my encyclopedia of quilt patterns. I wondered if whoever had planted them had known that. In the quilt pattern there was one star or "sister" in the middle and six surrounding it, similar to the constellation after which it was named.

I glanced at the literature and saw the roses were hybrids named for the seven Brown sisters and their mother. The rose in the center was, naturally, Rose Jewell, the others Capitola Jewell, Willowdeen Jewell, Etta Jewell, Daisy Jewell, Dahlia Jewell, Beulah Jewell, and Bethany Jewell. The last four were obviously the two sets of twins who had died. What took their lives? Back in the early part of the century, it could have been anything. Many of the cemeteries around San Celina had tiny gravestones erected because of an encounter with influenza or some infectious disease that was incurable before our current medical advances. I wondered if the grandmother, Rose Jewell, thought much about the babies she'd lost so long ago. I sat down on one of the stone benches and listened to the trickling of the four fountains situated in each corner of the center courtyard. Wine tasters wandered up and down the rows, exclaiming over the roses, marveling at their size, abundance, and variety.

"Quite an awesome bush, isn't it?" Susa Girard asked, sitting down next to me.

"It certainly is," I agreed, surprised to see her. "Just how old is the Rose Jewell?"

"At least sixty years old," she said. "It originally was up next to the house in a small rose garden that Great-Grandfather started. When he died, Grandma Rose couldn't bear to look at them, much less care for them, so they were moved down here, and gradually this garden emerged. Jose, our ranch manager, has been the main caretaker since Great-Grandfather died. And with the winery, they've now become quite the attraction. It's one of the biggest private rose gardens in California."

"So it says here," I said, holding up the brochure. We sat for a moment in silence.

"Benni," she finally said. "I just talked to JJ a little while ago, and she told me about the note she found in Bliss's possession. I have a confession to make."

I didn't say anything, but continued studying the slick brochure in my hands. This family had more secrets than a locker room of teenage girls, and it seemed as if I was destined to be a part of their clique.

"I . . ." She stopped, hesitated, then started again. "I was the one Giles sent it to. Bliss found it in my room and insisted on taking it." Her voice faltered, causing me to look up at her. The finely etched lines around her eyes tightened as the sun passed from behind a cloud and brightened the air around us. "She said it would be better if she kept it. That it looked too . . . incriminating for me to have it in my possession."

Keep it or destroy it, I wondered. It's true that it implicated Cappy big-time, and Cappy had a good enough motive just with the conflict between the winery and the ranch.

"When did Giles give it to you?" I asked.

"Monday morning." Her voice stayed low, and I had to move closer to hear her words above the laughing and conversation of other people.

"The day of the party?" Things were looking worse and worse for Cappy.

She nodded, breathing in short, shallow breaths.

"Did you show it to Cappy?'

She gave an ironic laugh. "I was going to wait until after the party so Bliss and Sam's evening wouldn't be ruined." Sitting this close to her, I could see her strong resemblance to Cappy in her firm jaw and proud chin.

"Do you have any idea what he meant by 'it'? What about the lily of the valley? Do you know the significance of that?"

"No."

"Why would he give the note to you and not Cappy?" I asked.

"I have no idea. Maybe he thought I'd be able to talk her into doing what he wanted. Maybe he thought he could scare her by getting me involved. My mother is . . ." She swallowed hard. ". . . very protective of her family. That's not a secret, I'm sure you know."

Maybe he's the one who should have been scared, I thought. "And what he wanted her to do was vote to merge the Seven Sisters winery with Norton Winery."

"Yes, but she never would have done that. It could possibly harm the breeding operation in a big way because the winery would take—some people would say destroy—all the best grazing land. And more important, we'd be beholden to someone else, to Giles's father, who Cappy's hated from the first minute they met. Nothing would convince her to vote to merge our holdings with theirs."

That's not what Chase had just told me. I kept that to myself. "Why does Cappy hate Giles's father?"

Her natural-colored glossy lips formed a wry smile. "Two peas in a pod is what I'd guess, though she'd throttle me if she ever heard that." She smoothed down her yellow cotton skirt. "Benni, I don't believe Cappy would ever hurt anyone. Not even to save her horses. Really, my mother does have a very high moral code."

I didn't answer. We never want to believe that people we know or care about are capable of terrible and cruel acts. One, it was too frightening to think we wouldn't know evil even when it sat at the breakfast table with us, and two, it was even more frightening to think we'd harbor that same evil within ourselves.

I cleared my throat, feeling awkward and apologetic. "I'll have to tell Detective Hudson, you know."

"I wish JJ would have come to me first." She left it at that, knowing better than to ask me not to. If JJ had gone to her mother first, there's a good chance it would have stopped there.

"He seems like a fair man," I said, folding the brochure over and sticking it in the back pocket of my jeans. "That note doesn't mean Cappy did anything, but Detective Hudson will probably want to talk with you both again." I tried to encourage her. "The fact you didn't show it to her helps, I'm sure."

Her face became still. A soft wind blew tendrils of gray-blond hair around her eyes, but she didn't blink or brush them away. "I know that JJ put you in an awkward position, what with your husband being the chief of police. I apologize for my daughter. Normally she would have come to me first, but these days . . ." Her voice trailed off again. It was a trait I was beginning to see was common for her.

"She just got scared. I was a convenient adult, I think. She was trying to keep you from being involved. Maybe she was afraid it would cause problems between you and Cappy."

"Thank you for listening to her and for being so kind to Bliss."

"You have wonderful daughters."

"Yes, they are." She stood up and used one hand to pull back her long hair. "It seems in spite of Moonie and me."

As she started walking away, a thought occurred to me.

"Susa, there's one thing I wondered."

She turned, her silvery eyes dark and questioning. "Yes?"

"Why did you leave Seven Sisters when the girls were so young? I mean, forgive my curiosity, but I just wondered."

"No great mysterious reason. Moonie just didn't feel comfortable in San Celina County or with my family. You can see why. Cappy and the aunts can be pretty overpowering, and my mother didn't like Moonie much."

An easygoing, hippie-type guy who preferred commune living to building an empire. No, he wouldn't be Cappy's dream husband for her only daughter.

"Is that all?" I asked, hoping for more.

An unreadable expression swept over her face—bewilderment, anger, sadness? I couldn't tell.

"Are you close to your family, Benni?" she asked.

I stuck my hands deep into the pockets of my jeans. "We have our squabbles, but, yes, I'd say we're close."

"No secrets?"

Remembering all that had happened last May concerning my own past and that of my mother and of my father's often frustrating reserve and lack of openness, I answered, "Every family has secrets, I think." I inhaled deeply, the overwhelming sweetness of the hundreds of roses making me slightly sick to my stomach.

"Maybe so, but there were too many unanswerable ones in the Brown family for my taste. Moonie and I wanted to raise our girls in a more open environment. And we did. I don't regret leaving at all. As a matter of fact, if it were possible, I would have never come back to Seven Sisters. But it's JJ's and Bliss's heritage. Good or bad, I couldn't keep it from them forever. I just worry that the malevolence I've always sensed permeated the Brown family will hurt my girls. Especially now that Bliss is going to have a baby. I'll never forgive myself if it does." She turned and walked away before I could question her more.

What secrets? Secrets terrible enough that the family could be blackmailed? Secrets terrible enough to kill to keep hidden?

Those questions churned through my brain when I walked back to my truck. I poured some bottled water into a tin pie plate for Scout. While he gratefully lapped it up, I contemplated my next move. My answer came when Cappy drove up in her old Jeep Wagoneer.

"Benni! One of the grooms told me you were here," she said, climbing out. Her expression appeared congenial and welcoming.

"I thought I'd come out and see if Bliss was working any of the horses. And I hadn't gone through the wine-tasting room and rose garden yet."

She reached down and scratched behind Scout's ears. "So, what did you think of them?" His tail wagged slowly.

"The adobe's been restored wonderfully. And the rose garden is spectacular."

"They should be. They cost enough."

Just the opening I needed. "What's going to happen now? Wasn't the winery mostly Giles's business?"

Her weathered face seemed to lengthen, and her lips and eyes narrowed to a thin line. I remembered the look. Suddenly I felt fifteen again.

"That still hasn't been decided," she said, her voice short. "Is there something I can do for you?"

I felt my face turn red. "No, like I said, I was just coming out to see if Bliss was working the horses . . ."

"She won't be doing that for a while. She's not happy about it, but I won't have her taking any chances with the baby."

I nodded. "Yes, I understand. I guess I'll go, then."

She looked straight into my eyes, a cold steel gray that didn't show a hint of her years. They were the same eyes that gave me no sympathy when, tears in my own hazel eyes, I fell off my barrel-racing pony for the fifth time. *Your own fault*, she'd said at the time. *God gave you thighs for a reason. Use them to stick to your pony the next time.* "That would be best. Give my regards to Dove."

"Yes, ma'am."

Her back stiff as an oak trunk, she strode toward her Jeep, then stopped and faced me. "Benni, no matter what Bliss says, please don't come out to the stables again without my knowledge. We have a strict routine with the horses, and new people make them nervous."

My face was hot enough to fry eggs. "Yes, ma'am."

On the drive back, Gabe's annoyingly smug voice silently reprimanded me for my snooping. *That's what you get*, it said. *Are you embarrassed enough to mind your own business now?*

At home, I took a quick shower and changed into new black jeans, my dressy Tony Lama boots, and a teal-colored silk tank top with a lacy V front. With black and silver Navajo earrings, I didn't look quite as much like I'd just come in from cleaning horse stalls.

And why, pray tell, is that suddenly important to you? I asked myself in the mirror as I fiddled with my curly hair, now past my shoulders, first braiding it, then pulling out the braid and touching it up with a hair pick to show off its thickness. I darkened my eyelashes with mascara and even gave a perfunctory swipe of blush to my cheeks. After staring at myself in the mirror for a truly embarrassing amount of time, I made a face at my reflection.

"You're pathetic. There's no way you can compete with her looks and style." I looked down at Scout's sympathetic gold eyes. "Is there?" His tail thumped twice on the carpet.

I grabbed his muzzle and shook it gently. "You didn't have to agree so quickly, Scooby-doo." After feeding him and giving him a rawhide chew, I headed downtown. It took me fifteen minutes to find a parking space, not unusual for a Saturday evening when there is a downtown event. Two blocks away, the Zydeco band Varise's Red Hot Daddies perched on the steps in front of the mission. The party was already in full swing when I reached the line to enter the roped-off area. After getting my hand stamped and receiving my authentic "Zin and Zydeco—the Only Way to Go" wine-tasting glass, I headed for the food booth set up by Momie Fontenot's Authentic Cajun and Creole Cookin'.

The tantalizing smell of the spicy Cajun sausage persuaded me to eat before I attempted to find Gabe. I took my paper plate of red beans, dirty rice, sausage, blackened chicken, and hot cornbread to one of the long picnic tables they'd provided behind the twenty or so wine-tasting booths. I sat down next to a group of four people dressed completely in black except for their zebra-patterned vests trimmed with sequins and matching Mardi Gras masks. One of the females had a long black feather boa trailing down her back. But this was a mostly casual affair, and T-shirts with silly sayings outnumbered the Mardi Gras costumes: "Forgive Me for I Have Zinned," "It's So Good, It's Zinful," "Zin-sational!" "Zinners Wanted."

Up front the band had announced their next number, a wild dance song called *Valse a Beausoleil*, and the zebra clan left to start dancing on the large concrete area in front of the band. I finished up my food and joined the crowd wandering from wine booth to wine booth, tasting the different zinfandel wines. All the booths were decorated with purple and green flags celebrating the Cajun theme and had bowls of unsalted crackers and bottled water for tasters to cleanse their palates between tastings. At the Seven Sisters booth JJ and another young woman poured samples of two different zinfandels—both named after Cappy's racehorses—Churn Dash Zinfandel and Dashing Rose Zinfandel. JJ's face brightened with a smile when she saw me.

"Do you have a minute?" I asked.

"Sure." She turned to the other girl. "Hold down the fort for a little while, okay?"

We walked over to the ivy-covered fence overlooking San Celina Creek. Across the water, people at the cafes were enjoying the Cajun music from afar. The energetic, addictive rhythms of the electric fiddle, squeeze box, and aluminum washboard had me itching to move my feet, too, and after my conversation with JJ, I was determined to find D-Daddy and claim my dance.

"What's going on?" JJ asked, chewing at a raw red spot on her lip.

"I went out to Seven Sisters today and talked with your uncle Chase. He also told me Giles had been fooling around with one of the tasting room employees. A twentyish red-headed lady with freckles."

Her tongue came out and licked her dry lips. "I think her name is Sheila. She's only worked for us for about six months, but I doubt that she's the first. I told you Giles wasn't faithful, but I never like to know any of the details. He'd come on to both me and Bliss. He was quite impressed with himself, to say the least."

"Do you think Arcadia got fed up and decided he'd fraternized with the help one time too many?"

She shook her head in doubt, her pale cheeks burnished gold by the early evening light. "Now that I've really thought about it . . . somehow I just can't imagine Arcadia doing that, even if she did know how to shoot. She's just not brave enough. What I mean is, she isn't nervy enough. Besides, she'd have cracked in a minute when the police questioned her."

"But her grandmother or her great-aunts wouldn't."

JJ's eyes widened. "No," she whispered. "They wouldn't."

I gave a deep sigh, feeling real empathy for her, one of the few innocent Brown family members. "I had another conversation with your mother. She told me you talked to her this afternoon. I'm glad."

JJ looked ready to burst into tears. "She said she was going to talk to you. I knew if you told the detective, she'd be questioned again, and I didn't want her to think I was sneaking around behind her back. It never occurred to me that Bliss got the note from her. I thought Bliss was only protecting Cappy."

"Your mom's pretty upset that Bliss and you are involved. She said she was sorry she came back and even sorrier you and Bliss are here."

"She's always tried to protect us, but now I think she needs our help. It's her family and, whether she likes it or not, ours too. So, now that you know who gave Bliss the note, what do we do?"

"I have a problem, JJ. I also ran into Cappy when I was there and foolishly tried to find out what was going on with the winery now that Giles is dead. I think I might have blown it with her. She asked me not to come out to the ranch again without calling first even though she knew that Bliss specifically invited me. She's suspicious, and I don't think I can safely ask any more questions."

"What are we going to do, then?" she asked, tears filling her eyes. "Bliss is the one I'm really worried about. She came over to my house after work this afternoon because she felt too sick to drive to the ranch. I'm afraid something bad's going to happen. She loves Cappy as much as she does me, Susa, and Moonie. I'm not sure how she'll take it if Cappy is the one who killed Giles."

"We don't know that yet. A note that may or may not be blackmail is only circumstantial evidence. That much law I do know. As for Bliss, talk to your mom and see if the two of you can convince her to stay with you in town for a few days. If she's not at the ranch, maybe she'll calm down."

"I'll try, but Bliss feels so darn responsible. Like she has to protect all of us every minute. We have to do something." She watched me expectantly, waiting for me to think of something. I felt like screaming, "Who put me in charge of piecing your family back together?" A slight tremble in her hand when she reached up and touched her blue-veined temple caused pity to well up inside me.

"I still haven't talked to Detective Hudson about all this," I said. "Or Gabe." Below us in a cafe courtyard, a group of people laughed uproariously at something. I was tempted to walk away from JJ and this whole situation and join them. "Once I do, it's out of our hands. Your family's going to come under some tough scrutiny."

"I know, and it's all my fault. I guess I should have gone directly to my mother with that note." She turned and grasped the metal fence, staring down into the bubbling creek.

Except doing that and then destroying it would have dug both her and Bliss deeper into a possible murder coverup, not to mention add another brick to the wall of Brown family secrets. "Do you really think Bliss could have destroyed that note and remained a cop?" I asked softly. "The guilt would have driven her crazy. Frankly, I think you did her a favor by bringing it out in the open. You did something for her that she couldn't do for herself."

Her face softened in relief. "All I really want is the pressure to be off Bliss. Do you think talking to Gabe and this detective will do that?"

"I have no idea, but I also have no choice but to tell them what I know. Maybe you shouldn't be telling me any more if you think it might compromise your family. If you need a lawyer, my friend, Amanda—"

"We have tons of lawyers," she broke in, her voice sharp. "What I need is a friend, Benni. Someone who isn't just out to pin this killing on anyone they can find without regard to who it hurts. As crazy as they all are, they are my family, and I care about them."

"I'm doing the best I can," I said, fed up with the whole business. "I'm not a trained investigator."

She wrapped thin arms around herself in a self-comforting hug. “I’m sorry, Benni. I just don’t know where to turn.”

“I’ll talk to Gabe and Detective Hudson, then get back with you.”

“Do you have to tell that detective it’s me, Bliss, and Susa who have seen this note? Can’t you just say . . .” Her thin nose flared in agitation, like one of her grandmother’s racehorses. “I don’t know . . . say . . .” A sob escaped from deep in her chest.

“I have to tell him the truth. No matter how Bubba Joe Bob he looks, he’s not a stupid man. He knows we have a relationship. He’d figure it out.”

She glanced over at the wine booth where the other girl was pouring frantically. The girl gave her a pleading look. “I’ve got to get back to the booth.” She turned abruptly away and headed back to the crowded booth.

Frustrated at being in a situation where I had no idea where to turn, I walked back over to the edge of the crowd to watch the dancers twirl and Cajun two-step to the band’s hypnotic beat. I scanned the crowd for my husband, determined to pry him away from his ex-wife long enough to drop all I’d learned today in his very capable lap. His dark head wasn’t visible to me even when I hopped up on a small concrete wall and peered over the bobbing heads.

“Señor Jose Friday, where are you?” I muttered, jumping down.

In the next moment, I felt a hand grab my elbow and a low, comically villainous voice whispered in my ear, “Lady, I got your number. Spill the beans before I lock you up.”

I twisted around to look up into Detective Hudson’s grinning face. Jerking my elbow from his hand, I said, “That dialogue is the most pathetic I’ve ever heard.”

"Almost as bad as my taste in boots?"

I glanced down at his feet. They were clad tonight in a pair of dark brown plain leather ropers with one scuffed toe. "Those actually look like they might have worked a day or two."

"They've seen their share," he said. "Are you looking for the chief? I think I saw him over at the Sierra Robles wine booth. Had the mayor, a couple of city council members, and a very striking Hispanic woman with him."

I ignored his barb. "We need to talk. I've got some information about the Brown family you should know."

"Figured as much. After your talk with Chase, the mother, Susa, and the Girard girl with the crazy hair, I had an inkling we'd need a consultation."

"You'd probably get more accomplished on this case if you'd spend less time following me and more time working on your own leads."

"Didn't have to follow far, Ms. Ortiz. The bench underneath where you and Miss Girard stood has great acoustics. You know, when dealing with a family with this much prominence in the county, I'd be keepin' my voice a li'l bit quieter if'n I was you. That's a little piece of country-fried advice from Bubba Joe Bob himself." His exaggerated Texas drawl mocked me.

A slow blush crept up my neck. "So, I guess I don't need to tell you anything, then. Later." I started to edge my way around a group of people bouncing on the balls of their heels to the music.

"Not so fast," he said, grabbing for my elbow again. But I was quicker and used my small size to weave through the crowd, leaving him in the wake of swaying human bodies. I'd talk to him tomorrow and fill him in on everything he hadn't overheard, but for now I decided to let him stew in his own juices. This continual feint and jab ritual we'd established was beginning to wear on me. Right now, the one person I really wanted to talk to was Gabe.

I finally spotted him across the open-air dance floor, sipping a glass of pinkish wine and talking to the mayor and a deputy district attorney who was running for DA next month. Next to him, looking very comfortable and happy, was Lydia.

He's still *your* husband, I told myself. I took a deep breath and started along the edge of the dancing crowd toward them. Before I could get very far, a hand grabbed mine, and in an instant I was out on the dance floor.

"Hey, *ange*," D-Daddy said, twirling me to the raucous, firecracker beat of a souped-up version of Hank Williams's "Jambalaya." "You ready to shake a leg?"

I laughed and fell in with his rhythm, letting him lead me into steps, twists, and twirls I didn't know were possible while the wild Cajun fiddler pushed the crowd faster and faster with his impossible-to-follow riffs. One song moved into another with only a few seconds for people to catch their breath and start again. Early in our third dance, after D-Daddy had twirled me around three, four, five times, I felt his hand leave mine and another, larger one take its place.

"Hey, Mrs. Ortiz," Detective Hudson said, smiling his Tom Sawyer smile. "Did I forget to tell you these were my dancing boots?"

"What?" I sputtered as he twirled me around three times and spun me around the crowded dance area. It took every bit of concentration I had to keep up with him. Somebody had taught this man how to dance. As we moved around the other couples, I glanced over the crowd, looking for Gabe, hoping with pure petty juvenile revenge that me dancing with another man would seriously annoy him. Naturally he was nowhere to be seen.

At the end of the song, breathing heavily, I jerked my hand out of Detective Hudson's and pushed my way through the milling people. He caught up and fell into step beside me.

"Man, haven't moved like that for months," he said, wiping his forehead with the back of his hand. "It's like riding a bike, though. How about you? Did you enjoy it?"

"Where did . . . ?"

"My mother owns a Cajun restaurant and dance hall in Beaumont, Texas," he said, winking at me. "That's where I was born and spent my delinquently formative years. Did I fail to mention I was half Cajun?"

Another exaggerated mother story. "Good-bye, Detective Hudson," I said, disgusted.

He continued walking beside me, not speaking again until we reached my truck two blocks away.

"What is in those notes you and the Girard girl were discussing?" His face was dead serious now.

"I'll call your office tomorrow and make an appointment," I said, opening my car door. "We can discuss it then."

He grabbed the door from my hand and slammed it closed. His swift and unexpected action caused me to jump.

"I don't think so," he said. Then added, "Ma'am."

I tightened my lips and told myself to breathe deeply. "Fine," I said and in a terse voice told him everything that had happened since JJ first came into my office this morning.

"Add that note with the conversation you *accidentally* overheard at the party, and it sounds an awful lot like blackmail," he said.

"So it appears," I replied, ignoring his gibe.

"Do you think Susa Girard knows what it is Giles Norton had on Cappy?"

"I have no idea."

"Looks like Officer Girard, Miss Girard, and their delightful mother and I need to chat again. And I'd like to take a look at that note and grave rubbing myself. What kind of flower did you say it was?"

"Lily of the valley." A cold breeze . . . or the thought of the grave rubbing . . . caused me to shiver. Goosebumps covered my bare arms. I slipped my hand in the back pocket of my jeans and touched the copies of the note and grave rubbing. I knew I should show them to him right now, but he'd irritated me so much, I decided to keep quiet. Let him get his own copies. "Maybe you should talk to Gabe before you talk to Bliss."

"I don't have to clear anything with Chief Ortiz. He's not *my* boss."

I frowned at him.

"Have you told him any of this?" he pressed.

"I'm on my way home to tell him now. We haven't crossed paths long enough to talk today. He's . . . we've both been busy."

He nodded, his eyes solemn. "Ex-wives have a way of taking up a man's time, that's for sure."

"Is there anything else, Detective Hudson?" I said coolly, not about to discuss Gabe or his ex-wife with him.

"Not right now, but I'll be in touch. You're doin' a bang-up job, Mrs. Ortiz."

"My last name is Harper," I snapped.

His thick eyebrows went up. "You don't say? You're one of them liberated women? Gotta maintain your own identity and all? I'm impressed."

"It's not because . . ." I started, then stopped, annoyed at myself for even bringing it up. "Oh, forget it." I started to climb in the truck, then turned and said, "When you talk to Bliss, please be careful. She's . . . well, she's not feeling too good and this . . ."

"Benni," he said softly. "I'm not going to browbeat a pregnant woman. Give this Texas bubba credit for having some class even if I do wear white-trash boots."

Again I felt my face go hot. It was disconcerting at times how well he read my mind.

He reached over and touched a finger to my cheek. I jerked back, surprised by the tiny jolt of electricity I felt. His knowing chuckle made me want to slap him. He mimed tipping his hat and said smoothly, "Thanks for the dance, darlin'. Most fun I've had since I landed here on the Central Coast."

I watched him walk away, my hand still itching to do something, like throw a rock at the back of his head or slap my own husband upside the head because his preoccupation with his ex-wife was putting me in this awkward position.

Gabe's Corvette was parked in front when I got home, but he wasn't inside the house. They were obviously still cruising around in Lydia's car. I took a quick shower and pulled on a cotton T-shirt and boxer-style shorts and was making myself a vanilla Coke when Lydia's Jag pulled up in front of our house. The clock above the stove read eight o'clock. Through the kitchen window I watched him get out of the driver's seat and walk across the yard, whistling softly.

"Hi," I said, sipping on my drink at the kitchen table. "Guess we missed each other tonight."

"Guess so. I was talking to Larry, that deputy district attorney who's running for DA and Lydia and he discovered they had some people in common. After tasting a couple of wines, we went over to the Thai restaurant for a quick bite. Lydia doesn't care for Cajun food."

"Oh." The ice in my drink cracked, sounding loud in the silence.

He pulled his dark green polo shirt over his head in one swift motion. "It's warm tonight, don't you think?"

"Anything new with Sam?"

He shook his head, throwing the shirt over a chair. "He's worried about Bliss, but other than that, we haven't really formulated a plan yet."

But you and Lydia are sure spending a lot of time discussing it, I wanted to say. Pride and pure-born Ramsey stubbornness kept me from saying it. I was determined not to appear the irrationally jealous second wife. I stirred the ice in my glass with my finger. "I talked to Detective Hudson tonight."

"Again?" A flicker of suspicion came over his face, then was gone. "Well, I'm glad you're cooperating with him. This has to be a tough case to investigate. What did he want?"

Starting with the note JJ found in Bliss's suitcase, I went through everything I discovered today. "Detective Hudson said he's going to have to talk to all of them again."

Gabe nodded, sitting down at the table across from me. "Yes, I can see why." He ran a hand through his thick black hair. "I suspected Bliss knew more than she was telling."

"Gabe, this detective. What do you know about him?"

He leaned back in his chair, his face concerned. "Just another detective, sweetheart. He's new on the force, but apparently has good references from Texas. Why, is he causing you some problems?"

"No, not at all," I said a little too quickly.

His eyes searched my face, but he didn't press for more information. "Just be cooperative, Benni. And try to get Bliss's sister and mother to take their concerns directly to him. I don't like you being that involved."

"Whether we like it or not, we're involved with this up to our eyebrows. And for your information, every time JJ has come to me, I've not only told her to talk to Detective Hudson, but also that anything she tells me I'll have to tell you and the detective."

"*Mi niña muy buena,*" he said, getting up. "Looks like I've finally got you paper-trained."

"Sexist pig." I took an ice cube and threw it at him. He gave a surprised grunt when it bounced off his bare chest.

Later that night, as he lay sleeping next to me, my wide-awake brain hummed like an agitated hive, and I mulled over the events of the day, especially the contents of the envelope Giles gave to Susa.

A grave rubbing of a lily of the valley.

I'll use it if I have to. Tell Cappy.

Was it a real tombstone somewhere? Unfortunately there were lots of cemeteries in San Celina County. It could take weeks to go through all of them looking for a specific tombstone. Narrow it down, that's what I needed to do.

As I drifted closer to sleep, the black crayon rubbing drew itself in my mind, and the refrain *Find the tombstone* reverberated like an echo. Where was this tombstone? And whose was it? And the most pressing question of all: What about it would cause someone to kill Giles?

10

GABE AND I spent the next morning, Sunday, laying around reading the newspaper. No one called or came by, and for a little while I could forget everything that had happened in the last week—Sam's announcement, Lydia's presence, Giles's murder, Detective Hudson's uncomfortable attentions. About noon we met Emory downtown for brunch at a new Mexican restaurant that was getting rave reviews—El Cantina Gallo. Over seafood enchiladas the conversation turned to Elvia's work habits. As usual, she'd been too busy to join us.

"This is her day off, and she insists on going in for a few hours," Emory complained over his empty margarita glass.

"That's just her," I said, scooping up some guacamole with a fresh, hot tortilla chip. The reviews had been right. "If you're serious about her, you'd better get used to it."

"She's driving me nuts," Emory moaned, gesturing to the waitress for another margarita.

My cousin was one of those Southern men who knew

how to wring every ounce of pleasure out of his leisure time. Though deep inside I knew he and Elvia were right for each other, there were definitely some surface issues that needed work.

"Welcome to the real world, Emory," Gabe said, laughing. "It only gets worse."

I elbowed him. "Hey, Friday, we're trying to encourage, not discourage. Remember?"

While we continued to dispense sage and silly advice to Emory, Elvia's brother Miguel walked in. He spotted us and waved. Then he spoke briefly to the man at the take-out counter and came over to our table, adjusting the paraphernalia hooked to his heavy leather police belt.

"How's things going, Miguel?" Gabe asked.

"Fine, Chief. Sunday morning watch is a piece of cake. All the drunks are sleeping it off somewhere. Last night was crazy, though."

Gabe nodded. "I figured when that new bar next to the Chinese buffet started selling beer for seventy-five cents it would be trouble."

"Gum Alley is unwalkable today," Miguel said. "Hope the city gets someone down there to clean it up soon. Puke and piss, that's all those skippies know how to do."

"Skippies?" Emory said.

"College students," Gabe interpreted. "Specifically the drinkers."

"And to think they'll be running the treasury when we're collecting Social Security," Emory said. "Lord have mercy."

"Can we change the subject?" I asked, staring down at my enchilada, which was looking decidedly less appetizing.

"Sure," Miguel said. "Actually, I came over to give you a message, Benni."

"Me?" I said.

"Tell Dove no."

I gave him a confused look. "What?"

"Just what I said. Tell her no. Absolutely not. No way."

"What?"

"Just tell her."

The man at the take-out counter called out his name.

"Gotta go," he said. He nodded at Gabe and Emory. "Later, *amigos*."

"Take it easy," Gabe said.

"Don't work too hard," Emory called after him.

"Ignore that comment," Gabe added.

I cut another piece of my enchilada. "Wonder what his message to Dove means."

"Who knows what our dear Dove has brewing in her box of tricks," Emory said.

"Talk about your mixed metaphors," I said.

"Keep quiet, sweetcakes. I'm suffering this morning. I don't need my English scrutinized."

"Whiny-baby. So are you going to the barrel tasting and artist's reception this afternoon?"

"Have to. I'm covering it for the paper. You two going?"

"Yes," I said.

"No," Gabe said.

I turned to him, surprised. "I thought you were going."

He took a sip of his Corona beer. "Didn't I tell you last night that Sam, Bliss, Lydia, and I were going to visit Lydia's mother in Buellton?"

"No," I said slowly. "You didn't."

"I'm sure I did. Or I must have told you this morning."

"And I'm sure I would have remembered," I said, feeling a slowly rising heat in my chest. "I didn't even know Lydia's mother lived close by."

"Lydia moved her there when she took the job in Santa Barbara. Sam wanted us to come with him and Bliss when they tell her about their engagement and the baby. I'm sure I asked you if you wanted to go."

"No, you're mistaken," I said, really starting to get mad now. "You never mentioned it to me."

Gabe's face set in that stubborn, contrary look that said he was certain he was right and I was wrong.

Emory's amused green eyes darted from my face to Gabe's.

"Well, do you want to go?" Gabe asked, his voice carrying an edge of impatience.

I inhaled deeply, my anger feeling like too much air in a helium balloon. "No, thank you," I said, as sweetly as I could manage. "I promised JJ I'd go to the barrel tasting."

"Fine." He turned to Emory. "Can you give her a ride there and home? I'm late already."

"Certainly," my cousin said serenely. "I'll take good care of your wife, Cousin Gabe."

Gabe wiped his mouth quickly with his linen napkin and slid out of the booth. He leaned over and kissed me on the forehead. "I'll see you tonight, sweetheart."

"Sure," I said.

After he left, Emory studied me silently until I finally blurted out, "Oh, for crying out loud, Emory. What can I do, hog-tie him and sit on his chest?"

He shook his head slowly. "I'm tellin' you, sweetcakes, that woman is plain after your man. You'd best be circling the wagons and filling up the muskets."

"Now you're mixing your historical references."

"So what are you going to do, pray tell?"

"First I'm going to the ladies' room, then I'm going to let you take me to the barrel tasting. The rest, as my famous kinswoman once said, I'll think about tomorrow."

"New lingerie. Many a man has been lured back home with a satin bustier and lacy garter belt."

I tossed my crumpled napkin across the table at him. "Turn blue."

As I was leaving the ladies' room, heading toward the lobby, a voice called my name. A voice I'd heard just a little too often lately.

"Why, Mrs. Ortiz . . . oh, excuse me, *Harper*. What a fine surprise it is running into you on this bright and sunny Sunday afternoon." Detective Hudson, shooting me his stupid grin, threw his arm around a small, buxom brunette wearing a front-laced blouse similar in style to the bustier my cousin was entreating me to buy to save my marriage. She filled it out much more generously than I would have, and Detective Hudson's physical preference in women was painfully obvious. His date, not cracking a smile, scanned me up and down, then discarded what she saw with the flick of an artificial eyelash.

"Hello, Detective Hudson," I said.

"Hud," he said. "We're off the clock."

"And I have someone waiting." I moved past them only to find myself stopped short by his hand grabbing my upper arm.

"I'll need to see you in my office on Monday," he said. "There's some ideas I want to discuss with you about our case."

"Sorry, I work at my real job on Mondays," I said, jerking my arm back.

Emory's Cadillac Seville was waiting for me out front. In exchange for the ride, all the way to Eola Beach I was forced to listen to another lecture on keeping my husband from the clutches of his evil ex-wife.

"That's enough," I declared when we reached the parking lot of the San Patricio Resort and Country Club. "I've heard every argument in your pea-sized, testosterone-fueled brain and I'm still going to do what feels right to me, so why don't you just dry up."

He feigned a hurt expression. "I was only trying to help," he said as we walked across the wide lawn toward the three blue-and-white circus-style tents.

"I think you're trying to ignore your own problems in the love department by becoming obsessed with mine. If Gabe's behavior is bothering you that much, then you say something to him about it."

"I might do that very thing, oh, naive one. But you have to admit it made you mad that he's spending another family-oriented day with the ex–Mrs. Ortiz."

Ignoring him, I handed my ticket to the woman wearing an aqua and black T-shirt with the South Counties Vintners' Association logo—two wineglasses clicking in front of an oak tree—and received my wineglass and tasting guide. Emory flashed his press pass and shook his head when offered a glass.

"I'll use hers," he said.

We entered the first tent where the wineries, twenty-seven according to our literature, had their booths set up. It was similar to the event last night except the booths carried all types of wines—merlots, ports, pinot noirs, chardonnays, syrahs, cabernet sauvignon, and some I'd never heard of—nebbiolo, sigiovese, moscato allegro, gamay beaujolais. The names sounded as romantic as a gondola ride in Venice. The only thing different about these wines was that they were poured from bottles that were hand-labeled since the vintages wouldn't actually be on sale for a year or two. The vintners were hoping wine lovers would take a chance on a young wine and order cases on speculation.

"I wonder if they have anything else to drink," I said, handing him my wineglass. Sure enough, in the middle of the tent were huge aluminum washtubs filled with ice and bottles of fruit juices, Snapple, and sparkling water. I headed toward the drinks, Emory dogging my steps.

"Admit it," he said. "You *were* angry when he told you he was spending another day with Lydia."

I faced my cousin. "Okay, I'm angry. Are you happy now? But what can I do?" He opened his mouth, and I quickly held up my hand. "Wait, let me rephrase that, because you have way too many suggestions. I'm trying desperately to keep this situation from turning into one that will cause a serious problem between me and Gabe. Yes, I agree he's spending a lot of time with her. Maybe too much. But this thing with Sam and Bliss is complicated, and Sam *is* their son. I can't change that. I just have to trust in his love for me, Emory. Please, don't make this harder for me than it already is."

His handsome face softened with a look of genuine contrition. He pulled me to him in a warm, brotherly hug. "You're right. I'm just makin' things harder for both y'all. I'll keep my big mouth shut from now on. But if you need anything, you let me know. Promise, now?"

I kissed his cheek. "Emory Delano Littleton, you know you'd be the first person I'd run to."

"Good. Now I'd better get to work if I'm goin' to have an article to turn in tomorrow. Let's meet back here in two hours."

"Sounds good. I'm going over to the artists' tent and see exactly how a wine label is created."

I grabbed a bottle of sparkling water, twisted off the cap, and walked over to the second tent. Inside were a dozen different platforms where artists, using a variety of media, worked on paintings and drawings destined to be incorporated into wine labels. Some of the artists talked to their audience as they worked, explaining how they came up with the idea for each particular wine label.

I wandered through the exhibit of original art displayed with the finished wine labels framed next to them. Seven Sisters labels were simple but elegant, with some of the last year's vintage's labels showing more variety with bold, brightly colored renderings of the rose garden, the adobe tasting room, and rows of thick, lush grapevines. Though I'd only seen her work on quilts, JJ's slightly eccentric, free-form style was apparent on these labels.

In a corner of the tent, JJ was working on a watercolor painting of a horse I instantly recognized as Churn Dash. I mingled with the crowd, watching her add subtle reddish shading to his brown coat. He was shown at a gallop, and in the background she'd painted in faint peaches and browns the pattern of a Churn Dash quilt. A photograph of the quilt made by her great-grandmother was taped to her stained easel. In her painting she'd captured the championship bearing of Churn Dash with the arch of his elegant neck straining toward an imaginary finish line and the subtle, powerful surge of muscles in his strong, solid hindquarters. She glanced up when someone asked her a question, caught my eye, and nodded at me. I waved and melted back into the crowd. I wanted to talk to her again about the grave rubbing, but this wouldn't be the best time or place to do so.

In the last tent the silent auction items were displayed, and the line for the gourmet buffet donated by local restaurants was at least a half-hour wait. The food didn't interest me since I'd just eaten, so I headed for the auction items. There were dozens of things to be auctioned—cases of wines, bed and breakfast packages, limousine wine tours, and wine dinners for six hosted by celebrity chefs. Seven Sisters had sponsored a contest and silent auction for wine bottles decorated by local artists. The entries were spectacular with each artist vying for the most creatively original bottle. The auction bids were way out of my price range, but the money went for a good cause—the Rose Jewel Brown Children's Wing at General Hospital. The artist won a free case of Seven Sisters' most exclusive handcrafted noble wines, wines that were like a stakes horse, the best of the best. An announcement from the stage informed everyone of the wine bottle design winner. On the stage behind the row of twenty or so decorated bottles sat Cappy Brown, her sister Etta, and dressed in white and sitting in a wheelchair, their mother, Rose Brown. Her face was lightly spotted with age, but her silver hair and soft makeup were perfect. She looked twenty years younger than her ninety-six. The advantages of wealth and good genetics, I supposed. She smiled at the audience with long, pale ivory teeth, giving a palm-out royal wave.

After a long speech of gushing gratitude by the president of the vintner's association to the Brown family for helping to sponsor the event and a retrospective of all the accomplishments and charities instituted by the Brown family and most of all, Rose Brown, Cappy addressed the audience.

"On behalf of my mother and the rest of my family, I thank you for your kind words. Her health being quite fragile, she is unable to speak, but she wanted me to relay to all of you how privileged she's felt to be a part of this county for so many years, how grateful she is for your generosity, and to encourage you to dig deep in your pockets today and support the Rose Jewel Brown Children's Wing. As Mother has always said, without the children we have no future. Thank you."

After the applause, the winner of the bottle contest was brought up to receive his plaque. An artist who'd painted a 16th-century–style Madonna and child scene in exquisite detail won over bottles painted like rocket ships, Marilyn Monroe, Chumash Indian petroglyphs, peacocks, and the Mission Santa Celine. Starting to get bored, I decided to go back to the wine-tasting tent to see if I could find Emory and convince him to leave early. The lines were five and six deep at each booth as people twirled their glasses, sipped, and pursed their lips, searching for that perfect wine. I looked over the crowd and didn't see my cousin's blond head anywhere. To kill time more than anything else, I sidled close to people and eavesdropped on their comments about wine, which amused me to no end with their pretentiousness. I wished I had a tape recorder so I could replay some of them for Gabe later tonight.

"Stylistically," said a man wearing a baby blue golf shirt and white tennis shorts as he twirled a glass of straw-colored wine, "this would appeal more to the American palate than to the European, don't you think?"

The woman with him, wearing flat gold sandals and a bright pink spaghetti-strap dress nodded and added, "Its aroma is full and pretty, but not quite as multidimensional as I normally prefer."

He took another sip and said, "Yes, it has a ripe flavor. A bit earthy and tart, which is refreshing, but the finish is a little rough."

"There are so many wines like that," she agreed. "More up front than on the finish."

"Many men, too," a deep, familiar voice whispered in my ear. A gentle, bearlike hand slipped under my hair and gripped the back of my neck.

I squealed and swung around.

"Isaac!" I said, giving him a fierce hug. His massive arms lifted me up and swung me around.

"Isn't that Isaac Lyons, the photographer?" the lady in the pink dress exclaimed to her companion. They gazed up at his six-feet-four-inch frame topped with hair as white as a snow owl's, their mouths slack with awe. A diamond earring in his ear caught an overhead light and twinkled. As did his dark raisin eyes when he winked at me.

Isaac set me down and smiled at the woman, his arm still around my shoulders. "Isaac Lyons?" he boomed. "Why, I heard he's bought the farm, that randy old goat. Rumor has it he was caught with another man's wife and took three shots to the belly, but he went down kicking. Hemingway would have been proud." His face grew serious. "Then again, that could have been Gregory Peck. They're often mistaken for each other." Before the woman could speak, he grabbed my hand and pulled me through the murmuring crowd.

"What are you doing here?" I asked as he led me out of the tent.

He pointed to a picnic bench out near the lagoon that flowed into Eola Bay. "Let's talk away from the madding crowd."

We sat down underneath the cool shade of an ash tree. He leaned back on his elbows and I straddled the bench, just looking at him, unable to believe he was really here. Isaac had come into my life and, more important, into Dove's last November, a little less than a year ago when we'd all become involved in a murder that took place on the ranch. Having no family of his own, he'd adopted ours, and we'd welcomed him with open hearts and arms. Well, I eventually did after a rather rough beginning. As famous as Ansel Adams, Isaac Lyons had traveled all over the world, been married five times, taken photographs of kings, popes, cowboys, ranch women, carnival workers, cotton farmers, bar maids and truck drivers. Not to mention five different presidents of the United States. But he was still as down-to-earth as homemade gravy and he was besotted with Dove, which revealed his excellent taste. After our rocky start, I gave this mountain-sized man my whole heart and treated him like the grandfather I'd never had. Dove and I completely agreed on how special he was and also agreed that it was a good thing he was forty years older than me, or we'd be cat fighting over his affections. He and I had kept up a regular correspondence via E-mail.

He was dressed casually, as always, in faded Levi's, a khaki cowboy shirt with embroidered red arrows on the yokes, and beaded leather moccasins. His long white hair was braided in a thick rope, the end tied with a piece of rawhide. It just touched the top of his hand-tooled belt.

"Do I pass inspection?" he asked, chuckling.

"Your hair's longer than mine," I said, flicking his braid. "My braid just barely clears my shoulders."

"So your grandma has pointed out. I told her I'm trying to catch up with her."

"Does she know you're here?"

His broad, wind-weathered face wrinkled in amusement.

"Forget I asked that. Of course she does. Why didn't she tell me?"

"I flew in last night. She wanted it to be a surprise. She was supposed to come with me today, but she's busy getting set up for tomorrow at the ranch."

"What's going on at the ranch?"

He shook his head, his little raisin eyes laughing at me. "Sorry, top secret. She doesn't want to have her idea stolen by another fund-raising group."

"This has to do with the senior citizen kitchen?" Then I remembered what she'd said yesterday about her prayers being answered by something I'd suggested.

"Apparently."

"Are you involved?" I poked his chest. "C'mon, Isaac, you can tell me. I won't tell anyone."

"Ha," he said, grabbing my finger and shaking it. "Not a chance, young Harper woman. I'm not procuring the wrath of Dove Ramsey down upon my grizzled old head. You'll find out soon enough."

"Okay," I said, giving in quickly only because I was so excited to see him again. "So, tell me what you're working on now. I'm sorry I haven't answered your E-mail in the last week. It's been insane around here, and I would have needed five single-spaced pages to tell you everything."

He stretched his long legs out and rubbed his knees. "Dove clued me in. I can't believe you're involved in another homicide investigation. Is Gabe ready to lock you in your room?"

I grimaced and picked at some loose paint on the wooden bench. "I'm not involved because I want to be, believe me. She told you everything, right? About Sam and Bliss and . . ."

"And Lydia," he finished.

I made my cauliflower face at him. "Ex-wives. Guess you know about them."

"Do I. Dove says she's quite a looker."

"She is gorgeous, I'll grant you that. And, I'd only admit this to you, actually she's a pretty nice woman from what I can tell."

"And after your husband?"

I made claws at him. "Not you, too. I don't know if she is. Dove and Emory sure are convinced that's the case. Gabe is spending a lot of time with her and Sam, but what with Bliss and the baby . . ." I shrugged.

"Sounds like you're the only one being rational about it."

I looked up into his penetrating, photographer's eyes. "What do you think? Am I being stupid and naive? I've never believed you can force a man . . . or anyone to love you. My cousin thinks I should invest in a closetful of Victoria's Secret underwear. Dove thinks I should stick to his side like glue. My best friend thinks I should spike Lydia's coffee with arsenic."

His thick white eyebrows moved upward.

"She's joking," I said, laughing. "I think. Anyway, I've basically done nothing except sit on the sidelines and watch. You're a man of worldly experience. What do you think I should do?"

He took my hands in his. "Benni, all I know is it takes years for a couple to become a 'we.' Ultimately, some relationships make it, some don't. Who knows why?" He rubbed his big thumbs over the tops of my hands.

"In other words, it's what I suspected. There's nothing I can do."

"He has free will. But then, so do you." He squeezed my hands. "Now let's talk about your murder case. Who do you think did it? Do you need another investigator?"

I slapped the top of his hands gently. "Did Dove ask you to look after me?"

He laughed and shook his head no. "She's so busy with this project, she's barely had time to spoon with me on the porch last night."

"Spoon? Excuse me, you need to clarify to a concerned granddaughter just exactly what that term entails. In detail, please."

"Not on your life. Anyway, I've photographed this Capitola Brown twice, back in the fifties when she was working the rodeo circuit doing trick riding and later in the eighties when I was doing a book on horse racing. Dove says it's pretty certain someone in the family did it. Any ideas who?"

I told him everything I knew so far. "It could be any of them, though that note points strongly at Cappy. To be honest, she's the only one I can picture having the nerve to pull it off. Dove told you the whole thing about the switched guns, right?"

"Yes, so the only lead you have is the grave rubbing. Can I see it?"

"Sure." I pulled it out of my purse and handed it to him.

He took a pair of tortoise-shell glasses from his shirt pocket and studied the rubbing. He handed it back to me. "I'm assuming you're going to look for it."

"How can I? There's too many cemeteries in San Celina County. There are probably some I don't even know about. That would take weeks and even then might be a dead end."

"So you're going to give up? That doesn't sound like you. The Benni Harper I know would be lying in bed at night trying to figure out the puzzle."

"Are you saying I shouldn't? Thank you, but I've already got one man encouraging me to go against my husband's request to stay out of situations like this."

"Who's that? And for the record, I'm not encouraging you, I'm only making an observation concerning your personality."

"You know, you can be real annoying sometimes."

"But I'm right, aren't I?"

"Sometimes I think my cousin Emory was right, and I should have been a detective. I don't want to get involved, but something in me won't rest until Giles's murderer is caught. And it's not because of some great humanitarian motivation, either. From what I understand, he was a real jerk."

"Even jerks don't deserve to be murdered. I think you've got a strong streak of justice running through you, and that's what compels you to get involved."

"You make me sound a lot more noble than I feel. How

about you running that speech by Gabe the next time he gets upset at me?"

His hearty laugh made me smile. "Not on your life. He has the power to lock me up, not to mention sic the parking ticket patrol on me. So, who's this other man you say is encouraging you to get involved?"

"A sheriff's detective assigned to the Brown murder. For some reason, he's gotten it into his fuzzy little Texas head that I'll be able to ferret out information from this family that he can't."

Isaac peered out from under his thick, white eyebrows, his mouth turned up into a wide grin.

"Oh, shut up," I said, good-naturedly. "Yes, he's heard about my other experiences. That doesn't mean I'm going to jeopardize my relationship with my husband or my stepson to solve his case."

"So, this detective. Does he wear starched Wranglers, a white cowboy hat, and fancy cowboy boots?"

My eyes widened. "How did you . . . ?"

He pointed behind me. I turned and saw Detective Hudson strolling across the grass toward us.

"Oh, for crying out loud," I said.

"Looks determined," he said.

When Detective Hudson reached us, Isaac stood up. I swung my legs around so I wasn't straddling the bench and leaned back on my elbows.

"What do you want?" I said.

"Isaac Lyons," Isaac said, holding out his big hand.

The detective took his hand. "*The* Isaac Lyons? The photographer?"

Isaac gave his deep laugh. "Depends on who's asking. I think I may have a speeding ticket in Wyoming I haven't paid."

"Ford Hudson. My friends call me Hud. I'm a detective

with the San Celina Sheriff's Department, and as far as I'm concerned, your need for speed is Wyoming's problem, not mine. I bought your book on state fairs. Great photos of the carnies. My mother was a photographer with *Life*. She owns a studio now in Odessa. Mostly weddings and babies, bread-and-butter photography."

"Liar," I blurted out.

Isaac gave me a puzzled, then reprimanding look. "Forgive my young friend's rudeness."

I shot Isaac a hard look. Sometimes he could be just a little *too* paternal.

Detective Hudson grinned. "That's okay, I'm gettin' used to it. She's like one of those snarly little terriers. Kinda grows on you after a while."

Isaac gave a small chuckle. "Yes, she does." Then he turned to me. "Dove instructed me to ask you to dinner tonight. She's making pot roast."

"I'll be there."

He kissed me on top of the head and whispered in my ear, "Play nice, Ms. Benni Harper."

Giving him my sweetest smile, I replied, "Suck eggs, Mr. Isaac Lyons."

He gave a great booming laugh and ruffled my hair. "Oh, Lordy, I've missed you."

"Shoot," Detective Hudson said as we watched Isaac stride across the grass. "Didn't know you ran in such fancy circles. Is he a relative or something?"

"What do you want?"

"For you to come to my office at ten o'clock tomorrow."

"Why?"

"Like I said so politely this morning, I have some ideas I need to discuss with you about our case."

"It's . . . not . . . our . . . case," I said. "Shall I say it slower? Write it in lipstick on your forehead? Send a telegram?"

"Do people still send telegrams in this computer age? What with E-mail and all. I've wondered about that."

Not answering, I stood up and brushed past him.

"Tomorrow," he called after me. "Ten o'clock. I'm the third office on the right. Just tell the receptionist I'm expecting you."

Back in the tent, the crowds were still thick and noisy. I waited for Emory at our assigned place, but as usual he was late. He meandered by ten minutes later.

"I have one more person to interview," he said. "Give me another half hour."

"Oh, Emory," I moaned, wishing I'd driven myself so I could leave. Knowing my cousin, it would be more like another hour.

"Go amuse yourself, sweetcakes. Don't be a whiny-baby."

I went back into the artists' tent, hoping to find a chair. Next to some potted trees, near the stage where Cappy had spoken, there were a couple of white folding chairs. I grabbed one and sat down, heaving a big sigh.

"Too much wine?" an older woman's voice inquired.

I turned and looked behind the potted trees and saw Rose Brown sitting alone in her wheelchair.

"Uh, not really," I said, standing up and going over to her. "I don't really like wine."

"Then what are you doing here?"

"I came with my cousin. He's a journalist and he's writing an article for the *Tribune.* "

Her eyes opened and closed slowly, like some kind of ancient, slow-moving animal. "I was beautiful once," she said.

"Yes, ma'am," I answered.

"He was a judge and a horseman. His horses were in demand all over the country. He required perfection in his horses, his law, and his women."

I nodded, thinking, *He sounds like a real prize.*

"Women adored him. Many nights he didn't come home at all."

Suddenly uncomfortable with the awkward personal turn to our conversation, I looked around, trying to find a polite way of escape. "I'm sorry," I said.

"Do you have a husband?" she asked.

I nodded.

"You'd better fix yourself up. He'll leave you for someone prettier."

In deference to her age and, I was assuming, her slight senility, I held back the temptation to tell her to mind her own dang business. "Excuse me, I need to meet my cousin . . ."

The next moment, Cappy walked around the corner and saw me walking away from her mother.

She hurried up to me. "What are you doing?" she snapped.

"Nothing," I stammered. "Your mother . . ."

A panicked look passed over Cappy's face. A few feet away, her mother sat smiling serenely in her wheelchair, her cloudy eyes focused on something behind me. "She's very elderly," Cappy said.

I looked back down at her mother who still wore that spooky, disengaged smile. Was she senile? She certainly didn't sound as if she was when she was insulting my looks. Maybe she was just mean.

"I have to find my cousin," I said, turning and walking quickly out of the tent.

Cappy caught up with me outside. "Benni, wait."

I turned and faced her, shielding my eyes from the bright afternoon sun. "Yes?"

"Sometimes she gets confused. Very confused." Her gray eyes bore into my squinting ones.

"I understand," I said.

She stared at me for a long, searching moment. Both her hands were curled in tight fists. "Do you?"

"I've worked with elderly people, Cappy."

Her lips tightened. "You always did learn quickly, Benni Harper. You knew how to focus. I liked that about you."

"Thank you," I said. She was definitely her mother's daughter. The sudden conversation switch confused me.

"But your one fatal flaw was never knowing when something was too much for you. You always wanted to ride the horses that were too big or too wild or try some trick beyond your capabilities. Sometimes recognizing your own limitations is the smartest thing a person can do."

"I . . ."

Before I could say anymore, she added, "Be smart this time. Ignore whatever my mother said. Don't get in over your head."

I watched her walk back toward the artists' tent, frustrated that she didn't let me speak, didn't let me tell her that all her mother did was insult my looks and, ironically, give me advice on how to keep my husband.

But without realizing it, Cappy had pointed me in another direction. It was obvious by Cappy's overreaction that Rose Brown knew something about the blackmail or Giles's death. The thousand-dollar question was What exactly did Cappy think her mother had told me? And how would I find out what Rose Brown knew?

11

I FOUND EMORY deep in conversation with a new wine maker who was waxing poetic about the quality of grapes this harvest season and the possibilities for San Celina County's growth as a major wine-producing region. I tugged on my cousin's sleeve and demanded his car keys. "I'll wait for you there."

"Fifteen more minutes," Emory said. "I swear."

Inside Emory's luxurious Cadillac Seville, I reclined the cushy leather seat, rolled down the electric windows for a cross breeze, and turned on the CD player, letting the butter-smooth sounds of George Strait soothe my irritated soul. I settled back, closed my eyes, and tried to forget the Brown family, wine, racehorses, my looks, my husband, and his beautiful ex-wife.

I was floating in a soft drowsy state, down a long, slow Southern river, just me and George, when a man's voice growled near my ear, "Dangerous practice . . ." I simultaneously jumped, screamed, and swung my hand out in defense, my heart racing like one of Cappy's horses.

"Dang it all!" Detective Hudson exclaimed, backing up and grabbing his mouth.

"You idiot! You scared the crap out of me!" I screamed. "Don't ever, ever, ever sneak up on me like that! Ever!"

"I was just trying to tell you it's dangerous to nap in an open car where anyone can accost you. Oh, dang, I'm bleeding," he moaned, still holding his mouth.

I climbed out of the car and went over to him. "For Pete's sake, quit your bellyaching. You're lucky it wasn't pepper spray in my hand."

He felt his rapidly swelling lip gingerly, then stared at the blood staining his fingertips. "Criminy, what do you do, sharpen your claws on a whetstone?"

"I don't even have nails." I held up my hands in illustration. Clutched in my right one was the plastic case from George's CD. The sharp plastic edge was obviously what I'd struck him with.

"Assaulted by a CD cover," he said, moaning again. "How will I explain that one at the office?"

"You wouldn't have to if you'd *stop following me*," I said, reaching back into the car and handing him a tissue. "Here, clean up your mouth and shut up."

He brushed away the tissue, pulled a pure white monogrammed handkerchief from inside his jacket, and brought it to his swollen lip.

I stared at it. "A handkerchief? I didn't know men still used those."

He gave a sick smile. "I don't blow my nose with it. I use it to pick up women."

"What?"

"You'd be surprised how many heartbroken women there are in bars. I give them the handkerchief to dry their tears, listen to their sad story, offer a little sympathy, a strong Texas shoulder to lean on, a drink or two, then slip them my card. I always get my handkerchief back clean and ironed and a very grateful first date."

"That pathetic line actually works?"

"Never fails."

"It's despicable."

Unperturbed by my opinion, he dabbed at his mouth again, flinching at the pain.

"What a lightweight. I'd sure hate to have you for a partner."

"The only blood that bothers me is my own," he protested.

I gave him a withering look.

"You know, you are the least maternal woman I've ever met," he said.

His remark hit me straight in the heart, and thanks to my expressive face, he immediately noticed.

"Oh, shoot, I'm sorry, Benni," he said softly. "I didn't mean that how it sounded."

"Forget it," I said curtly.

Emory walked up at that moment and asked, "What's going on?"

"Are you finished with your interviews?" I asked.

"Yes, but—"

"Then let's go."

Emory looked at me, then Detective Hudson, then back at me. "Are you all right? What did he do to you?"

"I said, let's go, Emory." I climbed into the car, buckled my seat belt, and stared straight ahead. We were out of the parking lot and well on the highway back to San Celina before Emory spoke.

"Need to talk about it?" he asked.

I put a hand up to my eyes. "Not right now, Emory. But thanks for asking."

He gave me a worried look, then turned the conversation

to Isaac with whom he'd chatted briefly at the tasting. "He and Dove are cooking something up. He says he'll tell me about it when they need publicity. Couldn't get him to spill a word."

"Me neither. I'm going out there for dinner tonight, though, so I'll give it another try. Why don't you come, too?"

"Can't. I have to get these stories written and dispatched to my editor for final approval. Then I'm going to see if I can pry my ladylove away from her office long enough for a romantic dinner down at the beach." His voice wasn't as chipper and optimistic as usual.

You'd better watch it, I silently told Elvia, *or this one's going to slip right through your fingers, and I know you'll live to regret it.*

We pulled up in front of my house, and it was immediately apparent that Gabe's Corvette wasn't parked in its customary spot in the driveway.

My cousin gave me a sympathetic look. "He'll be home soon, sweetcakes."

I patted his hand, still curled around the steering wheel. "We both got us some kind of troubles, don't we, Cousin?"

"Amen, sister Albenia," he said, leaning over and kissing my cheek. "I'll call you tomorrow and find out the scoop on Dove and Isaac."

Inside the house the answering machine blinked a single message. I hit play, anticipating Gabe's baritone voice. Instead, it was Detective Hudson's.

"Hud, here. Mrs. Harper, in the confused melee of being injured, I failed to inform you that I observed you conversing with the senior Mrs. Brown and I expect you in my office with a full report tomorrow morning."

"Fat chance, Detective," I muttered, pulling on my barn jacket. I left a note for Gabe telling him I'd be at the ranch and to come out if he got home early enough.

I stayed at the ranch until nine o'clock, catching up with Isaac and trying to pry something out of Dove about her fund-raising project.

"In good time, honeybun," she said, "in good time. Now you and Isaac go out on the porch and catch up while I make some phone calls." She stood on tiptoe and planted a kiss on Isaac's lips. "Come get me before you go to bed, sweetie, and I'll heat you up some warm almond milk."

"Yes, ma'am," he said, gazing down at her with pure adoration. She smiled back at him, her own soft peach face matching his glow. Not for the first time I wondered why in the world I ever worried about this sweet, sweet man hurting my gramma.

Out on the porch, we sat on the swing, rocking in companionable silence, watching the evening shadows turn the oaks to black matchsticks against a cobalt blue sky. I tried not to peek at my watch every five minutes and wonder where Gabe was and what he was doing.

"Get things straightened out with that detective?" Isaac asked.

I brought my knees up and rested my chin on them. "I know I sounded like a brat this afternoon, but that business about his mother being a photographer is a flat-out lie."

"And how do you know that?"

"In the few days I've known him, he's claimed his mother lived in four different towns and had as many different occupations. It's either some kind of stupid game he's playing, or he's a pathological liar. I'm leaning toward the latter."

Isaac stretched his arm across the back of the swing. "He seemed nice enough."

"Well, you talked to him for exactly two minutes, so I

wouldn't be trusting him with your life savings if I were you."

With his thumb and forefinger, he thumped the back of my head gently. "Your mouth is getting a tad too sharp for my taste, kiddo."

I sighed and leaned my head against his thick, warm shoulder. In the dark September evening, the crickets echoed the *squeak, squeak* of the porch swing being pushed by Isaac's foot. "I'm sorry. I'm just in a funk tonight."

"I noticed. You've been checking your watch about every ten minutes. Doesn't Gabe have a cell phone? Why don't you just call him and see when he's going to be home?"

"He leaves it in the Corvette, and they probably took Lydia's car to her mother's since Sam and Bliss were going, too." Inside the house, I could hear Dove's cajoling voice on the phone. Whoever she was speaking to wouldn't stand a chance. "Besides, I don't want to seem . . ." I thought for a moment, searching for the right word. "I don't know, possessive. Or paranoid. It's not like this has been going on for months. It's only been a week and a stressful one at that. If our marriage can't withstand a week of weird behavior, then we haven't got much of a marriage."

He patted my shoulder. "He's acting like a self-indulgent adolescent. I think you're showing remarkable patience."

"You don't think I'm being too passive? With what everyone else has been saying, I can't help wondering if I'm being a wimp."

"Wimp is a word I'd never use to describe you, my dear," he said, laughing. "And there's a world of difference between patience and passivity."

"The thing is, even though it irritates me, I think I understand what he's feeling. He's more insecure than people realize. One of the few things he told me about his and Lydia's breakup was her contempt for what he did for a living. He was working undercover, and I guess that's pretty hard on a family—his hours were erratic, he was moody and angry all the time, had trouble reconnecting with the real world when he wasn't working. I don't blame her for pushing him to get out of it. I'm not sure I could have lived with him either. But she said some pretty ugly things about his capabilities of make a living, of supporting his family, about his masculinity. She really hurt his ego, and he's never forgotten it."

"He told you all this?"

"Some of it. Some I pieced together myself."

"So you think he's out to prove she was wrong and in the process rub her nose in it a little."

"Something like that. At least, that's what it seems like to me."

"But you and he haven't actually talked about it."

I stretched out my legs, tingling from being in one position too long, and studied the tips of my boots. "No, with all that's gone on with Sam and Bliss and the murder, we haven't had much time to talk about anything else."

"You'll have to deal with it eventually."

"I know. And we will. I'm just trying to let it happen in its own time. That's one of the biggest lessons I've learned in the last few years. You can't make things happen before they're supposed to or make people do things they don't want to do. Besides, I can't help remembering how understanding and open-minded he was about me staying in my inherited house in Morro Bay last May. He was really there for me when I was acting a little nutso; it only seems fair that I should grant him the same grace." I gave him a half smile. "Providing it doesn't last longer than a week, that is. Then I may just have to get out my trusty bullwhip."

He chuckled. "For her or him?"

"Depends on how I'm feeling that day."

"Well, you're thirty years up on me on that grace thing," he said. "I didn't comprehend that little fact until I was well past qualifying for Medicare."

"I find that hard to believe."

"Believe it. Wisdom has nothing to do with time served on this earth. In my observance, it's learning to let go and let a higher power have the control you foolishly thought was under your puny command. Mr. Gabriel Ortiz is a luckier man than he realizes. Hopefully he'll understand that someday."

"Well, if he doesn't, there is always the bullwhip."

He laughed. "Lordy, I'd never want you mad at me."

I tucked my arm through his. "You are one special gentleman, Mr. Isaac Lyons, and I *was* very wise about one thing. Letting you into my life."

"And next to your gramma, Benni Harper, you are the light of my life."

I hugged his arm to me. "Ha, gratuitous flattery will get you everywhere with a Ramsey woman."

"So I've discovered."

"I'm not touching that comment with a ten-foot cattle prod."

WHEN I ARRIVED home, my lightened mood turned black again when Gabe's car was still gone. That bullwhip was looking better and better. I was in bed cruising the television stations when he came in at ten forty-five. I heard him call out to me, then listen to the message on the answering machine before turning out the living room lights and coming into the bedroom.

"What's that sheriff's detective talking about?" he asked, walking into the bathroom while unbuttoning his shirt. "You are cooperating with him, aren't you?" When I didn't answer, his head popped out of the bathroom door. "Benni, I asked you a question."

"Hello, Gabe. Yes, my day was great. How was yours? Of course I missed you as much as you missed me. I agree, it was such a long day without you. Of course I'll tell you everything, but, please, you go first."

He walked back into the bedroom slowly, his head tilted in wariness. "*Querida*, are you all right? Did something happen today to upset you?" The sight of the dark circles under his tired eyes softened my irritation.

I sighed, climbed out of bed, and went to him, pulling his shirt out of his jeans and running my hands up his warm back. Sarcasm wasn't going to solve this. "No, Friday, I'm just . . . It's nothing. I'm fine. You were later than I expected and I got worried."

"We ended up spending the whole day with Lydia's mother, and then she wanted to take us out to dinner. After we dropped Sam and Bliss off at JJ's house, Lydia and I started talking about Sam, and then one thing led to another. I'm sorry. I should have called."

I pinched his lower back. "Yes, you should have."

He jerked. "Ow! Okay, okay. It won't happen again, I promise."

I laid my cheek on his bare chest, his musky scent so familiar and yet still so mysterious to me.

His hand stroked my hair, and I rubbed my face against his coarse chest hair. "About that message from the detective . . ." he said.

"I'm cooperating with Detective Hudson as much as I can."

He grasped my shoulders and held me away from him, staring down into my face. "What's that mean?"

"Well, I . . ." I didn't know how to explain that the detective was asking me to do exactly what Gabe was asking me not to do.

"Benni, it's one thing when you defy me and get involved in investigations, but please don't embarrass me in front of another agency. I want you to do whatever Detective Hudson requests of you."

"But . . ."

"No buts. I'm too busy right now with Bliss and Sam to be worrying about you. Please, for once, curb your urge to snoop. If you have some information the detective needs, give it to him and then stay out of his way."

"It's not what you think, Gabe. Detective Hudson—"

"Has a job to do and doesn't need you getting in the way. No more discussion. You'll do as he asks, *comprende*?"

"Understood," I said, my voice cool. I pushed away from him and climbed back in bed.

He joined me a few minutes later. "Sweetheart, let's not argue. I know I sound like a drill sergeant sometimes . . ."

"That's putting it mildly."

"I'm really sorry. I'm just so preoccupied with this situation with Sam and this nutty family he's marrying into. I don't want to worry about you being hurt because you've gotten in over your head."

An ominous prickling rippled through me. The last part of his sentence almost word for word mirrored Cappy's statement.

"I know," I said, reaching under the covers, taking his hand and lacing my fingers through his. "I'll stay out of this as much as possible. I promise."

"Good," he said, bringing my hand to his lips and kissing it. "Lydia sends her regards. Said she was sorry you didn't come."

I'll bet, I thought, and the possibility ran through my

mind that I was indeed being naive, that my husband was being stolen right from under my passive little nose.

Then I went to sleep and dreamed fitfully all night of gravestone rubbings and clouds and wine bottles that sprouted legs and became racehorses, and beautiful Mexican women wearing cowboy boots in all the colors of the rainbow.

"IT'S A FULL moon tonight," Gabe said, glancing at the kitchen calendar the next morning. "All the loonies will be out."

"Isn't that an old wives' tale?" I asked. "I saw on one of those magazine shows some statistics that said that there wasn't any more crime on full moon nights than any other."

He stood next to the toaster in his jogging shorts, waiting for a bagel to pop up, his strong thighs still tight and twitching from their morning run. I watched him over my coffee through bleary eyes, feeling like, with all my crazy dreams, I'd only slept two hours instead of eight.

"Let that television reporter take the next seven p.m. to three a.m. shift during a full moon and see if he changes his tune." He grabbed his toasted bagel, juggling it from one hand to the other before dropping it on the plate across from me. As he spread grape jelly over it, he glanced at the morning headlines, then peered at me over wire-rimmed glasses. "Are you going to talk to Detective Hudson today?"

"I guess."

"You guess?"

"Okay, yes, I'll talk to him. I don't really have anything to tell him, though. The conversation with Rose Brown that he's putting so much stock in was nothing that would help him find out who killed Giles Norton."

"What was it about?"

"She rambled about her dead husband, how much he loved beautiful women and good horses."

"That's it?"

My big gulp of coffee burnt my throat. He waited while I waved my hand in front of my mouth. "She also told me I should fix myself up or you'd leave me for someone prettier."

He laughed out loud and took a bite of his bagel. "Lucky thing for her she's elderly and Dove taught you to respect your elders. I take it you didn't smack her."

"No, but I sure wanted to."

"You look fine just the way you are," he murmured, his attention distracted by the newspaper.

And is fine good enough? I wanted to ask, but didn't. I contemplated whether I should tell him about Cappy's reaction to my conversation with her mother. Since we had enough other things creating barriers between us these last few days, I decided to be as open and honest as possible.

"Cappy reacted real strange when she saw me talking to her mother."

His head came up. "How so?"

"She seemed to have the impression that her mother told me something she shouldn't have, that I should ignore what her mother said and to basically mind my own business."

He looked at me over his glasses again, his nonverbal agreement with her obvious.

"I'm no more involved than you," I said petulantly. "She didn't even give me time to say that her mother didn't reveal a thing, only insulted my looks."

He thought about it for a moment. "That bothers me. If Cappy is involved in Giles's murder and she thinks you know something . . ."

"It didn't feel like she was threatening me, Gabe. Besides, I don't think she'd hurt me. Don't forget, I've known her since I was a girl."

"That doesn't make any difference," he said, looking worried for the first time. "If she felt her family was threatened, if she or someone in her family committed that murder and it appears they did, how long she has known you won't matter one bit."

"I can't change what's already happened, but I can stay out of their way. Which I will. If JJ asks me to get involved anymore, I'll just say no."

"Good. And don't forget to tell all this to Detective Hudson." He shuffled through the paper and found the sports page. "You know, Benni, I am very happy you're keeping me informed on this."

I opened my mouth to tell him exactly what the situation was with the sheriff's detective, then stopped. I'd never been in such an awkward position. I knew there had always been a slight animosity between the sheriff's department and the city police, though the sheriff and Gabe seemed to like each other personally. Like rival cattlemen and sheepmen, they looked at their professions in different ways and were certain their way was the right one. This situation with Detective Hudson could cause a bigger rift between the two agencies. Maybe I could figure a way to get the detective off my back without running to Gabe.

IT WAS QUIET down at the folk art museum. Monday was our only officially closed day, and D-Daddy used it to do any major work inside the museum itself. Today he was patching up some places in the adobe and replacing a window that broke yesterday.

"Have fun on Saturday, *ange*?" he asked, stopping to

rub Scout's belly. "That boy, Hud, he's real Cajun. He does the dancing, him."

"Only half Cajun, D-Daddy. The other half is pure bullshit."

He threw back his head and gave a rich cackle. "That make him full Cajun, then."

I smiled and said, "Thanks for the dances, but next time don't let another man cut in, okay?"

He went back to slapping on the mixture he'd concocted to match the dusky white adobe walls. "I think he likes you, *ange*. Cajun men, we like the *jolie blondes*. Your police chief, he better be closer watching the chicken coop."

"It's not that he likes me. I just have something he wants."

D-Daddy nodded his head solemnly, his eyes twinkling. "Yes, ma'am, you surely do."

I felt my face warm at his words and gave a nervous laugh. "Not in his wildest dreams, D-Daddy."

I walked outside, passing under the green canopy of honeysuckle and ivy, to my office in the co-op studios. Except for two women in the common area basting a quilt, Scout and I were alone. I grabbed a cup of coffee for me, a dog biscuit for him, and checked through the mail and messages that had accumulated in my box. Then I got down to work, digging into all the letters, reports, and filing I'd gotten behind on, accompanied only by the comforting doggy sounds of my canine companion, the only male in my life I truly understood these days. I didn't even glance at the clock until my phone rang two and a half hours later. Ten-thirty-five and I'd already done a day's work. I was feeling pretty proud of myself when I picked up the phone.

"Josiah Sinclair Folk Art Museum. Benni Harper speaking."

"I'm still waitin'." Detective Hudson's audacious Texas

twang instantly deflated my good feeling. "Did you forget to set your alarm?"

I hung up the phone without answering, knowing I'd regret my impulsive action. It rang again ten seconds later. On the fourth ring, I reluctantly picked it up.

"Josiah Sinclair . . ."

"I know where you work." His voice wasn't amused. "Get over here now."

Ah, the wonderful arrogance of law enforcement officers. What he'd forgotten was that I was married to one. I've been through that be-nice-then-surprise-them-with-force psychological tactic too many times to count. "We both know I can tell you what you need to know over the phone. I don't have time to drive to the sheriff's office."

"I want to see your face when you're talking. That's the only way I can tell if you're trying to pull one over on me."

"Listen up, because though I promised my husband I'd cooperate with you and I try to keep my promises to him, I'm only going to tell you my story once. If that's not good enough, then I suggest you take it up with my husband, *the police chief.* Have you got a pad and pencil?"

There was silence at the other end. Ha, I'd managed to shut him up for one nano-second.

"Rose Brown told me exactly nothing yesterday," I said. "Write that down, detective. *Nothing*. She rambled on like older people do about her dead husband, his fondness for the law, horses, and women, not necessarily in that order. She then proceeded to tell me to fix myself up or my husband would leave me for a prettier woman. That was it. I got away as soon as I could because I've about had it up to my chin with people telling me how to keep my husband from straying and I've had it with you bugging me. Goodbye." I hung up the phone, waiting for it to ring again. When it didn't, I let out a deep sigh and went back to filing, trying to keep my mind off the whole darn Brown family and their internal family dramas.

About a half hour later, I was on my knees, filing in the S–T's, when my office door flew open and a grim-faced Detective Hudson filled my doorway. Scout jumped to his feet, his one German shepherd ear at full mast, a low growl rumbling in his throat.

"Oh, great," I muttered.

Detective Hudson took a step inside the office, and Scout's hindquarters went taut, preparing to spring.

I waited a few seconds before saying, "Scout, friend." Scout sat down and lifted a paw. I reached over and pushed it down. "Don't take that word to heart," I said to the detective. "I have to call you a friend or he'll chew those atrocious-looking boots to leather shreds." Detective Hudson's feet were encased today in navy blue ostrich quill boots. They were ugly, but even I could tell they were expensive.

"I have one more question about what Cappy Brown said to you after you talked to her mama, and since my ear is already half deaf from you slamming the phone in it, I decided I'd probably be more successful and safer continuing this conversation in person."

I turned my back to him and resumed filing.

"Benni, I swear I'll take you down to the station, then call your husband and tell him that though I've repeatedly asked you not to, you've been investigating this on your own."

I turned to gape up at him. "You'll what? Are you saying you'll tell my husband lies about me?"

Any resemblance to Tom Sawyer disappeared when his face hardened. "I'll do whatever it takes to solve this case." The unbending resolve in his voice told me to take that statement seriously.

I stood up, weary of this game. "Detective Hudson, my husband asked me to cooperate with you, and I'm trying to do that. I'm sorry if I was rude, but to be honest, you rub me the wrong way. One minute you're Mr. Texas-cutesy and the next you're Mr. Hard-ass Cop. I'm tired of being manipulated by you and by the Brown family. I'll tell you what Cappy said to me, and then you're on your own."

His dark, serious eyes studied me for a long moment, his hands resting on his hips. Then he said in a solemn voice, "You think I'm cute?"

"Geeze Louise!" I said, throwing up my hands. "That's exactly what I mean."

He grinned. "Just tell me what Cappy said to you."

I told him the same story I told Gabe.

"So obviously she now suspects you know more than you do. I sure don't like that idea."

"Neither did Gabe, but I'll tell you what I told him: I don't think she'll hurt me. I know it appears she is the most likely one to be involved with Giles's death, but I know her better than you and Gabe and I don't think she'd kill someone in cold blood."

His face had the same scornful and superior boy-are-you-naive look I'd seen on Gabe's. It must be a class they take in cop school. Condescension 101.

"Is there anything else you need?" I asked. "I've told you everything I know. Scout's honor."

Scout's ears perked up at the sound of his name.

Detective Hudson searched my face with wary eyes, then concluded, "You're telling the truth."

"You wouldn't know the truth if it bit you in the butt."

"Exactly what does the chief do to shut that smart-ass mouth of yours?"

"Good-bye, Detective Hudson."

He didn't budge.

"What else do you want? I've told you everything I know. Now go do your cop stuff." I waved him away.

He pulled a white sheet of paper from inside his tweed, cowboy-cut jacket. "I have a list of the nineteen cemeteries in San Celina County."

"We have that many cemeteries?"

"Want to go grave hunting?"

I hesitated. To be honest, although the thought of going with him anywhere was not the least bit appealing, the possibility of traipsing through graveyards was. I'd always been fascinated by graveyards, especially the old ones and to actually have a mission, the hunt for this mysterious tombstone with the lily of the valley carving, was tempting.

"Look out, she's weakening," he said, amused.

I glanced over at the phone, causing him to smirk.

"Need to call the chief and ask permission?" he asked.

I glared at him. "No."

"Then let's go."

I thought for a minute, then said, "Why don't we split the list and get back with each other later? That would be the smartest thing to do."

"No way, Detective Harper. With my luck, you'll find what we're looking for and then hold the information for ransom."

"I would not! You make me sound like a criminal or something."

"Outside of her own family, you *are* the only one involved in this case with personal ties to Cappy Brown."

I stood up and faced him. "Look, Detective, if—and I'm saying if—Cappy did kill Giles Norton, I would never protect her from prosecution and I resent you implying I would."

He dangled the sheet of paper in my face. "So, what's keeping you?"

I grabbed the list and scanned it. "I have to be back by six o'clock."

"No problem, I have a date anyway. Say, do you have a camera?"

I gave him an exasperated look while opening the bottom drawer of my desk and pulling out the small telephoto Canon I use around the museum. "For someone who claims to be so good at his job, you sure are unprepared."

"But I always manage to get my man . . . or woman. My conviction rate was the talk of the Houston PD."

"Right, and your mother trains tigers for the circus."

"Actually," he said, switching off the office light as we left, "Mother did work for Barnum and Bailey's once. She was . . ."

I groaned loudly, trying to drown out the latest lie. "I don't want to hear it."

"A clown," he finished.

"How appropriate. How utterly appropriate."

He insisted on driving, reasoning that not only could he deduct mileage whereas I couldn't, his truck was newer, had air-conditioning and a CD player. I didn't like him being in the driver's seat, literally or figuratively, but also couldn't argue his points. The temperature was already in the high eighties, and some of the cemeteries were over the grade in North County where it would most likely reach the nineties. With Scout riding happily in back, we started with the biggest cemetery, San Celina's.

In the cemetery's parking lot, my eyes darted briefly over to the newer section where my mother and Jack were buried. A tinge of sadness struck me, like it always did when I came here. I hadn't brought flowers to their graves for a couple of months. Maybe tomorrow after work . . .

"Everything okay?" Detective Hudson had obviously

caught my glance. You couldn't fault the guy's visual acuity.

"Fine," I said, closing the truck door. "Let's check the Brown family section first. It makes sense that he'd be blackmailing them with something from their own family."

He came around the truck and stood next to me. "Now, that's right smart. Where is this Brown section?"

"I have no idea, but I know who will. And I bet I could show him the rubbing and he'd be able to identify it in two seconds if it's anywhere in San Celina's Cemetery."

"You're not showing that to anyone," Detective Hudson stated flatly. "That's the only lead we have in this case, and the less people who know about it, the better."

"But it would make it so much easier—"

"No."

"Fine, we'll waste time traipsing around graveyards when we don't have to. Makes sense to me."

"Benni, you . . ."

I told Scout to stay in the truck and took off across the green expanse of the cemetery lawn toward the gardener's stone building, not interested in hearing anything he had to say starting with the word "you." Inside, Mr. Foglino was tinkering with an old riding mower.

"Hey, Mr. Foglino."

"Well, hello, Benni Harper," he said, standing up and wiping his greasy hands on the thighs of his gray mechanic's overalls. Mr. Foglino had been the head custodian at San Celina High School for thirty-two years. We'd all loved his wry, gentle sense of humor and the Tootsie Roll pops he passed out with gruff impartiality. When he retired, he went to work for his son who owned two local mortuaries and the San Celina's Cemetery. He'd overseen the digging of Jack's grave and many other San Celinans' graves with the same serious respect he'd exacted over the shiny floors of San Celina High School. Mr. Foglino knew a lot of secrets about the families in this town, including who visited whose graves, how many times, how often, and why. Like a good bartender, he'd probably heard more confessions than Father Mark down at St. Celine's Catholic Church and was just as discreet. He'd caught me a time or two sitting on Jack's grave, my face slick with tears, and wordlessly handed me a package of tissues from his overalls' deep pockets before going back to his mowing.

"How's life treating you?" I asked.

"Can't complain. Got job security and a new recliner. Life's good."

I laughed and gave him a quick hug. "I have a question for you. Where's the Brown section?"

I didn't have to say which Browns. His bushy gray eyebrows raised in question told me he knew who I was talking about.

"That family's sure had its sorrows," he said, scratching his cheek absentmindedly, leaving a thin streak of black oil on a cheek as weathered as barn siding. "Then again, haven't we all?"

"Yes, we have."

"How's that grandma of yours? Tell her I'm sure looking forward to Christmas and some of her delicious fudge. I dole it out to myself a piece a day to try and make it last longer."

"She's feisty as ever. I'll tell her to make you a double batch this year."

"And your daddy?"

"He's good. Been having trouble with some new heifers he bought up north. Prolapsed uterus and some leg problems in one. It's getting better now, though. His arthritis has been acting up a little."

"I hear you there. I tell you, getting old isn't for weaklings. You give him my sympathy."

"Sure will."

"Heard your cousin's back in town."

"Yes, sir. He works for the paper."

"He was a good, respectful boy, I remember."

"Yes, he was. He's grown into a nice man, too."

"Well, that's real fine."

I could hear Detective Hudson shift behind me, then let out an impatient breath. I ignored him. The one thing about Mr. Foglino was you couldn't rush him.

"So," Mr. Foglino said. "Hear you got yourself involved with another family's hullabaloo."

"Not on purpose. I was just there when it happened. I . . ." Then I grinned at him. "Well, yes, I guess I have. But I'm doing my best to stay away from any large falling objects."

He chuckled and wagged a crooked, dirt-stained finger at me. "You're a trial to that husband of yours, missy. You know that?"

"So I've been told a few times."

"How's he doing?"

"Ornery as ever, but I guess I'll keep him."

"He's a good police chief. We're lucky to have him."

"I think so."

I heard Detective Hudson shift behind me again and clear his throat. I turned around and frowned him silent.

Mr. Foglino looked back down at the engine of the rider mower. "Over east of the pyramid, and there's a restroom over there, too, for your ants-in-the-pants friend." He looked up, his pale old eyes amused. "I'm assuming that's why he's dancing around like that."

"Thanks," I said, winking at him. "I'll give Dove and Daddy your regards."

"That was a waste of a good half hour," Detective Hudson grumbled.

I cut across the springy graveyard grass weaving around gravestones. "You know," I said over my shoulder, "you'd get a lot more information out of people around here if you learned how to chitchat a little."

He grunted in reply.

We passed by the famous pyramid mausoleum with the single name WYLIE on the front. Made of concrete and patterned after the real Egyptian pyramids, it was an incongruous monument among the sedate white headstones and moss-covered angels that decorated most of the older graves. It had been there since the forties, and, as usual, there was scattered around the base the remnants of a teenager's late-night visitation, half burnt incense sticks, empty beer and soda cans, candy wrappers, crispy matchsticks. I remember sneaking out here a few times myself when I was in high school, spurred on by giggling friends and the natural attraction of being scared common in most people under twenty. It was regularly patrolled by police officers who calmly shooed its nocturnal visitors away. From the base, you could also see with great clarity the last drive-in theater screen in the county, a mute but irresistible draw to cash-strapped students looking for a cheap date.

"What's the story behind this thing?" Detective Hudson asked.

"From what I was always told, some rich rancher moved here early in the century and built this for his wife and three sons. The youngest son got in a fight with the father and left the ranch to find his fortune in Alaska. The other two stayed home, never married, and worked the ranch. All of them eventually died, leaving no heirs. They were entombed here according to the father's wishes. Everyone except the third son. According to the terms of the will, the monument can't be permanently closed until the last son's body is reunited with the family."

"Which is probably the last thing on earth *he'd* want," Detective Hudson said, his voice suddenly bitter.

I glanced over at him, surprised.

His face stared at the pyramid with a raw, angry look that hardened his farm-boy features. He caught my glance, and just as quickly a smile replaced the angry look. "Time's a-wastin', ranch girl. Which way?"

Puzzled by his swift change of emotion, I pointed to a group of expensive headstones behind the pyramid. He strode away from me, whistling a tuneless melody under his breath. I watched him, wondering what family situation he'd truly left behind in Texas.

We glanced over the fifteen stones that made up the Brown family plot. Inside the square concrete edging around John Madison Brown's and Rose Jewel Brown's large, dark granite headstones were the four tiny headstones of the babies who'd died. Just the baby's names and a small lamb were carved on each one—Daisy Jewel Brown, Dahlia Jewel Brown, Beulah Jewel Brown, Bethany Jewel Brown. I stared at the tiny headstones while Detective Hudson went from headstone to headstone looking for something that resembled the grave rubbing.

"Not a lily to be seen, carved or otherwise," he called.

On Rose Brown's stone her name and birthdate were already chipped into the black shiny granite. The only thing left to fill in was her day of death. I wondered if it bothered her to have a headstone with her name already chiseled in. I knew death was inevitable for all of us, but that was just a little too organized and concrete for me. I'd bought two plots side by side when Jack died, having been encouraged to do so by the mortuary, but buying and carving a headstone—that was a little too obsessively neat and tidy. Look at me now, married to Gabe. Where did I want my earthly remains to rest? Next to Jack or to Gabe? Which was more appropriate? Should Gabe be buried next to the mother of his child to make it easier for Sam and his future children to visit their graves? And really, did it matter? Multiple marriages sure made the business of dying complicated.

Oh, honeybun, Dove's voice sang in my head. *What does it matter where your old bones are when your soul is dancing with Jesus?*

"Nothing even close here," he said, coming back to where I stood. "What're you looking at?"

"Just these tiny headstones. Wondering what it was like for a mother to lose four of her seven children."

"Guess that's how it was back then. Even the rich didn't have access to very good health care."

"No one ever mentioned what they died of."

"With no antibiotics and horrible sanitary conditions, it could have been something as simple as the flu or as complicated as TB or diphtheria. It's a wonder as many people lived as they did. Dangerous times to be a kid . . . or an adult, for that matter."

"On the other hand, we've got drug-resistant bacteria and AIDS now, so who's to say it's any better?"

"Good point." He pushed his cowboy hat back on his head. "So, this didn't tell us much. Let's try the next one."

"Let me see that list," I said when we were situated back in his truck. "We should do this in a methodical way so we're not wasting time running all over creation. Do you have a map of San Celina County?"

He nodded over at the glove compartment, and I pulled out a large, detailed map. In a half hour I had the quickest route planned for sixteen of the nineteen cemeteries.

"Three of these I've never heard of, and they're not on the map," I said.

"Deborah Schlanser, the very kind and gracious public librarian who looked them up for me, said six were inactive. A couple for quite a while."

"That might be why they're not on this map. They're probably old pioneer cemeteries."

"Maybe she could tell us where they are. There must be some record somewhere."

"There probably is, but I say we should check the ones we can today and keep our fingers crossed that what we want is in one of them."

"Sounds like a plan. Hope you like country-western music. That's all my truck plays."

"As long as it's the old stuff."

"My kinda girl," he replied, putting on Bob Wills and His Texas Playboys.

We decided to start with the cemeteries closest to the Seven Sisters ranch then work our way north. By three o'clock we'd only investigated six with no luck. It was beginning to look like this would be more than a one-day undertaking. I had to force myself not to linger over the headstones, reading the inscriptions and wondering about the life of the person who died. The number of children's headstones amazed me, and by the early afternoon the constant reminder of the delicate thread by which our lives dangled started depressing me. Apparently it was starting to show after our seventh cemetery when Detective Hudson found me after going through my assigned section, sitting on the open tailgate of his truck hugging Scout.

"I think we need a break," he said. "You hungry?"

"Kinda." I glanced around the pine-shaded cemetery we'd just traipsed through. It was northeast of Paso Robles, an old cemetery that surrounded the Estrella Adobe, one of the many old adobes scattered around San Celina County. "No McDonald's out here. Guess we'll have to go into Paso

Robles. The Paso cemetery will probably take us a long time. It's pretty big."

"No need for McDonald's. I brought lunch." He went around to the cab and brought out a small cooler from behind the front seat. "Do you want beef or turkey?" He held up two wrapped sandwiches.

"Beef."

He handed me the roast beef sandwich and a can of Coke, then joined me on the tailgate. Though it was in the high eighties, a light breeze blew through the stand of dusky green oaks the truck was parked under, and the air was scented with wildflowers and pines, smelling sugary and slightly burnt, reminding me of the Mexican sweet breads Elvia's mother baked at Christmas.

We ate without talking, occasionally feeding bits of our sandwiches to Scout. It was so quiet we could hear animal life rustling in the cottonwoods and scrub brush around us. When I tossed the last bite of my sandwich to Scout, I started picking burrs off the bottoms of my Wranglers, my thoughts drifting to all the mothers who'd lost so many babies. Was it worse to have one and lose it or never to have one at all? The old poet was convinced that loving and losing was better than never loving at all, and at twenty years old I probably would have agreed with him. There were times now I wasn't so sure.

Detective Hudson stood up, causing the pickup to raise slightly, and dusted his hands off on his thighs. "Ready to get going again?"

"Sure," I said, giving up on the dozens of burrs. It'd been so long since I'd been out hiking this time of year, I'd forgotten about these irritating little things.

I sat inside the cab, staring out the window as Detective Hudson chattered about something to do with a dalmatian he once owned. A thought was niggling at the back of my mind, just beyond my reach, and I couldn't grasp it. Something that wasn't right, about either something we'd just seen or something Mr. Foglino said. Detective Hudson's conversation switched to something about the Thursday-night farmer's market, and I continued to half listen and stare at the passing golden fields. In Paso Robles, we stopped at a mini-mart so I could buy some water for Scout. The detective watched as I poured water in my hand and let Scout drink.

"You've been too quiet. What's going on in that devious mind of yours?" he asked when we got back into the truck and headed up the hill toward the cemetery.

"Nothing." Which wasn't exactly a lie. I was thinking about something, I just didn't know what it was.

Paso Robles's cemetery was the second largest in San Celina County. It overlooked the city and the rest of the valley. In the distance, the mountains you had to drive through to get to Bakersfield and Fresno were sharp-etched against the cloudless sky. We divided up the rows and agreed to meet back in front of the adobe-style restrooms when we finished. There was one small funeral going on down near the entrance, but nothing in the areas we would be concentrating on.

I was walking up and down the rows looking for a carving that resembled a lily of the valley, studying marker after marker, going over each Brown family member in my mind—means, motive, opportunity, then trying to imagine each of them coldly shooting Giles. I hated to admit it, but the only one who had all three and who I thought capable of pulling the trigger was Cappy. But would she kill another human being just to protect her horses or her lifestyle? Then again, what about her sisters? JJ had said all the women knew how to shoot. Was I just being naive by assuming that Willow wouldn't kill for her political career or her granddaughter's reputation or Etta for the winery, or for that matter, Arcadia out of that age-old reason, jealousy? If Giles fooled around on her as much as people implied, she could have just gotten fed up that night and shot him. Happened all the time. Except it didn't fit with the conversation I heard or the fact that someone had called the paper and said there would be something "big" happening at Seven Sisters that night. I ruled out Arcadia. If she'd shot him because of his affairs, it made more sense for it to happen at another time, though I was the first to concede that many homicides weren't planned, but were emotional, spur-of-the-moment acts.

That still left Susa to consider—her peace-loving, hippie persona notwithstanding. What did anyone really know about her? After what JJ said about Giles coming on to her and Bliss, maybe there was something he did that caused their mother to lose her gentle manner for a split second. Though she had spent most of her adult life away living on a commune, she was still raised by Capitola Brown, who would not have allowed shrinking violets to grow on the Seven Sisters ranch. Then there was Chase, certainly capable of pulling the trigger, though, as far as I could see, no reason to. Then again, he was the one left with the cute little tasting room girl in the tight red jeans. Could it have been an argument over something as trivial as who gets her next?

No matter which family member did it, there was no doubt in my mind that Cappy and her sisters were sharp enough and cool enough under pressure to cook up that gun switching scene even with a houseful of guests, including a chief of police. One thing I knew from watching my cousin Emory: Growing up with money often gave you a sense of invincibility, a feeling of entitlement that enabled you to forge ahead when others would hesitate. It could be an endearing trait, like Emory's pursuit of Elvia, an obnoxious one, like Giles's cavalier affairs, or a deadly one, like the killing of Giles Norton.

I started down another row, where a monument with a headless angel was laced with scarlet wild fuchsia. GONE HOME stated the simple words on the base under the name CAMPBELL—1902–1958. I leaned against the warm marble and wondered what had happened to the angel's head and how one went about replacing something like that. I was idly looking out over the green cemetery lawns, brightly splashed with dots of yellow goldenrod, when it hit me.

There were no dates chiseled on the Brown baby's headstones.

I rushed across the smooth grass to Detective Hud, who was ten rows away, and told him what I'd discovered.

"So?" he said, not nearly as excited as I was.

"So, that means something. Look at all the children's graves we've seen. They've all had the birth and death dates."

"Not that graveyard in Estrella," he pointed out.

I impatiently waved his words away. "A lot of those people couldn't afford expensive headstones. The Browns could. Why wouldn't they put the dates on the headstones?"

"Maybe because they didn't feel like it. You're reaching for something that isn't there. I think you've been in the sun too long."

"You're jealous because I thought of it and you didn't."

"And you're delusional. Go back to the truck and have a Coke."

"I'm sure I've hit on something, and we're not getting anywhere trying to chase down a headstone that resembles this rubbing. We could be looking for days, and I haven't got that much time. In case you forgot, this isn't *my* real job. Let's go back to San Celina's Cemetery."

"Even if you have hit on something, and I'm not saying you have, what possible good is going back?"

"We could ask Mr. Foglino. He knows tons of stuff about people buried in the cemetery and he's belonged to the historical society for fifty years. If anyone would know why the tombstones are blank, he would." I started back toward the truck. "Are you coming or not?"

He trotted up beside me. "We really should finish looking through this cemetery. We're just going to have to come back if you're wrong."

"I'm not wrong." Before he could answer, I added, "But even *if* I am wrong, I won't be coming back, you will, so it doesn't matter to me."

"Don't you have a cell phone? Can't we just call him?"

"No phone in the maintenance shed."

He complained under his breath, but kept following me. On the ride back down the grade toward San Celina, I chewed my thumbnail, hoping I wasn't leading us on a wild-goose chase. When we reached the San Celina's Cemetery, I jumped out before he switched off the engine, called out at Scout to stay, and ran over to the maintenance building. Mr. Foglino was just locking the weathered steel door.

"I'm glad I caught you," I said, panting.

"Whoa, slow down there, missy," he said, pocketing his huge set of keys. "What's up?"

Detective Hudson walked up beside me, then stood there with his arms folded and his legs spread, his body language stating his feelings about this extra trip. I ignored him and asked Mr. Foglino, "Why don't the four Brown girls' markers have dates on them?"

An almost indiscernible grunt came from behind me.

"Now, that's a real good question," he said, glancing over at the disparaging expression on Detective Hudson's face. "You've got a sharp eye."

I turned and gave the detective a triumphant look. He rolled his eyes and impatiently shifted from one foot to the other.

"Did he ever find himself a men's room?" Mr. Foglino asked.

"Ignore him," I said. "Tell me the story behind the markers."

"I reckon it's not real common knowledge, having happened so long ago and all, but the reason there's no dates is cause those little babies aren't really buried there."

A tiny jolt of electricity sparked at the base of my neck. "Why not?"

"Story goes that Rose Brown was so distraught over the death of her babies in such a short period, her family didn't want her reminded of them when she visited the family graves. Both her sisters and her mother's buried here. They all died during a flu epidemic, as well as some Brown cousins and John Madison Brown's father and mother, who came to live out here from Virginia after the Depression took everything they owned. Rose Brown used to come once a week with roses for all her kinfolk's graves until she went to live in that retirement home a few years ago."

"But there are markers for the babies now."

"That eldest Brown girl, Cappy, had them made up when her mother stopped coming to the graves."

"But she didn't have the bodies moved back?"

"No, guess she figured to leave well enough alone. Or maybe she's thinking about doing it after her mother passes on. Who knows with that Brown family? They've sure done a lot for our community, but I'm not sure the whole group is wound as tightly as they could be."

"What did the babies die from?"

He stuck his dirt-stained hands in the pockets of his overalls. "Don't recall hearing what happened. I'm sure it's in some old records. Back then—this was about 1926 or '27—babies were dying of all sorts of things that they can cure nowadays—flu, diphtheria, scarlet fever, measles, just plain old infections."

"Excuse me, I need to check in at the office," Detective Hudson broke in. He turned and strode away across the graves toward his truck.

"What's his problem?" Mr. Foglino asked, his dark, thick eyebrows a fuzzy hood over his amused eyes.

"He thinks I'm being silly."

"Don't you have enough problems with one police officer in your life?" he asked.

"Detective Hudson is not *in my life*. We're just working on this case together. So, you wouldn't happen to know where the babies are buried, would you?" I looked at him hopefully. At that point, I was willing to bet that grave rubbing we had would find a match when we found the babies' real graves.

"Sure do, out in Adelaida Cemetery. If I'd known that was who you was looking for, I could've told you earlier. They're up on the hill part of the cemetery, if I recall correctly. Only reason I know that is my mother's best friend's neighbor was the Brown's nanny for a little while. Remember hearing about the babies being buried up there back when I was just a little tyke."

"Was it common knowledge?"

"Don't really know, but I doubt it. It was so long ago, and no one thought overly much about babies dying back then. It happened in almost every family. Probably most people assumed they were buried here, and no one probably ever checked. Like I said, only reason I knew was because my mother and her friend talked about the oddness of them burying the babies so far from the family."

"It is odd. Adelaida Cemetery is pretty far away and over

the pass. It would have been a difficult trip back in the twenties."

"Probably isn't even active anymore. Those old cemeteries are a pain to upkeep. That one's got so many trees and hills and rocks. I haven't been there in years, but I'll bet it's gone completely wild unless someone's taken a notion to keep it up."

"Guess we'll go out and look for them."

"If you can talk your antsy-pants friend into it. He didn't appear to be real enthusiastic."

"If he won't go, I'll go on my own."

Mr. Foglino took his hands out of his pockets and scratched behind a bristly ear, his broad, tanned face troubled. "Be careful out there, missy. It's pretty desolate. Take that dog with you."

"I intend to. Thanks for the information."

He gave a curt nod. "Anytime."

I started to walk away, then turned around and asked one more question. "Your mother's best friend's neighbor. Do you remember her name?"

"Mrs. Knoll. Don't recall hearing her first name. Doubt she'd even be alive, though. I'm guessin' she'd be in her late nineties if she was."

"Thanks." As I walked toward the truck where Detective Hudson leaned against the side, his legs and arms crossed, I wrote Mrs. Knoll's name down on the back of my checkbook register.

"What're you writing down?" Detective Hudson asked.

"Just something I need to pick up at the store," I lied. Something inside told me to keep Mrs. Knoll's name to myself until I figured out how she fit into the picture.

"What did the old man tell you?"

"The babies' real graves are in Adelaida Cemetery. I want to go see them. Bet you fifty bucks we find the lily of the valley carved on them." I gave Scout a quick scratch under the chin, then climbed up in the cab of the truck. Proud of my detecting work, I smirked at Detective Hudson when he climbed behind the wheel.

He pulled out the San Celina County map, scanned it, and immediately started complaining. "This place is in the hills outside of Paso Robles! We just came from there. It's almost five o'clock. We'll never make it out there and back in time for my date at six-thirty."

"Drop me off at the folk art museum, then," I said evenly. "I'll drive out there myself. I'll call you tomorrow and let you know what I find." I turned and smiled at him. "You certainly don't want to keep Bambi waiting."

His face was puzzled. "Huh?"

"Miss Bodice Ripper," I clarified.

He frowned. "Her name's Heidi."

I turned my face to the window, hiding my smile. "Of course."

"Leave my love life out of this."

"You brought it up."

"This Adelaida Cemetery is out in the boonies. I'm not letting you go out there by yourself."

I turned back to him and said, "Excuse me, but you do not have the authority to keep me from going anywhere I please. Besides, I grew up in this county. I'm less likely to get in trouble out in Adelaida than you are."

His face turned a dull red as he started the engine, released the emergency brake, and slammed the truck into reverse. "We could do this tomorrow." Rocks and gravel scattered as he gunned the engine and pulled too quickly out of the cemetery's parking lot.

I swung around and made sure we hadn't lost Scout, who was doing his best to get a toe-grip on the detective's plastic-lined truck bed. "Take it easy, rhinestone cowboy,

I've got a beloved dog in the bed of this city-boy truck. And I'm not waiting until tomorrow to find out if the rubbing is from the Brown sisters' graves, and frankly I'm surprised you want to."

"Heidi hates being kept waiting," he grumbled.

"Then take me back to the museum, and I'll—"

"If I let you go out there alone and you get hurt, your husband will have my head, not to mention other parts of my body to which I've become quite emotionally attached. No way, ranch girl. We're going there together, look for these stupid graves, and then we're through for the day."

"You know, I can't believe you're not more excited about this. It's a break in the case."

"More like a paper cut."

"Who knows what it could lead to? Quit being so close-minded. I swear, those blasted police academies need a creative-thinking class. You cops have thinking skills as narrow as a possum's tail. This will give you a whole new line of questioning for the Brown family."

"What do you know? I have an extraordinary conviction rate so I must be doing something right."

"Dumb luck, most likely."

"And for your information, that Brown clan is one extraordinarily tight-lipped bunch. I've interviewed Cappy Brown and her sisters three times and gotten squat. Half my questions their attorney won't even let them answer. Except for the younger ones, who are not privy to any of the family's secrets, a person would have a better chance finding out the recipe for Coca-Cola than a truthful answer from that group. And for all your bragging, I didn't see you doing any better."

"Then every little *fissure* in this case should thrill you. Shut up and drive."

He tossed the map over at me. "Fine, you shut up and navigate."

I calmly folded the map up and tucked it into his glove compartment. "I don't need a map to tell you where to go." I smiled innocently at him.

His answer was an exasperated, animal-like grunt.

Cops must learn that sound at the academy, too.

It took us almost an hour to get to the cemetery, which was quite a few miles off Interstate 101 on a turnoff out of Paso Robles. We twisted through neatly trimmed walnut groves, past rows of new grapevines thick with emerald leaves, fat, purple fruit hanging heavy and sensual among the lush foliage, under stands of cottonwoods with their bright yellow, heart-shaped leaves and maples just starting their turn from green to yellow to brown. Twisted deciduous oak trees, their trunks massed with poison oak, and white-trunked sycamores shaded the narrow two-lane highway with long fingers of afternoon shadows. The peaceful, empty road caused both Detective Hudson and me to withdraw into ourselves, become quiet and introspective, only startled out of the drowsy monotony of the curvy blacktop when a flock of hen turkeys dashed across the road, causing him to slam on the brakes. I glanced back at Scout, who'd survived the stop fine since he'd wisely laid down in the bed.

"Sorry," Detective Hudson murmured

"Right at the next split in the road," I said.

The cemetery lay on our left with no parking lot, but merely a wide spot in the weeds. We climbed out and walked over to the rusty gate. It was closed, but not locked. I turned and called Scout, since there was no one in this old cemetery who would care if he romped among the grave stones. I left my purse in the locked truck and just took my camera, a pen, and a pocket-sized notebook.

I followed Detective Hudson inside the weed- and wildflower-choked grounds. Except for an old outhouse that was long past its prime, there were only the overgrown graves shaded by oaks that had been here two hundred years or longer.

"Mr. Foglino said he thought their graves might be up on the hill," I said, pointing to a hill in front of us with a sharp, steep embankment covered in brambles.

"Is there a road?" he asked, glancing down at his fancy ostrich boots.

"You should carry a pair of work boots in your truck," I said, pointing to a small, overgrown path behind the outhouse.

"Yes, Mom," he said and took off toward the path.

It was about a quarter mile on a steep path to the upper part of the cemetery. On the hilltop, the trees were thicker; the leaves and brush crackled like tiny firecrackers under our feet. Blue oaks laced with overcoats of Spanish moss gave the deepening forest a spooky, bayou feel.

"Watch out for poison ivy," I said, ducking under a still-leafy oak branch. "It's bad this time of year."

I saw him flinch and subtly pull his arms closer, though in reality I didn't see any near enough to cause us any problems. I laughed silently to myself, recognizing a nature neophyte when I saw one. I stepped over some wild grape vines, stopping a moment to pick some volunteer grapes and squeeze them in my fingers. The sweet smell perfumed the air for a moment.

A rustling sound ahead of us caused Scout to take off into the underbrush, his tail straight out, a low growl deep in his throat.

"What was that?" the detective asked, his voice slightly apprehensive.

I raised my eyebrows. He wasn't lying about one thing; he was definitely a city boy.

"Probably just a mountain lion," I said casually, watching his back stiffen and trying not to laugh. *Yep, that was a definite stiffening.* "But don't worry, most times they don't bother humans. You're not wearing any cologne, by any chance?"

He turned around, his sweating face trying hard not to show panic. "Why?"

I kept my face serious, chewing my lower lip for effect. "Just wondered. They're kind of intrigued by the smell."

"You're shittin' me."

I shook my head solemnly. "Wish I was."

His nostrils flared slightly.

"Aramis is their favorite," I continued, keeping a straight face. "But I've heard the lions around here have been preferring Polo lately."

He narrowed his eyes at me, his lips thin with irritation. "Very funny."

I giggled. "Yeah, I thought so."

He took off ahead of me, obviously angry, and I felt a small twinge of shame for putting him on. A very small tinge.

When we reached the graves, he surveyed the area and gruffly told me to start on the west end and work toward him. "You have your camera?"

"Right here." I held it up.

"Film?"

"Yes, Detective. They tend to work better that way."

"Then let's get to work."

He strode off toward the east side of the cemetery, his anger still apparent in his stride. I whistled for Scout who eventually appeared out of some scrub brush, his nose wet and dirty, his tongue hanging out in obvious pleasure at chasing the rabbit or squirrel that had probably made the sounds prompting my practical joke on the detective.

"Didn't catch it, did you?" I commented, when he sat down and furiously scratched behind his ear. "You guys are all alike, running through the brush, chasing nothing important, but thrilled to your bones you get to chase it."

He sneezed twice in reply.

I started on my end, doing my best not to miss any graves, easy to do in this old, very disorganized graveyard. I was assuming the four sisters would all be buried together, but since the fact they were even buried in this old cemetery wasn't logical, I didn't expect how they were buried to make any more sense.

Once again I was struck emotionally by how many of the dead were infants and small children. So many of these graves hadn't been disturbed or visited in years. One especially touched me, bearing the inscription NATHAN RAY MONROE—AUGUST 10, 1882–DECEMBER 12, 1882, "CROWN'D WITHOUT THE CONFLICT." The baby had been four months old when he died. Walking in and out of the light cast by the thick maples, cottonwoods, and oaks, I felt a chill, as psychological as much as physical, when I read the headstones. One whole family, a father, mother, and six children, surrounded by a rusty Victorian iron fence, had been wiped out by influenza during the same month in 1917. I sat down on a flat rock, overwhelmed for a moment by the tragedy.

"I found them!" Detective Hudson's voice echoed from across the cemetery.

"Scout, come," I called and started running toward the detective's voice, dodging broken markers and uneven sunken spots.

He stood in front of four identical markers, standing in

a row like a just-started fence. On the front of each of them was carved a lily of the valley.

"It *is* about the babies," I whispered.

Then there was a sharp pop, and something whizzed past my ear. With a howl, Scout started toward the trees.

"Scout, down!" I started to run toward him, then found myself flat on my chest, the breath knocked out of me. Detective Hudson's solid, muscular body pinned me to the ground.

"Don't move," he snapped. His thighs instinctively tightened around mine.

Move? I couldn't even get a breath. Gasping, I tried to talk. To tell him I needed oxygen. To tell him it felt like I was dying. I felt his hip bone jab into me as he struggled to pull his gun out of his holster.

Another pop cracked through the silence. Dirt and leaves jumped a few feet from our prone bodies. His thighs tightened again.

I moaned, trying to get a breath, trying to tell him to get off me.

"Hush," he said, pushing my face into the sharp, dry leaves. They scratched my face, and I squirmed, trying to get a hand out to push them away.

"Lie still!" His harsh voice caused me to freeze. My heart *thump-thumped* in my ears, sounding as loud as the ocean.

Though his body grew heavy on mine, gradually my breath came back, and I managed to take short gulps of cool, soil-scented air. As we lay there, the noise of the forest slowly resumed, the chirping of crickets and the chattering of birds telling us our assailant had departed. I could feel Detective Hudson's breath warm and rapid on my neck, then gradually felt the muscles in his arms and legs relax around me.

"Listen," he whispered. In the distance the rumbling sound of a truck's engine moved farther away.

"Good," I mumbled into the dirt and leaves. "You can get off me now." With the immediate threat of danger gone, our position was entirely too personal for my tastes, though I had to admit he had pretty nice thighs.

He laughed softly in my ear, his lips brushing against my hair. His thighs tightened around mine again, voluntarily this time. "I don't know, it was just starting to get fun."

I spit a leaf out of my mouth. "Get off me, you jerk." I shoved my elbow as hard as I could into his chest.

He laughed again, then rolled off me and stood up, reholstering his pistol. He held out his hand. "Someone sure isn't happy with us finding these graves."

Ignoring his offer of help, I scrambled up. "Where's Scout?" I looked around frantically for my dog.

He lay flat on the ground a few feet away, whimpering.

"Scout, come," I said. He jumped up and ran over to me. "What a good, good boy you are." He licked my face as I ran my hands over his body, checking for injuries. "Are you okay, Scooby-doo?" I crooned, hugging his thick body.

"Shoot, he's fine," Detective Hudson said, rubbing his lower back. "I'm the one who just pulled a muscle because of that dimestore Daniel Boone sniper. Bet you a taco dinner it was someone hired by the Browns. They must've been following us all day. Dang it all, I was so busy haggling with you I let them get the slip on me."

"So why didn't you go after them, Mr. Purple Heart, and find out who they were?" Hair at the back of my neck was damp from heat and fear. I lifted it up, letting the small breeze cool my skin.

"My mama might've raised a fool, but my daddy taught me never to get into a fight I didn't have at least a fifty percent chance of winning. No way was I running into those woods. They had the advantage and they knew it. There wasn't a chance this side of Lubbock I would be able to catch them."

"Hmmp," was all I said, tenderly touching a raw place on my cheek.

"Sorry I had to throw you down so hard," he said, tilting his head to look at me. His grin belied his apology. "But you were a perfect target."

"Some excuse."

"I saved your life!"

"Don't deny you enjoyed knocking the air out of me."

"Well, it *was* right peaceful for a few minutes there, what with your mouth not moving and all."

"Eat dirt." I walked back over to the babies' graves, took a notebook out of my back pocket and started writing down the information on the headstones.

Detective Hudson went over and picked up the camera that had flown out of my hands when the sniper shot at us. He turned it over in his hands, inspecting it. "Think this will still work?"

"I don't know. That's why I'm copying down the information."

He came up behind me and took a dozen or so shots of the markers. These did have dates, though nothing else appeared on the plain white marble stones except the lily of the valley.

DAISY JEWEL BROWN—May 1, 1925–November 3, 1925

DAHLIA JEWEL BROWN—May 1, 1925–March 12, 1926

BEULAH JEWEL BROWN—January 25, 1927–June 15, 1927

BETHANY JEWEL BROWN—January 25, 1927–September 9, 1927

"I wonder what they died from?" I asked out loud.

Detective Hudson shrugged. "Does it matter?"

I looked at him, surprised. "Of course it does! It's obvious that whatever Giles was blackmailing the family with has something to do with these babies. How they died might be the key. I mean, maybe someone killed them or something."

He pointed to the lichen-covered markers. "The dates of death don't support that theory. They most likely died of influenza or diphtheria or who knows what else. Look at all the other graves of children here. You're really reaching now."

"If they died innocently, why is someone shooting at us?"

He was silent for a moment, knowing I had him there. Then he said, "I don't know. Might just be that this person wanted to scare us off investigating altogether and after following us all day decided that out here in the boonies was the safest place for him . . ."

"Or her," I said.

He rolled his eyes. "Okay, Miss Feminist, *or her*, to shoot at us. I mean, when else would they? When we were at the folk art museum? Or in the San Celina's Cemetery? This was the best opportunity."

"Except we've been in other isolated graveyards today, like the Estrella one. Nobody shot at us there. They were warning us away from this particular cemetery."

"Benni, if they didn't want us to get here, they would have done something while we were out on the road. There's absolutely no evidence to support your theory."

"You haven't even looked for evidence to support it! You're dismissing it without any serious consideration. That's very poor detective work. I find it hard to believe your success rate is as good as you say with a pessimistic attitude like yours."

"Don't tell *me* how to do my job! Criminy, you can be a pain in the ass."

I ignored his comment and crossed my arms. He knew I was right. Eventually he'd admit it, though not without some whining.

Back at his truck, he searched the ground for tire tracks. The grass had definitely been flattened, but the dirt was too hard to leave any hints as to what kind of vehicle the shooter was driving.

"You know," he said, driving back down the winding country road toward the interstate, "there's a good possibility that all of this is a ruse to distract us from who the real killer is. Did you ever think about that?"

"Okay," I finally conceded. "You could be right. So where does that leave us?"

"Not much of anywhere, but it's something to consider. Do you happen to be carrying your cell phone?"

I dug through my purse and handed him the phone. While trying to ignore his exaggerated excuses to Heidi, I thought about what he said. If it didn't have to do with the babies, then why was Giles killed? His determination to take over the winery was still a possibility, so maybe it was Etta who shot him in a passionate moment, and her sisters helped cover it up. I thought about the Seven Sisters quilt pattern I'd looked up the other day—how it was a pattern of six stars revolving around one in the center, much like the constellation Bliss and I had searched for. Like the pattern and the constellation, there was a center to this, a something or someone all the other events circled around. Was it the grandmother, Rose Brown, and her four dead children? Or was it simpler than that—a moment of anger, a handy loaded gun, a family adept at covering up, showing a good face to the world? After he was finished with his excuses to Heidi, I tried calling Gabe at the office and got his voice mail. Then I called home and got the answering machine, a practice that had been happening a little too frequently this week.

The detective dropped me off at the folk art museum at seven o'clock, and we said a quick good-bye without any more discussion about what we should do next. He was anxious to get to his date, and I was eager to go home and tell Gabe about what had happened, come truly clean about how much I was involved. Then what? Those tiny graves kept reappearing in my head. I wanted to know more about the four babies even if they didn't have anything to do with finding out who killed Giles. I knew someone who worked in the county records department—a girl I went to college with. Tomorrow I'd go downtown and see if she could find their death certificates for me.

The house was dark when I got home. I immediately went into the kitchen and fed Scout, who was two hours past his regular dinner time and was giving me a soulful look telling me so. As I watched him gobble his dinner, I went in and checked the answering machine. There were only two messages—mine and an old one that told me Gabe had most likely been home and gone out again after listening to the message. It better not be Lydia's voice, I thought as I hit replay.

"Chief!" Miguel's voice croaked over the phone. "I'm down at General Hospital. I couldn't find your cell phone number so I hope you get this soon. Bliss took one in the shoulder. I thought you'd want to know." The message time was 5:02 p.m.

I ran for the car, yelling at Scout to stay. On the drive down there, all I could consciously pray over and over was, *Oh, Lord. Make her okay, please, please make her okay.*

12

INSIDE THE EMERGENCY room, there were a few families with sick, cranky children and the requisite medical personnel milling about. There was no sign of Gabe, Sam, or Bliss's family. I asked at the desk, and while the nurse was checking the computer, I spotted Miguel down the hall putting money in a coffee machine.

"Never mind," I told the nurse. "That's her partner over there." I rushed over to him. "Miguel, what happened? Is Bliss all right? What about the baby?"

He watched the liquid splash into the paper cup, not answering me for a moment. His hand shook slightly as he picked up the steaming cup.

"Miguel," I said softly. "Are you okay?"

He looked down at me, his eyes rimmed red, fighting tears with all his Latin-bred masculine resolve. I wanted to put my arms around his broad shoulders and hug him the way I used to when he was three and was startled awake from his nap by a bad dream.

He took a gulp of the hot coffee, then said, "She's upstairs. The asshole got her in the shoulder. She lost a lot of blood and, well, they say it shouldn't affect the baby, but they can't promise . . ." His voice choked.

"What happened?" I asked again.

"A friggin' traffic stop over by the bus station," he said. "She was driving today so she made the approach. He shot her before she could get halfway to the car. I fired two shots, hit his back window, but he got away." He took another gulp of coffee. "They caught him up in Paso about an hour later. He had a half gram of cocaine under his seat. She was almost killed for a stinking half gram of cocaine."

His hand jerked, causing some coffee to slosh onto the shiny hospital floor. He looked down at it, his face a mixture of agony and dismay.

"I'll get it," I said, taking a tissue out of my purse and bending down to wipe it up. "Is her family here yet?"

"They're upstairs. Fourth floor. She's in intensive care, but the doctors say she'll be all right. They just want to keep a close eye on her tonight." He gestured with his cup. Coffee splashed out on his hand. He flinched and said, "Shit."

"Here, give me that." I gently took the cup out of his hand and handed him a dry tissue. "Is there anything I can do for you?"

He wiped his wet hand, then handed me the damp tissue. "No, thanks. My shift's over, so I'm going home. They said there's nothing anyone else can do tonight, and she's got her family up there." His dark eyelashes were shiny with unshed tears. "I shouldn't have let her approach that driver. I should have taken it."

"There was nothing you could do. It's not your fault."

He gripped the butt of his gun and looked down at the floor.

"Bliss didn't like being coddled or treated special. It was

her turn, and she would have fought you to take it. It was just the luck of the draw, Miguelito," I said, using his childhood nickname.

He gave a tremulous smile. "Go on up. I'm sure the chief wants to see you."

I squeezed his upper arm, then walked over to the elevators. Upstairs, I asked the desk clerk which way to the waiting room. Halfway down the hall I could see Bliss's mother, JJ, and Cappy sitting together on a sofa. Gabe's back was to me. Lydia stood next to him, and Sam sat on the wood coffee table, his face in his hands. A doctor walked out of a glass door next to them, and they eagerly gathered around him, blocking him from my view. But even from down the hall, I could hear Sam's agonized cry and watched his mother encircle him with her arms. Susa and JJ clung together, weeping. Gabe stepped over to Lydia and Sam and put his arms around both of them.

I froze, not knowing what to do. Watching Gabe so tenderly hold his son and ex-wife caused a pain in my heart that I couldn't ignore, but to go up to them now seemed like a crass and self-serving invasion of privacy. Trembling, I turned and walked back down the hall and sat down on a chair near the nurses' station, wondering what had happened and what I should do. Was Bliss all right? Was it her or the baby? Or both? Finally I went up to a nurse with a friendly face, trying not to stutter, explained briefly who I was and asked if she could find out.

"Honey, I understand," she said. "I'm a number two myself. It's an awkward place to be at times like this. Let me find out for you."

She came back a few minutes later, her round face regretful. "Your stepson's girlfriend is going to be okay, but she lost the baby. I'm sure sorry."

"Was it the gunshot?" I asked.

She shook her head no. "Most likely not. Pregnant women are tougher than people realize. Unless she'd been shot right in the stomach, her baby, even at two or three months, was capable of surviving quite a lot of trauma. It seems strange, I know, but most likely she would have lost the baby whether or not she'd been shot. Most miscarriages are caused by chromosomal or genetic abnormalities that can't be prevented or treated. There's nothing for anyone to feel guilty about here."

"Thanks," I said.

Back at my car I couldn't help worrying that my decision not to break into the Brown and Ortiz family tragedy would be taken as a sign of not caring. At home, I cleaned up the kitchen and waited for Gabe and prayed for them all, especially Bliss, who would suffer with this the longest—her whole life. And I tried to erase the picture in my head of Gabe with his arms around Lydia and Sam. Jealousy had no place in this situation, but I couldn't get rid of the sad feeling that somehow Gabe had slipped away from me. When I wasn't paying attention, his old life, his old love came back and lured him away. *Fight for your man*, Elvia and Emory had encouraged me. But I knew fancy nightgowns, fierce demands, and pieces of paper that say you're a couple can't buy the human heart.

Finally I called Dove and told her.

"Those poor kids," she said. "Should I come out? Or is there a wagonload of people already seeing to them?"

"I came on home. Sam and Bliss seem to have plenty of emotional support. I'll send flowers and a note tomorrow. I don't know what else to do."

"Not much else we can do. Life's tragedies come and go. I don't have to tell you that. We stand up through them or we fall like saplings in a windstorm. All depends on how deep of roots you've grown before they happen. I surely do hurt for them, though. Losing a baby's got to be the hardest thing a woman ever goes through."

"Have you ever? Lost a baby, I mean?"

"Once. Lord, it was so long ago, but there's times it still seems like last week. A little girl in between your daddy and your aunt Kate. I was six months along, and she just came. Back then we didn't have the fancy incubators and such they have now. They let me see her before they took her away. Prettiest shaped head I'd ever seen on a baby. She looked perfect. But God knows best. It wasn't her place to be born to this earth."

"Do you ever think about her?"

Dove was silent for a moment, then said softly, "Every May 3rd."

"Oh, Gramma, I'm so sorry." So many dead babies in the last few days. It was more than my heart could manage.

"It was a long time ago, honeybun. Hurts don't go away, but they gentle."

"Is that a guarantee for all hurts?" I asked, trying not to sound desperate.

"Some take longer than others. And it all depends on the person. A hurt can soften you like a good, wool blanket, or, if you let it, turn you into a pile of dried leaves, ready to crumble at the first footstep. Your choice. Our hurts are what make us human. It's why God had to become a man, to see what it was we were all whining about, see if maybe He'd made things too hard for us."

Thinking of all the little graves in the Adelaida Cemetery, I said, "Sometimes I think He did."

"Well, He also came to rescue us and did a fine job of it, though some might not think so at first. And it's okay to have a doubt now and then. What riles Him is folks not carin' enough to even wonder. Now, come on out to the ranch tomorrow, because me and Isaac got something to show you. I think it'll cheer you up. And besides, I'm going to bake Sam some of his favorite peanut butter cookies, and I need you to fetch them to him."

"Okay. By the way, I have a message I forgot to give you from Miguel. We saw him on Sunday. He said, and I quote, 'No. Absolutely not. No way.' "

She laughed softly under her breath. "No problem. I'll just pull some strings, go over his head to his boss."

"What's Gabe got to do with this?"

She snorted. "I mean his real boss. Now, are you coming out?"

"What time do you want me?"

"Before noon. You can help serve lunch to the crew."

"The crew? The crew for what?"

"Never you mind. Just be here." She was quiet for a moment. "And don't worry. Things'll work out for the best with all this. That's a promise from me to you."

"Yes, ma'am," I said, wanting with all my life to believe her.

I was in bed reading when he came home around eleven.

"You heard?" he asked, his face shadowed with tired lines.

"Yes, I played Miguel's message when I got home at around seven o'clock. Then I went down to the hospital and ran into him outside the emergency room. He told me what happened. I . . ." I stopped and took a deep breath. "I was walking down the hall when the doctor was telling you all about the baby. It didn't seem appropriate for me to break in, so I decided to come home and wait for you." I looked up into his tired face. "Oh, Gabe, I'm so sorry."

He sat down on the edge of the bed. "Sam's over at the hotel with his mom. He wanted to sleep at the hospital, but Lydia talked him into going back with her. Her mother said they gave Bliss some drugs that made her groggy, so I'm not sure how much she's comprehended. Her shoulder's going to be okay, no major damage."

"How's Sam?"

"In shock, I think, but he's handling it pretty well. I'm proud of him."

"When this is all over, maybe you should tell him so."

"I will." His mouth opened in a wide yawn. "I'm exhausted."

"Why don't you sleep in tomorrow?"

"Can't, too many appointments. I'll be okay."

"Then come to bed."

He pulled his suit jacket off and tossed it on a chair. The rest of his clothes he left in a crumpled pile on the floor, telling me how tired he was.

When I turned out the light, he laid on his back and stared at the ceiling. I wanted to say something that would make him feel better, but knew there was nothing I could do but just be here. Under the covers I sought out his hand and held it tight. He cleared his throat in the darkness.

"I . . ." His voice faltered. "You know, I was just beginning to get used to being a grandfather. I never held Sam much when he was a baby. I was thinking that maybe I'd have been a better grandfather than I was a father."

I leaned over and kissed his bare shoulder, then laid my cheek on it. "Sam loves you very much."

"I know," he said, pulling me into his arms, holding tight.

The next morning he skipped his ritual jogging and was subdued over breakfast. I didn't force conversation, knowing one thing about this reticent Latino man I'd married; his grief was a private thing, difficult to share even with me.

"I think I'll send Bliss some flowers. When you see Sam can you tell him why I left last night? Let him know I'm concerned," I said, buttering an English muffin.

He nodded. "Sure, he'll understand. I'll drop by the hospital on my way to work, see how Bliss is doing. What are you doing today?"

"Same old stuff," I said, wondering if I should tell him about the shooting at the cemetery yesterday. His face, craggy with fatigue from a restless night and the anticipation of a day filled with questions and reporters and dealing with Sam's grief decided for me. He couldn't take one more thing to worry about right now.

After dropping by the florist to order Bliss's flowers, I went to the folk art museum more out of habit than any real need since I had caught up on all my paperwork yesterday and the exhibit was doing fine. After chatting with some potters over a cup of coffee, I went to my office and puttered around, sharpening pencils and cleaning out drawers. What I was trying to do was decide whether I should continue looking into Giles's murder. With Bliss engaged to Sam, I felt awkward about trying to prove one of her family members was a killer. What with Bliss's miscarriage and the sniper yesterday, I'd decided that me being involved was too risky . . . for my own life and for the relationships of the people I loved.

I was reduced to washing my small, wavy window when JJ walked in.

"Hey," I said, getting down off my footstool and giving her a quick hug. "How's Bliss?"

"They're letting her come home tomorrow. The wound wasn't very deep and . . ." She swallowed hard, her face contorting in grief.

"Sit down," I said, leading her to a visitor chair. I sat next to her, turning my chair so we were facing each other. "Are you okay, JJ?"

She sniffed and rubbed the back of her long-sleeved chenille sweater under one eye. She was bare-faced today, and her hair was soft and pixielike around her head. "Yes . . . no . . . Oh, I don't know. I'm glad Bliss is okay, but I'm sad about the baby. I just don't know what to do or feel."

"What you're feeling is normal. Just be there for Bliss, that's really all you can do. Let time soften things."

A deep frown narrowed her forehead. "I'm mad, too."

"At who?"

"My grandma. Do you know what she said at the hospital last night to me and my mother after everyone left? That it's probably for the best. That Sam and Bliss were too young to have a baby. How could she say that? Say that Bliss's baby dying is for the best?"

I shook my head, unable to give her an answer. It was a common, if insensitive remark I'm sure many people had said and thought in similar situations.

"How's Bliss's shoulder doing this morning?" I asked, trying to move the subject away from questions about her grandmother that I couldn't answer.

"Much better. Susa's with her right now. I just wanted to come find you."

"Why?"

"To tell you I'm leaving San Celina. When Bliss is healed up, my mother and I are moving back up north. She called my father last night, and they had a long talk. They're going to try to work things out. As for me, I just don't like it here. Seven Sisters and all its problems is something I don't need in my life."

"We'll miss you, JJ. I'll really miss you."

She leaned over and hugged me. "You're one of the few things I will miss." She reached down and petted Scout. "You, too, big boy." Then she stood up and straightened her long cotton skirt. "As for all the stuff about the secrets in my family and who killed Giles, I just don't care anymore. I really understand why my mom left when she was eighteen, why she didn't want us raised around Seven Sisters. Frankly, I'm hoping Bliss and Sam come up north when they get married."

"And I hope they don't," I said, smiling. "But I understand what you're saying."

Her visit helped me decide once and for all that stepping out of the investigation was the right thing. It was Detective Hudson's job, not mine, and right now I was too concerned about my husband and his son to worry about which person in the Brown family was a killer.

I was unlocking my truck, having decided to drop by Elvia's bookstore and catch up on the trials and tribulations of her love life, when Detective Hudson's red pickup pulled up next to me. Scout barked in enthusiastic recognition. The detective stepped out, wearing the plain brown ropers today that he'd worn Saturday night when we'd danced. The sleeves of his blue Arrow shirt were rolled up, revealing a large leather-band Swiss Army watch.

"You should've worn those yesterday for our cemetery tour," I said, glancing down at his feet.

"How's Officer Girard?" he asked.

"They said she'd be going home tomorrow." I looked at him curiously. "How'd you find out about her?"

"It was in the newspaper this morning, but I found out last night. When a cop goes down, believe me, it gets around even if it isn't someone from your agency."

"Did you hear she lost her baby?"

His eyes dropped to the ground. "That stinks. The gunshot?"

"No, the nurse told me that most likely there was something already wrong with the baby, that the gunshot didn't cause the miscarriage. It was just one of those things."

"My ex-wife lost one before Maisie was born. It's hard on a woman."

"That's the first time you've mentioned your daughter's name. Maisie. That's pretty."

He grinned shyly. "Don't get me started, or I'll force you to look at all my pictures. Then after that it's the home videos and refrigerator art. You'll never get free."

For the first time since we met, I almost liked Detective Hudson. "So there's at least one woman who has you under her thumb."

He nodded, laughing. "Benni Harper, you hit it right on the head with that one. Not to change the subject, but what did your husband say about our little wilderness experience yesterday?"

"I didn't tell him and I don't want you to either. He doesn't need any more worries right now. Actually I'm glad you dropped by, because it saves me a phone call. I'm off the case."

"You're chickening out on me when we're getting so close? You can't give up now."

"I'm not giving up, I'm just doing what I should have done from the beginning—let you investigate it alone. I should have never let you talk me into getting involved. We could have been hurt or killed yesterday."

He cracked his knuckles nonchalantly. "They were warning shots. If they'd wanted us dead, we would be."

I threw up my hands in exasperation. "And that doesn't bother you?"

"Not really." He studied the backs of his hands, then checked his watch. Early morning sunlight glinted off the reddish-blond hair on his forearms. His calm expression told me he wasn't kidding.

"You may have a death wish, Detective, but not me."

"It doesn't bother you that an innocent man was killed?"

"We could debate the appropriateness of the word innocent in his case, but, yes, of course, I care. But it's not my job, and I don't want to do it anymore."

He folded his arms across his chest. "I don't believe you."

"You'd better, because it's the truth."

"Okay, one last thing. Look at these and then tell me you still want to quit." He reached into his truck and pulled out a large, manila envelope.

I opened the envelope, pulling out four pages. They were pink with a fancy blue border. Across the top read *County of San Celina.* In the left bottom corner was California's state seal, in the right corner a same-sized circle saying County Recorder, San Celina County, State of California.

The babies' death certificates.

I glanced over them, looking specifically at the cause of death. The first one to die was Daisy. Pneumonia. Dahlia was next. Her cause of death stated simply natural causes. Natural causes was also written on Beulah's and Bethany's certificates. Though they tugged at my heart, they didn't tell us anything we didn't already know.

But . . .

What if someone *had* killed them? What if this person had gotten away with it all this time? I was reacting emotionally, I knew, and that was exactly what the detective was hoping for, that I also knew.

I handed him back the death certificates. "It says here they died of natural causes. Nothing else we can do unless the doctor is still alive."

"Which he isn't," Detective Hudson said. "I already checked. And his records were destroyed a long time ago."

"So that leaves us—no, make that *you*—exactly nowhere. I know I started you down this path, but even I can see when something's a dead end."

He slipped the certificates back into the envelope. "No, you were right. I wasn't thinking creatively enough and I also think you're right about Giles's blackmail attempt being something that involves these kids. Or at least something in the past that the Brown family is trying to hide. Now we just have to think of a clever and sneaky way to find out about this family's past." He smiled at me with encouragement. "Your specialty, Mrs. Harper."

I leaned back against my truck's passenger door. Scout came over and nudged my head, and I reached up and rubbed his chest. Detective Hudson was deliberately manipulating me with his flattery, and I knew it. Yet I was still pulled toward this case. If indeed they'd been murdered, even after all these years, the babies deserved justice. And Giles, whether he was a person I would have liked or not, deserved it, too.

"What would you do now?" he asked, his voice cajoling. "I mean, *if* you were still working on this?"

I closed my eyes briefly, irritated because his plan was working. "Someone should talk to Rose Brown again."

He scratched his cheek, trying to suppress the grin that lurked behind his feigned seriousnss. "My thoughts exactly."

I pushed myself away from the truck. "Guess that would be you since I'm not involved anymore. See ya."

"She'll never talk to me," he said, following me. "That's even if I could get in to see her. I'll bet you fifty-yard-line seats at a Cowboys game that those Brown sisters have already stepped up security around their mama."

"You're probably right, so most likely I couldn't get in to see her either." I opened my door and started to climb in.

"Your friends could, though."

I slowly turned around. "My friends?"

"You teach a quilting class at Oak Terrace Retirement Home, two floors down from Mrs. Brown. There are eight ladies in your class. Four of them have known you since you were six years old. And they've been involved with one investigation with you already, a year ago February during what was referred to as a Senior Prom. Very clever wordplay, by the way." He glanced down at his watch and smiled widely. "Today's Tuesday, and I do believe you have a class with them. Three o'clock. How convenient for everyone."

Surprised, I was speechless for a moment. First, because of his audacity. Second, because I'd completely forgotten that today was the third Tuesday of the month.

He smirked. "What's wrong, did you forget about the class? Come by my office after your meeting, please, and tell me what you find out. Note that I did say *please*." He tipped his Stetson hat.

I opened my mouth to snap back that I wasn't about to involve those ladies in a murder investigation, then closed it again. He knew I'd never be able to resist asking them about Rose Brown now, and I knew he'd eventually track me down anyway, so I said, "Okay."

He stepped back a foot, his hand gripping his chest dramatically, as if shot in the heart. "What? Benni Harper is being cooperative! Lord have mercy on us all, the end of the world is nigh upon us. A miracle has occurred."

"Oh, go milk a bull," I said childishly. I went back to my office to get the museum checkbook. A quilt made by the ladies had sold recently in our small gift shop, and I needed to pay them. When I returned to my truck, the detective was gone.

After a trip to the post office, I stopped by Blind Harry's. Elvia wasn't there, so I left her a note. Downstairs in the coffeehouse, while I was waiting for my mocha, I spotted

Sam at a table. I took my cup and went over to him.

"Hey, bud," I said, sitting down across from him. "How's it going?"

He wrapped his hands around his thick white mug. "Okay, I guess."

"Are you working today?"

He shook his head no. "I just dropped by to pick up my paycheck. I'm going over to see Bliss, but I needed to chill out for a while first."

His voice was so low, the soft buzz of late-morning customers swallowed his last few words.

"How is she doing today? Is she up for visitors?"

He drew in a deep breath, as if getting ready to lift a heavy load. "She's better. She's at her sister's house and doesn't really feel like seeing anyone. I'll tell her you said hi." He looked over at me, his dark brown eyes glossy with pain.

I reached over and put my hand on top of his. "How are you?"

He shrugged and didn't answer, already well trained in the stoic macho tradition of his Latino heritage. But a small portion of the vulnerable young boy he still was leaked out. "I can't sleep that good," he whispered.

I nodded and didn't answer.

Using both hands, he brought his mug up to his lips. After a sip, he said, "Tell Dove and Ben I'll be back out to the ranch tonight. I know I'm behind on my chores. Tell them I'll catch up this week."

"They understand, Sam. You take care now."

He nodded again, and I left him staring into his black coffee.

To relieve the sadness that had crept around my heart, I put Patty Loveless on my portable cassette player as I headed out to the ranch. I was singing along, agreeing with her wearily cynical view of male/female relationships, when I pulled into the long driveway of the ranch.

I slammed my foot on the brakes when I saw the fire truck, the paramedic van, a Highway Patrol car, and a San Celina PD car.

"Oh, no," I said out loud, my heart thumping in my chest, thinking Dove, Daddy, Isaac?

I JUMPED OUT of the truck and ran across the lawn to the house. It was empty. On the kitchen counter were casserole dishes covered with tinfoil and a half dozen pies and cakes. Voices came from behind the house, so I dashed out the back door and headed toward the barn. Outside the barn's double doors, a paramedic and a Highway Patrol officer stood shooting the breeze.

"My gramma?" I said, breathing hard.

"You mean Dove?" the paramedic asked.

I nodded.

"In there." He pointed to the barn. "But be careful, she's . . ."

I pushed past them and ran through the barn doors, expecting to see Dove stretched out on a gurney, hooked up to IVs, fighting for her life.

She was fighting all right, but not for her life.

More like for her lights.

"To the left," she yelled through my cheerleading megaphone. "Not that left, your other left. For cryin' out loud,

John, pay attention!" Big John, one of the members of the historical society, rolled his milky eyes at her and patiently moved the tall camera light to where she pointed. Behind her, Isaac sat on a director's chair, fooling around with a large square camera, grinning to himself.

Daddy walked by, carrying a small lamb whose unremitting bleats sounded like a broken car alarm.

"What's going on?" I asked him.

A resigned look on his face told me he'd been roped into this early and perhaps before he'd had his third cup of coffee. He stroked the head of the lamb, whose rhythmic cries didn't skip a beat. "Better ask your gramma, pumpkin. I'm just the hired help."

Behind him, in the middle of the barn, two women I knew from the San Celina Cattlewomen's Association were combing and brushing a white-faced calf who squirmed and called for its mama. Next to the calf, another two women, Edna McClun and Maria Ramirez, members of the Historical Society, were brushing and fiddling with the hair of another hunk of beef. A much bigger one.

And they were giggling like two schoolgirls.

A half naked Miguel, wearing only a pair of faded jeans and his gun belt, stood patiently still, his face slightly flushed, while the much shorter older women, standing on wooden milk stools, touched up his hair and dabbed bits of makeup on his smooth, brown, muscle-defined chest.

"Five minutes," Dove called through the microphone. "We've got February and March waiting in the wings. We ain't got all day."

I walked over to Isaac. "Okay," I said, laughing. "What's going on here?"

He looked up at the sound of my voice, his cracked-adobe face happy to see me. "It was your gramma's idea. I think she's calling it 'Hunks and Babes.'"

"What?"

He pointed at the bawling calf. "She said there's two things women go crazy over—handsome men and baby animals. She got the idea that a calendar showing both would sell like hotcakes. I think she's onto something."

"Not to mention the fact that the famous Isaac Lyons taking the photographs just might help sell a few."

He winked at me. "You know I'd do anything for Dove."

I put my arm around his massive shoulders and hugged him. "And that's one of the reasons you've captured my heart, you old grizzly."

The calf let out another plaintive cry.

"We're going to have to get this show on the road!" Dove yelled. "That baby's getting tired."

I went over to Miguel, who was still getting primped and powder-pouffed by the two ladies. "Miguel, baby," I said, giving him the thumbs-up sign. "Love your new career move. Let's do lunch. Have my people call your people."

He shot me an irritated frown. "My mother's making me do this."

"Ah," I said, nodding. So that was what the mysterious communication between him and Dove was about on Sunday. She had indeed gone over his head to his real boss. Unable to resist, I reached over and ran a hand over his ripply chest muscles.

"Nice and firm, aren't they?" Edna McClun said. She rapped on his left pectoral. "Like a good melon."

"The muscle definition is *muy bueno*," Maria Ramirez. "All natural, too. No steroids."

"He's certainly prime cut," I agreed, nodding solemnly. We all studied his chest closely. "I can't find a flaw anywhere."

"Would you people hurry up," Miguel complained, his

face a deep scarlet. "I've got a shift to work."

We looked at each other and burst out laughing.

"Don't worry about it," Dove said, walking by, the megaphone clutched in one hand. "I have connections with your chief who, by the way, will be Mr. April with chickens."

I turned to her, my mouth open. "Gabe's going to be in the calendar? He never told me!"

"Good," she said, her face pleased. "Then I know I can trust him to keep a secret."

"Mr. April? With chickens?"

"He won't take off his clothes," she said. "Says it ain't dignified. So we decided to go for a sophisticated look. He'll be in his tuxedo surrounded by baby chicks." She elbowed me. "Surrounded by chicks, get it?"

"I get it. Am I right in assuming all the men loitering around outside are today's models?"

She caught Elmo Ritter's arm as he walked by and asked, "Who's on the docket today?"

After adjusting his brown beret, he checked his clipboard. "There's Miguel Aragon, San Celina Police Department, and white-faced calf—Mr. January; then Bill Connor, Arroyo Grande fire fighter, with baby ducks—Mr. March; Ty O'Brien, Highway Patrol officer, with lamb—Mr. August, and Josh Dunbar, county paramedic with shih tzu puppies—Mr. June. We had to reschedule Mr. February, the SWAT team guy, cause the Siamese kittens didn't arrive. The cat lady called and said she couldn't get here until Friday."

"Fine," Dove said. "As long as we get everything wrapped by Friday afternoon so we can get it to the printer's next week." She turned and yelled into the megaphone. "Are we ready for action yet?"

"We're placing the calf now," Edna said, helping the calf's hairdressers position him in Miguel's arms.

"Oh, shit!" Miguel yelled, holding the bawling calf away from him. "What's this green stuff?"

The ladies jumped back from the splatter, laughing.

"Yes, it is," Edna said.

"Oh, man," Miguel moaned, looking down with dismay at the front of his jeans. "Don't you have any, like, house-trained cows or something?"

"Oh, no," Dove echoed. "Did you bring that extra pair of pants I told you to, Miguel?"

After getting him a new pair of jeans, Isaac cleared the barn set of everyone but him and Miguel.

While Isaac took Miguel's picture and then developed the film in the small darkroom he'd set up inside the house, Dove and I served lunch to the hungry models and helpers.

"Have you seen Sam or Bliss today?" she asked, unwrapping a huge Pyrex bowl of her famous potato salad.

"I stopped by the bookstore and talked to Sam. He seems to be doing okay, though kind of sad. He says Bliss doesn't want to see anyone right now, including him. He said to tell you he'd be back to the ranch tonight."

"My heart surely goes out to them."

A drop-dead handsome, black-haired man with eyes the color of blue jay feathers parked himself in front of Dove and held out a paper plate. He was dressed in jeans and an Hawaiian shirt.

"I thought you were on tomorrow's list," she said.

"Gotta work tomorrow. I called, and Mr. Lyons said he could fit me in today. Didn't he tell you?"

"Probably, but my brain's been a little full these days. Guess we do have to work around your schedule." She looked him up and down critically before giving him a small scoop of potato salad and one thin slice of ham. His face fell in disappointment. With an apologetic look, I followed her lead and put one roll on his plate.

"You can have more after the shoot," Dove said. "We don't want any paunchy stomachs. The camera lens sees every bulge. Did you bring your uniform?"

"Yes, ma'am," he said, eyeing her bowl of potato salad with longing.

"The shorts?"

"Yes, ma'am."

"Not them baggy ones. The short, tight ones."

"Yes, ma'am. Just like you told me."

"Good, the Doberman puppies will look real nice with the brown."

After he took his food outside, I asked, "What agency . . . ?"

"UPS," she said.

I laughed. "You're kidding."

"You know any woman who isn't half in love with her UPS man?"

Before I left for my quilting class, Isaac showed me the contact sheets of Miguel. "He's gorgeous," I said. He'd managed to make Miguel appear both dangerously sexy and adorably boyish. The calf's dark shiny eyes matched Miguel's, and the delicacy of the animal's fragile pink nose and gangly feet was a brilliant contrast to Miguel's smoldering sexuality. Dove's idea about men and baby animals was right on the mark. Just based on Miguel's photograph, I'd buy this calendar in a heartbeat. And one for each of my friends.

"A photographer's only as good as his subject," Isaac said modestly.

I checked my watch. As fun and distracting as this interval had been, I had to get to my quilting class. My stomach churned, remembering what I had to accomplish there today.

"What's going on, Benni?" Isaac asked. His discerning

photographer's eye had caught the change in my expression. Then again, I never have been the queen of deception.

I explained what Detective Hudson wanted me to do and my mixed feelings about it.

"Maybe you should talk to Gabe," he suggested.

I shook my head no. "He doesn't need that right now. It would just cause a big fuss between him and this detective and maybe some problems between the departments. What can it hurt to just quiz the ladies about the past? Knowing them, they'd bring it up anyway."

"Sounds like you know what you're doing, then." The doubt in his face was evident. "Anything I can do to help?"

"Not really, but you could do me one big favor."

"Name it."

I handed back the contact sheets. "Just don't make my husband look *too* sexy, okay? I've got enough competition as it is."

He leaned down and kissed my cheek. "You don't have a single thing to worry about. I guarantee you've wrestled that man's heart to the ground and hog-tied it for life."

I laughed, hoping what he said was true. "And without a bustier or a garter belt. Thanks, Isaac, you always know just the right thing to say."

"Old age and lots of bad road gives a man a certain cockeyed wisdom, I guess."

"Cockeyed or not, it works for me."

PERCHED HIGH ON a hill overlooking the twisting two-lane highway to Morro Bay, Oak Terrace Retirement Home was a group of salmon-colored buildings where many of San Celina's senior citizens were living the final years of their lives. It had an ambulatory side where the seniors shared rooms and ate in a communal cafeteria, but for all intents and purposes were on their own. Most of the rooms peered out over alfalfa fields and pastures where the seniors watched the cycle of life in the cattle that dotted the scrubby range. Then there was the hospital side. Death Row, the ladies in my quilting group called it without a bit of compunction.

"We're sorry," said Thelma, who at one time owned the largest feed store in the county and had sold me my first pair of spurs when I was seven years old. "We forgot you're a civilian." That's what they called the world outside their exclusive group. Now that I was married to a cop, I was used to their gallow's humor, though I'll admit the first time they called it Death Row, the shocked look on my face caused joyous titters to ripple through my group of eight regulars. Even the term *civilian* reminded me of how Gabe and his colleagues viewed those who didn't carry a badge.

And I guess what these ladies had was a badge of sorts. The badge of time, of making it this far with the ability to still laugh at and enjoy life. So when I proposed we name our group, since we basically functioned as an in-house quilt guild, the fact that they chose Coffin Star Quilt Guild didn't surprise me one bit. We even had black sweatshirts printed with our guild's name in fluorescent pink letters, which each of them was wearing today. The first time I took the ladies to a quilt show wearing the matching sweatshirts, we caused quite a stir and a whole lot of laughter.

They were all set up in the craft room when I arrived. We were working on baby quilts for Gabe's officers to carry in their police cars to give to kids taken out of violent home situations by Social Services. My function was less of a teacher than a bringer of news, donated quilting supplies and fabric, ideas, patterns, magazines, and gossip. There was nothing they enjoyed more than hearing everything that was going on at the folk art museum, Elvia's bookstore, the police station, and the Historical Museum. They especially loved it when I was involved in some crime, as I'd been a few times, and were generous with advice on how I should proceed. People's love lives intrigued them to no end, though Elvia and Emory's static romance was frustrating them, and Gabe and I had been getting on too well to suit them. So, just to prime them, the first thing I did was tell them about Bliss and Sam, their secret romance, her unplanned pregnancy, Lydia's arrival on the scene, the engagement party, Giles's murder, and then Bliss getting shot and losing the baby.

"Oh, my," Martha Pickering said, her hand digging in her sweatshirt sleeve for a violet-embroidered handkerchief. She dabbed at her white powdered temple. "That's more than a month of stories on *All My Children*." The others nodded in agreement, their fingers still quilting on the Tumbling Blocks quilt in the frame.

"That Brown family," Juby Daniels said, shaking her head. "They've certainly had their share of baby troubles through the years."

"Starting with Rose herself," Leona Shelton said. Leona was turning ninety-two this year and was our oldest guild member. Though I had to thread her needles for her, she still sewed a straighter, truer quilt stitch than I ever would, using her experienced fingers to guide her as much as her washed-out-denim blue eyes. She'd been San Celina's seamstress of choice for years and years. Her tiny shop downtown across from the courthouse had been the premier place among the rich and powerful for hearing about who was cheating on who, who was having a baby, and often whose baby it *really* was. She still remained a virtual encyclopedia of information of San Celina's citizenry. If you'd put her and Mr. Foglino together, they could have probably blackmailed the whole town.

"Do you remember when her babies died?" I asked casually.

Her pencilled eyebrows moved a notch upwards. "You know about them?"

I stopped stitching and sat back in my chair. "One of her great-granddaughters, JJ, is a quilt artist at the co-op. She told me how the Seven Sisters ranch got its name."

"I surely do remember," Leona said, turning her eyes back to the red and brown quilt. "Rose Brown about went crazy. All them funerals so close together. I made the christening gowns for every one of them babies. Hand-stitched lilies of the valley around the hems. Three hundred–count imported Egyptian cotton with Belgian lace trim. Some nun went blind making that lace, mark my words. Each of those babies was buried in them. I think about that sometimes, my beautiful stitches, that lovely lace, being eaten by worms."

The others nodded, murmuring at the waste. I flinched inwardly at the graphic scene it painted in my imagination. "So, how did they die? JJ didn't know." I looked back down at the quilt. It wasn't exactly a lie. JJ hadn't known how they died.

"Oh, they say it was just natural causes," Leona said, pushing her needle in and out, in and out. "But there was rumors."

"Really?" Martha said. "I was only fifteen at the time, but I don't remember people talking."

"It was kept pretty quiet. Those Browns were prominent folks even back then," Leona said, stopping to cough into a crumpled tissue. She wiped her mouth delicately and continued. "He was a judge, you know. Quite the ladies' man, let me tell you. Good-looking as that husband of yours, Benni, and with none of Gabe's scruples. Rumors were he could have any woman he wanted in their crowd and heard tell he practically did."

"What were the rumors about the babies?" I prompted.

"That somebody killed them, plain and simple," Leona said with a quick nod.

"Oh, my . . . oh, dear . . . oh, Leona, really," the women around the quilt exclaimed.

"Don't shoot the messenger," Leona said, sniffing. "That's what they were saying behind closed doors."

"But who would kill four innocent babies?" asked Mattie Lee Jones, who was the progeny winner of the group with 27 grandchildren and 18 great-grandchildren to her credit. She took great pride in constantly reminding the group of her huge, supposedly close-knit family.

"Mattie Lee," Leona said, "get your head out of that sandbox you call a life. Not many families qualify as the Waltons. Not even your messy group of misfits. Every day of this old world babies are hurt and sometimes killed by their own parents, sisters, brothers, and who knows who else. Why do you think we're makin' these quilts for the police department? And it'll be that way till Jesus comes back."

"Well, I just can't imagine it," Mattie Lee said, her pointy chin jerking up, insulted. "I think you're just spreading vicious old rumors without substance. And as for that remark about my wonderful family, I think—"

"Who cares what you think?" Leona said. "As a matter of fact, why don't you think about kissing my—"

"Leona! Mattie Lee!" Thelma said, her voice sounding the way it did when she caught us kids jumping on the expensive hay bales in back of her store. "Now, let's not set a bad example for Benni here. She's still at an impressionable age, you know. We have a responsibility."

Leona looked over at me and winked. Mattie Lee's chin moved an inch higher. I bit my lip trying not to laugh.

"Okay, just assuming . . ."—I gave Mattie Lee an apologetic look—". . . *pretending* that this horrible rumor had some truth to it, why do you think anyone would do such a terrible thing?"

Leona shook her head. "Who knows, Benni? With what I've seen in my ninety-two years I'm only certain about one thing. Just when you think human beings can't sink any lower, they do. On the other hand, there's more good bein' done out there than bad. So far, anyway."

"Maybe it was for the insurance," Selma Gonzales suggested. She'd been a legal secretary for fifty years and had a kind and intelligently practical view of every situation. "That's always a consideration."

"Did people insure babies back then?" I asked.

"Maybe one of the older sisters did it out of jealousy," Leona said. "Or the judge himself because he thought they weren't his children."

"Rose Brown committing adultery?" Mattie Lee exclaimed. "Why, I can't even imagine that."

Leona gave Mattie Lee a disgusted look.

"Maybe it was Rose's sister," Juby said. "She was an old maid. Heard she had a crush on the judge her whole life. Maybe *she* killed the babies out of jealousy."

"There was the nanny, too," Selma offered.

"Or the butler," Martha added with a giggle.

"Oh, girls," Thelma said. "They didn't have a butler."

I sat back in my chair, my head spinning. These ladies had just handed me even more suspects than I'd started with. That was certainly not my intention when I started questioning them.

"That nanny, Eva something-or-other," Leona said. "I heard she's still living."

Knoll, I filled in silently. The nanny who was Mr. Foglino's mother's best friend's neighbor.

"Still living?" Mattie Lee said. "My goodness, she'd be

ninety-six or -seven. Would she even be able to—"

"To what?" Leona said, narrowing one pale eye in Mattie Lee's direction. "Be *coherent?*"

Mattie Lee's face turned pink, and she leaned back over the quilt, stitching furiously.

"What was her last name?" I asked, just to double-check Mr. Foglino's information.

"Knoll," Leona said, her voice triumphant. "Her name is Eva Knoll. Pretty good for someone in her *nineties*, don't you think?"

"Does anyone know where she lives?" I asked, sitting forward in my seat. Next to talking to Rose Brown again, the nanny who was there when the babies died would be a great source of information.

The women shook their heads no.

"After the last baby died, she was let go," Leona said. "Rumors were she was paid to go away. That tells me there was something fishy going on."

"Did you hear where she went?" I asked, unrolling some white thread and snipping it off.

"Don't reckon she'd go far," Leona said, "if I remember right." She glared at Mattie Lee. "And I do believe I do. Her only family was her father and a child. A boy, I think. Most likely she settled in San Celina County somewhere."

"Do any of you ever see or talk to Rose Brown?" I asked.

"Huh!" Leona snorted. "Miss High-and-Mighty Brown leave her private tower and walk among the heathens? Don't think so."

"Now, Leona," Juby said, shaking her head of poodle hair. "You know Rose is not able to socialize." She gave me a kind look. "Rose Brown has her own suite on the other side of the home, near the offices. She doesn't take her meals with us. But she has good girls. They visit her regularly and hired her private nurses. Tell you the truth, I don't really know why she's here and not at her lovely home, but they say she didn't want to die there. I don't think she's quite all there, poor dear."

The conversation drifted slowly away from the Browns and back to their own lives and the doings of their children, grandchildren and great-grandchildren. I didn't push it, figuring I got what I needed—a confirmation of Eva Knoll's identity.

When our hour session was over, we had a quick business meeting. I showed them the check for the quilt.

"What would you all like done with it?" I asked. Though we had a guild account, they often liked donating it to the Oak Terrace Friendship Fund. It provided bingo and snack money for people in the retirement home who had no families and were barely making ends meet.

"Donate it to the Friendship Fund," Thelma said. "We have plenty in our account." The others nodded in agreement.

After hugging and kissing everyone good-bye, I went upstairs to the offices to take the check to the accounting clerk. After shooting the breeze with her, I walked down the long corridor toward the exit, passing by a large, airy sunroom. Normally crowded, it was empty this early evening. The large clock over the gurgling fountain read five o'clock. Dinner was served at five-thirty, so everyone was probably in their rooms getting ready.

Everyone except Rose Brown. She was, to my surprise, sitting in a wheelchair alone, gazing out the picture window at the English rose garden and beyond at the cars driving by on the highway below. I hesitated for a few seconds, then decided that this might be my only chance to speak to her, so I'd better grab it. She was dressed in expensive-looking camel slacks and a brown cashmere sweater. Good leather shoes covered her small feet. In her lap, on top of a nubby, hand-knitted throw, her hands clutched a neat leather purse that matched her shoes. She didn't turn around or even react when I walked up behind her and softly called her name.

"Mrs. Brown," I said again, a little louder, and walked around so she could see me.

She looked up, her aqua eyes cloudy with age. Really looking at her this time, I realized what a beautiful woman she must have been. And how much Bliss favored her.

"Mrs. Brown, my name is Benni Harper. We talked the other day at the wine tasting."

She nodded mutely. Her face was slack today, traces of spittle pooled in the corners of her pale pink mouth. It was hard to believe she was the same woman I'd talked to only a few days ago, but I knew how, at this age, good days and bad days were as unpredictable as our Central Coast winds.

"Can I ask you some questions? It won't take long, I promise."

She blinked slowly and nodded again.

I hesitated again. Questioning someone this elderly, this helpless, seemed cruel and heartless. And, considering her condition today, so much worse than a few days ago at the wine tasting, maybe even pointless.

And what about those babies? I heard Detective Hudson's voice in my head.

I swallowed and said, "I'm sorry about your babies, Mrs. Brown."

Her eyes looked into mine at the mention of babies. Her mouth started moving, trying to say something. I bent closer, trying to encourage her.

"My babies," she said, her voice low and harsh. "They died."

I knelt down next to her wheelchair. "Yes, I know. I'm sorry."

"Dr. Jacobs was so good to me. We drank tea."

"I'm sure he was." I wracked my brain trying to think of what I could ask her. "Mrs. Brown, do you remember Eva Knoll? She took care of your babies. Do you remember?"

Her eyes teared up upon hearing Eva's name. "The judge sent her away. He said she was a bad woman. She just flew away. Like a bird." A pale, age-spotted hand grabbed mine, pinning it to the cold handle of the wheelchair. "She wasn't bad." She squeezed my hand, then let go and crooked her finger at me to come closer. I bent toward her.

"Rouge," she whispered, her head nodding. "The men love it. They don't even know we have it on."

Great, more grooming tips. I tried to lead her back to the subject of Eva Knoll, maybe find out her whereabouts. "Where did Eva Knoll go?" Before she had a chance to answer, we were interrupted by a sharp voice.

"Excuse me, who are you?"

I stood up and faced the stern-faced woman dressed in a nurse's uniform. Unlike the rest of the employees of Oak Terrace, she wasn't wearing a name tag, so I assumed she was one of the private nurses hired by the family.

"I was just saying hello to Mrs. Brown. We met the other day at the wine tasting in Eola Beach."

The woman peered at me suspiciously and said, "She's not up to visitors today." She'd obviously been warned that people might come by and quiz her charge. She fiddled with the knitted throw in Mrs. Brown's lap, then pushed her out of the room without another word to me.

I stood there for a moment, contemplating what Rose Brown had just told me. Her husband had sent Eva Knoll away. Why? Had she been involved with the death of the babies? If so, why hadn't he turned her over to the authorities? I tried to sort out the things I'd learned. I had to find Eva Knoll, if she was still alive, and talk to her. But how? Then an idea formed.

Before going to the Sheriff's Department to tell the detective what I'd learned, I stopped by my friend Amanda Landry's law office to beg the use of her very capable investigator, Leilani, to locate Eva Knoll.

Amanda's office was above the Ross store downtown. It was located up a set of narrow, steep marble stairs. Inside the small reception room, Muddy Waters played gut-aching blues from a small stereo hidden behind a bushy green fern. Though I'd known Amanda for only a short time and we definitely rooted for different college teams—she was a diehard 'Bama fan—we'd become good friends. A faithful, dyed-in-the-wool Crimson Tide Alabaman, she'd followed her husband to San Francisco, and when that didn't work out, decided she loved the wild and woolly west enough to make it home. She'd worked for years as a prosecutor for both San Francisco and San Celina, but had sometime back started her own practice with an inheritance she'd acquired from her father, a rich Birmingham judge who wasn't famous for his honesty, integrity, or marital faithfulness.

Luckily Amanda inherited her late blues-singing mother's honesty as well as her weakness for down-and-out musicians.

"He's the best I ever had," she told me as I sat in her office, decorated in deep crimson and dark blue. Leilani was in her adjoining office using her numerous contacts and CD-ROM programs to get a lead on Eva Knoll. "I'm in heaven. I'll never give him up. Never." Her antique oak chair creaked when she leaned back. With the tip of a yellow school pencil, she scratched a spot in her thick head of auburn hair.

"We'll see," I said, having heard this song and dance before.

"I'm serious," she said, giving me her Mississippi-wide smile. The same gorgeous smile that won her almost as many cases as her spur-sharp intelligence. "He's perfect. Doesn't miss a thing. I go to bed happy every night."

"He's a musician. You know how reliable they are."

"He calls me Miss Mandy," she said, her eyes twinkling.

"And you let him live? He must be good."

She sat forward in her seat and pointed the yellow pencil at me. "I'm telling you, cowgirl, my house has never been cleaner. Did you know that place on your stove, where those little round things are?"

"You mean the burners?" Cooking was not one of Amanda's many talents.

"Did you know the thing they sit on, that whole top of the stove, lifts up? You should see what was under there. Disgusting! But, bless his blues-lovin' heart, he's thorough. He cleans *everywhere*," she said, heaving a big sigh. "He's not cheap, but, heavens to Dixie, he's worth it."

"Just don't get romantically involved with him," I warned, "or you'll be out a great housecleaner."

"Never," she declared. "Boyfriends come and go, but a good housecleaner, *that's* hard to find."

Within the hour, Leilani found the information I was seeking.

"She's still alive," Leilani said, her brown, fashion-model face as sober as a prison guard's. "Or at least someone who is signing her name and collecting her Social Security checks is."

"How do you find out things like that, Leilani?" I asked. "I mean, isn't it illegal or something? Privacy laws and stuff?"

"Never ask Leilani *how*," Amanda said, nodding thanks

at her investigator. "Just act like Elvis and say thankyou-verymuch."

"Thank you very much," I said.

"No problem," Leilani replied, her facial muscles not moving a bit. She turned and left the room, shutting the door behind her.

"Does she ever smile?" I asked Amanda. It was hard to imagine the two of them working together, considering how much Amanda liked to laugh.

"I think she cracked a small one when I gave her a Christmas bonus last year. Hey, who needs smiles when you can work the miracles she does. The DA's office still hasn't forgiven me for stealing her."

We both glanced at the address Leilani had found.

"A post office box in Mariposa Valley," I said. "That's out in the Carrizo Plains. I haven't been there in years." The Carrizo Plains was in the far eastern part of San Celina County. Except for a few desert dwellers and sporadic groups of bird-watchers and hikers, the barren Carrizo Plains was pretty much left to its own counsel. Back in the fifties, there was a small flurry of interest by some Los Angeles developers who claimed it would be the next Palm Springs. Some streets were built and lots sold. There was even a motel and gas station constructed for the benefit of prospective buyers. But some kind of complication with water rights doomed the project, and all that was left were some windswept streets, rusty gas pumps, and the shell of the fifties-style motel called the Mariposa Valley Inn.

"I had to interview a witness out there once when I worked as a prosecutor," Amanda said. "The only way to find anyone is to ask at the fire station. It's about a half mile past the old motel."

I folded the piece of paper and slipped it in my back

pocket. "I'll give it to Detective Hudson and let him take care of it."

"Hey, why are you doin' his work for him, might I ask?"

I smiled. "Just to show him I can. He's an arrogant Texan."

"Oh, my, a Texan. I dated an attorney from Fort Worth once. Emphasis on the word once. By all means, use all my resources to put him in his place."

"Thanks, Amanda. Again, I owe you one."

"Who's countin'?"

I used my cell phone to call Detective Hudson. "I'll be there in fifteen minutes tops."

"It's almost seven o'clock," he said. "Where have you been? Your class was over at four-thirty, and it's only a ten-minute drive."

"I'll explain when I get there," I said, hanging up before he could harangue me. I wasn't going to pay cell phone prices to be nagged at by the likes of a twangy-tongued detective. I called Gabe's office where I got his voice mail so I called my house, hoping to find him there. When our answering machine replied, I left a quick message, trying not to project where or with whom he might be.

I sat for a moment staring at Eva Knoll's address. She was a very old woman. Remembering Rose Brown and the guilt I felt about questioning her, I made a quick decision. What I was about to do would make Detective Hudson spit nails and quite possibly strangle me, but morally and humanely, it seemed my only choice. Before I went to his office, I dropped by the electronics store downtown and bought a small hand-sized tape recorder, the kind Emory used for interviews. I took it out of the box, slipped in one of the tiny tapes, and stuck it in my purse.

At the Sheriff's Department, the front desk clerk, a young woman with a painfully sunburnt nose and dressed in a Hawaiian print dress, was hefting her red patent leather backpack over her shoulder, getting ready to leave. The offices appeared to be empty except for the departing receptionist.

"Benni Harper?" the young woman asked. She picked up a green apple from her desk and took a bite.

"Yes."

"He's really pissed," the young woman said, around chews. "I'm a temp. Thank goodness. I'd never work full-time for these nutcases. And they're supposed to be the good guys? *Sheesh*. Third office to your right. See ya."

"Thanks," I called after her, wondering if I should maybe follow her out and phone my information in.

I knew Detective Hudson was going to be annoyed that I didn't run over to his office the minute my quilt class was over, but I hoped he'd be appeased when he heard I had the name and address, or at least the post office box number, of the nanny who cared for Rose Brown's children. Not to mention the information I'd just gotten from Rose Brown herself. Maybe the killer of the babies had been living in San Celina all along, out in the desolate Carrizo Plains. That still didn't explain why Giles would be killed, but I was confident that talking to this Eva Knoll would bring us one step closer to finding out who killed Giles and why.

When I came within his eyesight he bellowed, with a drill sergeant's snappy bark. "Where have you been? Get in here. Now."

"Unless you can the attitude," I snapped back, "I'm outta here." I added in a lower voice, "Jerk."

He came barreling out of his chair. "What?"

Keeping my voice calm, I said, "Quit acting like a Nazi. I got here as soon as I could. What is your problem?"

Without answering, he inhaled deeply, sharp points of

color staining his cheeks. He gestured for me to follow him into his office. He shut the door behind me and nodded at a visitor's chair against the wall. I glanced around the compact office where two black-and-chrome office desks faced each other. One held a scattered group of Little League, ballet recital, and soccer team pictures, used coffee cups, a crumpled McDonald's bag, a Beanie Baby snake, and stacks of files. The desk Detective Hudson sat behind contained only a green desk blotter, a black ceramic pencil cup filled with pens, a phone, and a picture of a redheaded girl about five years old sitting on the hood of his pickup truck. A sticker on his pencil cup showed a red circle with a slash through the word "whining." Between the two desks was a calligraphy sign that mocked the Serenity Prayer—"God grant me the serenity to accept the things I cannot change, the courage to change the things I can, and the weaponry to make the difference."

"Very inspiring," I said wryly, nodding at the poster.

"What did you find out?" he asked.

"Geeze, let me take a breath. What's the big hurry?"

"The big hurry is I'm getting my butt reamed out by my superiors because the sheriff is getting harassed from two prominent families—the Nortons and the Browns. One wants it solved, one wants us to quit poking around. I'll leave it to you to guess who's who."

"Well, sor-ry," I said, stretching out the word. "But that's still no reason to be such a jerk. In case you forgot, I'm not on the payroll, buddy. This is purely voluntary on my part, so save your nasty remarks and bad attitude for someone collecting a county paycheck."

He settled back in his chair, crossed his legs, and rested his hands across his flat stomach. Today he wore a pale yellow Arrow shirt and sedate, tobacco brown bullhide boots that looked like they cost a thousand bucks. "You're absolutely right, Benni, and please accept my sincere and heartfelt apology. I'm just feeling like the rope between the cow and the cowboy. Know what I mean?"

I nodded, suspicious at his suddenly genial mood.

"So, what do you have for me?" he asked, keeping his voice even and pleasant. But I sensed the tension and determination behind his good-ole-boy demeanor. He really, really wasn't going to like what I was going to tell him.

"I have the name and whereabouts of the nanny who worked for Judge and Rose Brown when she had the two sets of twins."

He sat forward in his chair, his face amazed. I have to admit one-upping him, to quote Dove, dearly gladdened my heart. "Shoot, that's great! But wait, that was back in the twenties. She'd have to be—"

"Ninety-seven and, according to my sources, still alive. Or at least someone is signing and cashing her Social Security checks."

He jumped up and grabbed his pale cowboy hat from the credenza behind him. "Let me have her address. I'm going to talk to her right now before she croaks on me."

I stood up and looked him squarely in the eyes. "No."

He stopped dead, his hat still in his hands. Anger flashed like a dust devil across his face, then was gone. He took a couple of slow, controlled breaths then asked, "Why not?"

I already had my answer thought out. "What's the difference between interviewing and interrogating?"

"What?"

"Tell me the textbook definitions."

"What are you talking about?"

"Tell me."

"Look, I'm not a barbarian."

"The definitions, please."

He gave a sharp, irritated sound, then said, "Interviewing

is a non-accusatory, fact-finding mission where you let the suspect/witness do the talking. Interrogating is an active, confrontational method of questioning where you give the suspect a psychological reason to confess."

"Now how old did I say Eva Knoll is?"

"Ninety-seven, but what's that—"

"She's an elderly woman, Detective Hudson. And no matter what she's seen or done, I'm not going to let you browbeat her. I'm married to a cop. I've seen the techniques. I've *experienced* them. I know a so-called interview can turn into an interrogation in two seconds. I'm not going to allow that to happen. We'll go see her tomorrow. It's too late tonight and it's a bit of a drive. Please note the pronoun *we*. And one other thing. I'm going to do the talking."

He threw his hat down on the desktop. "There is no way you are interviewing this or any other possible witness. Give me that name and address now."

"No."

"I swear, if you don't, I'll . . . I'll . . ." he sputtered.

"You'll what? Call Gabe and tell on me? Inject me with truth serum? Lock me up for the night?" I held out my wrists. "Go ahead, book me."

He literally growled at me, "Don't think I won't call your husband. I'll tell him you've interfered in this from the very beginning, that I've asked you repeatedly to stay out of it, that you're jeopardizing my investigation, and that I'll have to go to my superiors if he can't control you. I'll embarrass you and him in front of all his colleagues."

I smiled serenely, knowing I had him. "And you know what I'll tell him and your boss? That you cajoled and harassed me into helping you on this case. That you didn't have the resources or feel confident enough to solve it without the help of a lowly civilian. Worse than that, a *female* civilian. And then I'll give the story to my cousin, the journalist. He's always looking for amusing things to make fun of in his column. He'll make mincemeat of your burgeoning career here on the Central Coast. You'll be the laughingstock of every police agency in the county. Nope, you got me into this, and now I've got the upper hand. I suggest you deal with it."

He gave a nasty smile. "With your reputation, who do you think they'll believe? Admit it, I have you there."

That's when I pulled the ace out of my sleeve. Or rather, the tape recorder out of my purse. "They'll believe me, Detective, because I've been recording key conversations with you for days, and the tapes are in my safety deposit box." I wiggled the tiny tape recorder.

He stared at the recorder, opened his mouth and started to say something, then closed it. His brown eyes were dark and angry, and I tried to quell the anxiety in my chest and the truth on my face. It was the biggest bluff I'd ever attempted, me of the billboard face.

Slowly a smile tugged at the corner of his mouth. Then he let out a small laugh. Shaking his head, he said, "Oh, man, you're good."

Surprised, I laughed, too, and said, "Yeah, I know."

"With an ego to match mine," he added.

"Meet me tomorrow. Nine o'clock at the folk art museum."

"I'll be there with my whips and thumbscrews."

"I told you, Detective, no browbeating on my watch."

He lifted his eyebrows slightly. "My dear Mrs. Harper, who said they're for the old lady?"

In the parking lot I called home again to see if Gabe was there. When the answering machine took the call, I hung up.

The driveway was empty. Inside the house, it was apparent Gabe hadn't been home yet—no briefcase or dirty glasses in the sink. Another dinner with Lydia? Annoyed, I listened to my message to him on the answering machine, then the one after it.

"Sweetheart," he said. "I have a dinner with the city manager and then I'm going to drop by Lydia's hotel to talk about Sam. She and I have missed each other all day. I'll be home as soon as I can. *Te amo*."

"Yeah, me, too, Friday," I said, feeling sad rather than angry. I fed Scout, then heated up a can of soup and watched a couple of sitcoms on TV before falling asleep. The sound of the shower running awakened me, and I glanced at the bedside clock—ten-twenty.

"How was your dinner with the city manager?" I asked when Gabe climbed into bed.

"Fine," he said, turning to me and pulling me into his arms, nuzzling my neck.

I lay there for a moment, tempted by the masculine rasp of his beard, his gentle, seductive tongue, then pulled away. "I'm tired."

"All right," he said without argument. He kissed my temple, then settled into his side of the bed.

I lay there in the dark and listened to his breathing slow down until he fell asleep. The lacy curtains covering our bedroom window made snowflake patterns on the ceiling, and I watched them move and change, like all the lives surrounding me, like my own life.

SAM CAME BY the next morning and had breakfast with us, his dark eyes ringed blue with fatigue.

"How is Bliss?" I asked after Gabe left for work. I tossed some leftover bacon in Scout's dish. His happy tail beat against my leg.

"She's doing okay," Sam said, leaning his chair back on two legs. "She still won't talk about it, though. Says we just gotta move on." His young face looked troubled. "What do you think she means by that?"

"I have no idea, Sam," I said, taking his plate. "All I can suggest is give her time. Losing a baby and getting shot are both extremely traumatic."

"What should I do?"

"Just listen. Don't try to push her. Let her feel what she needs to feel. That's all I know to tell you."

"She told me last night she's thinking about taking a leave from the police department. She said she might go up north for a while with her mom and sister. Don't tell Dad. He doesn't know yet."

"How do you feel about that?"

"I don't want to go up north. I just got my life together down here."

I scraped a plate into the garbage can. "Only you can make that decision."

"Do you think it'll hurt our relationship?"

Determined to be honest, I said, "I have no idea, but it would be hard to build a relationship with someone if they aren't around."

"That's kinda what I thought. Maybe we don't love each other as much as we thought."

"Then again, maybe a separation will help you both see what you really want."

He nodded, his face miserable. "Like I said, don't tell Dad any of this. Or Mom. I haven't decided yet what I'm going to do."

"You have my word," I said, flattered he'd confide in me first. There was no doubt I'd miss him like crazy if he left.

He let the front of his chair drop on the kitchen floor

with a thump. Scout went over and laid his head in Sam's lap, and Sam massaged his ears, causing Scout to sigh deeply. "All I gotta say, *madrastra*, is being an adult sucks. It sucks big-time."

"Yes, I know," I said and poured myself another cup of coffee. "This I do know."

DETECTIVE HUD ARRIVED at the folk art museum at five minutes to nine. He wore a pink shirt, another tweedy Western jacket and black-cherry-colored boots.

"Just how many pairs of boots do you own?" I asked, walking out to his truck.

"Twenty-two," he said. "But that's nothing. My mother owns forty."

"The infamous mother. I don't even believe she exists."

He opened the passenger door, a bland look on his face. "Oh, believe me, she exists. Where's your hound dog?"

"Left him home today. It's a long, hot drive."

He came around and climbed into the driver's seat. "Okay, enough small talk. Where are we going?"

"Mariposa Valley."

"Where's that?"

"Out on the Carrizo Plains. Eastern part of San Celina County. Just get on 101 North, and I'll tell you where to turn off."

He put the truck into gear and pulled out of the parking lot. "Put on some music, or I'll punish your insubordination by forcing you to listen to me sing."

With Dale Watson singing low-down, truck-driving, honky-tonk country, I directed him to turn off on Highway 58 outside of Atascadero and headed east on the winding, two-lane highway toward Mariposa Valley. In the distance, the Temblor mountain range rose stark and forbidding against the white-blue morning sky. We passed small herds of cattle grazing among the long grasses, bunched together around an occasional wind-carved oak. Then the land changed to pure prairie, and the sky turned a deep solid blue. Birds flew high above us, swooping in the currents, too far away to tell if they were peregrine falcons or one of the many types of hawks that live out here on the desolate plains—red-tailed, Cooper's, marsh, and rough-legged hawks.

"Hard to believe we're in the same county," the detective commented. "How far are we going?"

"It's about seventy miles to the fire station. That's where the post office and the library is, too. I'm hoping someone there will give us an address."

We passed a huge sun-faded billboard. He slowed down and read out loud, "WELCOME TO MARIPOSA VALLEY—2 1/2-ACRE PLOTS—GOLF COURSE, POOLS, SHOPPING CENTER, GOOD SCHOOLS—TOMORROW'S PLANNED COMMUNITY TODAY." He glanced over at me. "What *is* this place?"

"That sign is almost as old as me. Back in the early sixties Mariposa Valley was apparently being advertised as the up-and-coming place to buy property. There were twenty-five thousand acres to be sold, as the sign said, in two-and-a-half-acre plots, and a whole town was going to be built. They wanted to name it Paradise Valley, but I think that name was already taken. Anyway, except for some die-hard desert rats of the human variety, the only things that prosper out here now are a lot of mule deer, lizards, coyotes, sandhill cranes, and the occasional rattler. The only time it really gets crowded is when the bird-watchers flock out here to add to their life lists."

"What happened to the developer's great plan?"

I reached for my purse and dug around for a rubberband. This time of year out here, it would probably get close to ninety, and the sun coming in the window was already turning my thick hair into an uncomfortable blanket on my neck. "It was missing one important element—water." I zipped up my purse, irritated because I spend a fortune buying those fabric-covered hair scrunchies, yet never seemed to have one when I needed it. "You have a rubberband or a piece of string or something?"

"Check the glove compartment."

I opened it, and next to the neat black leather map holder was a bright pink Barbie scrunchy. Good enough. I pulled my hair into a high ponytail and turned to stare out the window. "It shouldn't be real hard to find her. I don't imagine there's more than a couple of hundred people who live out here these days."

"Then maybe we can get this cleared up today."

"I sure hope so," I said.

We passed only one other vehicle in over an hour, a San Celina Sourdough Bakery truck. Except for a couple of wind-blasted farmhouses, miles of black sage, manzanita, and chaparral, and a cluster of rusty combines laced with shiny-feathered crows, we could have been driving on Mars. Every once in a while we passed an abandoned car skeleton, bleached almost colorless by the harsh, prairie elements, squatting among the grasses—a twentieth-century reminder of nature's uncompromising power. The desolation out here had always slightly unnerved something deep inside me and though I'd eat a plateful of hay before admitting it, I was glad for Detective Hudson's presence and especially the gun underneath his tweed cowboy jacket.

"We're almost there," I said when we passed by the closed Butterfly Cafe and the graffiti-decorated, abandoned motel. I pointed to our right at a group of buildings about a mile away.

Outside the combination fire station/community building a single person stood watering a struggling section of lawn. We pulled into the parking lot next to the only other car, a tan Toyota pickup. I was right about the temperature. The hot and dusty air hit us with a slap when we stepped out of his air-conditioned truck. The person watering, a tall, proud-looking Latina dressed in engineer-striped overalls and a white tank top, watched us curiously. There was something vaguely familiar about her, but I couldn't put my finger on it.

"Let me do the talking," I said in a low voice.

"I will not," he replied.

"You'll blow it," I spat.

He grabbed my elbow, then swung around to the front of me so his back was to the woman watering, blocking her from my view. "Look, I've been extremely patient so far, but I'm not going to let an inexperienced civilian screw up this chance for me."

"*You* look. The people who live out here aren't like regular people. Many of them are hermits and other loners who are very skittish about anyone they don't know. I have connections with some of the ranching families out here and so have a better chance at getting them to talk."

He stood with his hands on his hips, a condescending sneer on his face. "You honestly think you can do better than me?"

I folded my arms across my chest. "Yes, I do. If they find out you're a cop, they'll clam up, and we'll never find out anything."

He stepped aside and swept his arm out dramatically. "Then by all means, go ahead. But I'm warning you, if you blow it, I'll—"

"Fire me?" I finished. "Detective, just follow me, keep your mouth shut, and your gun ready."

"You are really asking for it, Mrs. Harper."

I ignored him and started toward the woman in overalls, putting on a friendly smile. "Hey," I said.

"Hey," she repeated, her handsome face open but wary.

"My name's Benni Harper, and this is . . . my friend . . . uh, Hud."

Squinting into the bright sun, she nodded at the detective. The hose she was watering with sputtered, and she turned around, straightening the kink in it. "Harper," she said, when the water started flowing smooth again. "I used to know a Wade Harper when I was a bartender in San Celina. A place called Trigger's."

"Wade was my late husband's brother. Trigger's closed awhile back. Lost their liquor license."

"I heard. So, you're Jack Harper's wife? I remember him, too, 'cept he was a lot quieter than Wade. He left good tips. Nice eyes." She put her thumb over the hose's metal lip to make a thin spray.

"Yes," I said, remembering Jack's gentle brown eyes. "He did have nice eyes. He died a few years ago in a car accident."

"That's rough. I'm sorry."

"Thank you."

She peered at me closer. "You know, I feel like I've seen you somewhere. Did you hang out at Trigger's, too?"

"Not much. But I know what you mean. You look familiar to me, too. I grew up in San Celina. My dad and gramma own a ranch east of the city."

She walked over to turn off the spigot. "Cattle?" she said over her shoulder.

"Yep, some Angus, some Santa Gertrudis, some Hereford crosses. My dad likes to experiment with different breeds."

She turned back to face me, her brown, oval face thoughtful, then said, "I got it! We sat across from each other at a Cattlewomen's Association Christmas luncheon about five years ago. Over at that Mexican restaurant near the Goodwill store. A lady next to you was talking about antique buttons."

"That's right," I said. "She had one that was worth two hundred dollars, remember? We were flabbergasted."

"Yeah, I remember. That was when I was still with my first husband, Danny Wheaton." She made a sour face that was more telling than words.

"I know the Wheatons. They own a ranch north of the city. Nothing but Black Angus. Danny and I went to high school together." *And he was a spoiled, rednecked jerk if I remember correctly,* I added to myself.

"That's them. Meanest bunch of people you ever saw. Especially the mother. Danny was her pride and joy, and he took full advantage of that."

"How'd you end up out here?" I searched my brain for her name, it was something unusual . . . Danny and . . . Rolanda, Renata . . . Riccarla. That was it. "Riccarla," I said.

A big grin spread across her face as she wiped her wet hands on her overalls, leaving dark spots. "That's a pretty good memory you have. Met my current guy when I left Danny and was working at Trigger's. Bobby's great. He's the mailman out here. I run the library three days a week and spend the rest of the time making bay leaf wreaths. I sell them at the Farmer's Market."

"You make those! They're beautiful. I bought one for my gramma last year. She loves it."

"Thanks. It keeps me off the street corners."

Behind me I heard Detective Hudson impatiently clear his throat. Ignoring him, I said to her, "Being the mailman, I bet your husband knows everyone who lives out here."

"Yeah, he does. Lived here his whole life. His family's land goes back to one of the original Spanish land grants. We live out on the old place. Real log cabin. Takes us forty-five minutes just to get to the station here."

"Guess you really like your privacy," I said.

"After listening to those Wheatons yammer for six years, you betcha." She stuck her hands deep into her pockets. "So, what are you two doing out here? Going to see the petroglyphs on Painted Rock? I think it may be closed right now. They've been having some trouble with vandalism."

"No, actually we're looking for someone."

Her face instantly closed down. "Is that so?"

"Yeah, all we have is a post office box and we really need to talk to this person." I smiled my friendliest, most disarming smile. "I promise, we're not process servers."

She gave a small smile. "Who're you looking for?"

"Eva Knoll."

Her face definitely took on a cool demeanor. "Why?"

"Just want to ask her some questions."

She jerked her head over to the fire station, her friendliness gone. "Might be better if you talked to Lukie. She knows Eva best."

"Lukie?"

"She's the fire captain. Closest thing we have to the law out here. Talk to her." A few feet away a faded green Chevy pickup pulled into the gravel parking lot. Five children under ten scrambled out of the bed and ran toward the small door marked LIBRARY. She waved at them. "My public beckons. Nice shooting the breeze with you. Tell Wade hey from Riccarla if you ever see him again."

Behind me, Detective Hudson gave a mocking chuckle. "A half hour of playing 'six degrees of separation' and she tells you to talk to the fire captain. Very impressive interviewing. I was taking notes the whole time."

I turned around and, without a word, punched him hard on the arm.

"Hey, hitting a cop is against the law," he said, rubbing the spot.

"Yeah, yeah, yeah. Let's go see the fire captain."

"Are you going to let me do the talking this time?"

"No, I *still* know these people better than you."

"Fine, screw up our only chance to find this old woman."

"I'm not going to screw it up."

Inside the sparsely furnished fire station office, it took three minutes to get from the fire captain, a tanned, athletic-looking woman dressed in the neat, green uniform of the Forestry service, that yes, she did know Eva Knoll, and no, she wouldn't tell us where she lived.

Behind me, Detective Hudson started to say something. I turned around and held up my hand for him to keep quiet. He glared at me. I glared back.

"Why not?" I asked her. "Like I said, we don't want to hurt her or anything. We just want to ask her some questions. Riccarla can vouch for my identity and integrity." I decided to pull out what I hoped was my ace in the hole. "I'm married to San Celina's police chief."

"You're Gabe Ortiz's wife? He's a nice guy. Talked to him about old Chevys a while back at a Chamber of Commerce thing. He said he's restoring his son's Malibu. Sixty-five, I think it was."

"Yeah, Gabe loves old cars. We have a restored 1950 Chevy pickup. Original interior. His dad bought it in Wichita, Kansas, the same year Gabe was born."

"Cool," she said, nodding appreciatively.

"About Eva Knoll . . ."

"I'm sorry, but I just can't."

"But, honestly, we won't hurt her. We just want to ask her some questions."

A deep crevice formed between the woman's clear blue eyes. "I'm not questioning your identity or integrity and I'm sure you're a very nice person, but things are different out here. Our motto is 'Don't ask, don't tell.' Folks move out here because they don't want to be bothered by people, and we try to accommodate them. Sometimes it's for illegal reasons. I'm not saying we don't have our share of drug labs, but most times it's just that they want to be left alone. We're a tight group. We look out for each other because we have to. If we called the Sheriff's Department it would take an officer over an hour to get out here. That makes us pretty independent and self-sufficient. Eva's our oldest citizen, and we all feel real protective about her. I can give her a message, and if she wants to get back to you, then it's her choice."

"But it's very important I talk to her as soon as possible. It's a long drive out here. Does she have a phone? Can you call her?"

Lukie hesitated for a moment, then said, "Sure, I'll try."

She punched the number in and waited. "There's no answer. Guess she's out back in her greenhouse. She can't hear the phone out there. Like I said, I'll give her your number."

I bit my lip in frustration. "Isn't there any way I can convince you to tell me where she lives?"

"Like I said we feel real protective of Eva."

"Please, if I . . ."

Her eyes widened slightly as she peered over my shoulder. "Well, that would do it. Let me write down her address for you." She turned back to her gray metal desk and started hunting through a Rolodex.

I whipped around to look at Detective Hudson. He was holding up his badge and wearing a smug grin.

"Smart-ass," I muttered.

"Now, now," he said, patting me on the shoulder. "Let's not be a sore loser."

After the captain showed us on the huge wall map where

Eva Knoll's house was, she said, "Please be careful. Eva's very fragile these days."

"I promise," I said, glancing over at Detective Hudson, who was expressionless, "we will do our very best not to upset her."

"WE'D HAVE THIS interview done and eating lunch back in San Celina if I'd done that sooner," he said.

"Oh, pipe down," I said halfheartedly, staring out the window. At the side of the road a gray pronghorn antelope, its stomach open and raw, sat waiting for the elements to clean it to bones. No animal control officer out here to shovel up death and dispose of it neatly. "And I meant what I said to the fire captain. If Eva Knoll shows any signs of getting upset, I'm going to stop you."

He just shook his head and started humming the Dwight Yoakam song "A Thousand Miles from Nowhere . . ."

It took us forty-five minutes to find her place. For a little while we drove along the edge of Soda Lake. A silvery-white layer of water glimmered, miragelike, across the flat lake. The surrounding prairie mounds covered with bunch-grass were mirrored perfectly in the lake's glassy surface.

"Read somewhere that was an alkaline lake," the detective said.

I nodded. "Usually it's dry this time of year, but we had a rainy summer. In the winter, you should see the sandhill cranes. It's quite a sight."

Eva Knoll's house sat at the end of a half-mile dirt road. With only a lone cottonwood for shade, the tiny slat-board house and the occupant seemed defenseless against the frightening expanse of prairie. When we pulled up, a huge rottweiler mix bounded off the front porch, its large, powerful teeth bared. The dog jumped against the side of the detective's truck, its claws scraping down the passenger door with a sound like chalk on blackboard. I instinctively scooted across the seat away from the growling dog.

"He's scratchin' the paint!" Detective Hudson cried. "Dang it all, this is a custom job!" He leaned over me to pound flat-handed on the window. "Get back, you sorry piece of taco meat!"

"Maybe you should get out and stop him," I said, pressing myself against the seat and laughing.

The look on his face could have melted cheese. "You wouldn't be laughing if it were your truck he was clawin'."

"You're right," I said cheerfully, then instinctively jerked back against him when the dog hit the side of the truck again. I cracked my window and called to the woman standing in the porch's shadows. "Mrs. Knoll? Mrs. Eva Knoll?"

"Who wants to know?" her cracked voice called back.

"Benni Harper."

"Okay, then, come on out. Lukie called about you."

She moved out of the shadows, dressed in a flowered housedress and holding a double-barrel shotgun. So much for Mrs. Knoll's vulnerability. I eyed the growling dog, then called back. "Uh, could you call off your dog?"

"Heidi, come on, girl. These people won't hurt you." The dog turned and trotted back to Mrs. Knoll on the porch.

I laughed at Detective Hudson's stunned face. "She does kind of favor your girlfriend around the muzzle, don't you think?"

"Let's get this done," he said stiffly, opening his door and walking around the passenger side. The shredded paint caused a deep moan to erupt from his chest.

"Oh, cowboy up, city slicker," I said. "Better your door than your face."

Though the dog sat quietly next to the old woman, we

were hesitant as we walked up to the shadowed porch. After a short introduction and a minute of letting Heidi sniff our hands, she rolled over and exposed her pale brown stomach, begging for a scratch.

"You're just an old fake, aren't you, girl?" I said, rubbing her muscled stomach. Detective Hudson stood a foot or so back, glancing over at his truck's ravaged door, still annoyed at the dog's disregard for his paint job.

"Oh, she can take a hunk out of you," Mrs. Knoll said. "Don't doubt it."

I straightened up and held out my hand. "I'm Benni Harper. You said Lukie called?"

Mrs. Knoll nodded, her short, white hair wispy about her dried-apricot face. Her handshake was firm and direct, like that of a young woman. "Said you needed to ask me some questions."

"Yes, if you don't mind."

She set her shotgun down on the corner of the porch. "Don't reckon I have much anyone wants to know."

"It's about Rose Brown," I said.

Her old face seemed to sink further into itself, and she stared out over my shoulder at something in the distance. She seemed lost for a moment in the past. She turned her ghost-lit eyes on me. "He the lawman Lukie was talking about?" she asked, nodding over at a silent Detective Hudson.

"Yes, he's with the Sheriff's Department."

"I don't have any use for the law. Won't talk to him. It's you or nothing."

I turned to look at Detective Hudson, raising my eyebrows in silent question.

He threw his hands up in frustration. "I give up."

"Come inside," she said to me. "You." She pointed at the detective. "Go sit in your truck. Sound travels around here, and this ain't none of your business what I got to say." The wooden screen door slammed shut behind her. Heidi remained on the porch, panting and watching me and Detective Hudson.

"I'm not sitting in my truck," he said. "I'm the one with authority here. If that batty old woman thinks . . ."

I put a finger over my lips. "You want to blow this just because of your overinflated ego? She's agreed to talk to *me*, so just humor her and go sit in your truck."

Looking as if he'd like to take a bite out of someone's leg, he stomped back to his truck.

Inside the cramped house filled with the accumulation of a lifetime of possessions, Mrs. Knoll was already sitting in a ratty blue velour armchair with beige doilies on the arms. Heidi had followed me into the house and settled in what was obviously her accustomed spot in front of a fireplace filled with charred bits of wood.

"Over there." Mrs. Knoll pointed with a spindly finger to a Victorian sofa across from her. I moved a pile of ancient *Life* magazines and sat down.

"Sorry for the clutter," she said. "I don't get many visitors."

We sat there for a long, silent moment. Finally I said, "Mrs. Knoll, I have some questions about the years you worked with Rose Brown out at Seven Sisters ranch."

"That was a long time ago, young woman," she said, her thin arms resting quiet and still on the chair's lacy arms.

"Yes, it was. But there's been some . . . trouble out there recently, and Detective Hudson and I think it might have something to do with what happened back then."

"What kind of trouble?"

I quickly told her about Giles's death and the circumstances behind it. Her face never changed expression.

When I finished, she took some time to answer. The

ticking of a large grandfather clock next to the door reminded me that an impatient Detective Hudson was fuming outside.

"Do you know . . . ?" I started.

She held up her hand. "That family will haunt me till I die. That's the plain truth of it."

"How?" I asked, hoping to get her started talking.

She gestured over at the table next to me. "See that picture?"

I picked up the round, copper frame and looked at the black-and-white photograph of a young boy sitting in the lap of an older woman who bore a striking resemblance to Mrs. Knoll. The boy appeared to be about two years old, and I recognized the facial features of a Down's syndrome child.

"That's my boy and my mother," she said. "He wasn't normal. Guess you can tell that. He had the best care, though. His whole life he did. Even when he got the cancer in his bowels. Had the best care. Private nurses. Big pretty headstone when the angels finally took him home. All because I kept quiet." She reached down and stroked Heidi's huge head, causing the dog to sigh deeply. "But now, I reckon there's no reason anymore. I'm old. I've been wanting to tell someone. You look like a nice young lady. Do you have any children?"

"No," I said. "No, I don't."

"Well, I'll tell you. You'll do anything for your kids. Leastwise, most folks would. Oh, you make your mistakes, all right. Maybe you're too easy or too hard. But most folks do their best. They *try.* Do you understand what I'm saying?"

"Yes, I think so."

"There's those, though, that just defy everything God ever intended. You want to believe they have a soul, but you can't imagine, can't imagine on this earth, why they do what they do. Do you understand what I'm saying?"

I nodded and didn't answer.

Then she told me a story that would darken a piece of my heart until the day I died.

14

"THOSE BROWNS NEEDED me, no doubt about it," Mrs. Knoll said. "Good nannies weren't any easier to find then than they are now, and the Browns really needed a good nanny, what with those three little girls under eleven and then the two sets of twins. Rose Brown had her hands full, and she wasn't raised to do nothing much but sit around and look pretty."

"When did you first come to work for them?" I asked.

"Right before the first set of twins was born. Oh, my, Mrs. Brown was big as a steamer trunk. By the time I came, those little girls of hers had been running wild for months. Took me a good long time, let me tell you, to get them civilized again. Especially that little Capitola. She was wild as a fox and liked it that way. Took me a week to comb all the knots out of her hair."

She shifted in her chair and wiped a bit of spittle that had pooled in the deep wrinkles around her mouth. I waited, trying to keep every part of my body still, though I was jittery with nerves.

"She was a handful, that little Cappy," the old woman reminisced. "The others, too, though not as much. That house was beautiful. It felt like a castle to me. I grew up around San Miguel in a little two-bedroom shotgun shack out in the middle of nowhere. Father worked for a farmer out that away. Mother was sick from the time I was real little. I started keeping house for Father when I was five years old. Could make a perfect angel food cake when I was seven, and that was on a woodstove."

"Incredible," I murmured. Then I asked, "How old were you when you went to work for the Browns?"

"It was in 1925," she said, almost inaudibly. "I was thirty-eight. Father said it was the best thing, what with Johnnie's condition and all. The Browns paid real good, and Johnnie's daddy took off right after he was born. Never saw him again. I sent money to my parents and visited when I could. The money helped a lot, Father said."

"Johnnie is your son?"

She nodded and pointed again at the picture on the dusty end table. "I visited him every chance I could get. He did okay out on the farm as long as Mother was alive. He didn't take much care, mostly just feed him and dress him, sit him on a blanket under a tree. I'd been with the Browns for about a year when Mother died. By that time, I'd already seen what I'd seen and I wanted to leave, but the judge offered to triple my pay, and with Father being all stoved up and not able to farm anymore, I was the only bread-winner. He and Johnnie moved to a little house near the San Miguel mission, and Father Xavier there gave him a job tending the mission gardens. It worked out real well because there was an old nun there who took care of Johnnie. I was real grateful for their kindness."

"What was it you saw at the Browns'?" I said, trying to focus her wandering attention.

Her age-spotted hand went up to her mouth as if wanting to physically hold back her words. "The first baby, Daisy, died of pneumonia," she said.

I nodded. That fit with the death certificate. "What about her sister?"

"Rose was so sad when Daisy died. Inconsolable. But the family and all her friends were right there helping her and taking care of things. Petted her and comforted her and told her she had to get up out of that bed, that her other little baby needed her, that her little girls needed her. Even her husband, the judge, started coming home at night. And her doctor, handsome fella, he came over every day, twice some days and talked and talked to her. They took to having tea in the parlor every day about four. She started wanting to live again, blossomed really. All that attention, she just craved it, and it fed her like an underwater spring feeds a lake. But then, like people do, they got back to their own lives. The judge started staying away again. He had his work and, though no one talked openly about that sort of thing then, his lady friends. Her doctor got busy with other patients and such. It was just me and her again, with the little baby and the girls and all the servants. The first time she came running down with the baby calling for me to fetch the doctor, the baby wasn't breathing, my heart just about broke for her. No one deserved that kind of sorrow. The doctor came, but by that time the baby was breathing again, and he sat with her down in the parlor and had his tea, and she laughed and carried on with him as if her baby hadn't been on death's door only an hour before. It didn't seem right to me, but I never was one to question about folks' ways much. They'd always been such a mystery. Still are for that matter."

She paused for a moment, breathing deep and hard. The effort of telling this story was wearing on her, but I didn't know how to make it go any faster. Like most things in life, it had its own pace, and I had to just let it unfold. She inhaled a phlegmy, rattling breath, and suddenly I was fearful that this might all be too much for her. *Should I stop?*

"Would you like some water?" I asked.

She motioned no with her hand and continued on. "It was after the third time the baby stopped breathing I got suspicious. It only happened when she was in the room, and since I tended that baby more than she ever did, it just didn't seem right to me. Every time the doctor came, and they talked and he fawned over her. I kept telling myself a mother wouldn't do that to her own child. Not just for a little attention. So I started kinda following her, watching her. Then I saw her do it."

"What?" I whispered.

"Hold the pillow over the baby's face. Her little legs just kicked and kicked. I screamed, 'Mrs. Brown!' and she looked up at me. Straight in my eyes she looked at me, set the pillow aside, and said, 'Yes, Eva?' Just like that, face as blank as a rock. 'Yes, Eva?' My blood ran cold as creek water."

"What did you do? Did you tell someone?"

Tears pooled in her pale eyes. "What could I do? Do you think anyone would believe me when I said Mrs. Rose Brown, wife of the richest man in the county, was a-tryin' to kill her own baby? So I made myself believe her when she said the baby had pulled the pillow over her face, and she was taking it off. I believed her because I wanted to. I had to. I kept telling myself that mothers don't smother their own babies. They just don't kill their own babies."

"Except she did," I said.

She nodded. "I was down at the stables with the girls, watching while they took their riding lessons. When I saw the doctor's car come barreling up the dirt road, and I knew in my heart this time it was bad."

"She killed Dahlia."

"Yes, and all the attention started all over again. Oh, such a funeral you can't imagine. Just like Daisy's. Hundreds of people. All the florist shops in town were empty. Judge Brown knew everyone, just everyone. A lot of people came, of course, trying to curry up to him. And during it all, I knew she'd killed that baby. At the funeral, she caught my eye and she knew I knew."

"No one suspected? None of the other servants? The judge?"

"Not that anyone said. To me, anyway."

"So, what about the other babies . . ."

"She got pregnant shortly after that. I stayed till past her delivering time. When she had another set of twins, I couldn't help but wonder what God was thinking, giving her those babies. They named them Bethany and Beulah. I struggled with what I should do, even went to the judge once, trying to tell him he needed to watch out for those babies, but I got too afraid, and my words got all jumbled.

" 'Eva,' he'd finally said in that gruff voice of his. 'I know working for Mrs. Brown's not the easiest thing in the world. I'll triple your pay if you'll stay. I know you need the money, what with your son and father. I'll see that Father Xavier at San Miguel gives him a little extra work, add to his pay. They'll be taken good care of, Eva. Trust me on this. I value your discretion.' "

She fingered the torn arm of her easy chair. "That's all he said. He valued my discretion. I had to look the word up to see what it meant. I knew then he was telling me to keep quiet. What could I do? If I lost my job with the Browns, there was no place to go. I was a good nanny, but by then it was hard times, and there was no work anywhere.

With my job and Father's tending the mission gardens, me and Father and Johnnie had it good. All I had to do was forget what I'd seen." She sighed deeply, causing Heidi to lift her head and whine. Mrs. Knoll patted the dog's head reassuringly.

"Things went okay for three months after the second twins were born. I'd even convinced myself that maybe I'd been seeing things. Then Beulah started having the breathing spells, and time after time Mrs. Brown would call for the doctor. I took to following after her, especially when she was around the babies. But she'd say, 'Now, Eva, let me care for my babies. Take the girls for a walk. They're looking a little peaked these days.'

"I'd take Cappy and Willow and little Etta for a stroll around the garden, and then, sure enough, the doctor would come driving up in his fancy car, spewing dust in his haste to get there. Finally Beulah died, and then Bethany. I was beside myself, not knowing what to do."

"Didn't anyone, Judge Brown, her doctor, *anyone*, suspect what was happening?" That seemed unbelievable to me, that all these babies kept dying and no one questioned it.

She shook her head slowly. "Lots of babies died back then. You go look at any graveyard and you can see that. If anyone else suspected she was killing her own babies, they never said anything. Like me, I reckon they just wouldn't, *couldn't* believe such a thing about anyone."

"Did you go to Judge Brown after the others?" I asked.

"I tried, but after Bethany, the last twin, passed on, he wasn't living at the house but one or two days a month. I think he knew something was going on. Maybe he just wanted to stay away from all that sadness. Maybe he didn't want to make any more babies for her to kill. I don't know. The one time I tried to say something, he stopped me and told me they wouldn't be needing me at the big house anymore. He gave me a year's pay and said he'd pay me a pension until I died. Got a check at the first of the month like clockwork. When my boy got sick, the bills were paid, and he paid for the funeral, too. Did the same when my father died. Then one day, after Father had been gone a while, the deed to this little house came in the mail. I moved out here around '42 and never saw any of the Browns again."

"And you never told anyone," I said.

Her glassy eyes seemed to clear slightly when they stared straight into mine. "Not until now. I figure there's no reason to hide it anymore. Those babies never got their justice, and I shoulder the burden for that. I should have told someone. I should have tried."

OUTSIDE, DETECTIVE HUDSON leaned against his truck, staring out at the bright, level horizon.

"Thought you'd never get through," he said, spitting a wad of gum out on the dirt. "So, what's the story?"

"She's ninety-seven. I'll be glad if I can even talk at that age." I looked back at the tiny desert house, bleached bone-white by the sun. A mental shiver rattled my brain. "Let's get on the road. I'll tell you on the way back."

We were halfway to San Celina by the time I finished my story.

"That's unbelievable," the detective said, his expression as incredulous as I still felt.

"I know. And somehow it's got to do with Giles's murder. I'm assuming he found out about this and was going to let it out. I bet you anything now that *Giles* was the anonymous caller to the newspaper the night of the party.

He was going to make sure this went public immediately if Cappy and the sisters didn't cooperate."

"And the great child-loving philanthropist, Rose Brown, would be exposed for what she really is—a baby killer."

I stared out the window. "The question is, what do we do now?"

He was quiet for a moment, then said, "I'm going to confront Capitola. Throw down the gauntlet and see what happens."

I twisted around to look at him. "I don't think that's a good idea. We don't know enough yet to confront her. We need to run this by someone who knows the legal stuff involved. You could blow it if you jump in too fast."

He thought for a moment. "Okay, I'll go talk to someone at the DA's office, then."

"That's still jumping the gun. I don't trust them to keep it quiet. I'm telling you, Detective, this is a very, very prominent family in San Celina. One whiff of this scandal, and the media will be all over you, me, the Browns, and Eva. If we found her without much trouble, so will they. I don't want . . . no, I *won't* let that happen. It might kill her."

Annoyed, he asked, "So what do you propose we do?"

"I know someone we can trust who'll be able to advise us without fear of leaks. Let me just run it by my friend before you set things in motion."

His face set hard and stubborn.

"Please," I said, ready to beg if necessary.

He hesitated, then said, "An hour. That's what I'll give this person. Then it's out of your hands, and I'm going to my superiors and the DA."

"Deal," I said.

AS BEFITTING A good attorney, Amanda's expression didn't change while I told her Eva Knoll's story. For once Detective Hudson sat quietly and kept his thoughts to himself. When I finished, she waited a moment before speaking.

"I'll be flour-breaded and deep-fried," she finally said. "I know some research doctors back east who'd give their left nuts to hear this. There's always been speculation it happened before the seventies when it was given a name, but most doctors always considered it a modern-day disorder. I guess there is nothing new under the sun."

"A disorder?" I said. "What do you mean?"

"If what this Mrs. Knoll told you is true," she said, leaning back in her executive office chair, "then it appears that Rose Brown had a syndrome called Munchausen by Proxy."

"Don't give me any psychological crap," Detective Hudson burst out. "She killed those babies. That's homicide in my book."

Amanda's normally mobile and smiling mouth turned

grim. "I agree wholeheartedly, Detective, but it's not quite as simple as that, at least in the law."

He started to protest, and Amanda held up a hand. "Let me see if I can explain. I prosecuted a Munchausen by Proxy case when I was working for the DA's office in San Francisco. Young mother regularly fed her two-year-old daughter syrup of ipecac to make her throw up whatever she ate. The child inhaled her own vomit, causing pneumonia a couple of times. She was literally starving to death, but it took doctors eight months to figure out what was causing it. Since the pneumonia qualified as great bodily harm, we eventually prosecuted the mother under torture charges, simply because we couldn't figure out what else to call it and get a decent sentence." She picked up a small Beanie Baby panda from the top of a pile of Beanie animals and absentmindedly stroked its back with her polished fingernails.

"How about plain old child abuse? Assault? Attempted homicide?" Detective Hudson said bitterly.

Amanda nodded, still stroking the furry toy. "It's certainly a form of child abuse, but the problem is it doesn't fit neatly into what we call child abuse under the law or any of those other things. Once we had all these tidy organized categories: You had physical abuse, you had molest, you had neglect. Now all of a sudden we have this insidious type of child endangerment whose physical manifestations are hard to distinguish from the behaviors of good mothers who are simply caring for very sick children. You have to understand, the mothers of these children often appear to be extremely loving and deeply concerned. It's dangerous for doctors, nurses, or social workers to accuse someone of Munchausen by Proxy, because they might be accusing a mother who is innocent. There have been cases where a slow-growing brain tumor caused vomiting or other symptoms that only the mother observed, and it took the doctors some time to find the tumor. If those mothers had been accused of this disorder, it would have been tragic for them and their children. As a society we are hesitant to believe that a mother would harm her own child. It's only the worst of these Munchausen cases that even make it to court. Most are so borderline that the prosecutor doesn't have a chance convincing a jury that a mother deliberately tried to harm her sick child, that indeed she was the one making the child sick."

She set the toy panda down and picked up a turtle. She took a pair of scissors, cut the tiny tag off the ear and threw it away. "I give these to the deputy DA in charge of the child abuse unit. Helps the kids to have something to hold when they testify. They're the perfect size for little hands." She put down the turtle and picked up a pale pink pig. "I cut the tags off so crazy adult collectors won't steal them."

"So you're telling us that lots of mothers get away with killing their babies with this Munchausen thing?" Detective Hudson broke in.

She tossed the pig in the detagged pile and picked up a bright red lobster. "Look, child abuse cases, even ones with real evidence of physical injury, are hard for juries to watch and rule on. Like I just said, something deep inside all of us does not want to believe or face the fact that some mothers hurt their children. And when there's not always overt evidence of harm and the mother appears loving . . . well, what can I say? More often than not, they get away with it. That's if they're ever discovered, which in most of these cases they aren't." Her mouth turned down with sadness as she clipped the tag off the lobster's claw.

"But why would anyone do that to their own child?" I said.

"The question of the year," she said, leaning forward and resting her elbows on the desk. "I'll give you the fifty-cent lecture. It has to do with power. Not having it and wanting it. Oh, there's lots of deeper issues, but it really comes down to that. Surprisingly, most of the mothers who do this have not come from overtly abusive homes. But they often come from homes where the father is emotionally unattached. Somewhere in the psyche of this young girl—and by the way, the majority of people who have this disorder are women—she develops what we call a 'character perversion.' In a nutshell, to get positive attention from her doctor, who is an authority figure substitute, she uses her baby and its imagined or manufactured illness. Their babies aren't even people to them, but more like objects used to gain them what they want, which is attention and praise. Some researchers have even gone so far as to compare the babies to fetish objects."

"But she killed her babies," Detective Hudson said. "If they were what she needed for attention, why would she kill them?"

"Very good, Detective," Amanda said, nodding. "You're right, most deaths in Munchausen by Proxy cases are accidental. Those mothers don't *intend* for their babies to die. But if they do, God help the next baby that comes along. They become the new fixed object."

I felt my stomach churn. Amanda was right; it was a hard thing to comprehend. The mother/child relationship was one we all idealized, even when we knew better.

"So, you're telling me," Detective Hudson said, "that she managed to kill four babies and no one had a clue? And why wouldn't she try harming the older girls?"

Amanda picked up a small moose with orange antlers, studying it critically. "He's pretty cute. I may have to buy one for myself." She looked back up at us. "First, it sounds like the first twin died naturally. Maybe the attention she received when the baby was sick set it off. As for why she didn't harm her older girls, who's to say she didn't and they survived whatever she did? We'll probably never know. The harm she did to them psychologically isn't as obvious. I'm telling you, Detective, I did extensive research on this subject, and there is very little information out there. As for people suspecting, there was one case file back in the fifties where seven children in the same family died from what they diagnosed as crib death before anyone started asking why."

Detective Hudson stood up and started pacing her small office in frustration.

"What do you think we should do?" I asked.

Amanda shook her head, bemused. "Accusing someone of this with so little proof, especially someone as prominent as Rose Brown, would only gain you a libel suit. Not to mention that it happened so long ago. I'm not clear as to why you found out this information."

I told her how we thought it was the reason Giles was murdered, that somehow he'd found out and was blackmailing the family.

"Then you've got a real sticky situation on your hands," she said. "It could be any of the family who killed him or none of them. And this could possibly have nothing to do with Giles's murder. It's intriguing, but I'd say it's information that, though troubling, is best filed under the good Lord's final judgment."

Detective Hudson let out a scoffing grunt. "I think I should confront Cappy Brown."

I looked to Amanda, questioning.

"That could be problematic," she said, watching him walk back and forth, finally saying, "Sit down, Detective, darlin'. You're makin' me dizzy."

He stopped, stared at her gorgeous, uncompromising smile, then did as she said without a peep of protest.

"Here's the deal," she said. "Everything I told you is pure speculation. Ruining the reputation of someone like Rose Brown over something you have no substantial proof for would, as I said before, not only garner you a libel suit, but also might hinder you finding the real perpetrator."

He frowned, knowing she was right.

"So, what should we do?" I asked. "We should do *something*."

"My advice? Go light a candle or say a prayer for those sad, pathetic people and get on with your life, because it's way beyond your control."

I stood up, hitching my purse over my shoulder. "Thanks, Amanda. I appreciate you taking the time to talk to us."

"No problem," she said, coming around the desk and wrapping me in a Ralph Lauren–scented hug. "You do manage to get yourself into some interesting situations." She held out a hand to Detective Hudson. "Good luck, Detective. Hope you find your killer."

"Count on it," he said grimly.

She grinned at me. "God bless the eternal cockiness of the native Texan male."

"YOU CAN DROP me off at the folk art museum," I said, as we walked out to his truck.

"Fine," he said.

I glanced over at him. "You okay?"

The only reply I received was an almost imperceptible shrug. He was quiet the whole drive over to the museum.

"Got a john in there?" he asked when we pulled into the driveway.

"Sure, back in the workrooms."

I was listening to the message on the answering machine for the third time when he walked past my office. "Detective, come listen to this."

He stood next to me, listening to Cappy's gruff voice.

"We need to talk," she said. "Call me." The time of the call was three-forty-five p.m. The exact time we were sitting in Amanda's office. It was now almost five.

He picked up the phone and handed it to me. "Call her and see what she wants."

"I bet she knows we went out to see Eva Knoll," I said, staring at the phone he held out. "She probably had us followed or she has a contact out there."

"That's what I was afraid of. Call her."

After finding it in my Rolodex, I punched her number with a shaking finger.

"We need to talk," she said again. "Can you come out now?"

"Right now?" I asked, looking at the detective. He nodded yes.

"Yes," she said. "But alone. I will only talk to you alone. I mean it."

I hesitated, then said, "I'll be there in about a half hour."

"Fine." She hung up without saying good-bye.

"I'll drive," Detective Hudson said, starting for the door.

"She said she'd only talk to me," I called after him.

He stopped at the doorway and slowly turned around. "I will not let you go out there alone."

"But what if this is our only chance to get a confession out of her? Can't you put a wire on me or something? Park around the corner and come if I need help."

His face tightened. "This isn't television, Benni. If you got hurt, I'd never forgive myself. Not to mention your husband would kill me. Probably *after* he cut off my balls."

I grabbed up my purse and snapped. "Fine, come along. It'll probably screw up any chance of her telling us anything, but far be it from me to endanger your masculine appendages." Deep inside, I knew he was right. But I also knew that Cappy most likely wouldn't admit to a thing with him standing next to me.

When we drove the long, twisting entry road to the ranch, we didn't see one solitary sign of life; the ranch was eerily empty. Even the wine-tasting room had only one car parked in front. Though Wednesday was not a busy day, tourist-wise, I expected to see some activity, a vineyard worker, a groom, or somebody walking around or working. We passed the stables where the hot walkers stood still, the chains swinging gently in the breeze, the training track and corrals clean and empty. I rolled down my window, catching a strong whiff of horse, but not a single nicker came over the breeze to shatter the immense silence.

We pulled up to the house and walked up the front steps. Detective Hudson rang the doorbell once, and ten seconds later Cappy answered the door. She was dressed in slightly dirt-stained blue jeans and a pale blue, snap-button Western shirt with the sleeves rolled up. Her brown, muscled forearms looked as dangerous as a man's.

"I said I'd only talk to Benni," she said, her gray eyes flat as steel.

"Don't blame her," he said. "I wouldn't let her come alone."

"Sit in the foyer, then," she said, pointing at a parson's bench. "Come into my study," she said over her shoulder as she strode across the glossy floor toward her office.

Detective Hudson hesitated.

"I'll be fine," I said in a low voice. "You'll be right out here."

"I don't like this," he answered.

"We don't have a choice," I said.

"She's right," Cappy called from her office.

He glared in Cappy's direction and sat down on the parson's bench.

Inside her office, she was already sitting behind her desk, under her mother's Churn Dash quilt. "Please shut the office door," she said.

I did as she asked, then stood there, waiting. *Calm down,* I told my nervous stomach. *Nothing's going to happen. She's not a killer and even if she was, she's not going to pull a gun on you with Detective Hudson sitting right outside the door. Besides, he's just a yell away and he's armed and experienced at confrontations like this.*

"Please, sit down," she said, her voice amicable, as if all I was there for was to do a little horse trading or perhaps sell her a good load of timothy hay.

I sat down in one of the green leather chairs that Detective Hudson had used the night of Giles's murder.

"Would you like a drink? I've got some bourbon here in my desk."

I mutely shook my head.

"Okay, then," Cappy said. "Let's get down to business so we can get this wrapped up. I've got a trip to the Los Alamitos racetrack with Churn Dash tomorrow. He'll be running his first race as soon as he qualifies. We're expecting great things from him. Maybe he'll end up siring our next Futurity winner."

I nodded, not answering.

"You're a very clever girl, Benni Harper," she said, picking up a smooth wooden letter opener, running it back and forth through her strong fingers. "And persistent. I knew once you got your teeth in this I would have a hard time forcing you to let go. So . . ." She set the letter opener down and blinked her eyes slowly. "Blackmail's an evil thing, wouldn't you agree?" she asked, her mouth set in a grim, pale line.

I nodded.

"So anyone who would commit it would also be evil and deserve to be punished."

I shifted forward in my chair. Was she going to confess to Giles's murder? Reveal it was someone else? Was she covering for someone? That has always been a possibility. "Who are you talking about?"

She stared at me, her eyes as steady and reflective as a knife blade. She didn't answer my question, but instead said, "I have a story for you. Do you like stories, Benni Harper?"

Without thinking, I held my breath, mesmerized by her control. Her every deliberate movement, her unblinking eyes, reminded me of an ancient, battle-scarred rattler poised to strike.

She started talking, her voice cold and emotional. She told me a story that had I not already talked to Amanda, I would have never believed. A story about a terrified seven-year-old girl who watched her mother gently place a pillow over her little sister Dahlia's face, pressing down until her sister kicked and kicked her tiny legs in desperation to breathe. Then picking the baby up and running out in the hall and down the stairs calling for help, calling for someone to call the doctor, the beloved family doctor. How she saw her do it again and again, placing the pillow so lovingly, so gently over her sister's tiny face. Each time, stopping just in time to call for the doctor. The little girl told no one, but held the secret tight inside her chest, not believing her mother capable of that, not a mother, not her mother.

Then Dahlia died, and at the funeral she heard her mother whisper, *My babies are together again.*

Every night the little girl prayed that God would make things all right. That Daisy and Dahlia would not be dead, that the memories in her head of the pillow being held over Dahlia's face by her mother's delicate white hands would go away. A year later when another set of twins was born, the little girl was relieved because she believed that God had answered her prayers and that her mother had been given another chance. But she watched her mother, followed her constantly, until her mother said in her soft, gentle voice, *Don't be always hanging around me, go play like your sisters, get some fresh air, let me be with my babies.* Then the new twins, Bethany and Beulah, died, too, first one and then the other. Her mother both times came running out of the nursery crying for help, calling for the housekeeper to call the doctor. At the funerals, Cappy could not stop staring at her mother's delicate white hands.

"Then it was over," Cappy said, her voice emotionless and dry as a desert. "My mother never bore any other children, and she went on to become a great advocate for the welfare of children in this county. Without her, thousands of children would be much worse off, even dead, for lack of medical care. My father used his political influence to help her achieve her goals. I left home at seventeen to follow the rodeo and didn't come back until after Father died and Mother needed me to run the ranch."

I sat quietly—horrified. Horrified by the story of a sickness I still couldn't imagine, by the matter-of-factness with which Cappy told her story, and with the fact that a seven-year-old would have to carry a burden like that, a burden that twisted her own thinking and loyalties to the point of murder.

When I could finally speak, I asked, "Do your sisters know?"

"Yes, I told them years ago. But we agreed it should

stop there. Our children and their children have never known and never will. It needs to end when we die. And it would have . . ." She left the statement open.

"It would have, except Giles somehow found out about the murdered babies."

A muscle in her cheek flinched at my graphic words.

"Probably, because of her senility, from your mother," I continued, "and he was blackmailing the family to force you to merge your winery with his father's. You, or somebody in the Brown family killed him to keep him quiet."

Speaking slowly, obviously choosing her words with care, she replied, "Giles's death was a tragic event. I know his family will miss him. I wish it didn't have to happen."

"You know I have to tell Detective Hudson. I have to tell Gabe."

"What is there to tell? I'll deny anything you claimed I said about my mother and her babies. As for the rest . . ." She shrugged. "You and I were just lamenting over poor Giles's tragedy."

Our eyes met, and in that moment I knew she'd killed Giles and I knew she'd never get caught.

"Now you, too, have a burden to carry," she said, her voice not unkind, but firm and, it seemed to me, tired.

My heart pumped wildly out of control. It took me a moment to find the voice to ask the question I knew I had to ask. "Why would you protect her all these years when she murdered your sisters?"

An almost astonished expression crossed her old face, as if she couldn't believe I'd ask such a ridiculous question. "She's my mother, Benni."

"But she *murdered* your sisters," I repeated, my voice a whisper.

For the briefest second, her expression changed. All the years of fear and shame and grief and disappointment seemed to converge, and I thought for a moment she might lay her head in her strong, capable hands and start sobbing. Then her back stiffened, and cool resolve again blanketed her face.

"We've talked long enough," she said. "Please go."

I stood up, my knees trembling, wanting to say something, but not knowing what. Finally I said, "You won't get away with this forever."

"Goodbye, Benni," she said, then took a deep breath and turned her chair around, dismissing me.

Detective Hudson was pacing the hallway when I came out of Cappy's office.

"What did she say?" he demanded.

Stumbling over the words, trying to keep my composure, I told him.

He pushed past me and stormed into her office, his face white with anger. "You sick, sorry piece of human garbage," he said. "You'd protect a woman who murdered her own babies just for some attention. You'd protect a woman who's lived a lie most of her life, this woman who professes to be a great lover of children. You'd kill another human being in cold blood for a woman who'd do that! Why?"

She turned her chair slowly around, her face as expressionless and cold as a smooth river stone. Had I really seen all those emotions on her face minutes before, or had it just been wishful thinking on my part?

"I don't know what you're talking about," she said.

His breathing sounded loud in the quiet room. "You won't get away with it. I'll find a way to see that you or your mother doesn't get away with this."

"You don't have that kind of power, Detective," she said, unmoved by his anger. "And you never will."

"Maybe not," he said, his voice steel-edged, "but I have

time. And if it takes me the rest of my life, I'll expose you and your mother."

"Excuse me," she said, picking up the phone, dismissing us. "I have some important phone calls to make."

He started to say something else, but I laid a hand on his forearm. "Let's go, Detective Hudson."

He turned and looked at me, ready to snap a reply. We stared at each other a long moment, and I saw a small muscle flutter in his smooth cheek. Without a word, I took his arm and led him outside without looking back.

Swallowing the salt that coated the back of my throat, I willed myself to stay calm. *Get away*, a voice inside me kept saying. *Just get away*. Away from this house with its ghoulish secrets, away from a woman so tainted by the evil she saw as a child, it destroyed her, too. Having lost my mother so early and yet going on to live a fairly happy life, I once thought foolishly that perhaps a mother's influence was not as great as all the psychologists claim. That was until my experience last spring with my own mother's secrets. I realized then that our mothers set the stage so early for who we are, what we think of the world, of ourselves, of the bare facts of what we perceive as good and evil, that even their absence, emotionally or physically, changes the very fabric and landscape of our lives. We didn't have to be like them, but we never escaped them, no matter how swiftly we tried to run.

On the porch I gently squeezed his forearm and said, "Detective, you have to let this one go."

"No," he said, his voice still hard, though I thought I caught a tinge of agony.

"Amanda's right. There is no proof. And the Browns are too powerful. No one will ever believe us."

"So you're saying we should just walk away? That she'll never have to pay for killing Giles Norton? That her mother should never have to account for those dead babies?"

I flinched at his words. "She'll pay. And so will her mother. The babies and Giles will be given justice. Just not by us. Not in this lifetime."

His face contorted with disgust. "You believe that crap? You really believe they will stand before some almighty God when they die and answer for this?"

"Yes."

He slammed his fist against a wooden post. "Why? Give me one good reason why you believe that."

I thought for a moment, knowing that nothing I would say would satisfy him right now, but gave him the only answer I had. "Because the alternative—that this is all there is, that they will get away with it—is too awful to comprehend."

He shook his head, his face pale in the bright porch light. "That's some fantasy world you're living in, Benni Harper. Some pie-in-the-sky fantasy world for kids and dreamers." He ran a hand over his face. "But I swear, there are times I wish I could join you."

I touched his shoulder. "There's nothing more we can do here."

He turned back to contemplate the fancy, carved front door. "That is the only thing you've said in the last ten minutes I do believe."

As we were pulling out of the driveway, the front door opened, and Cappy stepped out on the front porch. At first her face was hidden in the shadows. She moved, and for a moment I could see her full face in the hazy evening light. Her hand reached up and touched her throat. Was that despair in her expression? Sadness? Regret? I still wanted to think so. I truly wanted to believe it was. In the truck's side mirror, I watched her standing alone, still as a granite sculpture, until we turned the corner and she disappeared.

On the way back, we were both quiet. When I opened my purse for some tissue, I spotted the small tape recorder I had bought to fool Detective Hudson. It hadn't even occurred to me to turn it on. Then again, maybe it was illegal, maybe it wouldn't have made a difference. Things happened in the way they were supposed to happen. She has had to and will have to live with what she'd seen and done her entire life and, if I truly believed what I told the detective, for all eternity. I closed my purse and stared out the window.

When we hit the city limits, the detective started to say something, stopped, cleared his throat and tried again. "What I said to Mrs. Brown, I meant. I'm not giving up on this case." His knuckles were white on the truck's steering wheel.

"I didn't think you would."

He cleared his throat again, keeping his eyes on the road. "So, if I needed, say, someone to help me. Research and stuff. I mean, since no one else knows about this but you and me . . ."

"Yes, Detective, I'll help you."

He smiled to himself. "Good."

"I've been thinking," I said. "If I were to get a bunch of people together like the folk art museum board, the Historical Society, the Cattlewomen's Association, maybe some children's rights groups, and all the wineries in San Celina County, and we organize a yearly benefit ball to help abused children, would you get the Sheriff's Department involved?"

He laughed out loud. "All the wineries so that if Seven Sisters didn't participate, they'd look pretty bad?"

I nodded. "We'll rub her nose in it every year. I'll use every society connection I've garnered in the last few years, call in every marker Dove and I have, and make it the biggest event of the year. Bigger than the Harvest Ball that Seven Sisters sponsors for the children's hospital wing. We'll make it less fancy so more average people can contribute and be a part of it. We could make it three times as big as the Harvest Ball."

"You do that, Benni, and I'll make sure every sheriff's deputy and police officer in the county buys a ticket."

We smiled at each other. It wasn't much justice, but for the time being, it was all we had.

It was dusk now, and ahead of us off the interstate we could see the flickering lights of San Celina. I hugged myself, my heart cold in my chest. Next to me, the detective's face, one I'd grown used to seeing jovial and laughing, was still and expressionless, except for an occasional swift blinking of his eyes.

When we turned off on Lopez, he said, "I'll take you to the museum."

"Would you mind driving by the police station first?" I asked, suddenly wanting to see Gabe, hoping he was working late. I wanted to feel his arms around me, wanted to hear him tell me that, yes, he agreed, there would be justice for Giles . . . and the babies. Maybe not man's justice, but eternal justice. My husband had his cynical moments, but on that one point we agreed.

"Sure," Detective Hudson said, swinging his truck over one lane.

Gabe was walking out to his parking space, his briefcase in one hand, his other hand loosening his tie. The detective pulled up behind Gabe's Corvette and said, "You gonna tell him what happened?"

"Yes."

"Are you sure? Maybe he'll feel obligated to do something, tell someone."

"It's up to him, but don't underestimate my husband's

wisdom. He'll know the right thing to do. And I know he'd never do anything that might hurt me."

His mouth turned down, impressed. "That so?"

I nodded.

"Well, ranch girl, go tell your husband I think he's a pretty lucky guy."

My mouth opened in surprise. "Is that a compliment? Someone record this and save it for posterity. Detective Ford Hudson actually said something nice to Albenia Harper."

He gave a weak smile and said, "I'll deny it under oath."

"You would." I sat there for a moment, my hand on the door handle. "Are you okay?" Something in me felt like I was abandoning a friend in deep distress. Though I'd eat penny nails for breakfast before admitting it to him, I had developed a bit of a soft spot for him and his cocky Texan ways. I might even miss him. A little.

His eyes flickered, then he smiled his wide, country-boy smile. "Now don't you worry about me. I'm gonna go downtown, buy myself a couple of long-necks, see what's playin' on ESPN. I believe I'll even spring for a chili dog." His face softened. "Then maybe I'll go see Maisie. Read her a bedtime story. One about a kingdom where the good knight always wins. You know how kids love fantasy."

"That sounds like a good idea. Be careful driving home."

"That almost sounds like you care."

"I'll deny it under oath," I said solemnly.

"Plagiarist."

"A three-syllable word. I'm impressed." I gave him a small salute. "Good-bye, Detective Hudson."

"Not good-bye, Benni Harper. More like see you around."

As he pulled out of the police station driveway, he hit

his horn. "The Yellow Rose of Texas" blared across the parking lot, and I laughed out loud.

Gabe was staring at Detective Hudson's truck when I walked up. It pleased me to see his expression was not entirely happy. Maybe even a little jealous. He shook his head and tossed his briefcase in the front seat of his car. "He's watched too many *Dukes of Hazzard* shows. What were you doing with him?"

The picture of the tiny overgrown graves of the Brown babies flashed through my mind. How petty my problems seemed now. I reached up and touched his strong jaw, scratchy with five-o'clock shadow. The rough familiar feel made me swallow hard, the tears I'd been holding tight inside myself coating my eyes like mineral oil.

"*Querida*," he said, cupping my shoulders with his warm hands, "what's wrong?"

"Have you got dinner plans tonight?" I asked.

His face looked chagrined. "No, and I know I've been neglecting you." He looked over my shoulder. "Why did you say you were with that guy again?"

"Yes, you have been," I said, not answering his question.

"Got a phone call today telling me so. I swear I was coming home to apologize and talk about it tonight."

I swallowed over the thick, salty lump in my throat. "Who called you?"

"I won't mention any names, but I really hate it when members of the press are right about something, though it happens so rarely."

"I know you and Lydia had a lot to discuss these last few days."

"Yeah, well as my little Arkansas Razorback told me, maybe I was too worried about proving to my ex-wife what a success I turned out to be instead of paying attention to what my wife was going through. I'm sorry, sweetheart. I feel like a fool for not seeing it myself."

I sighed and touched his cheek. "Forget it, Friday. You're a fool, but you're my fool. And I knew whose bed you were coming home to at night."

"Until the day I die," he said, taking my face in his hands. "Now, what's with you and Detective Hudson? Please tell me it was business, not pleasure. Is there something going on with the Norton homicide I need to know about?"

"First, how's Sam and Bliss?" I asked, not quite ready to begin the story I would tell him. There was one thing I was glad I'd learned from Cappy, that the family secret had not been passed down. Maybe Sam and Bliss still had a chance.

Gabe sighed deeply, his hands slipping down to my shoulders. "Bliss asked for a leave of absence today. She's going up north with her mother and sister. I have a feeling she's not going to come back. You know, there's things in that family that bother me, though I can't put my finger on them."

"What about Sam?"

"He says they're going to take a breather for a while. He doesn't want to leave San Celina. That's all he would say. At their age I wouldn't be surprised if it ended their relationship."

"I guess only time will tell."

"I suppose so." He squeezed my shoulders gently. "Now, tell me why you're so upset."

"I need to talk," I said, feeling as breathless and vulnerable as a child. A mental picture of a seven-year-old girl watching her mother place a pillow over her sisters' faces caused tears to finally flow.

"You can talk to me. You know you can always talk to me."

I looked up at this man whose face I'd kissed so many times. This man whose cries of passion were as familiar to me as my own. This man who knew me and loved me and had promised to stay with me until the day he died. This man I trusted like no one else.

"It's about Cappy. It's about Giles's murder."

"Yes, go on."

"The thing is," I said, my voice hesitant, knowing what I was asking might not be possible for him. "Right now I need to talk to my husband. Not a police officer. Not a government employee. My husband."

Still holding me by the shoulders, he looked at me a long minute. I wouldn't ask him again. If he couldn't, I would understand. I would still love him and I would understand.

He slowly reached into his back pocket and pulled out his leather wallet where he carried his badge. He opened the car door and threw it on the floor next to his briefcase, closed and locked the door. Then he held out his hand.

"Let's walk," he said.